CHAPTER ONE

Hannah thought it looked like the saddest house in the world, a slate-roofed Cornish monolith with dark windows for eyes, looming out at them from under November rain.

Did houses have feelings, though? she wondered, studying it as they drew steadily closer. Could a house *emote*? Or was that all in the eyes of the beholder?

It was a question for a psychology student, perhaps.

Or someone clever like Santos, with that restless spirit of inquiry that had always got him into trouble. Hannah was not a particularly intellectual or superstitious person, however, and her beloved Santos was gone.

All she knew was that Kernow House was not the idyllic spot above the Atlantic she had envisaged on the flight over here from Greece. She was too polite to say so, of course. She didn't want to upset the lovely Bailey, who had insisted on driving her all the way out here to the very back of beyond. And the place was incredibly remote, nothing but fields and woods and hedges, barely another house in sight since they'd left the outskirts of Pethporro.

Instead she exclaimed, 'Oh, Bailey, what a gorgeous house! Huge, isn't it?' Then added, with a touch of genuine

concern, 'It's rather close to the edge of the cliff, though. I know you said it had extensive sea views, but this looks more like a gull's nest than a home.' She paused, frowning. 'Do we need to worry about coastal erosion in this part of Cornwall? What about subsidence?'

Not that she could see their surroundings with much clarity. The windscreen of the Renault hatchback had begun steaming up almost as soon as they'd left the cheery bed and breakfast where she was staying until all the paperwork had been finalised. Now it was more condensation than view, like staring through a foggy sauna window. Even so, Hannah could just make out the grey, storm-tossed Atlantic Ocean on the far side of the house, stretching into mist beyond a dramatic, rocky drop. Yes, hardly the Aegean, she thought, eyeing its grim, unforgiving swell.

Bailey shifted down a gear to negotiate another bend in the muddy, overgrown track. She was one of Hannah's late grandmother's solicitors, and while her build was petite, she was sparky and full of vitality. She had large blue eyes enhanced by lashes thick with mascara, soft coral pink lips, and a heart-shaped face that glowed with health.

'Well, I know it looks dodgy, but your grandmother had a ground survey done about ten years ago,' Bailey told her frankly, 'after a small landslide further down the coast.'

'Small?'

'A few rocks demolished a beach hut, I think.'

'Oh, is that all?'

'Anyway, the survey found nothing to worry about. But she had a good stretch of the cliff edge secured all the same.' Bailey laughed at Hannah's expression. She leaned forward,

using a fist to rub out a porthole on the steamed-up windscreen. 'Please don't look scared. A careful woman, was Trudy Clitheroe. Trust me, she wouldn't have carried on living here if she'd thought Kernow House was at risk of tumbling into the sea. As I'm sure you must know.'

A careful woman.

The very opposite of herself, Hannah thought, with a touch of despair. Perhaps if she had been more careful, Santos might still be alive. And she would still be sunning herself beside their pool, high above Athens, instead of staring out through near-horizontal rain at her gloomy and crumbling Cornish inheritance.

Her heart ached at the thought of him. He had been everything she'd ever desired in a man: fit and outdoorsy, good-humoured, ambitious; yet tender too, and a wonderful companion from the first day they met. *A friend as well as a lover*, that was how the saying went. And it had fitted Santos to a T.

He had always asked her advice before making a decision, always managed to drag a reluctant laugh out of her when she was down, always rang promptly when he was going to be late home. He had never forgotten an anniversary or birthday, he whisked her out to dinner whenever she was too bone-weary to cook, and he often brought her flowers and chocolates or a gorgeous new dress. For no reason other than he loved her and wanted to pamper her, he had said.

To describe Santos as an ideal man was to do his memory a huge disservice. He had been more than ideal, he had been *perfect*.

A man to grow up and grow old with.

The two of them would have been so happy together. If

fate had not intervened and brought her here to Cornwall instead. Like a penance for some sin she had no idea she'd even committed. Hannah knew she would never find another man as perfect as Santos. Not for as long as she lived.

And she had no intention of trying.

'I didn't know my grandmother at all. I never met her.' She hesitated, knowing that must sound odd. 'My mother told me she'd died when I was a baby.'

'How awful.'

'I expect Mum had her reasons. I just don't have a clue what they were.' Hannah frowned at the condensation on her window, wishing she could see out properly. 'And I can't ask her now, because she's dead too.'

'That's so sad.' Rounding the bend, Bailey slammed on the brakes and swore under her breath, her posture changing instantly. 'Oh, shit. Not today, for God's sake! That bloody, bloody man.'

Hannah, who had been rubbing a porthole on her own window, turned and stared at Bailey, uncomprehending, then peered ahead through the driving rain.

'Bloody, bloody man?' she repeated, perplexed. There was something big and white blocking the narrow track. It wasn't a man though. In fact, it looked very like . . . 'What the hell is *that*?'

'That would be a washing machine.'

'Well, erm, I can see that.' Hannah blinked at its hulking mass. She felt like she was going mad. 'I meant, what on earth is it doing there? Right in the middle of the lane?'

'Stopping us from getting to Kernow House, I should imagine.'

'But who would want to stop us?'

'Who indeed?' Bailey gazed out at the washing machine too, then at the heavy rain bouncing off its white top and sides like hail. Her shoulders slumped. 'Okay, fine, whatever. I've got a waterproof on the back seat. I'd better get out and try shifting the bloody thing to one side. See if I can squeeze the car past it.'

'You'll never manage it alone.'

'I can try.'

'Those things weigh a ton,' Hannah pointed out. 'They have concrete blocks in the base, to stop them jumping about during the spin cycle.'

Bailey looked at her earnestly. 'I can't ask you to go out in this God-awful weather, Hannah. Especially not to help me move a washing machine out of the mud.'

She seemed very determined, Hannah thought, a little taken aback by her vehemence. Bailey was in her mid-twenties, maybe two or three years younger than her. Yet somehow that severe black trouser suit and smart white blouse made her look even younger, like she was dressing the part of somebody she wasn't.

Back at the solicitors' firm, Hannah had got the impression that Bailey was keen to do everything exactly and meticulously. Perhaps a promotion was riding on this, or there was something else going on that she couldn't quite grasp. Or perhaps Bailey was always this nervy and wound-up. Not surprising if her way was habitually blocked by white goods, Hannah thought drily, and once again studied the rain-pelted washing machine a few feet ahead.

Who could have put it there? And why?

Her mind, usually quite fertile, drew a blank. But what was really odd was that while her companion was clearly annoyed, she wasn't surprised by the blockage in the middle of the road. Almost as though Bailey had *expected* something like this to happen.

That bloody, bloody man.

That alone would seem to indicate Bailey had a shrewd idea who'd left it there. But she wasn't elaborating for some reason.

'You're our client,' Bailey continued, in a tone that brooked no refusal. 'It simply wouldn't be professional to get you soaked.' She took a deep breath. 'No, this is my problem. You stay here in the dry, and I'll ...'

'Get totally drenched?'

Bailey, who was now struggling determinedly into her waterproof coat, paused and met her gaze. 'Okay, have you got a better idea?'

'We could abandon the car and make a run for it.' Hannah measured the distance between the Renault and the front of the old house, where she could see a porch with a very inviting overhang. Glancing down at her loose denim jeans and T-shirt, an outfit more suited to Greece than rural North Cornwall, she grimaced. She was going to have to learn to *adjust*, she told herself. 'We'll both get wet but only for a few minutes. And maybe by the time we've looked over the house, the rain will have eased off.' She studied the glowering dark clouds overhead with feigned optimism. 'Perhaps it'll even stop.'

'*Stop raining?*' Bailey laughed, a little wildly. 'You've really never been to Cornwall before, have you?'

But she agreed to the plan, and a minute later they were

both running headlong for the house through puddles and pelting rain.

As they ran, Hannah wrinkled up her nose, assaulted by a barrage of odours. Mostly agricultural, as her mother might have said disdainfully. Her mum had been brought up at Kernow House, but had run away at the age of fifteen to get a job in London. She had been very vocal about hating the countryside, and Cornwall in particular, for reasons that passed Hannah's understanding. Cornwall had always seemed such a mythical place to her, though admittedly she had never visited it before now.

Mythical . . . and very, very wet.

Reaching the porch first, Hannah flung herself under its shelter with a breathless cheer. Then looked down at herself in dismay. 'Bloody hell, I could enter a Miss Wet T-shirt competition. I'm soaked through.'

'Are you okay?' Bailey looked at her, clearly worried.

'I'm fine. Just a bit out of breath.' She shook her wet hair from side to side like a dog coming out of water. 'And in need of a towel.'

Bailey bit her lip, passing her a handbag pack of tissues. 'Here, help yourself. Maybe there'll be some towels upstairs that you could use. I think I saw some on the inventory. But I can't vouch for their condition.'

'Thanks.' She grinned, dabbing ineffectually at her dripping forehead with a tissue not much larger than her palm. 'My own fault. I ought to have bought some wellies and a raincoat as soon as I got off the plane.' Hannah tried in vain to scrape mud off her trainers. 'Well, at least I'm not wearing

heels. Otherwise I might have ended up falling into a puddle and drowning out there.'

'God, I'm so sorry.'

'Don't be, it's hardly your fault. Whoever owns that bloody washing machine is to blame. Or used to own it.' Hannah glared back at the appliance, still squatting glumly in front of the hatchback, smack bang in the middle of the only track that led to the house. 'I mean, who dumps white goods in the middle of the road like that?' She flicked back her wet fringe irritably. 'Cornish fly-tipping, I take it?'

Bailey did not immediately answer. She was busy unlocking the front door with a vast, rusty-looking key. Or trying to unlock it, as it didn't seem keen to open. 'Sorry?' She glanced over her shoulder at the washing machine, and said cryptically, 'Not entirely fly-tipping, no. But please, don't worry about it.'

The lock finally gave way, and she pushed the door wide with a smile. Her relief was tangible. 'Here we are. Kernow House. All yours, bar the shouting.'

'Is there going to be shouting?'

'Not if I can help it. Please, after you.' Bailey gestured Hannah inside, following close behind. Her heels clacked on the slate floor, disturbing the thick, dusty silence that felt as if it had been inhabiting the house for centuries. 'Right then. My boss asked me to show you around the property and answer any questions you might have. So ask away.'

Hannah cringed at the thought of being shown around the house, as though considering purchasing it. 'I don't need—'

'It's all part of the service, honestly.' Bailey gave her a lop-sided grin, then pulled her wet hair free from its ponytail

and began to wring out the ends. 'Okay, quick guided tour. You have Delabole slate flagstones throughout the downstairs rooms, except for the utility room, which is concrete. Original wood flooring on the upper levels. On your right is the living room, with a wood-burning stove. On your left the dining room, with an open fire. Straight ahead you'll find the kitchen and a couple of pantries. A recently-installed Aga, and a handpump that draws water directly from a borehole dating back to the eighteenth century.'

'A *what*? A handpump?' Hannah echoed. 'I didn't know stuff like that still existed. Is this where they filmed Poldark or something?'

'I know, I'm sorry.' Bailey made an apologetic face. 'Like I said, the Aga is new, but I'm afraid your grandmother never got around to updating the plumbing. Or the electrics, which are in serious need of repair.'

Flicking one of the archaic-looking light switches in the hall, Hannah was dismayed to see the light bulb overhead remain stubbornly unlit.

Bailey nodded. 'Yes, the electricity is off at the moment.'

'Brilliant.'

'But we can sort that out with a phone call back at the office. And I can put you in touch with a local electrician if you like,' Bailey said helpfully, watching her, 'get you quotes for any work that needs doing.'

'That would be very useful, thank you.'

'My pleasure.'

Hannah tiptoed awkwardly across the shiny slate floor, leaving behind a trail of muddy footprints, and peered in through the living-room door. It was a generous room with a

wooden settle, some ancient armchairs, and a large double window with a cushioned window seat. The wood-burning stove was unlit, raised on a handsome plinth of black slate, its door left open to display a swept grate.

If she was going to stay, she would need to buy some comfortable sofas.

If she stayed.

'Delabole?' she repeated, bending to admire the slate flagstones. The ones she hadn't smeared with mud, that is.

'That's the name of the Cornish quarry where the slate was mined. It's a few miles along the coast.'

Bailey had removed her waterproof, revealing the clipboard she'd tucked inside her jacket before dashing out into the rain. All the same, the headed paper was damp, curling at the edges. Over her shoulder, Hannah read: 'Knutson Solicitors. Kernow House Inventory', followed by a list in dense, small print.

'Right, shall we make a start?' Bailey smoothed out the paper and read from the list, heading back into the hall towards the other room. 'Dining-room contents.' She threw open the door. 'One antique dining table with eight chairs. Sideboard with silver service, five pieces missing. Two silver candelabra and one large pewter plate, all early nineteenth-century. Grandfather clock with—'

'Please,' Hannah interrupted her, smiling. 'I don't want to be rude. But it's okay, I can see everything for myself. I'd just like a few minutes first to . . .'

She had been going to say 'listen to the house', but then thought better of it. Bailey was a lovely woman, very friendly and eager to help, but she did not strike Hannah as someone

particularly sensitive to atmosphere. And this place had an ambience. Not sad, as she had feared from the outside, but warm, and somehow inviting. As though Kernow House had been waiting for her to arrive. Which was perhaps a little spooky, but not in a disturbing way.

'Get my bearings,' she finished lamely.

'Of course.' Bailey closed the dining-room door again and tucked the clipboard under her arm. To Hannah's relief, she did not sound offended. 'That's perfectly understandable. You go right ahead and explore, Hannah. Take your time. I'll wait out in the porch until you're done.'

'Thank you.'

From the front doorway, Bailey glanced back at her with a shy smile. 'You look like her, you know.'

'Sorry?'

'Like your grandmother, Trudy.'

'You knew her, then?'

'Oh, everyone hereabouts knew Trudy Clitheroe. Though to be honest, everybody knows everybody else in Pethporro. And their business. It's a tiny place. But that's Cornwall for you. There's no such thing as privacy here. Or secrets.' Bailey peered up the dark, winding stair toward the floor above, and added thoughtfully, 'Well, maybe a few secrets. In old places like this.'

Perhaps the solicitor was sensitive to atmosphere, after all.

'Maybe,' Hannah agreed.

'In fact, there was some talk of a secret passage a few years back,' Bailey added, with a quirky smile. 'Local legend, you know. But we've all looked, and couldn't find anything. Maybe you'll have better luck.'

'Great. Now I'm spooked. Thanks for that.'

'Sorry. Probably just nonsense, don't worry about it.' Bailey paused, her expression turning serious. 'Anyway, look, I'm very sorry for your loss. We all are.'

'We?'

'Knutson Solicitors. And . . . well, everyone in Pethporro.'

'Thank you,' Hannah said huskily, taken aback by the genuine emotion on Bailey's face. She felt like a fraud, given she had not even known Trudy Clitheroe was still alive. But it didn't seem like the right time to bring that up again. 'That's very kind of you.'

When Bailey had gone, Hannah turned slowly on her heel, listening to the rain pattering down on the roof and against the windows. She wasn't sure which room to explore first. The dining room with its antique table and silverware? Or upstairs, shrouded so mysteriously in shadow? Though the kitchen did sound intriguing, if a bit behind the times.

She trod along the hallway, leaving another trail of damp footprints on the slate flags, and pushed open the door. It creaked loudly. Rusty, stiff hinges. Hannah made a mental note to bring oil next time.

There was a long, antique pine kitchen table missing chairs and a leg, the corner propped up on a stack of dusty books. The wood was lovely, though. It might be worth salvaging, she thought.

Apart from a newish-looking Aga in soft, sea green, the only other nod to this being a kitchen was a white ceramic Belfast sink, set deep into the exposed stone wall and cracked across in several places, with a handpump above it.

How wonderfully nostalgic, Hannah thought wryly, giving the wooden pump handle an experimental crank. Water trickled out through a tangled mess of cobwebs. It would save on gym fees to be working this monstrosity several times a day. But she couldn't quite see herself vigorously handpumping water every time she wanted to make a cup of tea or boil some potatoes; that would have to go.

Reliable electricity was a necessity too. First on the list, in fact. Much as she loved the idea of creeping about this old house by candlelight, like a character out of a Jane Austen novel, she would need to charge her phone and laptop at some point. Not to mention watch television and go online. She would feel nervous using these old plug sockets until she was sure there was no risk of fire.

After peering into the two side rooms, both dusty pantries – one cold enough to serve as a morgue, should the need arise – she went back into the hall.

'Is there superfast broadband in this area?' she called to Bailey through the open front door.

All she got from the porch was a kind of muffled snort.

'I'll take that as a no,' she muttered, and headed for the winding oak staircase, wondering what the bedrooms would look like. And there was an attic too, she seemed to recall from the neat, hand-drawn plan of the house that had accompanied Mr Knutson's original letter.

She paused, one hand on the old wooden newel-post at the bottom of the stairs.

It was hard to believe this was all hers now.

She had never owned property before. She had never even owned a car, though she'd passed her driving test at

eighteen. Her home in Greece had belonged to Santos' parents. Now she would have an entire house to herself. Though it came with very little land, of course. Most of the surrounding woods and fields had been sold years ago to a neighbouring farmer, Mr Knutson had said when she rang to discuss the bequest. But there were some gorgeous, overgrown gardens out the back; Hannah had seen them through the kitchen window and fallen instantly in love. With a little work, she could see herself hanging washing out there in fine weather, and sunbathing in a deckchair, overlooking the sea . . .

She didn't care about land anyway. She knew nothing about being a farmer, and very little about garden maintenance. The closest she had ever come to horticulture was looking after a few houseplants as a student. Not with much success there, either, as those sad ex-ferns would testify.

Her heart knew a sudden pang as she imagined how different it would have been to be standing here with Santos. The two of them settling down at last. Starting a family. Maybe even getting married.

They had never been into old-fashioned gender roles, but it couldn't be denied that Santos would probably have known what needed fixing here; might even have been able to repair some things himself. And she wouldn't have felt so lonely and apprehensive with him beside her. They would have explored her grandmother's house together, rushing hand-in-hand from room to room, grinning like idiots at the wonderful stroke of luck fate had dealt them. A proper home of their own, with these dazzling views over the sea. It was a fantasy they had often whispered to each other in

bed, looking at property listings with a longing eye, saving their pennies where they could, hoping the business would expand enough to allow them to buy a modest city flat one day.

Now here she was, alone in this amazing Cornish house.

She missed Santos so badly.

But what could she do, except keep muddling through, pretending to be brave, pretending she could do this without him?

As her hand gripped the banister, Hannah heard the tiniest of sounds from upstairs. An almost imperceptible creak, like a floorboard relaxing under a foot.

'Hello?' she called up the stairs, not really expecting a reply.

Then somebody sneezed.

CHAPTER TWO

'Bailey, is it possible there's someone else in the house today?' she called over her shoulder, startled by the thought that they were not alone here. 'Someone doing repair work upstairs, perhaps?'

There was no reply from the porch.

Puzzled, Hannah went to the front door and peered out. Outside, the rain seemed to be slowing. There was no sign of Bailey, though. The cosy little covered porch was empty. Perhaps she had risked the rain to check one of the many outbuildings Hannah had glimpsed on their way in.

Hannah poked her head out into the drizzle. 'Bailey?'

Nothing but silence.

She couldn't see a van out there either. Or any other vehicle but Bailey's silver Renault hatchback. So it was unlikely to be a workman upstairs.

With a shrug, Hannah went back inside and gazed up at the narrow, oak stairway as it wound away into shadow. There was a thin carpet runner tacked into place on each step, once a bold green, each faded strip now covered in dust. On the wall at the turn of the stairs was an oblong mirror, reflecting a dark, empty landing.

She listened hard, but there were no further sounds from upstairs. Perhaps she had imagined the sneeze. It could have been ... Well, her imagination failed her there. A sneeze was a sneeze.

But even given the spooky Cornish setting, it was unlikely to be a ghost she had heard. She was no expert on the supernatural, but she guessed that ghosts didn't tend to get the sniffles. So either it was a squatter, taking advantage of an empty property in the middle of nowhere, or it was somebody there on legitimate business, maybe fixing something. Either way, Kernow House was now rightfully hers, and it was ridiculous to feel nervous or embarrassed about being there.

Taking a deep breath, Hannah trod heavily up the staircase, calling out, 'Hello?' as she went. 'Is anybody there? I'm the new owner.'

At the top of the stairs was a closed door. She tried it, but the door wouldn't budge. Locked? On the left were two further doors, opposite each other, both open. She poked her head around the first door, which was clearly above the kitchen. It was a small, dank bedroom with a mouldy-smelling four-poster bed facing a boarded-up fireplace, in front of which stood a blue china jug stuffed with ostrich feathers. The curtains were a muddy brown, threadbare velvet, drawn across to hide the sunlight.

The other room was brighter and more inviting: a large bathroom with a roll-top Victorian-style bathtub set on a raised platform, a folded wooden screen leaning against the wall beside it. Two square windows overlooked the Atlantic Ocean, a churning dove grey expanse misted with rain for as far as she could see. But the bathroom was also empty.

The mysterious sneezer struck again, breaking the silence.

'Hello?'

Hannah wandered back along the landing, intrigued now. Three further doors stood open to the right of the staircase. More bedrooms, she guessed, and was surprised on glancing through the first door to find a small, book-lined study with a battered, leather-topped desk near the window, a swivel chair standing behind it.

It was a shame she had never met Granny Trudy. Her rather volatile mum had fallen out with her and then lied to Hannah from a young age, pretending her grandmother was dead.

Luckily, Hannah had never felt the need for more family around her. Especially once she had fallen in love.

She had met the dark-eyed, dark-haired Santos on a busi-ness management course at university, and together they had moved to Greece. The country's economy was still in turmoil, but she'd landed a good job with his dad in Athens, helping to organise climbing holidays while Santos contin-ued with his education, taking a higher degree. Later, they'd set up their own specialist travel company, planning events and selling adventure holidays to young, active profession-als. For a few years, it had brought in enough for them to save for a deposit on an apartment of their own, while still living with his parents.

Then, only a short time after her mum had died, Granny Trudy had also passed away, her existence – or rather, recent lack of it – taking Hannah by surprise. She died peacefully in her sleep, according to the solicitor's letter when it finally

found its slow way to her in Greece, informing her that she was Trudy's sole beneficiary.

'I didn't even know I had a grandmother,' she had told Santos at the time, bewildered by the letter. Bewildered and guilty.

She had wanted to fly home for the funeral, to try and make amends for that long estrangement by seeing her grandmother laid to rest, at least. But Santos had been in hospital after a climbing accident in the Peloponnese, and she had not felt able to leave his bedside. 'Don't worry about me, darling,' he had said, insisting that she should return to England at once. 'It's only a minor fracture. I'll be back on the mountains again in no time.' Family meant a great deal to him, of course, and Santos had always been very fond of his own vibrant and inquisitive Greek grandmother. He had not understood her reluctance.

But how could she leave, given the state he was in?

Because he was fit and strong, he recovered enough to leave hospital after a few weeks, much to Hannah's relief. All the same, she had put her grandmother's legacy on hold – once she had missed the funeral, there did not seem to be any reason to hurry her return to England.

The sneeze came again.

'Hello?'

Determined to find the culprit, Hannah darted into the bedroom to the left of the study, and stopped dead. Another empty room confronted her, the curtains open this time across a large double window overlooking the track that led back to the main road into Pethporro.

There were books everywhere. Stacks of them, leaning

perilously against each other or the wall, and scattered across the floor beside the bed, which was another grand four-poster. This must have been Granny Trudy's bedroom, she thought, and stared at the now-unoccupied bed. Presumably her grandmother had passed her last hours here.

All alone.

It made Hannah furious to think how she could have been here, in Cornwall, looking after the old lady, if she had known about her existence. Instead, Trudy had spent those final days on her own, nothing but a book for company.

Guiltily, Hannah bent to check the book that was still lying open, face down, on the bedside table, and had to contain her disbelief when she dusted off the cover.

It was a racy romance!

'Way to go, Granny Trudy,' she said under her breath, and put the book back exactly as she'd found it.

Of course, much of this would need to be thrown away or cleaned up before the house could become habitable. And she had no help, unless she hired a cleaning firm. Living in Greece since university meant she had lost touch with all her old friends, and none of them lived much nearer than London anyway.

Her dad had only been around for the first few years of her life, then died unexpectedly of a brain aneurysm. For years, she had imagined that early bereavement was why her mother was so bitter and short-tempered. But as Hannah grew older, she'd realised that was just her personality. Then her mum too had died, shocking her to the core. She had thought nothing worse could happen to her.

Until the avalanche struck.

A tiny squealing noise brought her round in surprise.

Directly across the bedroom, on the sagging seat pad of a dilapidated tub armchair, was a squirming mess of dark, striped fur.

'So that's what I heard!' Hannah approached the armchair slowly, careful not to disturb its mewing occupants. Crouching down, she met the wary yellow eyes of a dark tabby staring back at her, clearly in fear for her newborn kittens. 'Oh, you're gorgeous,' she whispered. 'And so are your babies. But what on earth are we going to do with you?'

The tabby cat blinked at her. Then sneezed again.

'I hope you don't have a cold,' Hannah said seriously. 'This is a very damp house for someone with a cold.'

But the mother cat merely licked one paw in response, smoothing down her fur. She looked wet and bedraggled, as though she had gone out to hunt mice that morning and got caught in the rain. Once she dried off, she would probably stop sneezing.

It was hard to differentiate between balls of fur, but Hannah did her best to count how many kittens were in the litter, repeating the head – and stubby tail – count twice, just to be sure.

'Five kittens! Well, there's a turn-up. I suppose I shall have to share Kernow House with you. You were here first, after all.' Ruefully, she eyed the heavy rain now streaming down the window as another dark cloud scudded over the house. 'And it would be rude to turn you out of doors, especially in this awful weather.'

As she straightened up, a sudden movement out in the grounds caught her eye.

Bailey was standing in the middle of the field that ran alongside the track, getting thoroughly sodden despite her waterproof coat. She was talking earnestly to a man in a tractor, her head tilted up as she tried to have a conversation with him.

The man shook his head.

Bailey shouted something. Not crossly, but presumably because of the noise the tractor engine was making, since he had not turned it off.

Abandoning the litter of tabby kittens to their adorable mewing and squirming, Hannah went to the window, frowning.

It was hard to be sure at that distance, but she guessed the man to be a local farmer. He was wearing a flat tweed cap and a dark blue wax jacket, of the kind she had seen for sale everywhere in town. When Bailey shouted again, the man gestured towards the house, something angry about his body language. He seemed to be shooing Bailey away like a fly, as though she was annoying him.

Curious, Hannah leaned both hands on the cold window-pane and watched them.

Who was he?

And why was he in such a bad mood?

Bailey left the man with a shrug that spoke of her contempt for him, and trudged back towards the house in the rain.

The man in the tractor glared after her without moving. He tipped his cap impatiently back off his forehead, revealing thick black hair.

Then his gaze lifted to the house, and for a few seconds

Hannah could have sworn he was looking directly at her. Then he wrenched the steering wheel around, and the vast machine lumbered away in the opposite direction, bouncing across mud ruts and grass as it headed for a five-barred gate at the far end of the field.

Hannah ran lightly down the stairs, and was waiting in the shelter of the porch by the time Bailey got back to the house, her coat dripping, her shoes muddy and waterlogged. The petite solicitor looked flushed and dishevelled, her eyes flashing with temper.

'Who was that?' Hannah asked, burning with curiosity, though really it was none of her business. 'One of my neighbours? What did he want?'

'That,' Bailey told her in a caustic tone, pausing to wipe rain out of her eyes, 'was Raphael Tregar. And what he wants is Kernow House.'

CHAPTER THREE

Once they had locked up the house again, leaving the mother tabby and her litter to their own devices – presumably the cat had some sneaky way of getting in and out on her own – Bailey drove Hannah back into town. She was oddly tight-lipped about the guy in the tractor, evading Hannah's questions as though she had been sworn to secrecy. But a few hours later, Bailey swung by the bed-and-breakfast place, and suggested dinner at the local Chinese restaurant, a small place off the high street called The Golden Dragon.

Hannah, who had not yet acquired a car and had no way of cooking in her humble bedroom, readily agreed. She was starving, and had no desire to eat more fish and chips, which was all she'd been able to get the night before.

Besides, she guessed from Bailey's expression that the petite solicitor had something she was dying to tell her.

Seated in a comfortable alcove at The Golden Dragon, they ordered a carafe of iced water, a pot of tea each, and an array of Chinese dishes.

'I'm having a glass of wine,' Bailey said with a lopsided smile. 'It's been a long day. I can leave the car here and walk home. It's not far.' She hesitated. 'What about you?'

'I'll stick with the Chinese tea, thanks.'

The waitress seemed to know Bailey well, enquiring politely after her cat as she brought out the first selection of dishes. She gave Hannah a curious smile as she left.

'Did I say something funny?' Hannah asked, watching the waitress retreat into the kitchen.

'Pay no attention. She's just interested in you.'

'What, am I the talk of the town?'

'Something like that.' Bailey laughed at her expression. 'We don't get a lot of excitement round here out of season. Newcomers are a welcome source of gossip.'

'So Mr Knutson gave you permission to talk to me, did he?' Hannah was surprised when Bailey nodded. 'Seriously? I was only joking.'

'I didn't know how much to share with you back at the house. I'm sorry about that. Confidentiality, you know. But I asked Mr Knutson, and he said we should tell you everything we know. Just in case.'

Hannah was puzzled. 'In case of what?'

'Trouble.'

'That doesn't sound good.'

Bailey shrugged, and poured herself a glass of iced water.

'So let me get this straight,' Hannah said, leaning across the table to spear another morsel of Kung Po chicken. 'The guy on the tractor—'

'Raphael Tregar.'

'Yeah, weird name. Isn't that one of the Mutant Ninja Turtle names?'

'I have no idea.'

'Wow, this is spicy.' Hannah forked another bite – which

was delicious but a bit on the hot side – then scooped up some chicken with broccoli to cool her mouth. 'Great choice of restaurant, by the way.'

'It's the only choice.' When Hannah glanced at her, puzzled, Bailey added, 'There aren't many restaurants in Pethporro that open in the evening. Not at this time of year. Most are closed out of season.'

'Well, it's still great. This is very tasty too.' Hannah pointed at the king prawn chow mein with her chopsticks.

Bailey nodded between mouthfuls. 'I come here all the time with my partner.'

'You should have invited him along tonight. I'd love to meet him.'

'I will do next time.' Bailey helped herself to some chow mein. '*She* is at her Cornish language evening class, tonight.'

'*She?*' Hannah echoed, then grinned. 'Oh right, I see ... into learning languages, is she?'

'Actually, she's the teacher.'

'That's impressive.' Hannah swallowed, then downed some ice water to deal with the spicy aftertaste of the Kung Po chicken. 'So, going back to flat cap guy, he thinks he has a claim on Kernow House?'

'That's about it, yes.'

'And how exactly is something like that possible?'

'He claims his granddad won it in a game.'

'A game of what?'

Bailey looked at her directly. 'Cards, apparently.'

'He says his grandfather played my grandmother for the house in a game of cards – and he won?'

'I wish it were that simple.' Bailey shook her head. 'But no,

it wasn't Trudy who was the card player. It was your grand-dad. Jack Clitheroe was a bit of a gambler. And a drinker, I'm afraid. Not a great combination.'

Hannah grimaced, and poured herself some warm black Chinese tea. 'I've been known to do some drinking myself. Though I'm on a bit of a hiatus at the moment. So why didn't this guy's granddad—'

'Gabriel Tregar.'

'Another amazing name. Sounds Biblical.'

'Cornish too.'

'Of course.' Hannah played with the decorative china tea cup, tilting it back and forth. 'So why didn't old man Gabriel try to take the house before now,' she asked, returning to her original question, 'if he had a claim on it?'

'That's where it becomes complicated. And interesting.'

'Go on.'

'Gabriel Tregar passed away a few years back from natural causes. Heart attack, I think. He left everything to Raphael. But his will also contained an instruction that no one was to touch the house while Trudy was still alive.'

Hannah's brows rose. 'You think Gabriel Tregar had a soft spot for my grandmother?'

'More than a soft spot, if local rumour is to be believed.'

'Wow, a secret romance . . .' Hannah savoured her tea, watching as Bailey poked the last of the chicken dumplings with her chopsticks. 'No, you take it. I'm not a big dumpling fan.' She frowned, still trying to puzzle it out. There was obviously some mystery here that she knew nothing about. 'Is it possible Gabriel's grandson could be the rightful owner of Kernow House?'

'He's not his grandson. Raphael is his adopted son.'

Hannah stared at her. 'I'm sorry, *what*?'

'Gabriel never had any kids.' Bailey offered her the dish of chestnut mushrooms, but Hannah shook her head, listening intently. 'He had a lot of property and land, though, and he wanted an heir. I think there was a distant cousin who could have inherited, but Gabriel hated him. So about fifteen years ago, he fostered a boy from a children's home in Truro. And later adopted him.'

'Flat cap Ninja Turtle man?'

'That's right.'

Hannah thought back to the glaring man she had seen on the tractor. 'So how old was Raphael when Gabriel fostered him?'

'About sixteen. And a serious pain in the arse.'

'And what's he like now?'

'Clever,' Bailey said flatly. 'But cold with it. Knows how to manipulate people to get the best deal. He's on the local council, sits on committees, makes big decisions. He has his finger in a lot of pies in Pethporro.'

'Some people have a gift for getting their own way.'

'I think Raphael must have developed his "gift" later in life. He'd been permanently excluded from all the schools in Truro by the time Gabriel fostered him. By all accounts, he was kind of a savage as a teenager, always getting into fights with older boys. Gabriel brought him home to Pethporro and taught him a trade.'

'Farming.'

'Farming, fishery, and tourism. They're the main careers around here.' Bailey's smile was dry. 'He grew up devoted to

the old man, by all accounts. Even changed his name to Raphael to please him.'

'So he wasn't always named after a cartoon superhero?'

'His real name is Ralph.'

'Bloody hell. I'm almost disappointed.'

'Don't be.' Bailey took a deep swallow of wine, and gazed down into the glass. 'My partner's the same age as Raphael. She says he was a grim bastard even as a teenager.'

'And what age is she?'

'Thirty-one.' Bailey looked self-conscious. 'She's quite a bit older than me. I'm only twenty-four. But it works.'

'What's her name?'

'Penny.'

'Like I said, I'd love to meet her sometime.' Hannah dropped her chopsticks into her bowl, and then pushed it away, happily stuffed. 'I want you and Penny to be my first dinner guests at Kernow House. Even if it means eating takeaway by candlelight.'

'You're on.'

The waitress came over to take away their empty dishes. 'I'll bring the dessert menu,' she told them with a persuasive smile.

'I couldn't eat another thing, sorry,' Hannah said, shaking her head. 'The meal was delicious though. My compliments to the kitchen.'

It had been a delicious meal, and Bailey was excellent company. Yesterday evening had been horrible, sitting alone in her room at the bed and breakfast, listening to the rain and watching some trashy game show on television. She had gone to sleep with half a mind to sell Kernow House as soon

as she'd seen it. Take the money from the sale and run. Any-where, it didn't matter where, so long as she could curl up alone and feel sorry for herself.

Just as she'd been doing ever since Santos died.

His parents in Athens had been lovely, saying she was wel-come to stay and make a permanent home with them after their son's death. And Hannah had been tempted, at first. She'd been utterly bereft in those first weeks after the funeral. Bereft and devastated, unable to stop crying, unable to look at his empty place in their bed without breaking down. It had felt for a time as though his family were all she had left of him. But her true place was here. Not in Greece. Not stuck in the past, constantly reliving the tragedy that had stolen such a wonderful man from them. Granny Trudy had left Kernow House to Hannah for a reason. Yes, turning that dilapidated wreck of a house back into a home was going to be bloody hard work, but she was determined to make the effort.

For Trudy, if not for herself.

Hannah bent to rummage in her handbag, hair falling about her face in a blonde curtain, hiding the sudden and unexpected tears in her eyes.

Bailey looked horrified. 'No, please put your money away. Mr Knutson insisted this should be his treat. I'll stick it on the tab.'

'Thank you.'

'You're welcome.' Bailey leaned back in her chair, gazing at her curiously. 'But what about you? Will you get a job down here? Or are you planning to sell up once the house is in a saleable condition? Property that big, it'll be worth quite a large amount of money to the right buyer.'

'I'm not sure. I sold my business in Greece, so I have plenty of capital. But it won't last forever. I suppose this Raphael Tregar might make me an offer if he's so keen to get his hands on the place.' She paused, hearing the words come out and suddenly unsure. Kernow House had made quite a strong impression on her. As soon as she had walked through the door, it had felt like coming home. Which was ridiculous, considering she had never visited the place before. 'You never did say how legitimate his claim is.'

'Not legitimate at all. Apparently the entire thing rests on a gambling IOU, which isn't legally enforceable in this country as far as I'm aware. Besides which, it's written on a paper napkin.'

'A paper napkin?'

'That's probably why he hasn't approached us directly. Mr Knutson doesn't think it would hold up in court. Raphael may have been advised by his own lawyers not to bother contesting the will at all. He's quite wealthy, but costs could be prohibitive if the claim fails.'

'This Raphael sounds like a joker. He must be, if he thinks he can overturn my grandmother's will with nothing but a paper napkin.'

Bailey looked troubled. 'Maybe.'

'Hold on,' Hannah said, catching a flicker of something in the solicitor's face. 'I thought you were joking. Is there a real possibility Raphael could contest Trudy's will and grab the house from me?'

'Unlikely.' Bailey turned to ask the waitress for the bill. When she looked back again, she was frowning delicately.

'But Mr Knutson had a look at this napkin IOU, and apparently it does bear a credible signature.'

'Whose signature?'

'Your grandfather's, of course. Jack Clitheroe.'

'That sounds pretty conclusive to me.'

'Look, I wouldn't worry. It's probably nothing. The best he could hope for is to bully you with it. So don't let him, okay?' Bailey sighed and stood up, reaching for the jacket she'd slung over the back of her chair. She smothered a yawn with her hand. 'Sorry. Definitely time to go. I'll ask them to put the bill on our account.'

They wandered out into the street together. It was dark and cold, and there was still a thin rain falling on Pethporro and the sea, a pale gleam just visible beyond the sands of the town's horseshoe bay.

Hannah hunched into her coat, glad of its warmth. She glanced up into darkness. 'I can't believe there's any rain left to fall after this afternoon's downpour.'

'Oh, Cornwall has plenty more rain where that came from.'

The black road surface was shining under the yellow streetlights, and as they waited to cross the road, a car drove past, tyres hissing in the wet. It was getting late, just after eleven o'clock, but music was blaring out of the pub opposite, all the lights on inside, the hanging sign creaking as it swung in the wind. Through the pub windows, Hannah could see a cluster of red-cheeked men in tweed caps and wax jackets at the bar, chatting and laughing. Downing pints of local ale, no doubt.

'Maybe I should arrange a meeting with this Raphael guy,' Hannah said, thinking aloud. 'Sit down and talk about this in a civilised manner.'

'A meeting?' Bailey stared at her, wide-eyed. 'I'm really not sure that would be a good idea . . .' she began warily.

'Why not?'

'You must do as you see fit, obviously. But if there's any legitimacy to his claim, Raphael will try to get what he wants without the hassle of discussing it with you. He owns most of the land around Kernow House already.'

'*What?*'

'Didn't you look at the documents we sent you? It's all in there.' Bailey took a deep breath. 'About a year after Gabriel's death, Raphael started buying the old lady out, one field at a time, until there was nothing left but the cliff edge and the gardens you saw today.'

Hannah blinked. 'I knew she'd sold most of her land, but . . . not to this Raphael character. That's appalling. Why on earth would my grandmother do that?'

'I expect she was desperate. That money was all Trudy had to live on towards the end. And she wasn't using the land for farming, so it was useless to her. But she hung onto the house itself.' Bailey placed a reassuring hand on her arm. 'Trudy wanted you to have Kernow House. She was very particular about that.'

But Hannah's eyes had narrowed, staring sightlessly down the dark high street. Preying on helpless old ladies. Buying up the land one plot at a time.

The man was a charmer, all right.

'It was Raphael Tregar who dumped that washing machine in the middle of the track this morning, wasn't it?'

'He denied it when I confronted him, of course. But it's not the first time we've been up to the house and found the track blocked. Raphael must have heard you'd arrived in Pethporro and decided to make life difficult for you from the start.'

'Kernow House is habitable, isn't it?'

'Barely.'

'Barely will have to do. Because moving in straightaway is my best chance of keeping him out.' For the first time since Santos died, Hannah felt a sudden, fiery energy rush through her; her chest was heaving, her cheeks flushed. It was an odd sensation. But not unwelcome. There had been times over the past few months when she had felt almost as dead as Santos. 'Okay, let's have it. What else do I need to know about my neighbour?'

'There are plenty of unsavoury stories about him doing the rounds. He's ruthless, cunning, likes to play tricks on people. And he's not known for suffering fools gladly. Most people keep out of his way. I'm not saying he's dangerous, but I wouldn't want to antagonise him.' Bailey hesitated. 'Plus, he's got a reputation with the ladies, if you know what I mean.'

'Well, he'll get a shock if he comes calling at Kernow House.' Hannah smiled grimly. 'Forewarned is forearmed.'

CHAPTER FOUR

Two days later, after much online shopping, Hannah moved out of the bed and breakfast and returned to Kernow House in a taxi. Until she bought herself a car, taxis would have to be her primary mode of transport. Not ideal – especially given that her mobile signal seemed a bit wobbly once out in the sticks – but it was only temporary. She had spotted a scruffy forecourt displaying used cars for sale on the way out of Pethporro, and scribbled down their details on the way past. With the capital she had left over from winding up her holiday business in Greece, buying a cheap second-hand car should be her next step.

Bouncing over the track's deep mud ruts in the back of the taxi, Hannah was relieved to see that someone had surreptitiously removed the old washing machine from the track since her last visit. Had Bailey arranged for it to be taken away? That seemed unlikely given how busy she seemed, but at least the obstruction was gone.

Twenty minutes after she had formally moved into Kernow House, the electrician arrived under yet another heavy downpour. Hannah gazed up at the glowering skies with a sinking heart. She was beginning to suspect that rain would

be a near constant here, at least from October to March. Except for when it snowed, of course.

The electrician seemed cheerful enough despite the rain, a tall, lanky chap in grey overalls who winked at her as he trudged downstairs to deliver his verdict. 'A few minor issues here and there, but overall the wiring is sound. Good to see someone in the old place again. Houses shouldn't stand empty.'

'I couldn't agree more,' she said firmly.

'I'll need to do some more work upstairs tomorrow.'

'Of course.'

'By the way, there's a litter of kittens in the front bedroom.'

'I know.'

He grinned and held out a hand. 'I'm Jim.'

'Hannah.'

'Does Raphael Tregar know you've moved in?'

'Why do you ask?'

Jim shrugged. 'It's common knowledge he's had his eye on this place for years. I don't blame you for settling in before it's been fixed up. Better a few uncomfortable months than giving him a chance to get in ahead of you and change the locks.'

Her eyes widened. 'Is that a genuine possibility?'

'I wouldn't put anything past him.'

She did not know what to say.

'Well, good luck.' He bent to pack away his tools, then hesitated, glancing around at her. 'Look, it's not a major issue at the moment, but you might want to put a bucket or two up in the attic.'

She stared. 'I'm sorry?'

'The roof's leaking in a couple of places.' Jim picked up his toolbox. 'Probably just some loose slates. But something to keep an eye on.' He paused, covertly looking her up and down. 'Do you need a hand with that? I can carry some buckets up there myself if—'

'That's very kind of you, but I'll be fine.'

Brilliant.

A leaky roof.

She'd only just moved into Kernow House, and already there were problems. Rain-related problems, which she really ought to have expected. At least she had seen some old plastic buckets in one of the outbuildings on her first visit here, so she wouldn't be putting down saucepans to catch the drips.

But she had no time to collect them and carry them up: almost as soon as she had waved Jim off on the doorstep, agreeing a time for him to complete the work the next day, her new fridge and chest freezer arrived. Fortunately she had already swept the kitchen floor in preparation, and soon had them both in position and switched on.

Half an hour later, another delivery van came trundling up the track, this time laden with camping equipment she'd ordered from a shop in Pethporro. The man looked at her doubtfully, but she laughed, saying, 'Just put it all in the living room. Even the sleeping bag. I'll be camping out by the wood burner until the upstairs has been cleaned and readied for new furniture.'

Once all her purchases had been set up, her food shopping

arrived, along with some locally-sourced logs and kindling. Which was good, as it was mid-afternoon by then and Hannah was starting to feel chilly. The rain was easing off so she helped the delivery woman carry the food crates from the van into the kitchen, her stomach already rumbling in anticipation.

Swiftly, she stocked the now-humming fridge with fresh food, then lit a small fire in the wood burner to warm up the living room before dusk fell.

Heading back into the kitchen, she made her first mug of tea using the new camping stove and metal kettle, as she had been unsuccessful in getting the Aga to warm up. It was on full, and the top plates were closed, but so far the heat was negligible. The electrician's view had been that it might take a couple of days to get properly hot – hot enough to boil water, that is – so she would just have to be patient. While she waited, her new camping stove would have to suffice.

'Home Sweet Hovel,' she said, toasting her shiny new appliances. She had found a dusty array of mugs at the back of one of the kitchen cupboards, and rinsed them off under the handpump. Her favourite one was decorated with a faded map of Cornwall. This she raised to her lips in the bittersweet knowledge that her grandmother had probably drunk out of it too. 'Mmm, not bad.'

It was going to be fun, she told herself. An adventure . . .

An unexpected noise at the back door made her turn, startled. A woman's face was framed in the glass panel. She looked to be in her mid-fifties, or maybe older. Red-cheeked, huge-eyed, grey unkempt hair straggling down past her shoulders like rats' tails. But the most astonishing thing

was her height. She had to be easily six foot three, her vast figure completely blocking out the rainy light.

The woman mouthed something incomprehensible, and then banged impatiently on the pane when Hannah was slow to respond. Her fist was clutching two long furry ears that appeared to belong to a dead rabbit. The rest of the unfortunate creature only became visible when she raised it and waved it at Hannah like a trophy.

'Good grief.' Hannah put down her tea and went reluctantly to the back door; the woman clearly wanted to communicate something to her. Warily, she unlocked it and opened it a crack. 'Hello?'

'I be Lizzie.' Her voice was thick, like Cornish clotted cream, and when she smiled, she showed a disconcerting gap where her front teeth had been. 'Lizzie.'

Hannah waited, but there was no more forthcoming. As though the woman's name was an explanation in itself.

'Yes?'

'I catch 'em for Trudy, see.' The woman shook the dead rabbit again, a note of pride in her voice.

'Rabbits?'

'And rats.' Lizzie nodded enthusiastically. 'Specially them big 'uns. They come round the barn, and the old pigsty. I put out traps, then take the dead 'uns away.' She held out the carcass of the rabbit. 'The rabbits I give to Trudy for her stews.' She paused, then looked down at the ground, her voice suddenly mournful. 'Or I did, afore she done passed away. Now I bring 'em to you instead. Yes?'

'Erm, no thanks.' Hannah suppressed a shudder, and waved away the dead rabbit with as much courtesy as she

could manage. 'That's very kind of you, Lizzie. But I'm not a big rabbit stew person, I'm afraid.'

'Oh.'

'Sorry.'

'I could show you how to skin 'em and gut 'em.'

'Oh God, no thanks.' Hannah felt suddenly nauseous, and averted her eyes from the shaggy carcass being dangled in front of her face. 'Sorry, but whatever arrangement you had with Trudy, I can't . . . I can't possibly honour it.'

Lizzie's face crumpled, presumably at the realisation that she was not going to be able to continue bringing dead bodies to the back door of Kernow House.

'I s'pose you be wanting me to move on, then,' she said in a broken voice.

Hannah's gaze narrowed on the woman's face. 'Move on?' She looked Lizzie up and down. 'Sorry, where exactly is it you live?'

'Long Field.' Lizzie pointed vaguely behind the house, as though indicating the area along the raggedy cliff edge. 'In my van. Trudy said I could stay. After the fire.'

'The fire?'

'I was used to live the other side of Pethporro, years back. Only one night some boys got rowdy, set fire to my van.' She pulled back a sleeve to show Hannah burn scarring along her wrist into her forearm. 'Trudy gets me another rig, proper good-like. And says I can have Long Field to myself, no questions asked.' She shook the rabbit at her again, this time sadly, as though aware it was an empty gesture. 'One rabbit a week in rent. Besides I kill them filthy longtails for her, course.'

Hannah hesitated, watching in silent horror as Lizzie dragged down her dirty sleeve to cover her scars again. Poor bloody woman. Hannah could hardly start her residency here by kicking off the local rat-catcher – or whatever Lizzie was – and she had to admit it would be useful to have someone about to keep the vermin population down.

Before she could say a word though, a deep male voice said from behind Lizzie's tall, shambolic figure, 'I'd take Lizzie up on her offer, if I were you. To show you how to gut and skin her rabbits, that is.' The man was invisible, but his voice made her stiffen instinctively. It was almost a drawl, mocking her with every word. 'It's an old country skill, and one I doubt you possess.'

Lizzie blinked, gazing back over her shoulder at this newcomer. 'She said she don't want no rabbits,' she told him plainly, and then hurried past the man with a curt nod, and vanished around the corner into the yard.

At least she'd taken the smelly carcass with her.

Hannah straightened, her eyes widening. She did not need to be psychic to know she was face-to-face with her new neighbour, the conniving Raphael Tregar. His tone had given that away, not to mention his lord-of-the-manor bearing, strutting into her yard like a cockerel.

Meeting his cool, incisive gaze, Hannah sucked air into her lungs and took an instinctive step back. Then another one, for good measure.

He was gorgeous.

Somehow Bailey had neglected to mention that, she thought, studying his tall, broad-shouldered figure in the wax jacket and flat cap. He had a striking face, angular and

almost swarthy, suggestive of long hours spent outdoors in all weathers. It was the kind of face you had to look at at least twice, just to be sure of what you'd seen: it was straight-nosed, high-browed, with a strong jaw and intelligent eyes that held more than usual knowledge.

Not that looks were everything, of course. But goodness, they certainly helped sugar the pill when they came along with a reputation as dodgy as his.

In that brief moment of mutual appraisal, she saw his dark eyes sweep down over her body, then up again. His arrogant gaze studied her face before returning to fix on one particular part of her anatomy. And not the part she suspected he would ordinarily be found staring at on first meeting a woman.

'What the hell?' The mockery had died from his eyes. 'You're *Hannah*?'

'Yes.'

'Trudy's granddaughter?'

'Yes.'

'But you ...' His tone was oddly blank as his gaze rose to her face again. 'You're pregnant.'

CHAPTER FIVE

'Well spotted, Sherlock,' she replied in acid tones, and then attempted to close the back door on her unwelcome visitor.

Raphael Tregar thrust a muddy, steel-capped boot into the gap, effectively stopping the door dead. 'No need for that.' He recovered his poise, a quick smile on his lips. 'Sorry, we seem to have got off on the wrong foot.'

'More a case of foot in the wrong place,' she said, glaring down at his offending boot. 'I've had my fill of visitors today, thanks. I just want to get on with my work.'

'And I promise I'll only keep you a few minutes.' Dragging off his glove, he held out his hand. 'I'm Raphael Tregar.'

'So I guessed. Could you move your foot, please?'

His smile did not falter, even when she ignored his outstretched hand. If anything, it became more persuasive. 'Come on, Hannah. I was hoping we could become friends.' She felt a tug inside at those words, and deliberately hardened her expression. His voice was deep and gravelly, and yet softly Cornish too, his country burr like warm caramel. Damn him. 'We are next-door neighbours, after all.'

'Hardly.'

'There's only one field between our houses,' he pointed

out. 'That makes us next-door neighbours here in Cornwall. And it's not as though we can ignore each other forever.'

'I don't see why not. It's a pretty big field.'

Raphael half laughed, clearly taken aback by her obstinacy. 'Okay, I'm going to assume by your attitude that my reputation has preceded me. But really, you shouldn't listen to local gossip. I'm not all that—'

'Did you dump that washing machine in the middle of my drive?'

'It's not exactly your drive,' he said gently.

'Did you?'

His shrug was eloquent.

'Sorry, what was that thing you just did? That jerking thing with your shoulder?' She glared at him. 'Was that a yes?'

He sighed. 'I may have left a washing machine there temporarily, yes.'

'Dumped it.'

'Left.'

'*Dumped.*'

His smile was frozen in place now. More like a grimace, in fact. 'Look, I didn't come here to argue with you. I admit, I did leave a washing machine in the road ... *accidentally.*'

'Fell off the back of your tractor, did it?'

'Something like that.' His eyes duelled with hers. 'But I also removed it the same day. No harm done. So let's not quibble over details.'

'I couldn't agree more. No quibbling required. All I need is for you to go back to your side of that quagmire you call a field, and let me get on with my work.'

Hannah banged the door against his boot. Repeatedly. In the back of her mind was what Jim the electrician had implied – that Raphael Tregar had his sights set on acquiring Kernow House, and would do more or less anything to get his way. So even allowing the steel-capped toe of his boot over her threshold felt dangerous.

'Sorry,' she said in a burst, 'but could you possibly take your foot out of the way? I have a million things to do, as I'm sure you do too. It was nice to meet you. But I believe this conversation is at an end.'

His dark eyebrows arched upwards in frustrated disbelief. 'Are you always this . . .'

'Straightforward?'

'I was going to say rude.'

'Yes, if by "rude" you mean "unwilling to take any of your man shit".'

'My . . . *what*?'

'Man shit. Shit from a man.'

He looked bemused.

'Finished?' she asked with arctic politeness, and looked down at his offending boot. 'Then could I close my door, please, Mr Tregar?'

Raphael stepped back, almost automatically, and Hannah shut the door in his surprised face, then locked it and drew the top bolt across with a loud crack.

'Good riddance,' she mouthed at him through the glass panel, then dusted off her hands in a mime of satisfaction and marched out of the kitchen, slamming the door behind her.

In the dim corridor, Hannah leaned her forehead against

the cold wall, breathing hard, her shoulders trembling and her legs a little wobbly.

Oh. My. God.

She never argued with people. Well, almost never. And she was never rude. Not like that. But there had been something so infuriatingly smug about Raphael Tregar's smile, and every time he spoke, she remembered that stupid washing machine, rain bouncing violently off it, abandoned smack bang in the middle of her drive. Or road, or whatever it was. And his ludicrous, bare-faced claim that it was an *accident* . . .

She was furious.

Damn him.

And that woman with the dead rabbit!

Her first impulse was to run. To pack up, call a taxi – assuming she could even get a signal on her mobile – and get the hell out of here.

She could still sell Kernow House. It wasn't too late to change her mind. Someone would eventually buy the place if she put it on the market. Raphael Tregar, for starters. Though anyone with a large enough wad of money would do. Anyone interested in buying a ramshackle old barn in the middle of bloody nowhere, complete with newborn kittens and a leaking roof.

As soon as her legs felt less shaky, Hannah stamped upstairs and threw herself on the creaky old mattress in Granny Trudy's room, now covered with a sheet to protect her from any creepy-crawlies that might have made their home in it over the past few months. It wasn't exactly comfortable but she badly needed to lie down, and she was

worried her neighbour might still be hanging about the out-side of the farmhouse, peering through windows. The last thing she wanted was to get cosy on her camping bed in the living room, with all the dubious elegance of a warthog in a watering hole, and spot Raphael Tregar leering at her through a window.

The mother cat sat up in her mangy armchair, staring at her with huge green eyes.

'Sorry, puss, did I disturb your sleep?' Hannah ran a hand through her hair, groaning. 'Blame that bloody man, not me. He's a complete menace, isn't he? Coming here, upset-ting us both . . .'

In response, the tabby cat yawned, displaying two rows of razor-sharp teeth.

'Exactly,' Hannah said, baring her own teeth.

The cat stretched delicately and returned to licking her litter of kittens, presumably discounting Hannah as a threat.

She couldn't sell Kernow House. It had been her grand-mother's dying wish that she should live here. Or at least that's what she felt instinctively. She was *not* a coward. Raphael Tregar had got under her skin, that was all.

That smug bloody smile.

Breathing slowly in and out, trying to regain some calm, Hannah put a hand on her large belly and stared up at the ceiling.

You're pregnant.

Raphael Tregar didn't know anything about her. Not a damn thing. He had looked at her belly and made a few rude assumptions based purely on the fact that she was pregnant

and alone out here. An unmarried young woman, big with child, apparently hiding from the world in the back of beyond. No doubt he thought she had been impregnated and deserted by some feckless male. That she was lurking here out of shame and unhappiness. That she needed to be pitied, for God's sake.

'Damn him.'

Hannah groaned and rolled over, burying her flushed face in the sheet. He had better never come back to Kernow House. Or she would . . .

Well, she didn't know exactly what she would do. She was in no position to dump a washing machine on *his* drive. Besides, she had always thought tit-for-tat a very silly way of doing things, and it was beneath her dignity to be that petty. But harsh words would be exchanged if he came back, that was for sure. Home truths, and all that.

Assuming she knew what those truths were by then. Because right now, she was a mess of confusion and distress and churning hormones. Ever since Santos' death, she had been living from day to day, not daring to look back at what she'd lost, trapped in a long dark tunnel of her own making. Raphael Tregar had just punched a hole in that gloomy tunnel, letting in the brilliance of unwanted light and totally distracting her from what lay ahead. What she needed to do was patch that gap up, and keep trudging grimly on.

Yes, her neighbour was ruggedly good-looking.

But he was also major trouble. He was nothing like Santos, that was painfully clear. He was the kind of man mothers warn their daughters about. The kind who breaks hearts and dumps white goods in the road and wreaks

havoc in otherwise-ordered lives, and then walks away whistling casually, hands in his pockets.

Besides, there was only room for one other person in her life right now.

And that was her baby.

CHAPTER SIX

Within a week, she was the proud owner of a second-hand Land Rover. She had also hired a cleaning team to scrub the house and dispose of the worst of the rotting furniture, and arranged for the phone line to be reinstated. Until it was, however, she still had to rely on the café with free Wi-Fi that she had found in town for access to her emails, as her mobile phone coverage was too patchy. It was one thing to make a quick phone call standing on an upstairs windowsill with her head and one arm thrust out into the rain, and another to try surfing the net in such a precarious position. Especially when she kept catching glimpses of her difficult neighbour every time she popped her head outside.

He seemed to have got into the habit of driving past the house on his tractor, or parking it under a cluster of trees at the far end of the field and just staring from a distance.

Raphael Tregar was clearly trying to intimidate her with his random little visits and watchfulness. But he was not going to succeed.

*

One afternoon on her way to the café, Hannah dropped into the solicitors' offices to invite Bailey to dinner. 'And please bring Penny. I can't wait to meet her.'

'Thanks, I will do. She can't wait to meet you too.' Bailey looked at her carefully, no doubt noting the dark circles under her eyes. 'How are things up at the house, Hannah? You look tired. Teething problems?'

'A few difficult nights, that's all.' Hannah shrugged, though it was impossible to disguise the strain in her voice. 'Nothing I can't handle.'

'Well, if there's anything you need, just ask.' Bailey put a reassuring hand on her arm. 'I'd be happy to help. You know that, right?'

'Honestly, I'm fine.' She forced a smile. 'See you tonight. Seven-thirty?'

It was hard to lie to Bailey, who had been so friendly and open with her. But Hannah had her pride to consider. She did not want to admit that life alone at Kernow House was proving more problematic than she had anticipated. And not just because of her neighbour, the unpredictable Raphael Tregar.

Thank God it was not raining today, she thought, heading outside and peering up into a leaden sky that showed only the faintest gleam of sunshine.

It had rained almost non-stop since she had arrived in Cornwall, and everything she owned had been soaked through at least once. Her favourite cashmere cardigan had shrunk so badly that it now looked like it belonged to a child, so she had donated it to the cat. The litter of squirming kittens had been moved during the big clean-up to a

high-sided cardboard box in the kitchen, set close to the Aga for warmth, and her green sweater now lined the container very comfortably.

Hannah was increasingly glad of the cat and her kittens for company in the long evenings. She had never thought of herself as needy, nor fanciful, but Kernow House was not the easiest place to live alone. The upstairs floorboards had a tendency to creak suddenly in the middle of the night, and the wind had a way of whistling under door frames that made it sound almost like moaning in the dark.

She did not believe in ghosts, and refused to countenance the possibility that Kernow House was haunted. But there had been a few difficult moments over the past few nights when she had thought – or imagined, more likely – there might be someone else in the house with her.

She needed to get a grip on her lively imagination, that was all. Kernow House was her home now. There was no reason to be afraid of living there.

After shopping in the mini-market for that evening's supper, she headed across the street to the café. Luckily, Pethporro was so small, everything in the centre was close together, so it wasn't far to carry the heavy bags.

'A large Americano, please,' she told the waitress as she backed into an alcove seat, thrusting her bags onto the seat opposite.

The waitress, a well-endowed lady with curly black hair that looked suspiciously like a wig, gaped at her in incomprehension. 'A what, sorry?'

'Americano.' Hannah struggled to remember what she had ordered last time she'd visited the café. An English

breakfast tea, as she recalled. 'A black coffee. And I'd like it with some milk on the side.'

'Black coffee with milk on the side?' The waitress stared at her. 'You mean, you want the milk in a jug?'

'I suppose so, yes.'

'Why ever d'you want it in a jug? I can add the milk at the counter, you know. Before I bring it over.'

'But then it would just be a white coffee, not an Americano.'

'It'll be a white coffee once you add the milk, though, won't it?' The woman was nothing if not persistent.

Hannah slipped off her jacket, frowning. 'Erm, I guess so, yes. Technically speaking.' She studied the woman's expression and sighed. 'Fine. I'll have a mug of white coffee, thank you.'

'Coming right up.' The waitress squiggled something on her order pad, then shuffled off behind the counter, muttering to herself, 'Why not just say that in the first place? Them fancy drinks. Milk on the side, not in the mug.' She laughed and began to make the coffee, presumably addressing herself to the ancient man seated on a high stool behind the counter, whose purpose there appeared to be decorative rather than practical. 'Whatever next? Hot milk instead of cold, I suppose. Or that soya milk nonsense. Milk that's never even seen a cow. Not natural, that.'

The old man nodded and cackled, then sucked air noisily through his teeth.

Hannah grinned, and then opened her laptop and went online, using the free Wi-Fi code prominently displayed on every table. She had been searching for suitable jobs in the

area, with little success, and was pleased to see a new notification pop into her inbox.

Pethporro Boxing Day Pageant. Director required: good rates of pay, temporary part-time position, immediate start.

Intrigued, she clicked on the link, and read the job description with mounting excitement. It sounded like the perfect fit for her skill set. Hannah had spent several years now working in event planning and management – albeit for herself and Santos' clients, rather than for a large, bureaucratic organisation like a local council – but the skills were easily transferable, and she had always found it easy working in a team. She didn't foresee any problems.

'Pity it's temporary,' she muttered to herself, and glanced up to see the waitress pottering across to her, steaming mug in hand.

'Your white coffee,' the woman said pointedly, and set it down beside her laptop.

'Thank you.'

But she did not move away as expected. 'Bit late in the season for sightseeing,' she remarked, hovering beside her table. Her curious gaze swept Hannah's casual jeans and hoody, then paused on her laptop screen. 'You here on business?'

A little nettled, Hannah angled the laptop an inch or two away from her, so she couldn't read what was on the screen.

'No, I just moved here.'

The woman raised her eyebrows. 'From upcountry, are you? Some place where they do them posh coffees, I dare say.'

'I've been living in Greece, actually. It's all espressos there.' Hannah suppressed a grin at the woman's expression. 'That's a small, strong black coffee.'

'I dare say,' the woman repeated blankly. 'Greece, eh? Bit of a change in weather for you, then.'

'That's right. Especially with all the rain we've been having.' Hannah moved her coffee closer, though it was still too hot to drink, and added breezily, 'Well, I'd better get on with my work.'

The woman did not take the hint, continuing her relentless interrogation. 'So where are you living? Here in Pethporro? On the new estate, maybe?'

'Not quite in town, actually. I'm at a place called Kernow House.' Hannah saw the woman's eyes widen. 'Do you know it?'

'Trudy Clitheroe's place? Of course I know it. Everyone hereabouts knows Kernow House.' The waitress looked her up and down again. 'You Trudy's granddaughter, then?'

Hannah nodded.

'I'm Fenella,' the waitress said, and held out her hand.

'Hannah,' she replied with a quick smile, and shook the woman's hand, which was warm and oddly damp. She resisted the urge to wipe her palm on her jeans. 'Pleased to meet you.'

Fenella shouted over her shoulder to the old man, not taking her eyes from Hannah's face, 'What do you know, Bert? This here is Trudy Clitheroe's granddaughter. She be living out at Kernow House now.'

The old man cackled again and replied unintelligibly, producing something more akin to a series of dolphin squeaks and whistles than human speech, gesticulating towards her with a knobbly walking stick.

'Well?' Fenella demanded, gazing down at her.

'I'm terribly sorry,' Hannah said awkwardly, 'but I didn't quite catch what . . . what the gentleman said.'

'He asked if Raphael Tregar had paid you a visit yet.'

'Raphael Tregar again? Why is everyone in Pethporro so obsessed with that bloody man?' Much to her chagrin, Hannah felt her cheeks flare with sudden heat, and could have kicked herself for giving so much away. She stopped and fell silent.

'So you have met your neighbour, then. Aye, he's a handful. I still remember him as a lad, kissing the girls and causing merry hell round this town.' Fenella took a dingy-looking cloth from her apron pocket and gave the table a cursory wipe. 'All grown up now, and his bark's worse than his bite these days. But you never know with a man like Tregar.' She nodded and limped back to her counter with obvious satisfaction. 'Well, enjoy your *white coffee*.'

Hannah sighed, turning her attention back to the job application, which was to organise a Cornish pageant for Boxing Day in Pethporro, with a fancy-dress parade through the town and a party on the beach afterwards, to attract new visitors to the area and keep the place on the map during winter's downtime.

If it increased revenue for the town over the Christmas period, the council hoped it might become an annual off-season tourist event.

Glancing through the various specifications and guidelines, Hannah felt her heart pick up speed; she was already envisaging how the event would be run, and what she could do to make it a huge success.

But first she had to fill out the application.

To her relief – since she had no access to a printer at the

house – the form could be filled out online and emailed to the council. She completed it in nearly half an hour and attached her CV as a Word document, then sent it off, crossing her fingers that they did not already have a glut of suitable applicants. After all, she lacked one very important criterion listed on the job description, and that was local knowledge. But she felt confident she could enlist Bailey's help in making friends, and she was already starting to make a few contacts about the town.

Now all she needed was a little luck.

Driving home in the old Land Rover, splashing through puddles, Hannah felt a deep enjoyment in the freedom that having a set of wheels gave her at last. The clouds had rolled away and the sun was out, the lush green fields and slopes breathtakingly beautiful. There was hardly any traffic on the road, and she slowed to admire the occasional thatched cottage that dotted the piecemeal landscape. It was picture postcard territory, and exactly how she had always envisaged the wilds of Cornwall as a child.

Turning down the narrow, unsignposted lane that led towards Kernow House and the ocean, she once again felt a stab of regret that she had never got to know her grandmother. It was clear that Trudy had been quite a character, well-known and liked in Pethporro. But her mother had told her she was dead and had said there was no point in mourning the loss because Trudy had been 'a difficult woman'.

Now that Hannah was grown-up herself, she could see it was her mother who had been difficult, not Trudy. Sadly too late to make amends for that mistake, though.

As she approached the house, she hit the brakes and came to a standstill.

There was a huge green tractor parked facing her in the lane ahead, with her neighbour in the driver's seat. No flat cap this time, his dark hair was clearly visible through the mud-flecked windscreen as he lounged at his ease, leaning both elbows on the steering wheel, looking for all the world as though he had been waiting for her to return.

Raphael Tregar.

What the hell was he doing now?

CHAPTER SEVEN

Hannah stared at the massive tractor in silence, utterly confused. She did not know what to do. The lane behind her was very twisty, and not having driven for several years while abroad, she did not feel confident enough yet to negotiate it in reverse. And what if another car should come up behind her on one of the blind bends?

The tractor ought to back up. His route backwards was mostly straight, as they were fairly close to the house here and there was a pull-in not far ahead.

She did not fancy the thought of another confrontation with her nasty neighbour, but she'd be damned if she was going to end up in the mud. So she put the car in neutral, and waited for him to move, her engine idling.

Nothing happened.

Raphael merely looked at her with an expression of faint hauteur, as though he felt the onus was on her to get out of the way, not him. Except there was nowhere to go. The track leading to Kernow House was only wide enough for one vehicle at a time, and when one of those vehicles was a gigantic tractor, there was no room to manoeuvre whatsoever.

After several minutes of this impasse, Hannah swore

under her breath and fumbled awkwardly for the door handle, getting out of the car.

Avoiding the worst of the mud ruts, she stormed up to the front of the tractor. There was not really enough room to squeeze around and glare at him through the side window, so she narrowed her eyes at Raphael Tregar through the windscreen instead.

'What on earth are you doing here?' she demanded angrily. 'You're in my way. I need to get home and you're blocking the road.'

He mouthed something at her through the glass.

'Look, I don't have a clue what you're saying.' She was thoroughly exasperated now. 'I can't hear you. Why don't you get out of that thing and talk to me properly?'

Raphael mimed opening his door into the abundant hedgerow beside the tractor, making it obvious that getting out was an impossibility.

'Okay, if you can hear me perfectly well, then why can't I hear you?' Suspicious that he was only pretending not to be audible, she planted both hands on her hips and shot him a fulminating stare. 'Enough of this bullshit. I need you to back up, now. Got it?'

With a drily apologetic smile, he shook his head and gestured to her Land Rover, indicating that she should reverse instead.

'Look here, buster, I don't see why I should be the one to move,' she said hotly. 'The lane twists and turns like crazy behind me, but there's a pull-in only a hundred yards back for you. Besides, you weren't even driving when I came around the corner. You were just parked here, in the middle

of the road, deliberately obstructing its users.' She saw his lips twitch, and continued crossly, 'You must have known someone would need access eventually. Why park a tractor somewhere so inconvenient? What could you possibly be doing, stopped in the middle of a country lane?'

He held up a flask and a half-eaten sandwich, regarding her with what looked like amusement.

'Well, this is my drive, and you're bloody well trespassing,' she told him with a snap, very flustered now. 'Please back up at once, or I'll . . . I'll call the police.'

Hannah turned back to her car, determined to carry out her threat if he still refused to budge. She was sick of this man's unneighbourly behaviour. But a sharp rapping on the glass brought her up short. She glanced back to see Raphael Tregar opening the side window of the tractor. Then he called through the narrow opening, 'It's not your drive.'

'I beg your pardon?'

'It's not your drive,' he repeated easily. 'It's mine.'

She gaped at him. What an infernal cheek the man had! First blocking her way, then resorting to bare-faced lies as a defence.

'And how exactly do you work that out? This lane only leads to Kernow House. It's not a public road, it's a driveway.'

'That's true enough.' He nodded towards the lane. 'But the land it's on belongs to me, not you. I bought it from your grandmother a few years ago, along with her last remaining parcels of property.' His dark eyes met hers, and this time there was no mistaking the glint of laughter in them. 'So technically, you're the one who's trespassing.'

She felt as though the air had been knocked out of her.

'That's ridiculous. How can you own the driveway but not the house?' She shook her head. 'I don't believe you.'

'Then ask your solicitor. Ask Knutson. He's the one who handled the sales.'

Hannah felt an incredible anger take hold of her, and found it hard to control herself. Though she did not know why she needed to be polite, given how rude he was.

'I know what this is about,' she burst out, and saw his eyebrows rise at her tone. 'I've already spoken to my solicitor about you, and she told me all about my grandfather's IOU. It's obvious what you're doing. You want Kernow House for yourself, and you think you can get it by coming around here and intimidating me, blocking the road, making my life difficult. Well, you can get knotted. My grandmother left me this place, and I intend to live here, even if you own every blade of grass between my front door and town. Do you hear me? I'm not going to budge an inch, not for anyone.' She stamped back to her rusty old car and flung open the driver's door, tears of fury blinding her as she glared back at the tractor. 'So you'd better ask yourself, Mr Tregar, how are *you* planning to get home? Because if I'm stuck here all day, you are too.'

Then she climbed into the Land Rover and slammed the door shut.

God, the man was intolerable! She ought never to have got out of the car in the first place. That was exactly what he'd wanted. Now she had made a fool of herself in front of him. If he'd been smiling before, what must he think after that little rant? Her face was hot and her hands were trembling. She curled her fingers around the steering wheel and sat there in a breathless silence, chest heaving.

Damn, damn, damn.

Suddenly, Hannah became aware of a diesel engine turning over noisily and looked up to see the green tractor reversing, Raphael checking over his shoulder as he negotiated the narrow, leafy track. Shocked, she watched in disbelief as he reached the pull-in – a muddy semi-circle of grass where a five-bar gate led into a field – and carefully backed the tractor into the small space, leaving her room to pass.

Still a little shaky, she hurriedly started her own engine and lost no time in driving past him, her face averted.

Just before she reached the house, she glanced in her mirror, and saw the tractor was almost out of sight, trundling off down the lane.

She could not quite understand what had just happened.

Santos had been a pleasant, trustworthy kind of man, never sneaky, never deceitful. Like his beaming parents, he had valued honesty and courtesy above all else. In fact, she had grown accustomed to dealing with people the way Santos had done; with a frank smile and a handshake, always genuine, always straightforward.

By contrast, Raphael Tregar was an expert at manipulating people, at getting them to do whatever he wanted. Bailey had told her as much over dinner, and she had seen his skill first-hand, like the way he had tried to excuse his behaviour over the washing machine dumped on her drive. Today Raphael had got her precisely where he wanted her: helplessly out-manoeuvred, and angry enough to give way to a silly temper tantrum more suited to a five-year-old than a grown woman.

And then, after all that game-playing and ironic sandwich-waving, he had blinked first and backed up for her.

Did that mean she had won this skirmish?

Somehow Hannah doubted it.

She had made an elementary mistake, blindly assuming Raphael possessed even one iota of the kindness and integrity she had come to associate with Santos. The two men were chalk and cheese. Expecting Raphael to behave like a gentleman was a lesson in futility, and one she did not intend to repeat. She would know better next time, that was all.

But that did not stop her from smiling as she unpacked her shopping.

Hannah Clitheroe one, Raphael Tregar nil.

CHAPTER EIGHT

Bailey and her partner Penny pulled up to the house promptly at seven-thirty, and Hannah hurried outside to greet them, torch in hand. It was dark outside, though the sea was glinting mysteriously below the cliffs, and she did not want her first-ever guests at Kernow House to fall over a loose stone and break their necks.

'Hello,' Hannah said at the gate, waving the torch beam over the ground so they could see where to walk, 'do please come in. Thank goodness it's not raining tonight.'

'We brought wine,' Bailey said cheerily, squeezing past her into the small front garden. 'Shall I put it in the kitchen?'

'Yes, please. That's the centre of operations tonight. Though I've cleaned up the dining room and laid the table in there, so you won't need to suffer the indignity of a floor banquet after all.'

'Oh, what a shame,' Penny said promptly, grinning. 'I was rather looking forward to that; it sounded so romantic. But maybe we could still eat by candlelight?' She held out her hand. 'Lovely to meet you, Hannah. I'm Penny.'

Bailey's partner – a tall, long-legged woman with short, ash-blonde hair and high cheekbones – looked startlingly

like a model, even though she was dressed casually like Bailey in denim jeans and a sweater, with blue-and-white Converse trainers. Her dangly silver earrings caught the light of the torch and glittered as they shook hands, just dressy enough to make their dinner feel like a special occasion.

'The pleasure is all mine,' Hannah told her, and kept the beam on the path towards the front door. Bailey would be sure of her footing, but she didn't know if Penny had ever been to Kernow House before.

The lights were on inside, spilling out the front, and the house felt quite welcoming. If a little draughty, she thought, shivering despite her hoody as they stepped inside.

'I'm sorry if you're cold,' Hannah added as they headed down the hall, realising too late that she should have warned her guests to dress warmly. 'Trudy never got around to installing central heating, and though I've lit a fire in the dining room, and the Aga's running, everywhere else is a bit on the chilly side.' She followed them into the kitchen. 'Including the upstairs bathroom, I'm afraid, which has a distinctly arctic feel.'

'At least it's not an outside toilet,' Penny pointed out drily, and they all laughed.

Bailey made a face. 'I'd better cross my legs for as long as possible, then. I'm not good with cold toilet seats.' She put down the wine she'd brought and sniffed the air. 'What is that delicious smell?'

'Ratatouille, my signature dish.' Hannah lifted the heavy lid on the pan she had left bubbling on the Aga. Much to her delight, it looked perfect, all the vegetables still recognisable

but softly melting into the tomato-based sauce. 'I'm serving it with chicken breasts in garlic butter.' She paused, replacing the lid as an unpleasant thought struck her. 'Wait – Penny, you're not a vegetarian, are you?'

'You cooked me *chicken*?' Penny looked aghast for a few seconds, meeting her horrified gaze, then threw back her head with a deep, gurgling laugh. 'Don't look so scared. I'm kidding! Of course I eat meat. I eat *anything*.'

Hannah almost slumped in relief. 'Oh my God, that was terrifying.'

'Sorry, did I fail to mention my girlfriend is a prankster?' Bailey mock-punched Penny in the arm. 'Behave yourself, woman. Or I'll put you over my knee.'

'Promises, promises,' Penny said in a purr, much to Hannah's astonishment, and arched finely-drawn eyebrows.

'Hannah, you've done an incredible job in here,' Bailey said, grinning as she adroitly changed the subject. 'When I think what this kitchen looked like when you arrived . . .' She turned on her heel, inspecting the gleaming Aga, the well-mopped flagstone floor, the newly-fitted appliances, all lit by two rows of spotlights in the ceiling, courtesy of Jim the electrician. 'This is nothing short of a miracle.'

'And these little beauties are a miracle in themselves,' said Penny, crouching down beside the box in which the litter of kittens was sleeping. The mother cat opened one baleful eye, regarding these newcomers with little pleasure, though she seemed content as long as nobody came any closer. 'Bailey said you found them upstairs?'

'In Trudy's old bedroom, yes.' Hannah smiled, watching one of the kittens attempt unsuccessfully to scale the high

wall of the cardboard box, falling back weakly onto its siblings after a few seconds. 'I thought it would be warmer for them down here beside the Aga.'

Penny reached into the box as though to right the squirming kitten, then jerked back her hand in a hurry when the mother cat hissed and stretched out a paw, sharp claws showing.

'Okay, I get the message,' she told the protective tabby, and straightened up again with a nervous laugh. 'No touching.'

'It would serve you right to get a scratched hand, Penny. You should know better than to interfere with a new litter.' Bailey was studying the ancient handpump that was still Hannah's only source of water. 'Hannah, are you replacing this?'

'I've got a plumber coming tomorrow. He thinks it will only take a day or two to install a sink and taps. Which is a relief, as the new kitchen cabinets are scheduled to arrive tomorrow. Then this lot can be taken away.' She ran a hand along the scratched old work surface. 'I can't wait to see the final result. I chose dark oak cabinets, to fit the old-fashioned feel of the house.'

'That sounds lovely,' Penny said approvingly.

'But very expensive.'

Bailey glanced around at her, no doubt catching her rueful tone. 'Beginning to regret not selling up?'

'Not at all,' Hannah said, somewhat untruthfully, and busied herself finding two glasses. She turned to open the bottle of Spanish Rioja that Bailey had brought. 'Wine, both of you?'

'Not for me,' Penny said quickly, 'I'm driving tonight. I'll be fine with a cup of tea.'

'I'll join you.'

'Looking after Baby's health?'

'Dreary, I know. But it doesn't feel right, drinking alcohol when I'm pregnant. Not to mention the fact that I'm still a bit queasy at times.' She laughed, putting a hand to her ever-expanding waistline. 'Once she's born, I'll probably lie down under a wine vat for a week.'

'*She?*' Bailey repeated with an inquisitive look.

Hannah smiled. 'I had a scan. The sonographer said it was definitely a girl.'

'What you wanted?'

'Boy, girl, it doesn't bother me. I'll be thrilled as long as she's healthy.'

'Of course.'

'Sorry to ruin your plans, but I suspect you'll be too busy as a new mum for much wine-drinking.' Penny gave her a mischievous wink. 'One of my friends had a baby about six weeks ago. She says she barely has time to get dressed in the mornings, and when she does, the baby always seems to throw up on her. Mostly she just gives in and stays in her PJs all day.'

'Oh God.'

'Pay no attention to Penny,' Bailey said, shooting her partner a quelling stare. 'She's a doom merchant. I'm sure you'll have a wonderful time with Baby.'

'Thanks,' Hannah said drily.

Once she had poured a large glass of red wine for Bailey, Hannah filled the new electric kettle and put it on to boil. It felt strange to have guests at Kernow House, she thought. Perhaps she had grown more accustomed than she realised

to living alone here, which wasn't necessarily a bad thing given how jumpy she had become lately, hearing strange noises in the middle of the night. But it would do her good to have some company for once.

She made a mental note to ask Bailey who owned the lane that led to the house. Maybe later though, when they sat down to dinner together. It all felt a bit raw at the moment, and she was not sure she would be able to remain calm once Raphael Tregar's name came up. That bloody man seemed to have a talent for unnerving her.

'I do need to get a job soon or I'll go stir-crazy, stuck out here on my own,' she told them while she prepared the chicken. 'Though I may have found one, right here in Pethporro.'

'Really?' Bailey looked pleased. 'How wonderful. What is it?'

'Director of the Pethporro pageant on Boxing Day.' She shrugged, trying not to let her nerves show. 'Of course, I only applied this afternoon. But with my experience, I'm confident of getting an interview at least.' Turning away to make Penny's tea, she sketched out the parameters of the job description she'd found online. 'Event management is my forte. That was my job in Greece, essentially. So I can do that part with my eyes closed. The only problem is local knowledge. I don't have any, and it was specified as a requirement, so that could be a stumbling block for me.'

When she turned back, cup of tea in hand, Penny was staring at her openly, and Bailey was looking down at her feet, a frown on her usually friendly face.

The silence felt uncomfortable.

Hannah held out the mug to Penny. 'Is that enough milk?'

'Perfect, thank you.'

But her tone was off.

Worried, she looked from Bailey to Penny, sensing a sudden tension in the room. She wondered for a fleeting moment if they disapproved of her applying to run a local event when she was such a total newcomer. After all, she had never been to Cornwall before last week, let alone Pethporro. And now she was muscling in on a regional celebration.

Perhaps they felt it was a job for a long-term resident, and part of her suspected they might be right. But she desperately needed to find work if she was to stay on at Kernow House, which was rapidly turning into a money pit. The Greek travel business she had run with Santos had been so massively successful that she had sold it to a rival company for a substantial amount of money, but that lump sum would not last forever, not at the rate her home renovations were consuming it.

Or maybe they felt she should not be working when she was pregnant. The timing was a little tricky, it was true. By the time of the pageant on Boxing Day, she would be rather large. But as long as the baby didn't make a premature appearance, it should not become a problem. She knew plenty of pregnant women who had worked into their third trimester. And as a freelancer, what choice did she have?

'Okay, what's the matter? Is it because I'm expecting a baby?' She took a deep breath. 'Because she's not due until early March. I can't sit around here every day for the next four months. I'll go insane with boredom. Not to mention broke.'

'No, it's not that.' Bailey smiled, but it looked forced.

WINTER WITHOUT YOU | 76

'Honestly, it's just ... we didn't realise that particular job was vacant. Again.'

'*Again?*'

Bailey looked at Penny, who shrugged.

'I'm sorry,' Hannah said, putting down her tea, 'but you're going to have to explain, because I'm totally in the dark here. What am I missing?'

Bailey sighed, putting a hand to her temple as though her head hurt, then said quietly, 'Raphael Tregar.'

Hannah stared at her new friend, unable to keep the dismay out of her face. 'Him again? You're kidding me.'

'He's on the local council. Didn't I mention that?'

A sinking feeling swept over her. 'Oh God, yes. I remember now. You did say something about him being involved. I completely forgot. So you think he'll quash my application because of his claim on the house? Is that it?'

'Not entirely.'

'I'm sorry, I don't understand ...'

When Bailey said nothing, her face troubled, Penny looked at Hannah sympathetically. 'Didn't you wonder why it was being advertised so late? I mean, it's the middle of November and these big tourist affairs usually take six months to organise, sometimes a year.'

'Yes, but I thought ...' Hannah shook her head. 'I didn't stop to question it, actually. I was so keen to get the job.' She looked at Bailey grimly. 'Okay, you'd better tell me everything. Where does Raphael Tregar fit into the picture?'

'Can't we eat first?' Bailey asked, almost pleading. 'I'm not sure I feel strong enough to discuss him on an empty stomach.'

'What an excellent suggestion.' Penny gave Hannah a quick hug. 'Now don't look so worried. You'll give yourself indigestion. Look, why don't you go and sit down, and we'll serve the food?'

'No, you're my guests.'

'We insist,' Penny said firmly.

Bailey was nodding too, so it seemed fruitless to argue with them. She pointed out the plate cupboard and cutlery drawers, then wandered down the hall to the dining room alone, leaving the two women to bustle cheerfully about her kitchen, whistling as they served the dinner she had cooked.

The dining room looked lovely tonight, Hannah had to admit. The open fire was burning well now, and the wood-panelled room felt very cosy, firelight flickering over slate flags. The antique table was an eight-seater and rather large for the three of them, but by using only one end, she had been able to make it feel more intimate.

There was already a jug of iced water on the table. She poured everyone a glass, then lit the candles in the two silver candelebra and arranged them on the table, remembering Penny's request for a candlelit supper. By the time she had put more logs on the fire, stoking the hot embers with a poker, Penny and Bailey had appeared, bearing plates of hot food. They chided her for still being on her feet, so she laughed and sat down at the head of the table. It was true she was feeling a bit hot and flushed, but some of that was down to annoyance over Raphael Tregar; there was no point trying to deny his ability to upset her.

'I'm pregnant, you know. Not an invalid.'

'Hey, enjoy it,' Penny said, and placed a heaped plate in front of her with a dramatic flourish. 'We don't do this for everyone. This is the full silver service.'

'Well, it's very kind of you.'

To her relief, the ratatouille looked and smelt delicious, and the garlic chicken breasts were perfectly cooked. The other two sat down on either side of her, grinning at each other across the table. Bailey sniffed her food appreciatively.

'Gorgeous.'

'It does smell fantastic,' Hannah agreed.

'Shall I say grace first?' Penny enquired, knife and fork poised in the air.

Hannah blinked. She wasn't very religious, but . . .

'Of course.'

Penny took a breath, and then said pompously, 'Grace.' Then tucked into her dinner. 'There you go. All the formalities observed.'

'Idiot,' Bailey said, shaking her head at her girlfriend, but she was smiling.

They ate for a few minutes in silence, savouring the food. But Hannah found she was not enjoying her meal as much as she'd hoped. She was still thinking – and worrying, frankly – about Raphael Tregar. She couldn't seem to get the blasted man out of her head. Or out of her life. It was bad enough putting up with him haunting Kernow House. But now apparently he had the power to interfere with her job application.

'Bailey,' she said at last, 'who owns the track that leads from the main road to the house? I assumed it must be part of Kernow House.'

Taking a sip of wine, Bailey hesitated before answering. Her expression was carefully neutral. 'That would be Raphael Tregar too, I'm afraid,' she said. 'Your grandmother sold nearly all her land to him over the last few years. She needed the money for the upkeep of the property. The details will be in the bundle of documents Mr Knutson gave you when you took possession. All the sales records should be in the file, and a map showing your legal boundaries.'

'So Raphael wasn't lying?'

Bailey looked at her sharply. 'You spoke to him about it?' She exchanged glances with Penny. 'To Raphael himself?'

Hannah nodded, avoiding their curious gazes as she picked at her dinner. 'He was parked in the drive when I came home earlier. Right across the lane. When I told him to move, he claimed the track belonged to him.' She sighed. 'I didn't believe him.'

'Unfortunately, it's true.'

'So I own the house, but not the access to it?'

'He can't stop you gaining access. If he does, tell him you'll involve the police. He may be the landowner, but you have a right of way. Besides, he had some kind of amicable arrangement with Trudy about the use of it. I don't know exactly what that entailed – and I know it's hard when he's such a bully – but I'd suggest you avoid open warfare and try keeping to the same arrangement if possible.'

'Thanks for the advice,' Hannah said grimly, not relishing the thought of having to play nice with her neighbour from hell. 'I also met another of my neighbours.' When they both stared at her blankly, she added, 'Lizzie? She lives in a camper van in Long Field, apparently.'

Bailey nodded. 'Ah, yes. A lovely woman, but definitely a local character. Special needs of some kind. Been living out there for years.' Her smile was curious. 'Did she come round offering to catch rats for you?'

'That's the one.'

'Yes, she popped up out of nowhere when I was viewing the property with Mr Knutson. Claimed she was here to keep the place free of vermin, that she had a prior arrangement with your grandmother.' Bailey shrugged. 'We told her we couldn't pay for the service, but she didn't seem to care. Has she been giving you any bother?'

'None at all. I just wondered if you knew about her. Raphael turned up at the same time, and he seemed on reasonable terms with her.'

Penny gave a snort of laughter. 'So he's got one friend, then.'

'Possibly.' Hannah paused. 'While we're on the unpleasant subject of Raphael Tregar, perhaps you could tell me more about his connection to the Boxing Day pageant.'

Bailey flicked her a glance, then swallowed her mouthful of food. Putting down her knife and fork, she studied her plate thoughtfully. 'Well, as far as I know, there have been two people in charge of the pageant to date. Maria Sutton was the first. She started in early summer, commuting from Truro, so I think it was quite a strain for her straightaway. And she was young and inexperienced.' She grimaced. 'She only lasted about a month.'

'Do you know why she left?'

'I'm not entirely sure. But rumour has it Raphael hounded her out with his unreasonable behaviour. You know, constantly

disagreeing with her decisions, demanding changes at every stage, making her life generally uncomfortable.'

'I can believe that,' Hannah muttered.

'Then Jennifer Bolitho took over from Maria. Late twenties, more experienced, and a local too. She only lives down the coast at Boscastle, and her family's Cornish to the hilt, going back generations. So she ticked all the boxes with the council.' Bailey paused. 'To be honest, I thought Jennifer was still doing the job. But if they're advertising for the position again, she must have quit.'

Penny made a face. 'Just tell her, Bailey.'

'I'm not spreading gossip.'

'Why not? What else is gossip good for?'

Bailey sighed, and cocked her head at Hannah. 'Look, I can't be sure about this, so take it with an entire salt cellar, okay? But people around town are saying that Jennifer and Raphael ... Well, it's hinted that they are – or were – a couple.'

'Before or after she got the job?'

'That's the real question, isn't it?' Penny chipped in.

Hannah was surprised by Bailey's warily averted face. It was obvious the solicitor was uncomfortable with passing on local gossip, especially of such a salacious type. But since it did seem to have a bearing on her own situation – given she had just applied for the same job Jennifer had been doing – she pressed on regardless.

'In other words,' she said, 'if they've stopped seeing each other, maybe the office romance got awkward and she quit because of that?'

'Or he sacked her,' Penny said.

'But that would be monstrous. Sexual harassment in the workplace.'

Penny shrugged. 'That's Raphael Tregar for you.'

'Penny!' Bailey gave her partner a warning look. 'We mustn't jump to conclusions without any evidence. We don't know for sure what happened between them.'

'No, but we do know he's trouble,' Hannah pointed out.

'Precisely.' Penny speared a large piece of courgette, and nodded at her wisely over it. 'So if you still want that job, you have been warned.'

CHAPTER NINE

On Friday, the morning after her mini-dinner party, a telephone landline was finally installed at Kernow House. With it came broadband, which meant Hannah did not have to go into town to access her emails any more, or hang precariously out of an upstairs window, hoping for a signal on her mobile. Simply being able to pick up a handset and press the button for a ringtone felt like a triumph, as though she had rejoined contemporary society after long days of languishing in medieval world.

Sitting down at the kitchen table, Hannah opened her laptop, and immediately found an email waiting for her from the council.

'That was quick.'

Hurriedly, she clicked on it before she could lose her nerve and trawl through her less-daunting Facebook notifications instead. It was an invitation to attend an interview on Monday afternoon at the council offices, along with an apology for the short notice. To her relief, there was no mention of Raphael Tregar, and the email was signed by Patricia Cobbledick, council secretary. Nonetheless, Hannah felt ridiculously apprehensive as she typed her reply, politely

thanking the secretary for her response and confirming that she could make the time of the interview.

She studied the attached map. The council offices were in a new development, in a part of Pethporro she had not yet explored, but they didn't look hard to find.

'I mustn't blow this,' Hannah said aloud to herself, and smiled when the mother cat chirruped, watching her curiously over the edge of her cardboard box. 'Sorry, did I disturb you?' She got up and opened a pouch of cat food, squeezing it into the old saucer she had been using as a pet dish. The cat jumped lightly out of the box and began to eat at once, no longer concerned by her presence. 'If you want any more of this duck in gravy, pussy cat, you'd better hope I get the job. Because cat food costs money, and if I run out of dosh, you'll have to go back to catching your own dinner.'

Poor mice, she thought ruefully. Between the tabby cat and that odd Lizzie creature with her traps, it can't be much fun around here for rodents. But at least it meant the place wasn't overrun with tiny scampering feet.

She watched the cat lick assiduously around the saucer, hunting down the last remnants of the gravy. 'I also can't keep calling you pussy cat. I'll have to think up a name for you.' She bent and stroked the animal gingerly between the ears. To her surprise, she did not dodge away as usual, but stood a moment, eyes half-closed, purring loudly with pleasure, before hopping back into the box and curling up beside her kittens again. 'Contented little thing, aren't you? I wonder if motherhood will suit me as well as it does you.'

*

Hannah had two full days over the weekend to prepare for the interview, which suddenly did not feel long enough. Not when she would almost certainly have to face cross-examination from her nasty neighbour. Getting the right interview outfit would be key. She spent most of that morning rummaging through her best clothes, most of which hung inside Trudy's vast mahogany wardrobe, and decided at last on a knee-length camel-wool skirt with a forgiving elasticated waist, and a discreet cream blouse to cover her bump.

It made her look a bit mumsy, she thought, studying herself in the bathroom mirror, but there was no point, after all, trying to conceal that she was pregnant. At least one member of the council already knew about her condition, and she did not want to be accused of dishonesty.

Later that afternoon, she drove into Pethporro to do some shopping, braving the cold November winds with the help of a thick hat and coat. The deep heat of Greece seemed like nothing but a distant memory now. It hurt to remember those years – her idyllic life with Santos, cut so horribly short by his death – but she'd promised herself she'd never forget the love they shared nor the wonderful time they'd had together.

At least Santos had known Hannah was pregnant before he died. In fact, that had been why she wasn't with him on the day of the avalanche, otherwise she might have been killed too. He had insisted she take things easier once the pregnancy test proved positive.

'It's not just about you and me anymore,' he'd whispered in her ear as they parted that last time. 'You have to keep yourself safe, Hannah. Think about the baby. Okay?'

Hannah had resented the pregnancy at first, especially after he died and she was left alone with the pain of his loss. Now though, as her belly swelled and she began to experience vague little flutterings that might be the baby moving inside her, she felt more in touch with her body. She sometimes wondered if she ought to have stayed in Greece and made her home with his parents, as they had kindly offered, but without Santos there to make the days bearable, she had found them overprotective, their conservative lifestyle claustrophobic and even suffocating at times.

Hannah had not so much left Greece as fled to England, relieved to be free and independent again. Even if money was increasingly an issue.

She bought herself a loose orange smock top in the only clothes shop in town – which did not cater for pregnant women – and some new underwear. Clearly, if she wanted to wear anything more stylish than an outsized T-shirt in the coming months, she would need to buy maternity outfits online, or perhaps take a day trip to Truro.

Using a map app on her phone, she rapidly located the Pethporro hardware store. There, she bought herself an iron and an ironing board – both of which had been conspicuous in their absence among her grandmother's belongings – and after another spot of food shopping, mostly fresh fruit and vegetables, she drove home again to Kernow House, laden down with goodies.

The sky was darkening by the time she turned off the main road towards the house. To her relief, there was no tractor blocking the approach lane today, and no tractor in the adjacent fields.

No sign of Raphael Tregar whatsoever, in fact.

Had he grown tired of taunting her?

Carrying her new acquisitions around to the back door, Hannah became aware of an odd sense of pique at his absence. A pique that was swiftly quashed when she turned the corner and came face-to-face with Raphael Tregar himself, hands in his jeans pockets, lounging at his ease in the doorway.

CHAPTER TEN

'Bloody hell,' she said, recoiling with a gasp. 'You nearly gave me a heart attack, lurking around the corner like that!' She glared at him, too startled to remember that she was supposed to be behaving professionally towards him. So much for having grown tired of taunting her! 'What are you doing here, Mr Tregar? I thought I'd made it clear I didn't want to speak to you.'

His eyebrows rose steeply at her tone, and his mouth quirked in a crooked smile. 'Good afternoon to you too, Miss Clitheroe. Do you need a hand with those bags?'

'No, thank you.' She lifted her chin. 'Please go away. Whatever you have to say, you can do it through my solicitors.'

'I'm not here about my claim,' he said, his expression unrevealing. 'Though I can assure you, I do have a legitimate right to Kernow House.'

'If it's so legitimate, why haven't you approached anyone about it? You have to make a formal claim on the property, you know. You can't just sneak around, threatening people.'

'Is that what I'm doing, Miss Clitheroe? Threatening you?'

She badly wanted to shout, 'Yes, so piddle off!' at him, and then get inside and slam the door in his face a second time.

But she dared not.

Wanting access to her home aside, this man could potentially destroy her chances of getting a good local job in her field of expertise. The nearest alternative work – as a quick search of the internet had revealed – was in housekeeping or hospitality, and even those positions were scarce, this being the off-season. She couldn't wait until spring to start earning money, notably given her due date.

Play nice, she told herself, counting silently to five.

'Of course not.' Her smile was as fake as a fifty-quid Rolex. 'I'm merely a little confused. You say you have an IOU that grants you ownership of Kernow House, but you haven't made any move to enforce that legally.' She tried not to sound sarcastic, but could see from his ironic gaze that he was not fooled for a moment. 'Naturally enough, I'm curious to know, why the delay?'

'Because I haven't made my mind up yet.' Raphael Tregar looked her up and down, his eyes pausing on her prominent bump once again. 'But that's not why I'm here. I need your help with an urgent matter.'

'My help?'

'Do you have any wellies?'

She stared at him, bewildered.

'I need you to walk across the fields with me, and it's very muddy at this time of year.' He studied her trainers with a supercilious expression. 'Somehow I don't think those will survive the journey.'

'I'm not walking anywhere with you.' She brushed past him and put her key in the back door. 'I've got better things to do, thank you, then indulge your . . . mind games.'

'Mind games?' Raphael Tregar was close behind her, as though about to follow her inside the house. 'If I was going to play games with you, Miss Clitheroe, they'd have nothing to do with your mind.'

Her face was suddenly full of heat. The inference behind his words was plain. And to her chagrin, her imagination had already raced ahead, leaving her breathless and not sure where to look. She turned in the doorway, clutching her shoppings bags tightly against her chest as though they might constitute some kind of defence.

'What do you want, Mr Tregar?'

'A difficult situation has arisen, and I can't resolve it without your help. All I need is for you to put on some wellies and come with me. It shouldn't take long. But we do need to hurry,' he added, glancing back up at the sky, which was thickening with dark clouds, 'before dusk falls.'

'Not until you tell me where we're going, and why.'

Raphael Tregar sighed. 'I'll tell you everything, but only if you put your boots on. You do own a pair, I hope? Because you're in Cornwall now.'

Thankfully, wellingtons had been put on her shopping list a few days before, after she had ruined an old pair of trainers by tramping around the muddy back garden. So she was able to give him a fulminating stare, and state boldly, 'Of course I have some. What do you think I am? An idiot?'

'I think you're a city girl in the sticks, Miss Clitheroe,' he said with unerring accuracy. 'But I'm trying not to hold that against you.'

'Thank you so much,' she said sarcastically, and backed into the kitchen with her purchases. 'Very well. Since this is

apparently so urgent . . . But I have to put my shopping away first. Do you mind?'

'Sure you don't need a hand?'

He had followed her in, closing the back door behind him. He seemed very large all of a sudden, taking up more space than she had anticipated. Somewhat flustered, Hannah shook her head. 'No, I'm fine. Why don't you just tell me what this is all about? And please say it's important. Because it is getting dark, and the last thing I want to do is go trekking through the mud at dusk.'

'Naturally it's important or I wouldn't have come here in the first place.' He pulled out one of the pine chairs, then sat down on it and crossed his legs. His gaze swept the homely kitchen, noting the shiny new sink and taps, only just installed. 'Already making your mark on the old place, I see.' He sounded vaguely approving. 'I kept telling Trudy she needed to get rid of that handpump, especially since she found it particularly hard to operate in the winter months when her rheumatism was playing up, but she wouldn't listen.'

'Perhaps she couldn't afford to replace it,' Hannah said tartly.

'Perhaps.' He turned his steely gaze back towards her, folding his arms across a broad chest. 'And where were you, all that time? I don't recall Trudy ever mentioning that you had visited.'

Hannah began stuffing vegetables into the fridge without paying much attention to what she was doing, standing the celery next to the milk. She stared down at the salad bag in her hand, her throat choked with emotion. He was perfectly right, of course. But he didn't know why she had never

visited her grandmother. Her mother had lied to her, that was the simple truth, but perhaps Hannah should have questioned it. She ought to have realised her mum might pretend Trudy was dead, simply to avoid having to go back home. That was the kind of woman she had been, after all. Cold and unreliable and narcissistic, like all sociopaths.

Yet how to explain such a difficult thing? Especially to someone who had made up his mind about her long ago.

'I went to Greece after university, and I've been there ever since.'

'And before that?'

'It's complicated.' She thrust the salad bag into the fridge, and slammed the door so hard that everything inside rattled. 'Look, stop trying to change the subject. What's all this about, Mr Tregar?'

'Raphael, please.'

'I prefer Mr Tregar.'

'Even though we might be working together soon?'

She stared at him. 'You've seen my application? Why didn't you say anything before?' Slowly, her brain filtered his words. Her eyes widened. 'Are you telling me I'm going to get the job? Isn't that a little premature? I haven't even been interviewed yet.'

'Difficult little cat, aren't you?' Removing his flat cap, Raphael placed it on his knee, watching her through narrowed eyes. 'Yes, I've seen your CV. On paper at least, you look like a good fit. But I have no power to give you a job just like that,' he clicked his fingers, 'so please disabuse yourself of the idea. You'll be interviewed by the committee, and the committee will make the final decision.'

'Committee.'

'The pageant committee, of course.' His gaze locked with hers. 'Though I do happen to chair that committee.'

'Oh, I see.'

Her sarcasm was not lost on him. He laughed appreciatively. 'Look, you've got me wrong. I like to keep my private life separate from my public life. I'm not here about your application. Like I said, this is a different matter.'

'A matter that requires me to call you Raphael instead of Mr Tregar?'

There was that smile again. It was hard not to be swayed by his charm and good looks, which were both considerable, but Hannah was making a brave effort.

'It's not a requirement. More a special favour, let's say.' He tilted his head to one side, studying her. 'Plus, I'm the nearest thing you've got to a neighbour for miles. How tough could it be for you to unbend and call me Raphael? And for me to be allowed to call you Hannah instead of Miss Clitheroe?' His smile twisted slightly. 'Without wishing to incur your wrath, that is.'

She leaned back against the kitchen cupboard, and folded her arms. 'Very well, *Raphael*,' she said, with deliberate emphasis, 'what is it you want? Why are you dragging me out of my house at sunset?'

'It's Lizzie,' he said, and for the first time she heard a troubled note in his voice. 'She's got this ridiculous idea in her head, and you're the only one who can help.'

'Lizzie?'

'The woman who brought you the dead rabbit.'

'I know who Lizzie is. What do you mean, she's got a

ridiculous idea in her head? And how is that anything to do with me?'

'She's leaving,' he said bluntly.

'Sorry?'

'Lizzie has a certain black-and-white way of looking at the world. Probably some sort of undiagnosed autism. Anyway, she's worked herself up into a state over what you said to her that day. She believes you told her to leave Long Field, so that's precisely what she's doing.'

'What?'

'She's been camped there for years, in an old van that's barely roadworthy. In fact, I would have said it didn't even run,' he said brusquely, 'until this afternoon, when I came across it outside my farmhouse. Lizzie had driven it there, and not surprisingly, the rusty old heap had broken down after less than a mile. I found her tinkering with the engine, in floods of tears.'

'Oh no!'

'When I asked what was wrong,' he continued, as though she had not spoken, 'Lizzie insisted that you'd evicted her. She didn't know where she was going, only that she needed to leave her home.' His voice was cool and relentless. 'She's got nowhere to go, Hannah. No money and no relations. But she's got her pride, and she won't stay where she is not welcome.'

'I didn't tell her she wasn't welcome.'

'Didn't you?'

Hannah met his hard gaze, and struggled to remember what exactly it was she had said to Lizzie that day. Perhaps she had been overly abrupt with the woman. But that dead animal . . .

'She must have misunderstood. I said I didn't want her rabbit, that's all.' She frowned, perplexed. 'Anyway, Long Field is yours, as you were happy to tell me. Not mine. You own all the land around this house. So I can hardly evict her when it's not my property.'

'Lizzie doesn't understand any of that. When she moved here, that field belonged to your grandmother Trudy. As far as she's concerned, it now belongs to you. And you made it clear her services as a pest controller were no longer required.' His lips compressed. 'I heard you myself.'

'I didn't mean she had to *leave*.'

He stood up abruptly, fitting his cap back onto his dark head. 'Then get your boots on and come with me. You need to explain to her exactly what you did mean. Because once Lizzie has fixed that old engine, she'll be on her way for good. And it's not safe for her out there.' He made swiftly for the back door, not waiting for her. 'If anything happens to her, it'll be your fault.'

'That's hardly fair!'

Hannah trailed after him to the back door, where a brand-new pair of green wellies stood on the slate floor, immaculately clean and unused. She saw his glance rake over them, his lip curling, and knew what he was thinking.

Townie!

She dragged the boots on, not looking at him again, and snatched her raincoat off the hook before following Raphael into the gloom of the yard. It was past four o'clock, with rain spotting intermittently, the sky darkening into a chill November dusk. She thought of poor Lizzie, working on her

engine in the near-dark, distressed and unsure where to go, and was swamped by terrible guilt. Hannah had certainly not meant to evict the woman. Yet somehow that was the message that had got through.

If that miscommunication was genuinely her fault, then she had better fix it.

Walking swiftly, Raphael Tregar led the way along a winding and precarious cliff edge path, seemingly unconcerned by the terrifying drop to the ocean below. Long wet grass and nettles whipped at her legs, and her new boots were soon squelching through mud, spattered and unrecognisable. Hannah had only ventured that way twice, and on both occasions had hurried home after a few hundred yards of exploration, blown back by the strong, blustering Cornish winds. Even now, she was afraid she might lose her footing and plunge hundreds of feet to her death. But Raphael did not even glance back at her.

'You didn't come by tractor, then?' she asked, eyeing the darkening path ahead with foreboding, and secretly hopeful he might have parked it in one of the fields along the way. 'Or in a car?'

'I'm afraid not.' Finally, he glanced around at her and then pointedly at her no-longer-pristine wellingtons, his tone mocking. 'I take it you don't like *walking*?'

'I enjoy walking very much, thank you. I only meant . . . When it's so urgent, it would be quicker by car.'

'I didn't want Lizzie to know I was coming to fetch you,' he said shortly, looking away from her again. 'I told her I

was going to check on my flock. But I asked her to wait until I got back. I said I wanted to give her something before she left.'

'Your – I'm sorry, did you say flock?'

'That's right.'

'You mean, a flock, as in *sheep*?' Now it was her turn to look him up and down, somewhat dazed. 'You're a . . . a shepherd?'

'These days,' Raphael said, his look sardonic, 'we prefer the word *farmer*.' As Hannah continued to stare, he added, 'You see, some farmers grow crops. Other farmers herd cows. And some farmers—'

'Have flocks of sheep.'

'Precisely.'

'But where's your dog? Don't sheep farmers have . . . sheepdogs too? Not those huge, hairy Old English ones but the smaller black-and-white ones?'

'Yes, they do,' he said blandly. 'In fact, I have two of those to help me. I call them Merry and Pippin.'

'Merry and Pippin?'

She was staring at him so hard, she stumbled over a grassy hillock in the gloomy half-light, and would have fallen if he had not caught her by the elbow and jerked her upright again.

'Thank you,' she said, feeling foolish. Raphael withdrew his hand with an abrupt nod, and they continued walking. But suddenly she was aware of him in a way she had not been before, and it was not an entirely comfortable sensation. 'Sorry, you named your dogs after the two hobbits in *Lord of the Rings*? As in, Frodo's sidekicks?'

'Precisely,' he said again.

'I love those novels.'

'So do my dogs.'

Raphael Tregar was definitely mocking her, damn him. She could not resist a little mocking in return. 'Does that mean you see yourself as Frodo?' He gave her a hard look but did not reply. She smiled to herself, guessing she had hit a nerve. 'So, do you have a crook?'

'Excuse me?'

'A shepherd's crook. Do you have one?'

Her new green wellies squelched noisily in the mud. They were getting absolutely filthy, she thought ruefully, but then glanced at Raphael's black ones; they appeared to be more sludge than rubber.

'Yes.'

'What do you use it for?' When he turned his head, his eyebrows raised, she added, 'I've always wondered. Being a townie.'

'Of course.'

She suppressed the urge to stick her tongue out at him.

'Well? Do you hook sheep with it?'

'Yes.'

'Round the neck?'

'When they're running away from me.' His tone was dry. 'When they're facing me, I hook them by the leg.'

'Oh, poor things. Doesn't that hurt?'

He threw back his head and laughed, a rich, amused sound. 'You're funny.'

'I didn't mean it as a joke.' A little stung, she traced the line of their path ahead as it turned away from the cliff

edge and trailed inland across a rough, muddy expanse of grass. The setting sun had sunk below the cloud line and was in her eyes now, but as she squinted she could make out the distant, ragged outline of buildings several fields away. His farm? 'How much further is it?'

'Tired?'

'No, I just . . .' She heard him laugh again, and gritted her teeth. 'I was worried Lizzie might leave before we get there.'

He was silent for a moment, the only sounds the wind rushing over the field and the constant roar of the sea below them. Then he said, 'Less than half a mile. But it's easy walking.' He paused. 'Lizzie won't leave. I left her with the dogs, asked her to keep an eye on them.'

'Wouldn't she expect you to have taken them with you? If you really were checking on your flock?'

'I doubt that she gave it a second thought.' It was getting darker now, and she could no longer see his face clearly, but she heard the smile in his voice. 'Lizzie's very fond of the dogs. And they like her too, which is surprising.'

Hannah frowned, instantly assuming he was being rude about the other woman. 'Why is it so surprising? Because Lizzie is a bit different?'

'No,' he replied patiently, 'because sheepdogs are working animals, not pets. They don't tend to make friends easily. But they've always let Lizzie fuss over them. What did you think I meant?'

This time it was her who did not answer.

The field came to an abrupt end a few hundred feet on. Hannah had hoped to find a lane on the other side, but to her

dismay it was just another field, in an even worse state than the first. They climbed over an old wooden stile, one after the other, Raphael going first and offering her a hand, which she declined disdainfully. She misjudged the distance in the gathering gloom, however, as she jumped down and slipped on a loose, unseen stone. Arms flailing out to save herself, she landed on her hands and knees in the gooey mud, then tried to get up too quickly and ended up falling face- and chest-first straight into the mire.

'Oh, for God's sake!'

'Are you hurt?' he asked.

'No, just completely caked in mud. At least, that's what I hope it is.'

'Here,' he said calmly, once more holding out a hand.

'I'm fine, I just need . . .' Hannah slipped again, spattering herself with yet more sludge, and grabbed hold of his legs to steady herself. Her cheeks flared with heat as she stared up into his dark face. 'Sorry, I . . .'

'No need to apologise. I've taken a tumble here myself once or twice. It's really slippery.' He seized hold of her coat at the back, like she was an unruly kitten, and dragged her to her feet with little attempt at delicacy. 'Nothing broken, I take it?'

'No, but I look like I've been mud-wrestling.'

'It can't be that bad, surely?' He looked her up and down, then his mouth twisted in another of those annoying crooked smiles. 'Well, maybe a little. I ought to have warned you about the uneven ground on this side of the stile. Especially now it's so dark.'

He started walking again with his long-legged stride,

leaving her to scamper after him, her boots squelching unpleasantly with every step. They were walking uphill now, she realised, the path rising steadily the closer they got to his farm.

'Don't worry,' he said, 'there's no real harm done. You can wash up at my place. I may even be able to lend you a clean T-shirt.'

Yes, five sizes too big, she thought grimly. But said nothing, concentrating on staying upright and not losing sight of his tall, lean figure in the growing darkness.

'This is Long Field, by the way,' he told her, and gestured with one arm at the broad stretch of field to his right, invisible to her except as a mass of shadowy nothingness before the land abruptly ended and the pale gleam of the ocean began.

'So called because it's so . . . erm, long?' His eyes gleamed in her direction, but he said nothing. Frowning, Hannah added, 'I can see part of this field from upstairs in Kernow House. I recognise that big oak.'

'That's right.' Raphael pointed to a particularly rough patch of grass close beside the old tree, where she could see deep ruts and ditches, and a collection of stones piled together as though part of a makeshift wall. 'See over there? That's where Lizzie's been living. I hope you can persuade her to come back here. Otherwise I'm not sure what will happen to her.'

'She told me she'd had trouble with some locals a few years back.'

'The Cutler's Estate bastards, yes.' His voice was grim now. 'Some people have so little going on in their own lives, they

feel the need to make other people miserable, almost as a form of entertainment. Especially people who can't fight back.' He glanced over at her. 'Lizzie was safe here in Long Field. Anyone planning to harass her would have had to cross my land to reach her campsite, and my dogs would let me know about any trespassers. But once she leaves . . .'

'I get the picture.'

'Good,' he said. 'Let's just hope she's still where I left her.'

CHAPTER ELEVEN

To her relief, when they reached the lane beyond Raphael's farmhouse, Lizzie had not disappeared but was sitting in the lit cab of her camper van, two dogs perched on the front seat beside her. The dogs, seeing their master, began to bark and pressed their noses against the glass, which was partly steamed up. Lizzie turned to stare into the darkness at once, her face pale and distraught, unable to see properly who it was.

Hannah went straight to the driver's door, and knocked gently on the side window. 'Hello, Lizzie,' she said, with as bright a smile as she could manage. 'It's Hannah Clitheroe, Trudy's granddaughter. Do you remember me?'

Lizzie did not answer, but her face, lit up by the cab's overhead light, showed tearstains and bloodshot eyes.

Hannah turned and pointed at Raphael, who was waiting silently behind her in the dark lane. 'Raphael told me you were leaving. I am so sorry to hear that.'

Her eyes wide, Lizzie wound the driver's window down an inch, speaking through the gap. 'But you said . . .'

'I know I told you that I didn't want any . . . erm, rabbits. But that doesn't mean I want you to leave. Far from it. We had a misunderstanding, that's all.' Hannah tilted her head

to one side, her smile persuasive. 'Will you please consider coming back? Both of us would be so happy to see you in Long Field again.' She hesitated. 'If you need a hand with the engine, I'm sure Raphael—'

'It's all fixed,' Lizzie said, interrupting her.

'Well, then. Why not just drive back into the field and set up camp there again? That's where you belong, after all.' Hannah softened her voice, seeing the other woman's uncertainty. 'That's your home, Lizzie.'

'You do want my rabbits, then?'

Hannah suppressed her instinctive shudder. 'Maybe one . . . every now and then. But I'm not really a big rabbit eater. Perhaps you should keep most of them for yourself.' She glanced back at the motionless Raphael. 'Or give them to Mr Tregar.'

He shot her a dry look, then came up to the van, patting the rusty bonnet as he addressed himself to Lizzie. 'Engine all sorted now, is it?'

'That's right,' Lizzie said, talking to him through the narrow gap, her manner still hesitant. But she was clearly relieved to see a more familiar face, and even managed a sad little smile for him. 'It'll do for now, any road.'

The two dogs had stopped barking but were still pressed up against the windscreen, wagging their tails furiously, responding to their master's voice.

'Thank you for looking after Merry and Pippin for me,' he told Lizzie. 'But you can let them out now, before they steam up the whole van.'

Lizzie opened the driver's door, and when Raphael whistled, the two sheepdogs jumped past her and down into the lane.

He laughed and fussed them as they milled about his feet, then clicked his fingers. Both dogs sat down in the same instant, tails thumping. Hannah was impressed. But of course they were fully trained working dogs, as he had said, not pets.

Raphael glanced up at Lizzie as she pulled the van door shut again. When he tapped on the glass, she looked worried, then wound down the window to speak to him.

'Y– yes?'

'If you want to turn the van around, Lizzie,' he said calmly, 'I'll open the gate for you. So you can drive back into Long Field.'

Her mouth agape, Lizzie stared from Raphael to Hannah, peering at their faces in the darkness. 'She do mean it, then? I can go home, no questions asked?'

'She means it.'

'Oh, thank you. Thank you pretty.' Her expression deliriously happy, Lizzie turned on the engine, and the old diesel van shuddered noisily into life. She bent to scrabble on the floor, then straightened a moment later, red-faced and breathless, with a bulging sack in her hand. This she handed laboriously out of the window to Raphael. 'For you and she, then. As a special thank you.'

'That's very kind of you,' he said solemnly, then held out the sack to Hannah. 'Hold that while I open the gate, would you?'

And so Hannah found herself holding a smelly old sack that contained what she suspected to be the corpses of several – hopefully recently – deceased rabbits. She held it out at arm's length, pretending to be pleased with the gift,

but couldn't prevent her nose wrinkling up as it was assaulted by the earthy, unpleasant odour.

She was quite impressed with herself for not tossing the sack aside in disgust. But she did not wish to offend Lizzie again, especially as the van's headlights were now on, shining full in her eyes.

Raphael threw open the five-bar gate, then guided Lizzie back through the narrow opening into Long Field. She waved a farewell at them both through the window, then shouted something inarticulate as the van lurched unevenly away across the mud ruts.

'No problem!' he called after her, apparently able to understand her garbled speech, his own hand raised. 'Speak to you tomorrow!'

He watched until she had driven several hundred yards across the muddy grass towards her tree, then whistled to his dogs, who had run enthusiastically after the van, and closed the gate again as soon as they were back in the lane.

Still dazzled from the bright headlights, Hannah took a few uncertain steps into the dark, looking down at her feet and not seeing Raphael until he was nearly on top of her.

'Oh God!'

'Steady, there,' he said, and grasped her by the shoulders. His laughter was mocking again, soft in the darkness. 'So you got your rabbits after all.'

'Ugh.' She pressed the smelly sack against his chest. 'Please, take them.'

'I've got a better idea.' Raphael turned her firmly, steering her toward the shadowy outline of his farmhouse on the other side of the lane. His voice was low in her ear. 'Lizzie

wants you to have one.' He clearly felt her recoil, adding, 'Now come on, you're not going to upset her by refusing, surely?'

'Lizzie won't know I didn't take one.'

'She will if I tell her.'

'Oh, you . . . !'

'Come inside the house,' he said easily, 'and let me show you how to skin a rabbit for the pot. It won't take long.'

She stopped dead at that horrid suggestion, and he bumped into her from behind. One of his dogs stopped too, and jumped up at her, both paws on her muddy jeans, sniffing her audibly. Like dog, like master, she thought in exasperation, pushing the cheeky animal down as she turned to face Raphael.

'You've got to be kidding.' She pushed the sack at him again. 'These dead rabbits stink to high heaven. There's absolutely no way—'

'Townie!'

His taunt made her livid. 'Now listen here . . .'

'You smell a little ripe yourself, you know,' Raphael told her suddenly, interrupting what she had intended to be a rant against his arrogance.

'I beg your pardon?'

He took the sack and then sniffed her up and down, just as the dog had done, leaving Hannah frozen in embarrassment. Did she really smell bad?

'Sorry to break it to you, but I don't think that was all mud back there. From the smell, I'd say you fell in some sheep shit.'

'Oh God, your bloody sheep . . .'

'Don't shoot me. I'm just the shepherd, remember? I don't produce the stuff.' He sniffed her again, and laughed. 'But I do recognise dung when I smell it.'

'I'm going home,' Hannah said coldly, and took a few determined steps away from him.

'In the dark? Do you even know where you're going?'

She stiffened with fury and humiliation as he came after her. 'You may have dragged me out here, but I can find my way home, thank you,' she told him, though part of her knew she was taking a ridiculous risk.

'Don't be a fool.' He came around to stand in front of her, blocking her way. 'You don't know these fields, and the wind's getting up now. You're more likely to get hopelessly lost and plunge off the cliff instead.'

'I'll take my chances.'

'Okay, Miss Crosspatch, it's a free country. You can walk home on your own, smelling like ... well, like a sheep, frankly, or you can come inside where it's warm, have a hot wash, and borrow some clean clothes. Then I'll drive you back.' He was standing very close to her, she realised. It was so dark that she could barely make out his features. She caught a faint whiff of his aftershave, which was citrus-fresh and masculine, and it made her even more aware of her own foul odour. 'What do you say to that?'

CHAPTER TWELVE

Don't tempt me, she thought wryly, though replied aloud, 'Well, for one, I couldn't possibly fit into any of your clothes.'

'Who said they'd be mine?'

Curious now, Hannah peered into his face, wondering what exactly he meant by that. Did he have a girlfriend who left her clothes at his place? Or maybe a live-in lover? Bailey had mentioned that Raphael Tregar had been seeing someone, but had finished the relationship. Perhaps he was secretive about his girlfriends though and nobody knew for sure.

She studied the grim outline of his farmhouse, and then shrugged. Raphael Tregar was a total pain in the arse. But he was right about this, unfortunately. It was foolish to insist on walking home alone in the dark. And, to be honest with herself, she was beginning to regret having suggested it. The field beyond the gate looked cold, pitch-black, and bleakly desolate. And she could recall how close the path had been to the cliff edge in places.

Besides, she did reek something awful.

'Okay,' she said testily, 'but if I throw up, it'll be your fault.'

He sounded startled. 'Throw up?'

'When you're skinning the rabbit.' She could not help shuddering again. 'They look so cute running about with their little bobtails. But I'd rather not see what's inside them, if it's all the same to you.'

'You're strange, do you know that?'

'Says the man who stalks women in his tractor.'

He merely quirked an eyebrow at her, then headed off without checking whether or not she was following him.

The farmhouse was surprisingly cosy inside, dark wood panelling everywhere, and reminiscent of a rabbit warren with narrow corridors on every side leading to closed doors. Raphael tossed his keys into a bowl on the hall table, flicked on some lights, then jerked his head in a rough 'follow me' gesture. She ought to be counting the turns, or maybe even leaving a bread trail, Hannah thought wryly, quickly bewildered by the odd architecture. Ahead, he turned off the corridor and went down a few steps towards a grimy-looking doorway.

She hung back, having heard what sounded like a faint cry from upstairs, and peered up a dim staircase to her left.

Raphael turned in the gloom, opening the door at the bottom of the steps, and frowned over his shoulder at her. 'You coming?'

She hurried after him. 'Sorry, I was just wondering . . .'

'If I had a mad wife in the attic?'

Hannah had not been thinking that. Not *exactly* that, she thought guiltily.

'No, but I am now.'

He gave her a straight look, then groped along the wall for the light switch. 'Hot or alcoholic?'

'What? Your mad wife?'

'Some men would be happy with both.' The room was a kitchen, she realised belatedly, following him inside. He shook the kettle, then filled it under the tap. 'Look, I'm assuming you don't want to learn how to skin a dead rabbit. But I need a cup of tea before I go out again in this weather. Want one?'

She could smell herself now. Much more strongly in this enclosed space. 'Perhaps I should have a wash first.'

'Upstairs.' At first she feared he was being suggestive, then he pointed at the door in a brusque manner. 'Far end of the landing, you'll find a bathroom. Towels in the airing cupboard outside the door. Heating's been on a couple of hours now, so the water should be hot.' He met her eyes ironically. 'Don't use it all. I'll need a bath myself later.'

'The stairs? It looked quite dark up there.'

'Here.' He unhooked a small, aluminium torch from the wall above the kettle and casually tossed it to her. To her relief she caught it without fumbling. 'My bedroom's next to the bathroom. You can grab yourself a clean T-shirt after you've showered. Middle drawer of the dresser.' His eyes narrowed on her face suddenly. 'And no mooching about in there. I was only kidding when I said they wouldn't be my clothes. Just take what you need and don't poke about in my stuff, you understand?'

Good grief, he was hard work.

'Why on earth would I want to poke about in your room?'

She headed out of the kitchen, adding under her breath, 'And I'm not a *moocher*.'

She was glad of the torch a few moments later, groping her way up a dark, wooden staircase that was like something out of the Addams Family. Her torch beam picked out a few thick cobwebs high above her head, and at least one pale, long-legged spider scuttled into the shadows as she approached. More than once she considered turning back, and only fear of Raphael's laughter, and the growing awareness of her sheep-like smell, drove her on. Not to mention her curiosity to explore this old farmhouse.

My bedroom's next to the bathroom. No mooching about in there.

What could he possibly have to hide?

There was a light switch on the landing, thankfully, so she was able to switch off the torch and pop it in her coat pocket. She found the bathroom easily enough, and instantly tiptoed into the room next door. Why not, after all? He himself had said she could go in, and besides, the door was partly open.

Mooch, mooch ….

She did not turn the bedroom light on, though, in case Raphael suddenly appeared and found her exploring. This way, she could pretend to have only popped her head around.

Raphael's bedroom was nothing like the rest of the chaotic farmhouse from what she could see by the hall light. For starters, it was immaculately tidy. There was a small desk and chair to one side, a shut laptop sitting on the desk beside a lamp; she imagined him sitting there long into the early hours, trolling forums under an assumed name, being

mean to people, and had to stifle a snort of laughter. She paused before the dresser, but did not bother looking for a T-shirt yet. The curtains were not closed. Hannah slipped across the room for a peek, trying not to set off any tell-tale creaking floorboards. The kitchen was probably directly beneath, knowing her luck.

The double windows overlooked dark, chilly fields towards the sea, its pale glitter just visible in the distance. She thought of Lizzie out there on her own, and shivered. She did not think she could live alone in a van like that. Not in winter, anyway. Though the summers must be quite lovely here on the Cornish coast.

Turning away, she clicked on the torch again to examine the books on his low bookcase. *Mooch, mooch.* Mostly sci-fi and thrillers on the top shelf, by the look of it, and a row of larger farming hardbacks underneath. *A Farmer's Life. Everything You Need To Know About Sheep. The Shepherd's Calendar.* A few books of poetry too, which surprised her. Some had pages marked with strips of paper.

Hmm.

His bed had a black metal frame and headboard, and a duvet cover the same stern colour. Less likely to show the dirt, she thought cynically. Then her gaze fell on a small, framed colour photograph above his desk. She wandered back that way, shining her torch beam on the picture, which was under glass.

It was Raphael as a young man, possibly still a teenager. He looked fresh-faced and even a bit spotty, a thick wedge of hair over one eye, clad in dirty boots, dirty jeans, dirty blue plaid shirt. Basically, he looked like he'd just spent the day

rolling in mud. He was standing in front of an equally muddy tractor, an older man beside him laying a casual arm across his shoulders. He did not appear to have fallen in the same watering hole as Raphael, though his wellies were heavily scuffed, and he was sporting a rosette on his sleeveless padded jacket.

She peered at the older man, studying his weather-beaten face by the light of her torch. That had to be Gabriel Tregar, Raphael's adopted father.

He must have been quite good-looking in his youth, she thought. He had a lovely smile too. A surprise then that Raphael tended towards such grim, monosyllabic utterances, with this charming man as his role model. Still, it was clear from the fact that Raphael was still here, farming the land, instead of having sold up and moved on, that he had loved Gabriel. Unless he stayed on simply in order to grab Kernow House when the opportunity arose.

'That was my dad.'

She jumped, dropping the torch at the sound of his voice in the doorway. 'Oh, you startled me!'

Raphael stood there, hands in his jeans' pockets, watching her with lazy eyes. 'Well, if you will go mooching in other people's bedrooms, despite having been asked not to . . .'

Hot-faced, she bent to retrieve the torch, and the overhead light came on at that moment, flooding the room. 'I wasn't mooching, I was simply . . .' She straightened, and saw the ironic look on his face. There was no point pretending. Not with this man. 'Yes, all right. I was nosing about where I shouldn't have been. And I'm sorry. But I was curious.'

'Evidently.'

'So this is you and Gabriel Tregar.'

He looked at her sharply. 'You know about him?'

Oops.

'Local talk, you know the sort of thing,' she said dismissively, and hoped he did not press her for more details. She did not want to land Bailey in trouble by admitting she'd been gossiping with her about the Tregars. 'I know this was his farm, that's about it. And that he – that you . . .'

'Gabriel adopted me, yes.'

'Right.' She smiled. 'He looks like a nice man. Very kind.'

She transferred her attention to the photograph again, studying it assiduously. She had not wanted to mention that she knew he was adopted. Not after the proud way he had declared 'That was my dad' on entering the room.

'Yes, he was kind. Kind but troubled.' Raphael strolled over to the framed photograph and studied it as though for the first time. 'This was taken at the Royal Cornwall Show by Ted Petherick. That was Ted's tractor, as I recall. Gabriel won a prize that year for his ewes. He was so pleased, he asked Ted to take this snap of him wearing the rosette.' He made a face, leaning forward. 'I haven't looked at this photo properly for years. God, I was young then.'

'You're hardly ancient now.'

He grinned, which disarmed her, and glanced sideways, examining her face in much the same way as the photograph. 'I'd guess we're nearly the same age. I'll be thirty-two in January. What about you? Twenty-nine? Older?'

'Twenty-seven,' she said tartly.

Raphael smirked, and looked down at her empty hands.

'No T-shirt yet? Couldn't you find the right drawer? I'll grab one for you.'

'Thanks.'

She followed him across the room while he dug about in the middle drawer of his dresser. It was awkward, standing there in his bedroom, the wind outside beginning to howl about the house. The place was like Wuthering Heights, she thought grimly.

'Don't you get lonely,' she asked, 'living all the way out here on your own?'

He dragged out a T-shirt, and held it up against her. It was a plain dark blue. He looked at her, his expression quizzical. 'I could ask you the same thing.'

'I've only been at Kernow House a short time. You must have been here by yourself for, what, nine or ten years?'

He looked at her through dark eyelashes. 'About that, yes.'

'So I guess you must enjoy solitude. Otherwise, you wouldn't still be doing it.'

'I have help, sometimes. Charlie comes in for lambing and shearing.' He shrugged. 'But I don't mind being alone.'

Feeling suddenly awkward, she took the T-shirt, thanking him. 'I'd better have my shower and get on home. Towels in the airing cupboard, right?'

Finally by herself, Hannah leaned her forehead on the back of the bathroom door and closed her eyes. What the hell was she doing here in his house? Apart from washing off sheep swill, that is. She felt a sudden desire to be back home, safe and alone, surrounded by her own things. She'd grown accustomed to her own company, she realised with a shock. She enjoyed waking up in an empty bed, and

pottering about the house, speaking only to the mother cat and her increasingly noisesome kittens. It was awkward to be in somebody else's house, to be forced to make conversation. Especially with a man who might have a hidden agenda in becoming friends with her.

Becoming friends?

Raphael Tregar did not want to be friends, she thought wryly. Not unless she'd lost the ability to spot a man who wanted to get her into bed.

CHAPTER THIRTEEN

To her surprise – although Hannah had steeled herself to expect a difficult situation – the interview with Pethporro Council did not go as badly as expected. Apart from a few obvious personality clashes in their midst – and having the Dark Lord of Gloom as their chair, of course – they were a cheerful enough bunch, five men and two women, the men in tweed jackets with leather elbow patches, one woman in a stiff woollen suit with chunky jewellery and too much make-up, the other – the woman who'd replied to her application, Patricia Cobbledick – more casually dressed.

To her relief, none of them seemed fazed by her obviously pregnant tummy. But perhaps they were so desperate to get their pageant organised at the last minute, they would have taken *anyone* so long as they were vaguely competent.

'When is it due?' Patricia Cobbledick asked enthusiastically, nodding at her bump. She was the council secretary, and had drastically short grey hair, with dangly silver earrings that rested on her shoulders and caught on her red woollen jumper in a way that was almost mesmerising. 'My daughter is expecting a baby. She's eight months gone. How about you?'

'Not quite that far yet,' Hannah said, smiling drily, 'so don't worry, I won't be having the baby halfway through your Boxing Day pageant.' She put a hand on top of her belly. 'Early March. That's when she's due to make an appearance.'

'Oh, you know the sex, then?' Patricia leaned forward across the table, smiling at her in an encouraging way. 'Nancy's expecting a boy. Perhaps the two of you could meet up sometime and talk babies?'

'That would be lovely.'

Hannah straightened in her chair, wondering what the others thought of her. They all seemed aware that she was a newcomer to the area. The first thing she'd been asked was how she would cope with not knowing Pethporro and its residents intimately. But they had not asked her to elaborate on her reply that she was good at getting to know people quickly. Even though, given her new-found hermit status, that answer had not been entirely truthful.

At the centre of the panel, looking dark and sardonic as usual, sat her neighbour and nemesis, Raphael Tregar. He had not passed comment on her response either, but one eyebrow had quirked, which had been enough to worry her.

He had taken her home the other night after her shower, saying almost nothing on the drive. She had got the impression there was something on his mind, but she did not know him well enough to ask what it was. Besides, she was too eager to get home, saying a hurried, 'Thank you, good night,' as she slammed the car door shut and ran inside, her hair still wet from the shower.

Today, he looked amused. Well, almost amused. It was hard to tell, the way his mouth kept pulling to one side,

usually when she was answering a question. Not to mention that mobile eyebrow.

'Frankly, I could do this job with my eyes shut,' Hannah told the panel. She sat back, hoping they did not think that was either hyperbole or arrogance. 'I realise the pregnancy could be an issue for some of you, but I trust I've answered most of the questions to your satisfaction.'

There was that eyebrow again.

'The bottom line is,' she added firmly, not looking at him, 'my CV speaks for itself. I have plenty of ideas, energy and experience. I'd love to run the Pethporro Boxing Day pageant for you. And short-time employment is precisely what I'm looking for at the moment. So I hope you'll agree that I'm the perfect choice.'

The panel glanced at each other thoughtfully, saying nothing.

Raphael shuffled the papers in front of him, then looked at her and said, 'Well, thank you for being so honest.'

Patricia Cobbledick, on his left, whispered something in his ear.

Raphael gave the council secretary a nod, then said, 'Would you excuse us, Miss Clitheroe? There have been a few other candidates interviewed today, and we need to have a chat amongst ourselves.' He nodded to the door behind her. 'If you could wait outside, please, it shouldn't take long.'

'Of course,' she said briskly, and left the room.

The hallway outside the committee room was empty, much to her relief. Her nerves were so jittery after that grilling,

she did not fancy having to exchange small talk with anyone or explain her presence there.

Hannah sat down on an old wooden bench, smoothing out her smart woollen skirt, and tried not to feel anxious. It was only a job, and she could always try something else if this didn't pan out. Maybe one of the work-from-home possibilities she'd been scrolling through last night. Those jobs had looked boring, though, not to mention low-paid, and might prove impossible to keep, given her less-than-reliable Wi-Fi connection at the house. And the fact that there were no other candidates in sight, the council buildings echoing with silence, was a positive sign.

Rain was falling again outside, the waiting area gloomy with it. The weather sounded wintry out there, a driving sleet dashing against the walls and windows. It was a melancholy sound, and one not exactly designed to soothe her nerves.

She tried to recall what Bailey and Penny had said about the previous pageant director. Jennifer, was it? That she and Raphael might have been an item, and he may have got her sacked after they broke up. Or she might have left under a cloud because they'd argued. It was an awfully large amount of unknowns.

Raphael Tregar did not look like a sex pest, of course.

But did they ever?

Also, he'd kept his distance the other night when Hannah was in his house. And she was glad about that. Absolutely. No disappointment at all.

She thought of Santos, his dark good looks, the warmth in his eyes, and bent her head.

There was no contest between the two men.

'I miss you, Santos,' she whispered to the black-and-white tiled floor, and managed a half-smile before the tears came to her eyes.

Never again. Never, ever again . . .

The door opened.

She looked up to find Patricia Cobbledick beaming at her from the doorway to the meeting room. 'Could you step back inside for just a few minutes, Miss Clitheroe? The committee would like to talk to you again.'

CHAPTER FOURTEEN

After coffee and a celebratory slice of chocolate cake at Fenella's café, she hurried through the rain to Knutson Solicitors, eager to share her good news with someone she knew. Mr Knutson, on the phone in the main office, waved and nodded her through with a friendly smile. Bailey looked up as Hannah knocked on the door to the smaller office marked Private, then pushed aside a mound of paperwork at least ten file boxes high, blowing out her cheeks.

'Lovely to see you,' Bailey said at once, but her smile was worried. 'Everything okay out at the house? Tregar been bothering you again?'

'Quite the opposite.'

Bailey put down the documents she had been rifling through and gazed at her, curious now. 'Okay, spill.'

'I got the job,' Hannah told her at once, unable to conceal her delight.

'You're kidding. The directorship of the pageant?' Bailey glanced from her swollen tummy to her face. 'Seriously? Even though you're expecting?'

'They didn't seem to care about the baby.'

'Good God. They must be desperate.'

'Thanks,' Hannah said drily.

'Oh no,' Bailey said hurriedly, standing up, 'I didn't mean it like that. Sorry, I'm sure you're really good at that kind of thing.'

Hannah laughed. 'It's fine, I know what you meant.'

Bailey made a face. 'Penny is always telling me off about that. Classic foot in mouth syndrome. Honestly, I'm really pleased for you, and Penny will be too. I can't wait to tell her.'

'Thanks,' Hannah said, and then added as an after-thought, 'Look, maybe I can entice you and Penny out for a drink one night? I need to meet more people locally, and you two seem to know everyone. Can I be totally shameless and pick your brains about this pageant, and who I might ask to get involved? There would be a round in it for you. Quite a few rounds, possibly.'

'Absolutely. In fact, I was just about to suggest it. And there are some lovely pubs around Pethporro. Not that we're a couple of lushes, you understand.' Bailey laughed. 'But we do like a tipple now and then.'

Hannah hugged her as a thank you, and then said good-bye, heading back out along the high street. She was on her way to an antenatal appointment at the local clinic. It was her first pregnancy check-up since coming to Cornwall, and she was a little apprehensive about it. The air was damp and cold, but at least the rain had finally blown away and the sun had come out. The wind caught at her blonde hair, which she had kept down for the interview, quickly reduc-ing it to a tangled mess.

But she doubted the nurse would care much about her appearance. She would no doubt be far too busy: the antenatal

clinic was only held once a month, at the one doctors' surgery in Pethporro. Hannah had been lucky to get an appointment this soon. It was either that, she had been told, or drive all the way to Truro for a check-up.

Three other mums were waiting in the clinic when she arrived, all of them in varying stages of pregnancy. There was a young woman who looked much further along than her, with striking cheekbones and ultra-short hair. Hannah studied her covertly, and decided that she recognised those eyes, and that thin-lipped smile as the woman flicked through a glossy magazine.

She leaned forward. 'Excuse me, but are you Nancy, by any chance?'

The young woman looked startled, lowering the magazine so that it rested on her large bump. She was wearing a pretty, flowery top, and a pair of those ubiquitous jeans with an elasticated waist that seemed to be the most practical maternity outfit around once you were past six months. 'Yes, how did you know? I don't think I've seen you round here before.' She stole a quick glance at Hannah's stomach. 'When are you due? In the spring?'

'Hey, not a bad guess. Early March.' Hannah held out her hand, and Nancy shook it in a friendly fashion. 'Your mother told me about you. I'm Hannah Clitheroe.'

Nancy looked even more startled, her eyebrows thinly arched. 'Hannah Clitheroe? You're living out at Kernow House?'

'That's right. I take it you've heard of me?'

'Only that you had applied for that job as pageant director. Such a pity about Jennifer Bolitho. I liked her.'

Hannah was curious. 'The previous director? What happened there? Did she run into difficulties with the job?'

'I'm sorry,' Nancy said hurriedly, laying aside the magazine she had been reading. 'I don't actually know anything about it. I shouldn't have said anything. It's none of my business, really.'

Hannah looked at her steadily.

'It's just that ...' Nancy leaned forward, lowering her voice so that the other two pregnant women in the room could not hear her, 'I wouldn't want to get on the wrong side of Raphael Tregar.' She looked suddenly anxious. 'You won't say anything to him, will you?'

'Not a word.'

'Thank you, thank you.' Nancy sat back and smoothed her flowery top over the burgeoning swell of her stomach. She was younger than Hannah. Early twenties, at a rough guess. 'It's not that I'm afraid of him, you understand. My mother says he's a very nice man,' she said naïvely, 'once you get to know him.'

'Oh, I'm sure.'

'But he does look rather ...'

'Scary?'

'Please don't tell him I said that.' Nancy gave a nervous laugh. 'It's those eyebrows, don't you think? So stern.'

'Maybe we should pluck them for him.'

'God, what a thought!'

'I met your mum today, at the interview. She thought we should get together and talk about our bumps.'

Nancy's face cleared. 'That sounds fun. I'm not working at the moment, and though it's nice not having to get up

early, there're only so many Netflix shows you can watch before you feel like stabbing yourself in the eye.'

Hannah was amused. 'Couldn't have put that better myself. Maternity leave, is it? Where were you working?'

'The local primary school. I'm a teaching assistant.' She smiled, adding optimistically, 'Though I plan to be a teacher some day. If I can get the right qualifications, that is, or do a training course.' She hesitated. 'What about you? I mean, what did you do before coming to Pethporro?'

'I ran outdoors adventure holidays in Greece and around Europe. Walking, climbing, skiing, sailing – that kind of thing.'

'That sounds amazing!'

'Amazing, but very time-consuming. I don't think I took a holiday myself in the past three years. Not until coming here, in fact.'

'So you and your husband—'

'I'm not married,' Hannah said quickly, then added, seeing the horrible question already forming on Nancy's lips, 'He – he's dead. The father.' She put a hand to her belly. 'Santos died in an avalanche, and I didn't want to stay in Greece without him. I'm on my own now.'

'Bloody hell, that's awful. I'm so sorry.' Nancy looked at her with wide, sympathetic eyes. 'I don't know how I'd cope without Matt. I know it's a cliché, but he's my rock.' She reached across and touched Hannah's arm, impulsively. 'I think you're very brave. Having a baby is hard enough without having to go through all this alone. If there's ever anything you need . . .'

'Well, as a matter-of-fact,' Hannah glanced down at the

discarded magazine, recalling that Nancy had been reading an article about an American beauty pageant, 'what do you know about floats?'

Nancy looked puzzled. 'Swimming floats?'

'Carnival.' Hannah grimaced. 'Apparently, the woman who was running the pageant before me – Jennifer – hired a bunch of them, but didn't leave any notes behind that would tell us what she intended to do with them.' She looked at Nancy imploringly. 'Any inspiration?'

'Oh God, plenty, trust me. This sounds like exactly what I need.' She grinned. 'My mum's a dear, but forget talking about our bloody bumps. How about we get together and dream up ideas for these floats instead? That would be far more interesting than yet more baby talk.' Nancy rummaged in her handbag and produced a small black diary and pen. She looked at Hannah expectantly. 'How about Friday lunchtime?'

The antenatal nurse was Caroline, a tall, elegant woman with blonde hair swept into a chignon on the back of her neck. She had a low, musical voice that was hard to interrupt, so Hannah didn't try. She took Hannah's details for about fifteen minutes, checked her pulse and blood pressure, and then finally said, 'Pop up on the bed so I can listen to Baby. Just loosen the waistband on your skirt so I can . . . That's it. Cold on your tummy, okay?'

After squirting Hannah with ultrasound goo, Caroline ran the handheld device over her hard, swollen bump. They both listened to the baby, who sounded like an industrial washing machine, as usual.

Caroline seemed pleased. 'Good, steady heartbeat, no signs of distress. How are you feeling yourself?'

'Well enough, physically.'

Caroline's gaze moved to her face. She straightened. 'Having other problems?'

'Only my wacky emotions.'

'Sorry?'

'They're constantly up and down at the moment. I'm like a human yo-yo.'

'That's perfectly natural when you're pregnant. It's all the hormones rushing about your system. I wouldn't worry too much.'

'I wish I could be that relaxed about it. Sometimes it feels like I'm losing my mind.' Hannah took the scrap of blue paper Caroline had handed to her, and wiped the ultrasound gel off her belly. 'I've just got a new job, you see. I don't want to screw up.'

'A new job?' Caroline cleaned the equipment and began putting it away. 'You can get down now,' she said automatically, then added, as she began to wash her hands, 'I hope the work isn't too strenuous.'

'Only mentally,' Hannah said drily. 'Though that's bad enough. I'm working for the council, running the Pethporro pageant.'

Caroline stiffened, standing at the sink with her back turned. 'I see. You know Jennifer Bolitho was organising it before you?'

'I did. Though she left for some reason, so I'm doing it now.'

'Well, watch out for Raphael Tregar,' Caroline said, turning

to look at her. She leaned against the sink, arms folded across her chest. 'You must have met him. Chair of the pageant committee. He's trouble.'

'Roving hands?'

'I don't know about that.' Caroline pursed her lips. 'But let me put it like this: if Raphael Tregar was a sailor, he'd be the sort with a girl in every port.'

'Thanks for the warning. It's not the first time I've heard it.'

'Well, he's not a very popular man.'

Hannah swung her legs around, and then jumped down from the examination table. She staggered on landing, suddenly light-headed.

'Careful.' Caroline took her arm, steadying her with a quick smile. 'Better come and sit down for a minute. Easy does it.'

'What happened there?'

'Blood pressure, I expect. It was quite low when I checked it just now. Nothing to worry about but you need to be aware of it. That can happen in pregnancy. Watch out for abrupt changes of position. Standing up suddenly, bending over – anything that could cause you to lose your balance.' Caroline bent to check her pulse, then nodded, seeming satisfied. 'And you don't want to fall over, do you? Not with a passenger on board.'

'No more dancing the limbo, in other words?'

'Exactly.'

Caroline did not smile; she didn't appear to have much of a sense of humour. But some people were like that, Hannah thought wryly. Whenever she made a joke, they would look

mystified, or not react at all, as though unable to work out if she was being funny or not.

'I'd better book you in for your next check-up,' Caroline said, looking distracted. 'And would you like to attend any of our local antenatal classes? To help you prepare for labour and the first few weeks of motherhood?'

'I probably should, yes.'

Having handed her a leaflet of antenatal class dates and locations, Caroline sat down and keyed into the computer. 'Right, let's have a look which clinic dates are available for next month . . .'

On her way back to the car after her appointment, Hannah studied the antenatal class leaflet with a sense of foreboding. She had never been much of a joiner herself, despite being good at organising groups. All the other expectant mothers would probably have been going for months, and she wouldn't know any of them. Except possibly Nancy, if she was going. But it was important to make the effort. Hannah did not like to admit it, but she was feeling increasingly apprehensive about having a baby. She had dismissed the situation at her interview, and made light of it just now when Nancy called her 'brave', but she had no real, hands-on experience with infants.

And the nearer she came to her due date, the more she secretly worried about giving birth. How much would it hurt? What if something went wrong during labour? And most of all, how on earth would she cope after that, all alone with a baby in that great draughty farmhouse?

She had turned down offers of help from Santos' parents,

determined to be independent, and kept insisting to every-one that she would be fine on her own. But in truth, as the weeks went on and her belly grew, the baby was becoming more of a reality. Hannah certainly did not feel very 'brave'. Perhaps classes would help with that, much as she felt awk-ward meeting other mothers-to-be.

Besides, if she was to make a success of this new job, she would need volunteers. And going to a local antenatal class was a fantastic way to make friends quickly.

Her phone buzzed in her handbag. It was a text from Bailey.

Call me.

Puzzled, Hannah rang her friend back at once. 'What's up? Did I leave something in your office?'

'I'm really sorry.' Bailey sounded worried. 'I don't want to spoil your day.'

'Oh hell.' Hannah closed her eyes. 'I knew this was too good to last. Go on.'

'Do you remember Lizzie? Your other neighbour?'

'Am I ever likely to forget her?'

'Well, the postie just dropped by our place. According to her, Lizzie's camped out on your doorstep.' Bailey took a deep breath. 'And she's crying.'

CHAPTER FIFTEEN

Hannah hurried back to Kernow House as quick as she could, which meant she nearly ended up in the hedge at one point, driving rather too fast for the narrow Cornish bends. The skies were darkening and it had started to rain by the time she reached the drive up to the house. Sure enough, Lizzie came limping into sight at her approach, feeling her way along the outhouse wall. The woman looked distressed: her eyes were red, her face blotchy, and her hair even more dishevelled than usual.

Hannah got out of her car and strode towards her. 'Lizzie, whatever's the matter?'

'Mr Tregar, he—' Lizzie began haltingly, and then burst into fresh tears, sinking against the grey wall of the outhouse.

'Good God, what has that awful man done now?'

Lizzie looked astonished. 'No, not awful. Not him.' When Hannah waited, frowning, she said in a stumbling way, 'Mr Tregar, he dropped me off here in his car. He wanted me to go home with him at first. But I said no.' Her face closing up, she added darkly, 'I don't like men.'

'Some of them are okay,' Hannah said drily, but did not press the point.

She walked around to the back of the house, with Lizzie trailing behind her, and found a heap of the woman's possessions lying higgledy-piggledy beside the back step, already damp with the rain that was falling now in a fine drizzle.

'I don't understand. Why have you brought these things here, Lizzie? What's this about?'

'They're mine.'

'Yes, but where's your van?'

'Back in the field. Only Mr Tregar says I have to leave Long Field.' And she began to cry again.

Hannah stared at her. 'Please don't cry, Lizzie. Look, I'm sorry to be so obtuse. But I don't understand. I thought we'd cleared all this up. You can camp in Long Field if you wish. Nobody is going to move you on.'

'But Mr Tregar, he says my van ain't fit to live in. That I have to get out. And come here. To you, if I won't go to him.'

'To him?'

Hannah was not only mystified, but concerned for Lizzie now. What on earth was Raphael up to? Had he taken it upon himself to evict this unfortunate woman from Long Field, after all? The only reason she could think of was to annoy her and make her life bloody uncomfortable. Yet why would he do that?

Unless he was still determined to get hold of Kernow House . . .

She felt a flush of temper fill her cheeks. 'Slow down, Lizzie. You'd better start at the beginning.'

'I shouldn't have moved her.'

'Her?'

'The van. I shouldn't have moved it. That's what started all this. Now the rain's a-coming in, and everything inside is soaked. Even my old bed. I saw Mr Tregar out in the field, and I showed him what had happened. And he said, I can't sleep there no more.' As if to prove a point, Lizzie sneezed dramatically, three times in a row, and then wiped her nose with the back of her sleeve. 'I'm sorry, Miss Clitheroe. It's my fault. He says I'm not to go back, that I'll catch my death in it. But I don't want to be no trouble. I'll sleep in the barn if I must.'

'There's no question of you sleeping in a barn, Lizzie. Mr Tregar was quite right to bring you here.'

Nonetheless, Hannah's heart sank. Although she had been feeling lonely, she had an enormous amount of work to do with this new job. And she was not sure that Lizzie was entirely the perfect housemate. But what else could she do? The poor woman was distraught. As well she would be, if she'd lost her home to all that recent heavy rainfall.

'Come inside out of this rain, and we'll see what we can do to get you comfortable.'

Lizzie followed her into the kitchen, looking about herself suspiciously. 'I don't like houses.'

'Well, I'm afraid you'll have to get over that,' Hannah said briskly, and filled the kettle while her new lodger prowled about, examining the kitchen in wary silence. 'There's a spare room upstairs you can have. I'm in the middle of redecorating, so there's no wallpaper or paint at the moment, but I don't suppose that will worry you. Only there's no bed either.'

'Don't matter. I can sleep on the floor.'

'No need for anything so drastic, Lizzie. I need to order

new beds anyway, as all the old ones had to be thrown out. The question is, how long will they take to arrive?' Hannah looked at her speculatively. 'Do you mind sleeping on a camp bed for the time being?'

Lizzie shook her head. 'I don't mind anything. But I don't like the wet.'

'Who does?' Hannah smiled at her. Already the woman was starting to look less distressed. 'Now, let's get this kettle on, then we'll bring your things in and get you sorted out.'

Once they had carried Lizzie's slightly damp possessions upstairs to the room next to the bathroom, Hannah laid out some dry clothes she could borrow.

Lizzie looked shocked. 'I can't take your things. That ain't right.'

'Honestly, it's fine. I can't fit in most of these anyway. You probably won't either, actually, you're much taller than me. Oh, wait!' Triumphantly, she dragged a bag out from under her bed. 'A friend of mine bought me this, but it's the wrong size. Massively too long in the leg. It's a rabbit onesie.' It was actually Santos' lovely mum who had bought her the garment, with overlarge matching slippers, as a parting gift. She'd been worried that England would be too cold for Hannah after the heat of Greece. And even though none of it fit, Hannah hadn't had the heart to give the pieces to a charity shop. To her, the outfit represented a little bit of her previous life. But Lizzie's need was greater. 'There are slippers too.'

Lizzie handled the pink rabbit outfit in mute astonishment. She turned it over, prodded the white bunny tail, then held the onesie up against herself.

Hannah got the impression she had never owned anything remotely like it. Or even anything pink, for that matter.

'If you don't like it, don't worry. I can find you something else.'

'How does it . . . How do you . . . ?'

'Oh, it's an all-in-one. A onesie. You step in and zip it up the front. Here, like this.' Hannah showed her how it worked, then handed Lizzie the fluffy matching slippers. They were pink and white, with long bunny ears that flopped about. 'Size nine. Too big?'

Lizzie took the slippers. She stroked one soft bunny ear, still blank with astonishment. 'No, I'm a nine.'

'Well, then. Keep them, they don't fit me.'

Lizzie blinked, then said, 'Thank you. Thank you.' Then added, 'Thank you,' again, more emphatically, as if unsure that she'd said it right before.

Downstairs, Hannah made them both a nice pot of tea, and put some cake slices on the table. 'Please, help yourself.'

She watched with a strange sense of satisfaction as Lizzie tucked in hungrily to some raspberry sponge. It was shop-bought rather than home-made, but she didn't seem to mind.

So now there were two of them living at Kernow House. Hannah could not pretend to be wholly delighted by this turn of events. She was still a little suspicious that Raphael had sent Lizzie to her out of spite, rather than kindness. Or was she being overly sensitive? And mean, too. Lizzie had rejected Raphael's offer of accommodation, after all, so Kernow House had been a second thought on his part, not a first.

'You want that other slice?' Lizzie pointed at the remaining cake. When Hannah shook her head, she grinned and

hungrily devoured that slab too. 'Ah, tastes good,' she managed to say, between crumbly mouthfuls. 'I like cake.'

'I *love* cake.'

'Suppose you don't want it today because you're fat enough.' Lizzie nodded at Hannah's stomach. 'You need to do more walking. Out over the hills. That's what gets rid of fat. Not riding around in a car all day.'

Hannah suppressed the desire to laugh. She put a hand on her belly, and smiled instead. 'This isn't fat,' she said. 'At least, I hope not. It's a baby.'

Lizzie's eyes widened, fixing on her face. 'A baby?' she repeated in a whisper. 'Who done it? Who hurt you?' She put down the last piece of sponge, as though her appetite had fled. 'Not Mr Tregar?'

Hannah caught her breath.

For a moment, she couldn't reply. And not because it meant talking about Santos.

This poor woman. What had happened to Lizzie in the past to make her associate pregnancy with . . . well, with what sounded like sexual assault? It almost did not bear thinking about. Except that she ought to think about it. And talk about it too, with Lizzie herself.

But not yet. Lizzie was too unsure about her at the moment. They would need to become friends if she was to trust her enough for a conversation like that.

'No, of course not.' She poured her some more tea, having spotted her eyeing the teapot in a thirsty manner, and smiled when her new housemate picked up the cake again. 'The father of my baby was a lovely Greek man called Santos. Sadly, he died and . . . now I'm on my own.'

'Not ... on ... own ...' Lizzie said awkwardly, through the final mouthful of raspberry sponge, and then swallowed. She wiped her mouth. 'You got me now.'

'I certainly have, Lizzie.'

'Though don't tell nobody about that onesie thingy.' Lizzie made a face. 'It looks right comfy. But it's so ...'

'Pink?'

Lizzie nodded heartily. 'With a bunny tail too. Kiddy pyjamas, that's what them are. And them slippers with ears ...' She laughed. 'Wouldn't want the likes of Mr Tregar to see me in that get-up. He'd think I never growed up.'

Hannah laughed too, and then glanced down at her tummy in surprise, having felt again that funny fluttering sensation she was beginning to associate with her bump. Only this time, the fluttering had been somehow harder, more defined.

Had the baby just kicked?

CHAPTER SIXTEEN

Rain continued to fall for the next couple of days. The windows stayed dark, streams swelled to rivers, rivers burst their banks, and the farmyard became a boggy morass. Wellingtons were required just to dash across to the car under the relentless downpour. Hannah had promised to walk out to Long Field with Lizzie and inspect her leaking van to see if anything could be salvaged, but the weather was so dismal, she persuaded her to wait, at least until it stopped raining. She herself had plenty to do, mostly online or on the phone, making plans for the Boxing Day pageant and carefully going through the existing concepts left behind by Jennifer, noting where tasks still had to be done or she wanted to make changes.

On the third day after Lizzie arrived at Kernow House, Raphael rang very early in the morning, startling Hannah and galvanising her sleepily out of bed to answer the phone.

'Tregar here.' He sounded terse, almost impatient. 'It occurred to me you might need some interim support before our next committee meeting. How are things going?' He cleared his throat. 'Getting to grips with the job yet?'

Dazed, still partly in a dream where she had been

running across a field, chased by black-and-white heifers with huge, snuffly muzzles, Hannah did not immediately put the question together with the answer.

'Job?'

'For God's sake, woman, the pageant is less than five weeks away. There's no time for you to sleep in.'

Standing in her crumpled pyjamas, phone handset to her ear, Hannah glanced around at her bedside clock. 7.45 a.m. Was he kidding?

She counted silently to five before replying, aware she did not want to lose this job before she had even started it properly. Raphael Tregar was no longer just her infuriating neighbour, she reminded herself. Now he was her infuriating boss too.

Oh, the joy.

'Sorry, I didn't actually hear the question. Over the noise of the . . . erm . . . coffee percolator.' She grabbed up a magazine she'd been reading in bed the night before, and scrunched up the pages next to the phone, then put it back to her ear. 'I was just making up a flask, ready to attack my planner. What were you saying?'

'We should meet.'

She was taken aback. 'Again?'

'I told you,' Raphael said drily, clearly unconvinced by her magazine-percolator noises, 'you've very little time to pull all this together, and you're new to Pethporro. I don't want this to slip away from you.'

'I've already arranged to talk to some local people, get to know the town better.' Tomorrow was the lunch with Nancy.

Not exactly 'local people', but with any luck it was a first contact that would lead to many more. 'So you see—'

He interrupted her. 'I'm glad to hear it. Nonetheless, you need support or you won't get this job done in time.'

She pulled a face at the thought of being helped by Raphael Tregar, and was instantly glad this was not a Skype call.

'Right, okay.' She closed her eyes. 'When? Where?'

'How well do you know the rest of the North Cornwall coast?'

'Only what I've read online. Plus the brochures I picked up at the Pethporro Tourist Information Centre.'

'I'll pick you up at eleven. Time you took a field trip.'

She looked out at the rain, which was less persistent than it had been, but still falling, and bowed her head. 'Not more fields, please . . .'

'Pardon?'

Had she said that out loud?

'I said, yes please, that sounds wonderful,' she lied quickly. 'I'll be ready at eleven. Wellies?'

'Wellies.'

'I'll bring my planner, so you can see where I'm up to.'

'Good idea.' He paused. 'How's Lizzie? Is she staying with you now?'

'She is.' Hannah frowned, surprised by his enquiry. 'And not doing too badly, after the initial shock of having to leave her van. She's settling in nicely, in fact.' She hesitated. 'Thank you for dropping her off the other day. That was very . . . erm . . .'

'Neighbours look out for each other in Cornwall,' he said,

his tone dismissive. 'Well, I'll see you at eleven. Don't keep me waiting.'

He rang off, and she stared hard at the handset before replacing it on its cradle. Raphael Tregar was so difficult to read, she thought. Brusque and even unpleasant at times, then acting the concerned neighbour. And now she would have to spend possibly an entire afternoon in his company.

She glanced back at the clock. Plenty of time to explain to Lizzie that she'd be out most of the day, then grab a shower, do her hair and make-up, and cobble together some kind of breakfast.

She only hoped he wouldn't turn up in his tractor.

It was only while she was in the shower, blindly rinsing shampoo out of her hair, that Hannah suddenly recalled the gossip about Jennifer Bolitho, her predecessor of the Boxing Day pageant. She and Raphael had become an item, or so rumour had it. Then things had turned sour between them, and she had left the job abruptly.

Raphael had seemed very much hands-off with Hannah at the farmhouse the other night, but perhaps he preferred women who were under his control in some way. Had she just agreed to spend the afternoon with a predatory boss? Was this 'field trip' along the Cornish coast actually Raphael making his first move on her?

To Hannah's very poorly disguised relief, Raphael turned up in a sleek convertible BMW rather than the tractor. The roof was closed, of course, although it had miraculously stopped raining only an hour before. The car was black, without any discernible trace of mud upon it.

'I didn't see this at your house the other night,' she said suspiciously, climbing into the front passenger seat. 'Did you steal it?'

'Only in terms of having liberated it from my garage, which may be how you missed it,' he told her in caustic tones, then turned the car around in the yard with infuriating ease. He looked edible as always, she noted with her usual flicker of annoyance. Black jeans and a casual white V-neck jumper, coupled with a leather jacket that looked both elegant and expensive, hugged his athletic figure. So much for the Farmer Giles persona. Today he could have been a rock star, or a famous actor, roughing it in the wilds of Cornwall. Except for his rugged walking boots.

Only nice men should be that good-looking, she thought, and then looked quickly away when she caught his eye. God forbid he should ever guess what she was thinking. Though that little twist of his lips seemed to indicate that he had a pretty good idea.

Before driving away, he lifted one hand to wave goodbye to Lizzie, who was standing motionless at her bedroom window, looking like a ghost, before waving wildly back.

'I hope she'll be okay on her own,' Hannah said, suddenly guilty. 'Perhaps I ought to have asked her to come along too.'

His look of horror nearly made her laugh.

'So where are we going?'

'I thought we could start with the classic tourist traps . . . Tintagel Castle, Boscastle, St Ives.'

'Oh, I've seen that TV show set in St Ives.'

This cultural reference was apparently not going to earn

her any brownie points. Not with Raphael Tregar, anyway. He gave her a repressive glance, and then lapsed into silent concentration on the street, driving swiftly through the wet lanes towards the main coast road. Rather too swiftly for her tastes. A little alarmed, Hannah clung to her seat, watching him corner at what could only be described as an insane speed, then transferred her left hand to the hanging strap above the door.

'In a hurry?' she asked at last, goaded into comment.

'Not particularly.'

'I'd hate to see you driving when you are, then,' she muttered, swaying from side to side like someone in a tube train.

Again, the repressive sideways glance. 'There's a lot of ground to cover before dusk.'

'You think we'll be out that long?'

'I should imagine so.' Abruptly, he pointed off to the left, startling her. 'Llamas!'

She turned her head, trying desperately to spot what he was showing her. There was a large sign, featuring a massively outsized llama, and an arrow pointing inland. She glimpsed a field – green, wet and muddy, like all the other fields they had passed so far – with a one-second sighting of a few large, furry-looking creatures in the middle, rather like sheep on stilts. Then a hedge flashed between her and that tantalising glimpse, and she looked to the front again.

'Did you see them?' He sounded almost eager.

'More or less.' Hannah decided that honesty would not serve her well in this situation, and might even lead him to turn the car around for a second look. 'Very interesting.'

'I'm a big fan of llamas.'

'Really? You surprise me.'

He seemed perfectly serious. 'They're unusual,' he said, staring ahead at the road. 'Plus they bring in tourists. Nobody wants to look at fields of sheep. Not unless it's a rare breed, with horns and what have you. But llamas are worth the effort. I may farm them myself one day. You never know.'

It was hard not to laugh, but somehow she managed it.

'You're not wearing wellies,' she said accusingly.

His gaze met hers for an instant, then he grinned and focused on the road again. A vast tractor at a crossroads ahead suddenly pulled out in front of them, trundling along at what felt like five miles per hour after the suicidal pace they had been doing.

Raphael swore, despite being a tractor driver himself. He braked hard, swung out to see if the road was clear, and then overtook the vehicle effortlessly.

'Bloody idiot!'

Hannah gritted her teeth and clung onto the strap as he accelerated away. It was a little hypocritical, perhaps, for her to feel ill at ease because of his speed. She enjoyed driving fast herself, after all. But it was different when someone else was behind the wheel, wasn't it? Especially someone she did not entirely trust.

Trying to distract herself, she looked at the Cornish landscape instead. And it was enchanting. As they crested a hill, she caught a brief glimpse of the sea on their right-hand side, turbulent and grey, stretching all the way down the North Cornwall coast into misty haze. Then the road dipped

again, and the soft grey line of the Atlantic was once more hidden behind straggling, thorny hedgerows.

'So who is he?' he asked idly, settling to an easy sixty miles per hour as they hit a stretch of straight road with no traffic on it.

'Who is who?'

'The father of your child.'

CHAPTER SEVENTEEN

She stared at him, stunned into silence by his question.

'Is it a secret?' Raphael asked after a moment, seemingly unembarrassed by the fact that she had not replied. 'Because I should warn you, we don't do secrets in Pethporro.'

She pulled herself together. 'Of course it's not a secret.'

Haltingly, she told him about Santos. Not just their relationship and the life they had led together, but his death too. The avalanche. Raphael listened without saying anything. With anyone else, she would have thought it a sympathetic silence. But with Raphael Tregar, it felt different. Not judgemental, but not neutral either. He was thinking while he listened to her story. Thinking about her, and her life choices, and possibly her future too.

'I always knew there'd be a serious accident one day, the way he threw himself into so many dangerous activities. But there was no stopping him. Santos could be wild at times, you see. Unpredictable. He hated the idea that he might be holding back out of fear, that he wasn't giving one hundred and ten per cent to everything. He was almost reckless . . .' Hannah stopped. That had not come out right. And she felt disloyal making even mild criticisms of the

man she had adored. The man she *still* adored. Uncomfortable, she shifted the conversation away from her past, and toward the work that now bound them together. 'But he was very skilled at communicating. That was his forte as a businessman. I learned a lot from him about successful event management. How it's all about getting the right people on side.'

'Did you love him?'

'Sorry?' Her heart hurt and she felt almost offended. Deliberately, she let it show in her sharp tone. 'That's a funny question. Of course I loved him. We were having a baby together.'

If she had expected him to apologise, she was disappointed. He merely shrugged, as though dismissing that as a premise.

Turning off the A39, Raphael headed west down a narrow, winding road that seemed to go on forever, passing fields of sheep – no more llamas, she noted – and dark, bare fields ploughed in deep ruts. Finally, he slowed the car slightly, pointing ahead as they descended towards the ocean. A gap in the hedgerows had opened up, and she could see houses shining white in that curious cold light that always seemed to follow heavy rain, as if the buildings had been washed clean. Beyond them, the ground fell sharply away until it met the heavy grey swell of the Atlantic Ocean.

'Boscastle,' he said, expressionless. 'We'll stop there for coffee, shall we? Unless you're hungry. We could have lunch instead, if you like. There are some good places to eat along the harbour.'

Boscastle.

The name was familiar to her, and not just because she had looked at the map before coming out. What was it?

'They had a terrible summer flood here about ten years ago,' he said, as though guessing her thoughts. 'Nobody died, thankfully. But quite a few properties were damaged or destroyed, and the lower bridge to the harbourside had to be completely replaced. It was a total catastrophe, and it took them several years to bounce back from it.'

'I remember seeing it on the news.'

'They have better flood defences now,' he said, and shot her a look. 'So don't worry. I know the weather forecasts have been warning about floods in Cornwall after all this heavy rain, but we should be safe enough.'

She murmured an appropriate reply, but something was nagging at the back of her mind. *Boscastle.*

'The woman who was running the pageant before me,' she said innocently, 'didn't she come from this town?'

His hands tightened on the wheel. But his expression did not change. 'That's right. Jennifer Bolitho. Though Boscastle is a large village, really. Right on the sea, very picturesque little place. It's most famous for its old harbour and the blow-hole under the Point, just before the entrance to the waterfront. That's worth seeing. And there are stunning cliff walks,' he added. 'Perhaps we could wander along them before lunch.'

She hid her smile. Raphael was beginning to sound like a tourist guide. Which almost certainly meant he was hiding something.

'A good friend of yours, wasn't she? Jennifer, I mean.'

Now, at last, his lip curled. 'Fishing for gossip, Miss Clitheroe? Tut tut. I thought you were above all that, being a Londoner.'

'Londoners love to gossip just as much as you country folk,' she said deliberately, and was rewarded with an irritable glance. She turned her head, looking out at the quaint, Cornish houses lining the zigzag road down to the waterfront. Large, solid, their shoulders to the roadside, the houses were slate-roofed, many of them covered in wisteria or clinging ivy, dark green leaves shining after the recent rain. 'Besides, I've lived in Athens for the past few years, not London. And I can tell you now, the Greeks enjoy nothing better than a good gossip over a glass of retsina.'

'Beware of Greeks bearing retsina?' he asked drily.

She smiled, but all thoughts of a clever retort fled as Raphael slowed, rounding the final, tight bend towards Boscastle, and she saw the village bunched up below them. Picturesque was an understatement, she thought, her eyes widening. It was an archetypal Cornish seaside settlement tucked into a valley bottom, all grey roofs and squat, whitewashed walls, with a narrow river rushing between the houses and under a stone bridge on its way to the sea. The place looked like it had been there forever, a cluster of houses surrounded by wind-bent trees, and steep, wooded slopes on every side.

'Oh, how beautiful!'

'I'm glad you approve. Boscastle is one of my favourite places in Cornwall; I come here quite frequently. Though it's best out of season – it's always swamped with tourists in the summer.' He drove over the bridge, past shops and

restaurants twinkling with Christmas lights and festive window displays, and towards a riverside parking area. 'Lunch is my treat, by the way,' he said casually, backing the BMW neatly into an empty space. 'A thank you for coming with me today.'

She was surprised. 'I thought this was an essential fact-finding trip to increase my local knowledge. All part of the job, et cetera.'

'And so it is.' He gave her a look that was difficult to read. 'But that doesn't mean you had to agree to come. Especially in your condition.'

He went off to buy a parking ticket while Hannah got out of the car and stretched, a little annoyed by his reference to her pregnancy. Once again, someone calling it a 'condition' – as though she were sick, not carrying a baby, which was a perfectly natural thing for a woman to do. Almost in response, she felt again that brand-new jabbing sensation against her side. The baby agreeing with her, perhaps. Or having a good old kick. She flattened her palm to the spot, trying to pinpoint it, and jumped when Raphael's deep voice said, 'Are you okay?' close to her ear.

She turned. 'Do you have to creep up on people like that?'

'I wasn't creeping,' he said with a touch of asperity. He slid the parking ticket onto the dashboard, then locked the car and frowned. 'Perhaps we should forego the cliff walk.'

'Because of my "condition"?'

'I'd rather not have an argument over semantics.' His smile was lopsided. 'Come on, let's walk into the village.'

Suppressing an impulse to tell him to go to hell, Hannah reluctantly fell into step beside him, and for a moment

there was silence. But of course it had been too much to hope he would not press the point.

As they stopped to look in the window of a small art gallery, he said coolly, 'You may like to pretend to the world that you're not pregnant, Miss Clitheroe. But trust me, you are. And you can't hope to hide it anymore.' He nodded to the reflection of her rounded belly. 'Going round the place pretending you've had too much to eat won't work for much longer. That is a baby. Not a chicken and mushroom pie.'

'Why am I always Miss Clitheroe when you're being patronising? My name is Hannah,' she pointed out, a sharp edge to her own voice. 'And I know this isn't a chicken and mushroom pie,' she added, pointing to her belly, much to the bewilderment of an old couple coming out of the gallery. 'I got an A in biology at school. I know what goes where, and the potential consequences.'

He looked at her sideways, his lips twitching. 'Good to know.'

They walked on past several more galleries and souvenir shops, some of them closed for the season, and past the bridge onto a riverside walk. The harbour lay ahead, with a row of white-washed Cornish cottages and a smattering of low-built shops on either side of the gradually widening river. She could see why the place attracted so many tourists in the summer. Even in cold weather, it was very appealing, with windows lit up to dispel the wintry gloom, and jolly Christmas carols playing in the shops.

'Are you hungry now?' he asked as they crossed the lower bridge towards the harbour, and stopped to look down at the water below. 'It's windier than I expected,' he said,

though in fact there was only a slight breeze coming off the sea and ruffling Hannah's hair. 'We could go straight to lunch, rather than walk along the cliffs first.'

'I'd rather work up an appetite, thank you very much,' she said crossly, aware that he saw her as fragile simply because she was pregnant, and she strode on without wait- ing for him.

He caught up with her a moment later. 'Good grief, woman, you're touchy today. Was it something I said? Or is it the hormones speaking?'

Hannah shot him a furious look, clenched both fists, and began to count out loud, her voice uneven as she struggled with a very strong desire to punch him on the nose. 'One . . . two . . . three . . .'

Raphael barked with laughter. 'All right, don't thump me when you get to ten. Message received. No more pregnant lady jokes.'

'Look, mister,' she said sharply, rounding on him, 'I've done mountain-climbing. Off-piste skiing. Extreme sports. Just because I'm expecting a baby doesn't mean I need to be wrapped in cotton wool and treated like an invalid.'

He threw up his hands in a gesture of defeat. *'Mea culpa.* I won't say another word about your . . .' He made a face, as though searching for the right word and then discarding all the various possibilities. 'Erm . . .'

'Don't.'

He laughed. 'The cliff walk it is, then.'

The tide was out when they reached Boscastle harbour, a few small fishing boats moored on their sides in silt, their

ropes thick with green algae. It was much colder near the open sea, almost chilly, but Hannah was running warm because of her pregnancy and it didn't worry her too much. The tang of salt on the air was invigorating, and reminded her of childhood holidays at Southend, except that the Cornish coast was rather more rugged and dramatic than the long, flat stretches of sand that she remembered. Not a donkey in sight, either.

'The writer Thomas Hardy loved this place.' Raphael sank both hands into his jean pockets as though he regretted not having worn gloves. 'He came to Cornwall when he was about thirty, I think, to fix up the church of St Juliot, just down the valley. It's quite a well-known story. He had a romance with a woman called Emma, who was visiting the vicar there. Hardy married her in the end, though I don't think it was a very happy union.'

Hannah was delighted by the story. 'How fascinating; I didn't know that about him.'

'I believe they have a display in the visitor centre about Hardy's visits to Boscastle. We could take a look on the way back.'

'I'd like that,' she said, genuinely interested. 'When I was a teenager, I saw the film of *Far from the Madding Crowd*, and thought it was amazing, so I got the novel out of the library. I loved it, and went on to read most of Hardy's other works too. Though *Jude the Obscure* is a bit grim.' She looked back over her shoulder at the village, all dark stone and slate, and nodded. 'I can perfectly see why he loved Boscastle. It's so dramatic, and there's such a sense of history here.' She paused. 'Are you a Hardy fan too?'

'I like his poetry, even though it's unfashionable. Perhaps *because* it's unfashionable.' Raphael grinned. 'But I could never get on with his prose. Too elaborate and Victorian for my tastes. I was a slow developer as a reader, and it led me to prefer simple stories. To be honest, I'm more of a contemporary thriller man, myself.' He paused, stepping aside. 'Here, after you.'

He let her go first as they reached a narrow channel between the cliff wall and the harbourside, the path ahead riddled with old iron posts and rings for mooring boats, and abandoned lobster pots. On the other side was a short flight of stone steps set into the rock. They climbed these carefully, as the surface was a little icy, and reached a jagged outcrop of rock overlooking the entrance to the harbour.

She gazed over the edge at the grey-green sea, churning far below, and frowned at a sudden sucking-and-booming sound from below them. 'What on earth was that?'

'The Boscastle blow-hole.' He laughed at her expression. 'See over there, on the other side of the harbour? That's Penally Point. There's a cave under the cliffs. That's the blow-hole, or what they call the Devil's Bellows. Water gets sucked into the space, and then blown out again by the change in pressure around low tide. It makes a loud noise, like an underwater explosion. Or a sea-beast roaring,' he added with a grin, 'depending on how lively your imagination is.'

They listened for a while to the sucking noises of the blow-hole, and then walked up the narrow cliff path, pausing for the occasional rest as it grew steeper. The air was

quite sharp and cold the higher they went, catching at Hannah's lungs near the top. But the view over the Atlantic was superb and well worth the climb, she thought. She shielded her eyes against the light, staring down the west coast as far as it was possible to see, the rocky outline eventually stretching into grey haze. It was achingly beautiful.

'Why did you decide to come to Cornwall?' he asked suddenly, startling her. 'You didn't need to move here. You could have sold the house.' His smile was disquieting. 'Saved yourself the hassle of starting afresh somewhere so ... remote.'

'I know,' she agreed, the sea breeze blowing a wedge of blonde hair into her eyes as she turned to face him. She pushed it back impatiently. 'But after Athens, I suppose London felt too alien and soulless. Especially with winter coming. Besides, I've spent most of my life in cities. I wanted a change. I wanted ...' She paused, looking around at the rugged cliffs and flat, endless ocean. 'This.'

'So you weren't running away?' he asked softly.

'Running away from what?'

'I don't know. Your past?' Raphael lowered his incisive gaze to her stomach, a look which she instantly resented. He might have employed her, but that didn't make her personal life any of his damn business. 'Your future too, perhaps?'

Hannah drew a sharp breath. The sheer nerve of this man!

'Please don't presume to know me, Mr Tregar,' she said sharply, 'or the details of my life. I can't run from a past I didn't even know I had. And if you think you can persuade

me to part with my inheritance by getting close to me, you'd better think again. Kernow House is mine now, and I have no intention of letting anyone take it away.'

Without waiting to hear his reply, she headed back the way they had come, hurrying down the cliff path in a precipitous manner. But she was not used to the altered balance of her body that had come with pregnancy, and almost lost her footing.

Wavering, her shoe slipped on some loose stones, and she only recovered herself with difficulty.

'Hannah, for God's sake, be careful!' he called after her, and she slowed her pace, aware of the sheer cliff edge to her left and the sea below it.

He caught up with her along the harbourside, his face tight with annoyance. But to her relief, he did not say a word, accompanying her in silence. She wondered if he was angry with her for speaking to him so bluntly, and whether he might take it out on her in some other way, maybe by obstructing her work. From the things Bailey and others had said about him, she had the impression anything was possible with Raphael Tregar. But for now, he merely seemed to be brooding.

They were just passing the Museum of Witchcraft – a place Hannah decided to visit on her own next time she came to Boscastle – when a woman about her age, with long, dark hair and a heart-shaped face, came out of the door and stared at them both as though she could not believe her eyes.

'Raphael?'

He turned his head, stopping abruptly. There was an odd expression on his face, an emotion she could not immediately place. Could it be dread?

A second later, he was smiling politely. 'Hello, Jennifer,' he said, not looking at Hannah. 'Good to see you again.'

CHAPTER EIGHTEEN

'Hello, Raphael,' the woman said huskily. 'I thought I saw you earlier. But I couldn't quite believe it. What are you doing in Boscastle, of all places?'

Raphael hesitated, clearly reluctant to start a conversation, and then nodded towards Hannah. 'Just showing a friend around the harbour, that's all.'

So this was Jennifer Bolitho.

She was certainly a very attractive woman, Hannah thought, looking her up and down as covertly as she could manage at close quarters. She also seemed a little tightly-wound, if that was the right expression. There was a tension about her, as though she were permanently on her guard, or about to do something violent. And her smile had a reckless edge to it. Altogether, she was the sort of woman that Hannah would ordinarily try to avoid.

No avoiding her now, of course.

And she had clearly already made her own assessment of Hannah, that much was obvious from the way she stuck out her hand, saying, 'Hello, I'm Jennifer. Pleased to meet you,' tagging '*Hannah*' onto the end of the sentence with curious

emphasis, as though she did not believe that to be her real name.

'Pleased to meet you too,' Hannah said promptly, and shook her hand. She managed one of those openly fake smiles that she detested in other people. 'Do you live here? I'm so envious. Boscastle is a marvellous place.'

'Yes, I live up the hill there. At Forrabury.' Jennifer dazzled her with a brilliantly fake smile of her own. 'But how about you? Is that a London accent?'

Hannah nodded. 'I live in Cornwall now though. That's how I met Raphael.'

'Really? How fascinating.' Jennifer looked from her to Raphael, and back again. There was a barbed note to her voice as she asked, 'So you live in Pethporro?'

No doubt deciding to intervene at this point, before their lively exchange descended to fisticuffs, Raphael cleared his throat. 'That's right. At Kernow House, in fact.' Not bothering with the fake smile nonsense, he added, 'Hannah is Trudy Clitheroe's granddaughter. So we're next-door neighbours.'

'Well, how amazing.'

'And she's taken over planning the Boxing Day pageant for us.'

Ouch!

'Goodness, is that so? That must be hard work. Especially considering how new you are to Cornwall.' She smiled at Hannah, her teeth showing between lips coated in rich scarlet lipstick. 'You'll have your work cut out for you there.'

'I expect I'll manage.'

The white teeth gleamed again.

'Of course you will. The pageant will be a triumph, I'm sure.'

Raphael cleared his throat for the second time. Perhaps the poor man was sickening for something, Hannah thought cattily. 'Well, we must be going,' he said. 'Wonderful to see you again, Jennifer. Give my love to the Ripper.'

Then he linked his arm with Hannah's, and began to pull her away.

'Goodbye,' Hannah said, looking back over her shoulder at the woman. 'Wait! Do you still have any notes about the pageant kicking around? If so, I would love to see them. Perhaps we could have a drink sometime?'

Jennifer's face was like stone, but she replied, 'Raphael has my phone number. Give me a call.'

'Will do.'

'Come on,' he said under his breath, interrupting this brief exchange to drag Hannah back towards the shops, the two of them now locked arm-in-arm. 'Time for lunch. You must be hungry after all that climbing we did.'

They were walking so quickly now, she got a stitch in her side and started to pant. The pain was oddly intense. 'Ripper?' she asked once they were out of earshot, to take her mind off it.

'Her cat.' He grimaced. 'One of those skinny Siamese cats, always yowling. He liked to sink his claws into me almost as much as she did.'

Once inside the restaurant, the pain in her tummy subsided, and so did the slight flickers of panic that had accompanied it. But it was a timely reminder to her that life had changed, however much she kept trying to deny it. She was expecting

a baby. That was now her reality, and she had to stop pretending she could go on the same as ever, doing what she had always done, without altering her life choices.

'Wine?' he asked as they were seated beside a window overlooking the river, and she shook her head. 'Of course not. Sorry.' Raphael ordered them both sparkling water. 'I'll join you in not drinking. I am driving, after all.'

They waved away the festive three-course Christmas lunch, ordering a light single course instead. Raphael glanced at his watch, muttering something about their walk having taken longer than expected; he hoped they could still make a quick stop in Tintagel before dark. No doubt he had given up on reaching St Ives, she thought wryly. As soon as the waitress had brought them fresh cutlery and napkins, and then hurried away, Hannah looked across at him, her eyebrows raised.

'Jennifer came out of the Museum of Witchcraft. Does she work there?'

'She doesn't work in the museum itself, but she's a frequent flier there. So to speak.' He made a wry face at her blank expression. 'Sorry, a little broomstick humour. Jennifer writes books about folklore and country magic, and so on. I expect she was browsing the exhibits for some inspiration. It's a habit of hers when researching a new book.'

Folklore and country magic?

That might explain the slight air of mania, she thought. No doubt Jennifer was back at home by now, twisting barley stalks into a Hannah-shaped doll, ready to stick pins in it.

'So what happened between you two?' She moved an over-large floral centrepiece so she could see him without

peering around either side of it. 'I was told you and Jennifer were an item at one point.'

'We dated.'

'Oh, very revealing.'

He glared at her, then made a noise under his breath. 'I made a mistake.'

'And she paid for it by being sacked.'

'Good grief, of course not. What do you take me for? Some kind of monster?' The waitress arrived with the water and two glasses, and he sat back, studying the red-and-white checked tablecloth with apparent fascination until they were alone again. Then he met Hannah's gaze with something akin to anger. 'I suppose that's the popular story she put about before leaving Pethporro. Her way of getting some paltry revenge on me. Hell hath no fury like a woman scorned, and all that.' He downed some sparkling water, and spluttered on the bubbles. 'Charming.'

'So you deny it?'

'I deny that she was sacked. She chose to leave entirely of her own accord.' He put down his glass. 'Yes, we were involved. But only briefly.'

'Define briefly.'

'One night, after a friend's party.'

She winced. 'I see.'

'Unfortunately, Jennifer was rather more interested in me than I was in her. She wanted us to keep seeing each other. I declined, politely.' He wiped himself with a napkin. 'Things got messy.'

'Perhaps you ought to have kept your hands to yourself, then.'

His eyes narrowed on her face. 'With hindsight, yes. But at the time, after a few too many glasses of wine . . .'

Their meals arrived, and they let the topic drop. There was a print on the wall beside them, an old sepia photograph of Thomas Hardy, and they discussed his books again. And the novelist's romantic fling in Boscastle. Every now and then, Hannah's gaze drifted out the window towards the river.

'Shall we drive on to Tintagel?' he asked when she eventually pushed aside her plate. 'I'd like to show you the old ruins of the castle there, before it closes at dusk. They have a café. We could grab a coffee.'

'Sounds good.'

While he paid for lunch, she gathered her things and wandered outside. There were a few spots of rain and the wind was getting up, but the dark clouds seemed to be moving away from Boscastle, further north. Towards Pethporro, she thought with wry resignation.

Hannah studied the street curiously. Towards the end of their meal, she had spotted Jennifer standing across the road from the restaurant, arms folded, staring in at them through the window with a sad and furious expression.

She had not said anything to Raphael, and he did not appear to have noticed.

There was no sign of her now.

Raphael came out of the restaurant, shrugging back into his leather jacket. 'Ready?'

CHAPTER NINETEEN

Tintagel Castle proved to be a magical place, just as it always had been in her imagination, the supposed birthplace of the legendary King Arthur, built precariously on top of a rugged island outcrop, a short bridge connecting it to the mainland. Beyond it stretched the Atlantic Ocean, all the way to America, flat under the grey mizzle of persistent rain some miles out. But it was not actually raining in Tintagel, as Raphael pointed out when she rummaged in her bag for an umbrella. And even if it had been, the icy winds sweeping across the top of the old castle ruins would soon have turned any umbrella inside-out.

'Looks like it's pouring again up towards Pethporro though,' Raphael said when they reached the remains of the great hall, studying the same clouds to the north that Hannah had.

'Not more rain!'

'I wouldn't be surprised if the river bursts its banks. Hope the properties along the waterside have been sandbagged. Some of the older cottages are particularly vulnerable to flooding.' He checked his watch. 'We'd better not stay too long. I may be needed.'

'Council duties?'

'Someone has to do it.'

They strolled from one side of the island castle to the other, stopping to read the tourist information boards at each important feature, and Raphael told her the history of archaeological digs there, a topic on which he seemed particularly knowledgeable. 'Gabriel was interested in the history of this place,' he said when she queried it, and shrugged. 'I guess some of that rubbed off.' He smiled. 'Thomas Hardy came here too. The legend goes that he got himself locked in after closing, and had to shout and wave his handkerchief to get the curator's attention.'

She laughed. 'So what was Gabriel like?' she asked curiously.

'Solid, dependable, a good farmer and a kind man. Deeply secretive about his private life too. So secretive, in fact, I thought for many years that he didn't have one.'

'Meaning, he did?'

Raphael looked out to sea. 'After he died, I found some letters among his things. And a few other items that led me to believe so, yes.'

'Such as?'

'Some paintings and rough sketches.' He paused. 'Of your grandmother.'

She caught her breath, fascinated now. 'Bailey, one of my grandmother's solicitors, hinted there might have been a secret romance between them. So he painted her? And there were letters too? What do they say?'

'I told you, Gabriel was a very private man. I doubt he would want me to share something so personal. I'm sure

you wouldn't share your grandmother's secrets. Assuming she had any, that is,' he added coolly, 'given that she was a married woman.'

Hannah stared at him until he looked away, beginning to walk on along the path. She did not know what to say.

Had Trudy had a secret affair with Gabriel Tregar behind her husband's back?

She hurried after Raphael, buffeted by mounting side winds as they turned at the headland, heading back towards the bridge to the mainland.

'Raphael, wait!'

She felt her bottom vibrate, and stopped, fumbling for her phone in her back pocket. It was a text message from Bailey.

I need an urgent chat. You free?

The phone only had one signal bar out here on the very edge of Cornwall, and as she watched, it disappeared again. No doubt that was why Bailey had texted, rather than simply rung.

An urgent chat?

That sounded serious. She hoped her friend was not in trouble.

On the drive back to Pethporro, under dark, threatening clouds, Hannah kept checking her phone every few minutes. Once the signal looked stronger, she risked calling Bailey back.

'It's Hannah, what's happened? Are you okay?'

'Hannah, thank God.' Bailey sounded distressed. 'I'm okay, and so is Penny, but our cottage isn't. We're ankle-deep in water here.'

Raphael, driving, glanced at her sideways. 'What's up?' he mouthed.

'That sounds bad. You live beside the river, don't you?' she said loudly. 'Has it burst its banks, then?'

She did not want to reply to Raphael, nor say anything that would indicate to Bailey that she was with him. Bailey would only read more into it than there was. Especially after the eager way she and Penny had linked Raphael and Jennifer after only one night together (if he was to be believed about that). Besides, the local gossip mill was probably already grinding where the two of them were concerned. Why give it more grist?

'Yes, and the water level is still rising. Hang on a tick.' Bailey shouted something, the phone muffled, presumably against her chest, then said into the handset, 'Sorry about that. Colonel Mustard keeps trying to climb the curtains.' *Colonel Mustard?* 'We put down sandbags, but not enough. There was a sudden fierce downpour about two hours ago, and Penny rang to say water was coming in. By the time I got here, the downstairs was completely flooded.'

'You poor thing.'

'We've already rung the insurance company, but apparently they've been inundated – sorry, no pun intended – with calls today. So we're on a list to be seen. Meanwhile, the place is basically uninhabitable. I mean, there's upstairs, but there's no electricity. Plus, the flood water isn't exactly clean, and everything smells so horrible . . .'

Bailey was crying, she realised. Hannah's heart squeezed in anguish.

'Don't worry, I'll come around as soon as I can and help

with the clean-up. All I need is your postcode for the satnav.' She glanced out of the car window, trying to guess how far they were from Pethporro, but it was getting dark and she did not know the area well enough. 'I'm not at home right now. I, erm, drove out to explore the coast today. But I'm on my way back. I can probably be there in less than an hour, ready with my mop and bucket.'

'That's really kind of you, Hannah. But our neighbours are all mucking in for the clean-up. We don't need any more helpers.'

'Oh.'

'That wasn't why I got in touch.'

'Whatever you need, Bailey,' she said immediately, ignoring Raphael's intense scrutiny. 'Just say the word.'

'Look, I know this is a massive imposition, but is there any chance you could put me and Penny up at Kernow House? Just until the water's gone down and the cottage is liveable again?'

'Oh God, absolutely,' Hannah said, secretly relieved that she would not be required to don waders and mop out water. 'Stay as long as you need, Bailey. You know there's plenty of space at mine. In fact, I've just been fixing up some of the upstairs rooms with proper beds, so you won't even have to sleep on the floor.'

'Thank you so much.'

'Don't mention it. Do you need me to pick you up?'

'No, we've got transport. But we do have quite a few things to bring with us. Will that be okay?'

'Of course, bring whatever you like.'

Bailey hesitated. 'Well, when I say things ... I actually mean pets.'

'Pets?'

'Colonel Mustard. He's our ginger tom.'

'Oh, a *cat*.' Hannah smiled, realising what Bailey had meant before about Colonel Mustard climbing the curtains. 'Sure, bring him along. I hope he doesn't mind other cats, though. The kittens are nearly big enough to get out of their box.'

'Then there's Shilly and Shally.'

'Erm . . .'

'Our two geese.' Bailey added hurriedly into the silence, 'I know that sounds odd. But they're no trouble, honestly. They don't even live indoors.'

'Right, okay.'

'Then there's Slowtop.'

Hannah closed her eyes. 'Please tell me that's not a goat.'

'Tortoise.'

'A tortoise . . . okay, I can deal with that.' Hannah paused. 'Any more?'

'No, that's it. Thank you so much, Hannah. You're a star.'

Twinkle, twinkle, Hannah thought drily, ringing off a few minutes later and dropping her phone back in her bag.

She wondered what geese liked to eat, and hoped she had made the right decision, saying yes to all these animals as well as Bailey and Penny. It sounded like quite a menagerie was about to descend on the quiet farmhouse. Well, it would make a change from living all on her own, she thought, not without a sense of trepidation.

Raphael studied her profile, then looked back at the road ahead. 'Flooding in Pethporro, I presume?' He sounded terse, switching on his headlights as dusk thickened along the coast road. 'Those low-lying cottages along the river?'

'Yes, you were spot-on in your prediction. There was a heavy downpour a few hours ago that led to a flash flood.' She looked at him. 'Actually, I'm surprised your phone hasn't been ringing too.'

'I turned it off.'

Typical, she thought, but merely said, 'That explains it. Anyway, my solicitor has a paddling pool for a living room now, poor woman. She's in real trouble. I've said she and her partner can pitch up at mine for the time being.'

'With a few animals in tow, I'm guessing.'

She sighed. 'Picked up on that, did you? Well, I could hardly say no, could I?' She stared out at the dark fields. 'What do geese eat?'

'City girls.'

'Ho bloody ho.' Then her eyes widened. 'Oh God, I forgot about Lizzie. She's on her own at the house.' She glanced across at the luminous dial of the speedometer. His pace had slackened somewhat since the phone call, presumably because he found it harder to tear down the road at break-neck speed while earwigging on someone else's phone conversation. 'We'd better hurry. What if they turn up before we get back? Lizzie's easily spooked. She'll probably think the place is being invaded.'

'She might not be far wrong,' he said under his breath, but duly accelerated, catching the urgency of her mood.

Rain began to fall again abruptly, a dark, heavy curtain descending across the landscape. Raphael's windscreen wipers dashed the large drops away as soon as they landed, but visibility was still poor.

'Will you come in with me?' she asked suddenly as they

reached the outskirts of Pethporro, many of the houses ahead flashing with Christmas lights now that darkness had fallen. People trying to feel festive despite the appalling weather, she thought. 'Lizzie knows you better than me, and I'm not sure how she'll take the news. Especially the part about the geese.'

He sighed. 'If I must.'

It was raining hard by the time Raphael dropped her off at the front door. Maybe even harder than the first day she came here, she thought grimly, making another run for the house with her head down.

He kept his headlights on until she was safely inside, then she heard the car splash through puddles as he drove around to park in the backyard.

The farmhouse was in darkness when she entered, except for a faint glimmer of light coming from under the kitchen door. Hannah groped for the light switch in the hall but when she flicked it, nothing happened. Power cut, she wondered, due to the floods? Or had a fuse blown? They were a good few miles from the river here, and too high anyway for any floods to affect them, but she supposed power lines might have come down in the town, and caused outages elsewhere.

There was a thundering sound throughout the house. Rain drumming incessantly on the roof and windows.

'Lizzie?'

Hannah followed the glimmer of light to the kitchen door, and pushed it open to find candles stuck into empty old jam jars on the table, and Lizzie bent over the sink in her

pink rabbit onesie and bunny slippers, tangled wet hair trailing down her back. She gave a tiny shriek and looked around at Hannah with a start.

'I thought you was a ghost!'

'Sorry. I didn't mean to creep up on you. The noise of the rain . . .' Hannah took off her dripping raincoat and hung it on the back of the door. 'What on earth happened to the lights?'

'They just went out.'

'Power cut?'

Lizzie shrugged helplessly. 'I was trying to make toast. But the crust got stuck, didn't it? So I put a knife in, see if I could work the damn thing loose.' She turned back to the sink. 'Then the lights went out.'

'I see.'

'I remembered where Mrs Clitheroe kept her candles. And them jars. Always handy to have an old jam jar about the place, she used to say.'

'Good thinking. Sounds like we'd better have a look at the fuse box.'

Uncomfortably wet, Hannah took a linen tea towel from the drawer and dried her face with it, and then began rubbing at her hair. She glanced in the sink to see what Lizzie was doing. Then wished she hadn't.

'Lizzie,' she said hesitantly, 'you must make yourself at home, of course. *Mi casa es su casa*. But what are all your clothes doing in the sink?'

'They got soaked,' Lizzie said flatly, scrubbing away. 'Muddy too. So I took 'em off.'

'We've got a washing machine.'

'Don't know how to work it.'

'Oh.' Hannah felt guilty. 'You should have said. I'll show you when you've finished there, if you like.' She paused. 'Did you go outside? In this God-awful weather?'

'When the toast got stuck, there was a terrible noise. Shrieking it was, right in my ears. Then the lights went out. I couldn't bear it. So I ran outside in the yard, even though it was dark.' Lizzie shrugged. 'After a bit, the shrieking stopped. So I come inside again. But by then I was soaking wet, wasn't I? Damn bloody rain. I slipped over too. Fell in the mud. Proper Noah's Ark weather out there.' She looked around at Hannah, a little wary. 'You know who Noah was?'

'Of course.'

'They said *he* was mad too.'

Hannah sighed, and tossed the damp tea towel aside. 'I don't think you're mad, Lizzie. Just confused.' She paused, eyeing her pink onesie and fluffy bunny slippers with sudden misgiving. 'Erm, I invited Mr Tregar to come inside for a few minutes. Sorry, I meant to say.'

Lizzie stopped scrubbing and turned to look at her in horrified accusation. 'But he can't see me like this. I'm in me onesie.' She lifted one fluffy slippered foot. 'And me bunny slippers.'

'I know, I'm sorry. I didn't realise.'

At that moment, the back door opened.

It was Raphael.

'Get out!' Hannah shouted urgently.

In the same instant, a mortified Lizzie fled past her and through the kitchen door, a hand clamped over the white bunny tail on her onesie bottom.

'Lizzie, it's okay – !' But she was already gone.

The back door closed.

Mere seconds later, she saw headlights in the yard, and heard Raphael's powerful engine roar into life. No doubt he was now mortally offended at having been yelled at to go away. Either that, or he had caught a glimpse of Lizzie's cute pink onesie and retreated in male confusion.

'Wonderful,' Hannah muttered, wishing, not for the first or probably the last time, that she was not pregnant and could have a glass of wine.

She located the tripped switch in the fuse box, reset it so the lights came back on, and then hurried upstairs.

Lizzie was already holed up in her bedroom.

'I'm really sorry, Lizzie!' Hannah knocked gently on the door, but there was no reply. 'Honestly, I don't think Raphael saw what you were wearing. Not even a glimpse. Do you want to talk about it?'

CHAPTER TWENTY

Roughly an hour after Raphael's precipitous departure, she caught the flash of headlights outside and made her way to the back door.

The house was quiet. Lizzie had stoutly refused to come out for a chat or to let her in. So Hannah had given up and left her to mourn her lost dignity alone.

The rain having eased somewhat, she pulled on her wellies and squelched outside to greet her new arrivals. The vehicle that pulled up was a large black van she had never seen before, muddy and battered, with some lettering on the side that she could not make out in the dark. But she recognised Bailey and Penny sitting in the front, looking drawn and exhausted, with another woman driving.

Bailey threw open the passenger door and jumped down, narrowly missing a deep puddle. 'This is so kind of you! Seriously, we can't thank you enough, Hannah. What a lifesaver.'

'Don't worry about it. What can I do to help?'

Penny climbed down from the van, her face pale, wet hair plastered to her forehead. 'Listen, you don't need to do a thing. Except maybe put the kettle on. We had no electricity at the cottage, and I'm gasping for a hot cuppa.'

'At least let me carry something,' Hannah insisted.

The woman who had been driving the van came around the bonnet, hand outstretched in greeting. Her hair looked very bushy, somehow at odds with the shape of her head.

'Remember me?' she said, and laughed at Hannah's blank expression. 'I'm Fenella, from the café in Pethporro. First time you came in, you asked for an Americano, or some such foreign drink.'

'That's right,' Hannah said, surprised.

Penny clapped her on the back. 'Don't look so nervous. Fenella is Bailey's mum. This is her boss's van, but they need it back first thing tomorrow for work so we have to empty it tonight, I'm afraid. Just show us where we can toss our stuff, and we'll try not to be too much of a nuisance.'

'Of course.'

Hannah led them through the house, telling them not to worry about water stains or muddy boots; there were no carpets down so any mud trails would be easy enough to clean up later.

On the first floor, she threw open the door to an empty bedroom. 'I hope this one will be okay for you. It's a bit draughty, but it's the biggest room on this floor. And it has a double bed.'

'Well, that's me sorted for sleeping,' Penny said, studying the new mattress still wrapped in plastic sheeting, and winked at Bailey. 'You'd better take the floor, darling.'

'I think you'll find it's the other way around,' Bailey replied with an answering grin, adding '*darling*' on the end with delicate emphasis. 'I'm too good for the floor.'

Fenella, who had followed them up the stairs with a

heavy suitcase in either hand, dumped them and said breathlessly, 'You'll both be on the floor if you don't shut up and help me unpack that van.'

'Sorry, Mum,' Penny said at once, looking far from sorry, and pinched Bailey's bottom on the way out of the door, who jumped and gave a muffled shriek. 'We're on the case. If you'll pardon the pun.'

Bailey glared at Penny. 'You know she doesn't like it when you call her mum,' she hissed.

Penny grinned.

'I'd better find you some sheets,' Hannah said, stifling her laughter when she saw Fenella's outraged expression.

She went rooting about in the airing cupboard, where her grandmother had left a surprisingly neat stack of sheets, pillowcases and towels. They didn't smell damp, so she popped a selection on Bailey and Penny's bed. There were no duvet covers, but her grandmother had not been a duvet woman. However, she did keep a stockpile of ancient blankets in a chest on the landing. Hannah shook out some of the less raggedy-looking ones and added them to the linen pile.

While Fenella and Penny were carrying in a chaise longue – directed by Hannah towards the sitting room – also salvaged from the cottage, Bailey took her aside. 'All joking aside, Hannah, we're both incredibly grateful to you for putting us up. Especially when you're so new to the area. Invading your privacy like this . . .'

'I'm happy to help, honestly I am.' Hannah paused. 'Bailey, I don't want to be rude, but . . . is that a wig your mum's wearing?'

Bailey nodded, saying, 'Cancer.' But she smiled when Hannah began to apologise. 'No, it's fine. It does look odd, I know. Mum had several rounds of chemo last year, and her hair fell out. So she started wearing wigs, and I guess she just decided she liked them.'

'Is she – is she better now?'

'In remission.'

'Thank God.'

'Look, we really can't thank you enough for letting us stay here. If there's anything we can do to make it up to you, just ask.'

'No, you're welcome. But there's something you should know.' Hannah lowered her voice. 'You two are not my only house guests at the moment. You remember that issue with Lizzie crying on my doorstep?'

Bailey's eyes widened. 'Old Lizzie's living here too? How did that come about? I thought she had some kind of camper van?'

'It's a long story. Long and involved.' Hannah rolled her eyes, then headed back towards the kitchen. 'Come on, let's get you settled in first. Then I'll tell you all about it, I promise.'

A terrible, unearthly yowling noise stopped them both at the door.

'What the hell was that?' Hannah opened the door to the kitchen, and looked around warily, not sure what lay in wait for her. 'Good grief.'

She had expected to find a ghost, at least. But the explanation was rather more prosaic. It seemed that one of Bailey and Penny's menagerie had come into contact with her own

mother cat and litter of kittens, and a battle royale had commenced. A huge, overweight ginger tom stood in the middle of the kitchen, facing off with Hannah's tabby. His tail was puffed up, his back arched, and lips drawn back from vampiric-looking teeth, trying his best not to overbalance despite the fact that he only had three legs.

Following her into the kitchen, Bailey gave a nervous laugh. 'Ah, I see you've met Colonel Mustard.'

'What happened to his other leg?'

'We're not sure,' Bailey admitted. 'We found him hopping about the streets of Pethporro a couple of years back. No chip, and though we put up posters, nobody claimed him. The vet said he might not even be a local cat, that anyone could have driven down from upcountry and dumped him.'

'How awful.'

'I know, right?' Bailey crouched to stroke the huge tom, making a reassuring sound under her breath as she tried to smooth the raised fur on his back. 'Anyway, we took the poor thing in, and gave him a name and a home. The Colonel's getting a bit fat now, I'll grant you that. Too many of those moreish cat treats. Cat crack, Penny calls it, and makes me ration it out.'

She straightened, the cat struggling in her arms, apparently oblivious to the furious flailing of his tail. 'He's lovely though. Very friendly.' Then she added, as Hannah reached out to scratch him between the ears, 'But he does bite sometimes.'

Hannah drew back instantly. 'Good to know.'

The mother cat had retreated to her box when Bailey picked up Colonel Mustard, and was now licking her kittens furiously.

Bailey handed the tom to Penny, who had appeared in the kitchen. She put him out the door and returned to gaze into the box. 'Gosh, they're growing fast. Adorable little creatures. Look at those big eyes! They'll be all over the house soon, getting underfoot, causing mayhem.'

'That's what I'm afraid of.'

'Have you given her a name yet?' Bailey asked, nodding to the tabby.

Hannah shook her head guiltily.

'I sense a cat naming ceremony coming up,' Penny said ironically, and laughed when Bailey glared at her crossly. 'Come on, it's what you're good at. The naming of pets. And now you have, how many, six more cats to do? Speaking of animals,' she added, looking at Hannah for guidance, 'where should we put Shilly and Shally? Only they're starting to peck their way out of the van.'

'Oh God, the geese,' Hannah said faintly, and followed her to the back door. The yard was pitch-black, a sharp wind blowing in off the invisible Atlantic. 'I'd completely forgotten about them. Perhaps the shed, for tonight? It's empty, except for some old bags of compost, and the door shuts securely, though it doesn't lock.' She unhooked a torch from the wall by the door. 'Over there, behind the van.'

'Thanks, that sounds perfect. We'll look for somewhere more permanent in the morning, when we can see what we're doing.'

Fenella passed them, returning a few minutes later with an unwieldy binbag and what looked like an old, brownish-black rock. She held out the latter, saying, 'Here, could you take this while I carry these clothes upstairs?' and then

disappeared, leaving Hannah with a smooth and surprisingly heavy object in her hands.

'Okay,' Hannah muttered, peering down at the rock-like object, 'what is this, and what am I supposed to do with it?'

'That's Slowtop,' Bailey said cheerily, her eyes widening when Hannah nearly dropped him in shock. 'Careful there!'

It was not a rock, Hannah realised, but a tortoise.

Speechless, she carried him under the kitchen spotlights for a better look. Under the light, his tiny grey legs could now be seen, flailing about as he scrabbled for solid ground.

Bailey took him from her, grinning. 'Poor old boy. You don't have a clue where you are, do you?' She placed him gently on the slate floor and watched as his head poked out of his shell, gazing about this unfamiliar place with dim, accusing eyes. 'He's about a hundred years old in tortoise years. Still partial to a spot of lettuce though. I don't suppose you have any in the fridge?'

'Iceberg okay?'

Bailey made a face. 'Organic little gem is Slowtop's current favourite but he'll cope. Leave it out of the fridge for half an hour first, though. He doesn't like chilled food.'

'I'll bear that in mind.'

'Well, while you two thrash out the particulars of Slowtop's dietary requirements,' Penny said, 'I'm going to put the kettle on, since making a pot of tea appears to have been forgotten in all this chaos.' She approached the sink, kettle in hand, and recoiled. 'Good God. What happened here?'

Puzzled, Hannah came to look over her shoulder. The sink was a stinking mess, packed with wellingtons and clothing that were filthy beyond description; there was mud

everywhere, silting up the plughole and spattering up the sides of the basin.

She closed her eyes briefly, and then looked up at the ceiling. 'Lizzie. I forgot all about her. She was cleaning her things here, and then Raphael came in, and she ran upstairs like the devil was after her.'

'That woman has good instincts,' Penny muttered.

'Poor thing, she's probably wondering what on earth has been going on, with all this banging about. She's used to living on her own in a van. This place must seem like Piccadilly Circus.' She looked at Penny pleadingly. 'If you don't mind making the tea, I'd better go up and check on her. I'll clean this out later.'

'Consider me your tea genie.'

Upstairs, Hannah listened at Lizzie's door, but all was quiet inside. No loud sobs, at least. Which she decided a good sign. She took a deep breath, and then knocked on the door. 'Lizzie? Are you in there? I'm sorry about earlier. May I come in yet?' There was no reply. A little concerned now, she knocked again, this time more loudly. 'Lizzie?'

When there was still no answer, she decided to try the handle.

Rude and intrusive, maybe.

But she felt instinctively that all Lizzie needed was a little reassurance. She was used to living on her own, after all, and sharing a house must be rubbing her nerves raw.

The door opened easily, and she peered inside. The overhead light was not on, but the small bedside lamp was. By its

soft glow, she saw a heaped pile of bedclothes in the middle of the bed.

The pink onesie lay abandoned on the floor.

Ditto the fluffy bunny slippers.

'Lizzie?' she whispered, and then tiptoed to the bed. Silence. She hesitated before prodding the large, motionless hump under the blankets. 'Is that you under there? It's okay, I'm on my own. Raphael's long gone. You can come out now.'

'He saw me onesie. That's not right.'

'I don't think he saw anything, actually. He never came into the house. I yelled at him and he went away again.'

The hump shifted, and after some odd fumbling and creaking, a tear-streaked face peeked out at her from under the covers. 'You sure?'

'Pretty much.'

Hannah sat down on the bed without asking permission, and enjoyed a moment of rest after an impossibly busy day. Her calves, she realised, were aching. All that bloody cliff climbing, she thought. Followed by rather too much to-ing and fro-ing with bags and boxes, helping her friends move in.

She patted Lizzie's shoulder through the covers. 'Look, why don't you put on some clothes and come downstairs? I've got some new house guests. Bailey and Penny. They're friends of mine, and very nice people. Maybe you heard them arriving?'

'I heard 'em.' Lizzie sounded grumpy.

'Well, they got rained out of their home too.'

Lizzie sat up at that disclosure, looking around at her with

sudden interest. 'I saw the van out the window. Is that where they live?'

'Erm, no. They live by the river in town. But the river burst its banks and flooded their cottage. So they don't have anywhere to stay, just like you.'

'Can't they stay someplace else? Them noisy types.' Lizzie did not seem impressed with the new arrivals. 'Tramping up and down them stairs like a herd of elephants. I had to stick my fingers in my ears just to get a little peace.'

'Yes, sorry about that. They brought a vanful of things with them. I hope you weren't too startled. I did mean to tell you they were on their way, but everything got out of hand so quickly. By the way, just to let you know, they had to bring a few pets too.' She paused, biting her lip at Lizzie's wary expression. 'How are you with geese?'

CHAPTER TWENTY-ONE

Unable to persuade a strictly anti-goose Lizzie to get dressed and join her new housemates, Hannah visited the loo, splashed her face with water, and changed her own clothes from the day's outing before tramping back downstairs. She was feeling rather more human when she walked into the kitchen to find Bailey and Penny arguing over the sink, a heap of sodden, mud-streaked clothes and boots on the slate floor beside it. Bailey was brandishing a sink plunger and Penny had an ancient container of some sink cleaning solution in her hand, each of them trying to nudge the other out of the way.

'What on earth?'

'The sink's blocked,' Bailey said, and wiped a muddy hand across her forehead. She sounded almost hysterical. 'We need to use the plunger.'

'No, we don't. That would be a complete waste of time. This stuff is what we need to shift the blockage.' Penny held up the bottle, which featured a rather worrying black cross on a red background. 'Honestly, Bailey's mum swears by it. She says it can dissolve anything. Even teeth.'

'Where is Fenella?' Hannah asked, taking the bottle away

from Penny under the pretence of studying the instructions on the back.

'Gone home. She's got work in the morning.'

'So have I,' Bailey said tartly.

'This stuff looks a bit toxic. It would probably kill my septic tank.' She glanced at Penny. 'Where did you find it?'

'Under the sink.'

Hannah shook her head. 'That explains a lot. My grandmother . . .' Abandoning that disloyal thought, she threw the cleaning solution in the bin. 'I'm afraid Bailey's right. The plunger is the only way to go. But I'll do it.' Prising the wooden handle from Bailey's iron grip, she pushed both women gently towards the door. 'Go upstairs and have a wash, get in your PJs or whatever, then we'll sit down together and have some food and that long overdue pot of tea. Or something stronger if you prefer. You must be exhausted after the day you've had.'

Bailey and Penny limped away without any further argument, and Hannah looked down at the mud-encrusted sink with a sigh.

'Oh, Lizzie . . .'

Wearily, she set to work with the plunger, heaving the thing up and down over the plughole, and running both taps for good measure. She was so involved in this noisy process that she did not hear the back door open.

It wasn't until Raphael's heavy hand landed on her shoulder that she realised she wasn't alone in the kitchen. Not expecting it, and having just seen a gigantic spider scuttle away behind the bottle of washing-up liquid, Hannah let out an almighty shriek, and jumped violently, spinning around at the same time.

'What the hell?' Raphael leapt backwards in alarm. He put both hands in the air, a gesture of surrender, and shook his head. 'Good grief, you're jumpy. Didn't you hear me knocking?'

'What, over the sound of the taps?' She thrust the plunger towards him, splattering him with mud and water. 'I nearly had a stroke.'

'Don't get ahead of yourself, darling.'

Her eyes widened. 'I didn't mean it like that.' Then she saw his shoulders shaking, and realised he was taking the mickey. She lunged forward with her weapon. 'Oh, you . . .'

He stepped back smartly, but too late. She had already marked him.

'Oops.' She suppressed the desire to snigger, and withdrew the plunger, though she continued to hold it defensively in front of her, just in case of retaliation. 'Sorry.'

Looking down, he studied the imperfect, muddy circle left on his cream sweater, and then raised his gaze to her rubber-capped tool. 'You look like a Dalek.'

'That's not very polite, all things considered.'

'Sorry?' He glanced at her prominent tummy, and grinned. 'No, I meant, with the plunger. Not that you look . . . round.'

'What do you want, Raphael? I thought you had gone home. It's getting late, and things have been insane here. I haven't even had a chance to sit down with a cup of tea yet.'

'The end of the British Empire as we know it, then?'

Hannah glared at him, then tossed the plunger into the muddy sink. 'Is it so much to ask for you to leave me alone for five minutes? Look at the state of this place. And now the sink is blocked.'

Raphael moved her to one side. He dragged off his stained sweater, and rolled his shirt sleeves to his elbows. 'Blocked sink? Why didn't you say so? This is my forte.' When she tried to intervene, he shot her a quelling look. 'Didn't you say something about a cup of tea? Because that would be very welcome.'

'Why aren't you at home?'

'I drove there, only to find you had left your handbag in my car. I couldn't come back right away since I had to do the rounds with the dogs first and check on the sheep, but I returned as soon as possible. Only to find you giving mouth-to-mouth to your sink.' He stopped scrabbling about in the plughole, and frowned over his shoulder at her. 'Where on earth did all this mud come from?'

'Lizzie.'

'I should have known.' He gave it some serious welly with the plunger while she set about making a fresh pot of tea. 'Good grief, half a garden has gone down here. Where is Lizzie, by the way? Did you throw her out for crimes against plumbing?'

'What do you take me for?' She was outraged by this suggestion, glaring at his back. Not that he could see her. 'She's upstairs, getting some clothes on.'

He looked startled. 'Sorry?'

'I take it you didn't see her before you left?'

'What, you mean when you barked at me to get out, and I inadvertently caught a glimpse of Lizzie rushing off in some kind of rabbit costume?'

She closed her eyes briefly. 'Oh dear. I wouldn't mention that to her.'

'Don't worry, I've blanked it all from my mind,' he said blithely, and continued to pump at the sink with the plunger, his grip strong, his movements powerful but measured. It was rather attractive to watch, she realised, and hurriedly looked away. 'Much as I like Lizzie, women dressed as animals are not really my thing.'

Hannah opened her mouth to make some sharp retort, then shut it again without saying a word. She had suddenly experienced the most bizarre sensation of jealousy, given that she was not remotely interested in Raphael Tregar.

Surprised at herself, and more than a little uncomfortable, she went into the hall to call Bailey and Penny downstairs for tea. That was when she found Lizzie lurking on the stairs in a grim-looking bathrobe.

'Feeling better now?' she asked solicitously, and Lizzie nodded, muttering something about mushrooms, which seemed to be a non sequitur. Hannah decided not to pursue it. 'Raphael is in the kitchen. Is that okay?' She studied Lizzie's threadbare robe. 'I can get rid of him if you want.'

Lizzie looked pained. But she stomped into the kitchen, and Hannah heard her say cheerfully enough, 'You been flooded out too, Mr Tregar? Don't worrit yourself, Miss Clitheroe's got plenty rooms for us all.' Apparently being seen in a tattered dressing gown was far preferable to a pink bunny outfit. There was the sound of a cupboard being opened and shut. 'Got sponge cake too. Raspberry. Want some?'

Bailey and Penny came down the stairs in matching blue pyjamas and carpet slippers, holding hands and smiling broadly; their argument had clearly been forgotten.

True love, Hannah thought wryly.

She took them aside before going back into the kitchen. 'Raphael Tregar is here,' she whispered. 'I thought you ought to know. He just turned up.' She nearly added, 'to return my handbag', but then realised they didn't know she had spent the day with him. Nor did she want them to know. It wasn't a decision she felt made much sense, given his reputation, and she would rather not be forced to defend it.

Since the two women were still looking at her expectantly, she finished rather lamely with, 'He's been going hammer-and-tongs at the blocked sink. So I can hardly throw him out.'

'Well, as long as he's making himself useful ...' Bailey sounded uncertain.

'Actually, I think he may be having cake now. With Lizzie, no less.'

Penny looked interested. 'Cake?'

They went into the kitchen, and found Raphael backed up against the sink, Lizzie attempting to force cake on him. He looked at them almost pleadingly.

'Ah, Hannah, I cleared the blockage,' he said, and slipped past Lizzie, wiping his hands on a tea towel. 'Now I really ought to be getting back. I left your bag on the table.'

Bailey looked from him to Hannah and back again, her look perplexed. 'Bag?'

'She left her handbag in my car earlier.' He grabbed up his cream sweater and pulled it over his head.

'Car?' Penny mouthed at her while he was lost inside his sweater.

Hannah shrugged helplessly.

With a blank expression, Bailey turned to look at the handbag, lying on the pine kitchen table like a key exhibit in a murder case.

'You went out together?'

Hannah felt her cheeks grow warm and wished herself anywhere but there. How could he? In desperation, she snatched at the plate of raspberry sponge cake that Lizzie was still clutching and stuffed some in her mouth. 'Work,' she said between mouthfuls of cake, covering the crumbs with her hand. 'We had to drive down to . . . down the coast.' She swallowed. 'It was all work-related.'

Raphael looked at her. 'Speaking of, I'd like to see your notes sometime this week. Find out how you're getting on with the pageant. Time's getting short.'

'Of course.'

She followed him to the back door, mainly to put some much-needed distance between herself and the other three women, who were all staring at her as though she had sprouted a second head.

Raphael hesitated on the threshold, staring up into the cold, black night. Rain was still falling, but less heavily, and there was an icy feel to it now, as though the weather had turned wintry.

'Thanks for your help tonight,' she said gruffly.

'No problem.' He turned to look at her, his smile somewhere between sardonic and inviting. 'I wouldn't have missed it for the world.'

'Missed what?'

'You, and those three, all living under the same roof?' There was a sudden shift in awareness as his gaze locked

with hers. She felt breathless, and battled against the urge to kiss him goodnight, not even sure where such a thought had come from. He was her nasty neighbour, for God's sake, not to mention also her employer now. 'I give it twenty-four hours.'

'Until what?'

With that lopsided smile she was beginning to know so well, Raphael Tregar mimed an exploding mushroom cloud with his hands. Then he ducked out under the rain, making a dash for the shadowy outline of his car.

'Goodnight, Miss Clitheroe. Sweet dreams.'

CHAPTER TWENTY-TWO

On Friday, she met Nancy for lunch in 'downtown' Peth-porro, which was basically one main road and a few sidestreets crammed with tiny shops, some of them closed out of season, and the occasional restaurant and café. The place Nancy had chosen was a small family-run bistro, with fake snow already on the windows and a Christmas tree in the corner, its branches laden with lights and sparkly baubles. Tiny elvish and fairy figures adorned wads of cotton wool snow on a shelf above their alcove table, surrounded by strands of tinsel. Just to ensure everyone understood the significance of this décor, piped Christmas carols filled the air at a deafening volume.

'Sorry, any chance we could turn down Good King Wenceslas before he breaks my eardrums?' Hannah asked the harried-looking waitress as she dashed past, plates of hot food balanced along each forearm, and got a muttered reply. She looked back at Nancy, her smile resigned. 'Perhaps if we lean close together, we won't have to shout at each other.'

Nancy pressed her rounded belly against the tablecloth. 'Um . . .'

'I have that problem too.' Hannah studied the menu, then

semi-yelled across the table, 'The food looks good, though. At the risk of sounding like a walking cliché, do you come here often?'

'Once or twice a month,' Nancy barked back at her, just audible above the opening strains of *When Santa Got Stuck Up The Chimney*. 'Try the vegetarian chilli, it's amazing. Unless you're a meat-eater?'

'Guilty as charged.'

'You ought to get on well with Raphael Tregar then. You know he's a sheep farmer?'

Hannah nodded, joking, 'Calls himself a shepherd though. Apparently, it's more a calling than a profession. He wanders about the fields like Moses, tending to his flock, even after dark. I haven't seen his staff yet, but I bet it's *massive*.'

The music volume dropped dramatically halfway through that last sentence, and she blushed in the silence that ensued, aware of a few disapproving glances being cast in her direction.

Nancy stifled her giggles under a napkin.

The waitress arrived and snapped open her order pad. By her dour expression, she had heard the *massive staff* comment too. 'Today's special is finished,' she told them. 'Soup is leek and potato. No substitutions.'

'Veggie chilli and rice, please,' Nancy said meekly.

The waitress looked at Hannah, who smiled brightly and asked, 'How big are your sausages?'

'The usual size.'

'In that case, I'll have lamb chops, please.' She looked at Nancy once they had ordered drinks and the waitress had

bustled away again, and gave a shrug. 'Well, since we were talking sheep . . .'

'Is it true you've got a houseful of people?' Nancy asked, taking her by surprise.

'I have three house guests. How on earth did you know that?'

'Pethporro grapevine. It's very efficient. You sneeze at breakfast, by teatime everyone knows you've got a cold.'

'Good God.'

'Word is, you're starting a women's commune out at Kernow House. With Raphael Tregar dropping by whenever he likes.'

Hannah was startled. '*What?*'

'Oh yes, quite a throwback to the heady days of the sixties, I heard someone say in the newsagents this morning. Anything goes at Kernow House.' Nancy leaned her elbows on the table, her eyes sparkling with amusement, and whispered, 'You know the kind of thing. Free love, grow-your-own cannabis, tie-dye robes, and lurid Wiccan rituals in the dead of night . . .'

'You're pulling my leg, aren't you?'

'Maybe a little. But you might want to join the Women's Institute. Or make some home-made jam for the Pethporro Christmas Fair. Anything to mark yourself out as unremarkable.'

'I'm beginning to regret agreeing to meet you today.'

'Sorry.' Nancy took out a spiral-bound notebook and turned carefully to a page of tightly written script. 'But maybe this will cheer you up. I made some notes that might be useful to you: ideas for the pageant, names of people you

could call on for help, local companies that might sponsor a float, et cetera. I hope you don't mind, or think I'm interfering in your work.'

'Mind? You're an absolute star!'

A little flushed at such praise, Nancy grinned. 'Well, it was just something for me to do, now I have all this spare time. More interesting than my usual diet of Netflix and Kindle romances.' She made a face. 'Maternity leave sounded so good when I was still at work, but now . . . Would you like to hear some of my ideas?'

'I want to hear all of them. Don't leave anything out. Though I feel awkward now. Let me buy you lunch, at least, in exchange for your brain power.'

'Okay, it's a deal.'

Hannah grabbed her iPad and opened it to Notes. 'Go on, I'm listening.'

But while Nancy talked, and Hannah took down her ideas, nodding from time to time at a particularly excellent suggestion, her mind had shifted to an entirely different place. A less pleasant space, where the carols sounded suddenly shrill and hollow, her lamb chops tasted like greasy cardboard, and she felt belittled and humiliated by the spiteful gossip about Kernow House.

She winced.

'You okay?' Nancy asked, and put down her notebook. 'Was it a step too far, that last one? A female Santa?'

'No, I think it's a brilliant idea. And exactly right for the times. No job a woman can't do, right? Though I'm not sure about the beard.' Hannah rummaged in her bag for some paracetamols, and took two with a few sips of water. 'Don't

mind me, I've got a bit of a headache. I was up quite late last night.'

'Dedicating a ceremonial knife by the light of the full moon?'

'Yes, ready to use on my neighbours.' She paused, looking at Nancy in sudden uncertainty. 'Speaking of which, you said the local gossip mentioned Raphael Tregar too. Something about him visiting the house whenever he chooses?'

'Just some harmless fun, don't get too worked up about it. There's not much else to do in Pethporro on these long winter evenings,' Nancy said frankly, 'except indulge in idle gossip.'

'But what if Raphael catches wind of it?'

'He won't.'

'You sound very sure.'

'Because I am. Raphael Tregar never listens to gossip,' Nancy said firmly. 'He never listens to anyone, in fact. Except his own ego, perhaps.'

'Is he really that bad? I mean, don't get me wrong, he can be pretty overbearing at times. And he does love the sound of his own voice. But he doesn't seem to be the monster I'd been led to believe.' Her voice tailed off as she saw Nancy's pitying expression. 'What? Why are you looking at me like that?'

'Oh, no reason.'

'Nancy!'

'Look, don't get me wrong, I can't fault your taste in manflesh. Raphael Tregar is a very hot, very sexy male. No argument there. I've had a few naughty thoughts myself, just passing him in the street.' Grinning at Hannah's

surprise, she picked up her glass and drank the last of her cloudy lemonade. 'But he's also a serious troublemaker for any woman with her head screwed on.'

'Troublemaker?' She kept hearing that word in connection with Raphael Tregar, and a niggling doubt in the pit of her stomach told her that Nancy – and everyone else in Pethporro, apparently – was probably right. 'Define your terms.'

'Apart from the way he scowls at everyone, you mean?'

'Please.'

'Okay, how about a control freak?' Nancy began to tick off Raphael's faults on her fingers. 'A womaniser? A serial heartbreaker? A complete loner who never lets a woman into his life, except for one thing – and one thing alone?' She dropped her hand to stroke the top of her bump, looking across at Hannah with a touch of acerbity. 'And we both know where *that* leads.'

'You're sure about this? You couldn't have got him wrong?'

'It's what people are saying.'

'But who, specifically?'

Nancy shrugged. 'Just people.' She checked her watch. 'Oh God, the time. I've got a mindfulness class. Shall we get the bill?'

CHAPTER TWENTY-THREE

Three days later Hannah was still making phone calls and plastering the living room walls with sticky notes, trying to make the ideas Nancy had given her for the pageant a reality. When she got off the phone with Fenella, who had agreed to help with the catering at the post-pageant event, she wrote down their arrangement on one of her three whiteboards, then took a few steps backwards to study her work.

There was a dreadful screech as her heel landed on something soft, and Bailey's ginger tom scrambled frantically into the hallway, heading for the stairs.

'Oh no, I'm sorry!' Hannah dropped her marker pen and ran after the offended cat, who looked even more panicked at the pursuit. 'Did I tread on your tail?' She clucked her tongue. 'Here, pussy pussy.'

But 'pussy pussy' – which usually worked so well for the mother cat, now dubbed by Penny as The Cat With No Name – did not appear to be part of his vocabulary. Unless it was just the way she had said it. Ears flattened to his head, Colonel Mustard fled up the stairs, moving with remarkable speed for a cat with three legs.

Penny came out of the kitchen in a smudged apron, frowning, her hands covered in what looked like flour, but might have been icing sugar. A wonderful smell of baking accompanied her.

'What on earth was that eldritch shriek?'

'My fault, I'm afraid.' Hannah looked up the stairs, but the cat had vanished. 'I trod on Colonel Mustard's tail. He's gone into hiding.'

Licking her fingers, which suggested the white substance all over them was icing sugar, Penny shrugged. She did not seem bothered, studying the message board above the phone cradle instead. 'Bloody cat. He's always sneaking up behind people without so much as a purr, and then acting cross when they don't see him in time for evasive manoeuvres.' She nodded to the message board. 'Did you ever get back to Raphael, by the way?'

'No.'

'He rang three times yesterday.'

'I was busy.'

'You should probably at least email him.'

'I did,' Hannah said flatly. 'To tell him I was busy.'

'He said he wanted an update on the Boxing Day pageant.'

'And I will talk to him. But not today. Today I have sod all to report. Nothing has been finalised yet, so there's no point in a status check.'

Penny looked at her speculatively. 'You two have a row, did you?'

'I don't know what you're talking about.' A little flushed, Hannah tried calling the cat again, clicking her fingers this

time too. But there was no sound from upstairs. 'Will he come back down on his own, do you think? It's just Lizzie keeps forgetting to shut her bedroom door, and apparently she found Colonel Mustard curled up on her bed yesterday.'

'Oh dear.'

'She likes cats, she told me. But not when they leave smelly offerings in the corner of her bedroom.'

'I'm sorry. What a pest he is. At least your kittens stay in the kitchen.'

'That's because most of them are only as big as my foot.'

'I'll wash my hands, then help you look for him. I don't want Lizzie suffering because of us and our wandering menagerie. There was enough of a fuss when she encountered the geese for the first time.'

Penny pushed back into the kitchen, and Hannah followed her, glad to escape her hideously complicated pageant plans for a few minutes. The smell of baking was even richer here, and she sniffed appreciatively.

Penny grinned, glancing at the wall clock. 'Fifteen more minutes and out it comes.'

'What are you baking?'

'Christmas cake.'

'How lovely.' She gave the bowl of icing a stir. 'Wow, this is thick.'

'It has to be for Christmas cake. Royal icing. You can buy the stuff in strips, ready-made, but they never sit flat enough. Plus, it doesn't taste as good as the home-made stuff.'

'Which is why you were licking your fingers.'

'Busted.'

'Look, I don't want to drag you away from the Aga if you're busy. I can find him on my own. He's probably under someone's bed, that's all.'

'No, it's fine.' Penny covered the bowl with a damp tea towel. 'I can't do any icing until later anyway; I have to wait for the cake halves to cool. Then I have to put on the almond paste.' She ran the hot tap, washing off the last traces of white powder from her fingers, then dried her hands. 'Right, come on, let's find that mangy cat before he outstays his welcome.'

Lizzie had gone in search of rats, as she often did in the mornings, despite there now being two rat-catchers on the property, so her room was empty. And fortunately Bailey was at work. So there was nobody to see them wandering the house, calling 'Colonel? Colonel Mustard?', for which Hannah was much relieved.

Frustratingly, there was no sign of the ginger tom in any of the first floor bedrooms, though Hannah got down on her knees and searched under every bed, table and chest of drawers, just in case he had found a cosy corner to hide in.

After several minutes of calling, and clicking their fingers, and making sundry other ridiculous cat noises, Penny finally said, 'Are you sure he came upstairs?

'One hundred per cent.'

'Well, he doesn't seem to be on this floor.' Bemused, Penny glanced up at the ceiling. 'Is there another floor above this one? Like, a second floor?'

Hannah hesitated. 'There's an attic. The staircase is next

to the bathroom. But it's all cobwebby and grim. I've only been up there a couple of times, and I wasn't planning to go back.'

'Cobwebs or not, we'll have to take a look. Bailey will never forgive me if I lose Colonel Mustard.' And Penny headed off in a determined fashion to find the attic stairs.

'I'd better get a torch, then,' Hannah called after her. 'There's no electricity up there.'

She ran down to the kitchen. By the time she got back up to the attic floor, she found Penny cradling a very dusty-looking cat, who looked at her with a wounded expression.

'Sorry I trod on your tail,' Hannah told him, feeling a little ridiculous for speaking to a cat like it was a human. But he was probably used to it. 'There was no reason to run away though. It was an accident. Not deliberate.'

Penny cuddled the tom, semi-squashing him against her breasts like a baby. 'Who da silly puddy tat, den? Poor, poor puddy tat.' She looked up, catching Hannah's eye, and made a face. 'Sorry. Force of habit.'

They both looked around the attic. Penny had opened a cobweb-festooned curtain across one narrow window, letting in the pale daylight. It was icy cold, and a wind was blowing, rustling things unseen. There must be a broken window somewhere in the shadows, Hannah thought. The place was a mess. Old pieces of furniture, a broken door leaning against a half-full bookcase, what looked like a gramophone player with its lid down, the obligatory rocking horse, and crate after crate piled high with chaotic bric-a-brac, some of it spilling out onto the dusty floorboards.

Penny took an unwary step into the shadows, and gave a cry, recoiling with a loud crack.

'What in hell's name was that?' Hannah also backed away, her heart beating fast. It was silly to be scared of an attic. There was nobody there but the two – or rather, three – of them. But still, she could not shake off an eerie feeling. 'Penny?'

Penny let Colonel Mustard, who had been struggling violently to be free, escape her arms. He dashed to the door and back down the stairs without a backwards look. 'I think . . .' She bent over, her voice muffled. 'I kicked the bucket. Literally.' She straightened with a battered metal bucket in her hand, water sloshing noisily inside it. 'What's this doing up here?'

'My fault, sorry. The roof was leaking when I first moved in. I put a few buckets around to catch the drops.' Hannah shuffled forward and gazed up at the roof beams above where the bucket had been. There was no sign of daylight, thankfully. 'A nice man called Stewart came and fixed it for me – loose slates, he said – and I thought I'd taken them all down again.' She looked back at the floor. There was a puddle, but only from where Penny had nearly knocked the bucket over. 'I must have missed that one.'

'I'd say,' Penny said drily, and gave one leg of her jeans a little shake as though it was damp.

Hannah shone her torch beam over a crate in the corner. There was a small wooden box perched on top of some old books, a delicately carved inlay decorating its lid. 'Hey, what's that?'

She went over to investigate, treading carefully in case any of the floorboards were rotten. The box was locked, but when she shook it, she could hear something inside. Paper? And something small and possibly metallic rattling about.

She ran the torch beam over what looked like Chinese patterns carved into the wooden lid. 'I'm taking this downstairs for a closer look.'

'I'll grab the bucket.'

Hannah glanced at her. 'Sorry,' she said again.

'*De nada.*' Penny followed her out of the attic and down the narrow steps, bending her head to avoid the low beams. 'It's all useful practice, anyway.'

'For what?'

'For when I kick the bucket for real.'

Colonel Mustard was nowhere to be seen when they got downstairs. Perhaps he had decamped to the library with a length of lead piping, Hannah thought wryly. However, the smell of fruit cake was everywhere, the air rich and tangy.

And with a slight hint of burning . . .

'Oh shit,' Penny muttered, and pushed past her, water sloshing about in the bucket as she ran for the kitchen. 'My Christmas cake!'

While Penny salvaged her baking amid shrieks of anguish, Hannah sat down on the rug in the living room, surrounded by Post-It notes and crumpled pieces of paper, to examine the Chinese box she had found. She turned it over gently,

listening to that tantalising rustle and metallic tinkle from inside. A key, perhaps? A ring? Or some other piece of jewellery?

It was a beautiful piece of artistry, whatever it contained. It seemed to have been kept with loving care before its ignominious trip up to the attic. There were no discernible scratches on the wood, except beside the gilt lock, and the wood had been oiled at some point in the past. It still had a slight sheen to it, and a faint scent of linseed.

She wondered who had stuck the box up there in the attic. Her grandmother? That might suggest the contents were not so important, after all – or perhaps that Trudy no longer cared about them.

Unless someone else, clearing the house after her death, had taken the box up to store it along with other personal items, not thinking twice about it.

Running her fingertips over the fabulous Chinese patterned inlay on the lid, she found it hard to believe that anyone would be soulless enough to keep mere trinkets in a box like this. Or documents fit only for the shredder – long out-of-date bank statements, medical records or dreary shopping receipts. And why would it be locked, if the contents were uninteresting?

No, it had to contain something special.

Briefly, she recalled what Raphael had said about Gabriel, and having found a stash of old letters from her grandmother. Sketches and paintings too.

Her heart beat a little faster.

'Okay, where's your key?' she asked the box, glaring down at it.

Not surprisingly, it did not reply.

Reaching for her Perspex cube of assorted stationery items, she chose a thin metal paper clip, and unfolded it out into one long, slightly crooked, strip. This she inserted gingerly into the keyhole, and wiggled it about.

Nothing happened.

She wiggled it about some more, holding the box to her ear and listening for any sound of a click or shift inside the lock's delicate mechanism.

Silence.

'Damn.' Withdrawing the bent paper clip, she frowned down at the impenetrable seal. 'That always works in films.'

Disgruntled, she put her makeshift lock-pick and the Chinese box aside, and looked up at her whiteboards instead, all three of them covered in an increasingly frantic scribble. Maybe Bailey would have some ideas about opening the box. She seemed like the sort of person who could get into anything. Especially if she wasn't supposed to.

Meanwhile, there were still the main characters in the pageant to be decided.

Hannah sighed, studying her notes.

A traditional Cornish Christmas was their theme, and using the few files left behind by Jennifer Bolitho, Hannah had cobbled together a list of eager handbell ringers, carol singers, first-footers, and a troupe of elvish helpers from the local primary school – the latter courtesy of Nancy's former class. Hannah had also arranged for some of the specialist costumes to be made by a retired wardrobe mistress, Mrs Chorley, who had spent half a lifetime working in the theatre before moving to Cornwall. But those were all minor

considerations. The key characters in the pageant still eluded her.

'Gog and Magog,' she said, slowly reading the list from the whiteboard opposite in hope of fresh inspiration. 'The Cornish Giant. The Black Dog. The Lord of Misrule.'

The Lord of Misrule.

Well, she thought drily, that role practically casts itself.

CHAPTER TWENTY-FOUR

'Not a cat's chance in hell,' Raphael said.

He bent to pick up the sheep pinned between his legs, struggled along with the wild-eyed animal for a few feet, then pushed it firmly into a pen. He shut the gate to keep it secure, then straightened, wiping his hands on his thighs. His hair had fallen over his forehead, and he knocked it back impatiently, looking around at her. 'Did you walk all the way out here just to ask me that?'

Without waiting for a reply, he whistled for his dogs, who left the rest of the flock at once and came running across the steep field with total obedience, like he was the Pied Piper.

'It's important. Or I wouldn't ask.'

'I'm sure it must be important, city girl.' Raphael looked her up and down, taking in her jeans and waterproof jacket, his gaze lingering on her muddied green wellingtons. 'And I'm glad to see those boots are being put to some proper use at last.' Hannah hated the sarcasm in his voice. 'But the answer is still no.'

'You want the pageant to be a success, don't you?'

'Don't tell me I'm the only person who can play the Lord

of Misrule,' he drawled. 'Because that's bullshit, and you know it. Besides, I'm too busy to take the part.'

'Why?'

He hesitated. 'None of your business.'

'Because you say so?'

'Something like that.' He stroked one of the dogs, then turned abruptly and set off back towards his farmhouse, its grim stone walls nestled below them like some brooding animal in the thickening afternoon light. 'Besides,' he said over his shoulder as she stood staring after him, 'I thought you were in a mood with me.'

'A mood?'

'You haven't been returning my calls. Or replying to my emails.'

'I . . . I've been busy.'

He said nothing, but shrugged and kept walking, dragging a tweed cap out of his coat pocket and swinging it onto his head. Christ, she thought wearily, staring at his back. It's like being back in the bloody playground. He said, she said. And all the usual nonsense in between.

She stumbled downhill after him, catching up with his long strides with difficulty. 'Hey!' He stopped and looked around at her. 'I'm sorry, all right? I should have got back to you. But things have been difficult.'

'Why?'

The incisive question threw her off balance. 'I had lunch with a friend the other day. She said a few things that made me uncomfortable.'

'What friend?'

'Nancy Swan.'

He grunted. 'Pat's daughter.'

'That's right.'

'So what did this friend say to upset you enough to stop taking my calls?' He turned, and there must have been something in her face that gave it away, because he stiffened. 'Is this still about Jennifer Bolitho?' When she said nothing, he added sharply, 'I told you, there was nothing between us. Nothing serious, at any rate.'

'You think a lot of yourself, don't you? I'm in a mood with you, so you automatically assume it's because I'm ... what, jealous? That I'm attracted to you, and upset because some other woman is still holding a torch?'

Hannah opened her mouth again, meaning to say more, but the truth of her words hit her hard, and for a moment she was winded, speechless. She did find Raphael a teensy bit attractive. She could not deny it to herself, though she might deny it to his face. She had been at pains to pretend he looked like the back end of a barge as far as she was concerned; he would become insufferably smug if he knew the truth. But *jealous*? Genuinely jealous, not just a fleeting moment of pique?

Impossible.

Jealousy could only exist if there was love. And there was definitely no love involved here. Not one jot. All her affection was still reserved for Santos. And she had no intention of betraying his memory with a man like Raphael Tregar.

Luckily, he took her silence for contempt.

'No,' he said, 'I think you're unprofessional. Whatever the local gossips say, there was nothing between me and

Jennifer except a one-night stand. You don't have to act like I'm about to leap on you every time I try to talk to you about work. And you'd better find yourself some other Lord of Misrule too.' He strode off towards his home, not looking back this time. 'I've got better things to do than live up to everyone's expectations by playing the villain.'

Hannah trailed home over the fields, feeling wretched and low and angry at herself. Somehow – and she had no real idea when it happened – she had become *friends* with Raphael Tregar. To the extent that losing his good opinion made her squirm with unhappiness and embarrassment. She could have understood snatching at him for support if she had still been living on her own. He was her nearest neighbour, after all, even if several waterlogged fields and a few dozen sheep lay between their houses. And loneliness was a terrible burden. She had felt it acutely at the beginning – despite pretending that she was happy and independent – and as winter had set in, and the rains had begun to fall, she'd felt increasingly isolated and apprehensive about the coming birth, unsure how she would cope with a young baby by herself.

But with recent events – Lizzie moving in, then Bailey and Penny too, not to mention their unusual menagerie – she'd not had time to feel lonely.

On top of that, the child she was carrying felt more like a blessing with each passing day. A final gift from her beloved Santos, someone to love as she had loved him, someone to care for and share her life with. She would need to keep Kernow House if she wanted to give Santos' child a happy

and settled home life. Which meant keeping the predatory Raphael Tregar at bay.

Why then did she feel a sense of loss?

Back at the house, she found Bailey home early from work, and Lizzie apparently in the bath. From above came the sound of her off-key singing, coupled with gurgling from the hot water pipes. Bailey and Penny were cooking dinner 'for everyone', and refused her help.

So there was nothing to do but for Hannah to take off her coat and slope back into the living room, fast becoming her work study, to stare at her whiteboards and Post-It notes.

While she was working, the baby kicked; she put a hand to the spot, automatically murmuring, 'There, there,' as though she could hear and understand her. She would have to get a cot soon, Hannah realised with a sudden shock. Nappies, blankets, first baby clothes. Or was it bad luck to buy baby clothes before the birth? She seemed to recall her mother, always superstitious, saying something about that once . . .

'Obby Oss,' Lizzie said helpfully from the doorway.

Startled, Hannah turned. 'Gosh, you made me jump. I didn't know you were out of the bath.'

'Sorry, I was walking quiet so as not to disturb the kitty-cats.' Lizzie's head turned toward the whiteboard, seemingly mesmerised by her squiggles and rough notes for the pageant.

Hannah followed her gaze. 'What's up, Lizzie? What have you seen?'

'You done missed one out.'

'One what?'

'One of them scary men,' Lizzie said, pointing at her list that ended with the Lord of Misrule. 'For the Pethporro pageant.'

Eager for some fresh input, Hannah grabbed up a board marker. 'Okay. Which one have I have missed out, Lizzie? Tell me, I'll add it to the list.'

'I already told you, when I come in just now.'

'Oh yes.' She frowned. 'Hobby, or something, wasn't it?'

'Obby Oss.'

'I'm sorry, I don't—'

Lizzie mimed riding a horse, grinning wildly. 'Obby Oss. There's always Obby Oss in a Cornish pageant. Riding up and down, scaring everybody, and making the little 'uns scream for all they're worth.'

Hannah spelled the two words out on the board, and then glanced back at Lizzie for confirmation. 'Like that?'

'Dunno how to spell it.' Lizzie laughed, suddenly cheerful. 'But you need the Obby Oss, for sure. Or it can't be proper Cornish.'

'Got it.'

She would need to look it up on the internet. Though Lizzie seemed very sure of her information. And now that Hannah thought about it, the name 'Obby Oss' did ring a bell. Very faintly, somewhere at the back of her mind. Some nightmarish creature out of her mother's tales – usually disparaging, and no doubt intended to put her off visiting the place – of a rural Cornish upbringing.

She gave Lizzie a grateful smile.

'Thank you, Lizzie. That's really useful. If you have any more

ideas like that, come straight to me with them, please.' She underlined Obby Oss three times in thick red marker pen, much to Lizzie's delight. 'Honestly, I need all the help I can get.'

Dinner that evening was a raucous affair.

Bailey and Penny had cooked a vast pan of toad-in-the-hole, accompanied by petits pois, a mountain of mashed potatoes, and gravy so thick you could stand a spoon up in it. They did a great double-act as they served this humble meal, Penny in a soiled apron, waving a ladle and shrieking like one of her own geese, and Bailey, red-faced and sweating, running around with hot dishes and once nearly slipping on an oil spillage.

'I'm not your bloody slave, you know,' Bailey kept telling her partner as they cooked, to which Penny eventually retorted, 'That's not what you said last night, pet. Now get those spuds strained and mashed!'

Hannah stifled her giggles and made herself useful by laying the kitchen table. As an afterthought, she put two red, Christmassy candles in single candleholders and lit them. It looked quite pretty, she mused, with a cloth napkin at every setting and candle flames reflected in the glassware. She found a bottle of elderflower cordial in the fridge, currently her favourite tipple, and opened some red wine for the others.

'We desperately need to put up some Christmas decorations,' she told Bailey, glancing about the rather austere-looking kitchen. 'Tinsel, holly wreaths, mistletoe, and a Christmas tree, of course. Not to mention lights. I must sort that out soon, otherwise people will think we're a bunch of total Scrooges.'

'We had some lovely decorations at the cottage.' Bailey

made a face. 'But I expect they're a bit damp now. What a shame.'

'Any news on the flood damage?'

Bailey shook her head. 'The insurance assessor had a look at the property yesterday, but she said they can't get back to us with an official quote for at least a fortnight, they've had so many claims to process. Meanwhile, she suggested we keep receipts for any costs we incur trying to dry the place out. It's a bit depressing, really.' She paused, suddenly looking uncertain. 'Are you okay with us staying on here for a while?'

'Oh God, of course. Stay as long as you like, I love having you here. In fact, I didn't realise how quiet this place was until you two moved in.'

'I'll take that as a compliment,' Penny called over her shoulder, wrestling with a vast oven pan bulging with crisp, golden batter and sausages.

Hannah laughed, and went to call Lizzie down from her room, where the woman habitually retreated whenever anything noisy or unexpected was happening in the house. It was probably living on her own for years in the middle of a field that made Lizzie shy of company, Hannah thought, watching as she edged towards the table with an air of trepidation.

'What's this, then?' Lizzie said, sitting down and gawping at her plate.

'Toad-in-the-hole.'

She stared up at Penny in horror. 'Toad? *Toad?*'

'Pork sausages in batter, my lovely,' Penny replied with a laugh, her accent pure Cornish.

'Oh.' Lizzie hesitated, then laughed too. 'Sausage toads.'

'That's right.' Penny pushed a bowl of steaming petits

pois towards her. 'Here, help yourself to some veg. That's the way, take as much as you like.'

Hannah took the seat next to Lizzie and watched the two women work. She had not been exaggerating when she told Bailey it was good to have them in the house. She thoroughly enjoyed their sharp banter and to-and-froing over the Aga, grinning as she listened to the playful insults, feeling as though she were back in sixth form among her friends. Though it seemed more like a family dinner once the four of them were seated around the kitchen table, chatting and laughing, and passing around her grandmother's china gravy boat, its spout dripping.

Penny broke into her thoughts. 'So, how did you get on with the Lord of Misrule? Did he agree to do it?' Hannah had confided her plan to Bailey and Penny last night and they'd been amused by her optimistic belief that Raphael would agree to take part in the pageant himself. 'I bet he said no.'

'And you'd be right to risk your money.'

'I knew it. I used to work in market research and you soon learn to spot the "no, thanks" brigade on the high street. That man's got "no" written all over him.'

'Bailey told me you teach Cornish now,' Hannah said. 'Is that a full-time job?'

'You mean, when I'm not clearing up after Bailey?' Penny laughed, ignoring Bailey's cross face. 'No, definitely part-time. I teach Cornish both on and offline, and write the odd article for language journals. Otherwise I do as little as possible. My darling mum died a few years back and left me enough to buy that cottage, with a bit left over. So I'll be okay for money so long as Bailey here doesn't get the sack.'

Penny grinned at her girlfriend, then unscrewed the lid on a pot of mustard and scraped a little of the bright yellow condiment onto her plate.

'Mustard, anyone?' She offered it around, but they all shook their heads. 'Huh, your loss. Clears the sinuses, this stuff does.'

'I make it a rule never to eat anything named after a cat,' Bailey said truculently.

Penny crooked an eyebrow at her. 'The mustard came first. Not the colonel.'

'Not to mention the board game,' Hannah put in helpfully.

'Precisely.'

They all looked at Colonel Mustard, who was sitting up on a spare chair at the end of the table, blinking as he begged shamelessly for sausage.

'Board game?' Lizzie repeated, staring from the pot of mustard to the cat in obvious bemusement.

'Cluedo,' Hannah said, then saw her blank expression and added, 'It's a game where there's a murder at the start, and you try to work out who the murderer is.'

Lizzie's eyes widened in disbelief. 'A murder?'

'Not a real murder. It's just a game.'

'Doesn't sound like a very nice game to me,' Lizzie said in a mutter. 'Pin the tail on the donkey, that's a nice game.'

Hannah nodded slowly, cutting into her toad-in-the-hole. The batter was delicious – light and fluffy, but with a crisp finish, exactly how she loved it. 'Maybe we could have something like that at the Boxing Day pageant. Pin the tail on the Obby Oss, for instance.'

Penny looked at Hannah thoughtfully. 'Perhaps you could be Lord of Misrule? There's no law that says it has to be a man.'

'Lady of Misrule?' Hannah was intrigued. 'It's a thought.'

'Speaking of unruly ladies, guess who I saw in town today?' Bailey said, her tone mischievous.

'Don't,' Penny said repressively.

Unsure what they were talking about, Hannah frowned. 'No idea, sorry. Do I know any unruly ladies?'

'What, apart from her mother, you mean?'

Ignoring her partner's quip, Bailey leaned across the table, her look very earnest. 'You don't know her, Hannah, but we've discussed her before – Jennifer Bolitho, the woman who was running the pageant before you. I saw her walking down the high street as I left work, all dolled-up like she had a date tonight, and swinging her shopping bag like it held a severed head.'

Penny winked. 'No prizes for guessing whose head.'

'I can imagine,' Hannah said, and shuddered. 'She's probably a perfectly lovely woman when you get to know her. But she is a bit scary-looking, I have to admit.'

This accidental disclosure got their immediate attention.

'What?' Bailey demanded, staring. 'You've *met* her? You've met Jennifer Bolitho?'

'Erm, yes.'

'Where?'

'In Boscastle, actually.'

Penny paused with her mash-laden fork partway to her mouth. 'Well, you dark horse. When did this happen?'

CHAPTER TWENTY-FIVE

Hannah took a deep breath, her cheeks growing warm under their joint scrutiny. Then she decided to come clean about her coastal trip with Raphael. It had been weighing on her mind anyway. She was lying about it, and for what? To avoid embarrassment that she had spent time with him? He was not an ogre, she had discovered. Unfortunately, he wasn't exactly Prince Charming either. Though she didn't want them to think she found him . . . interesting. Not in that way, at any rate. She also refused to betray Santos' memory even for a second, and hated that her friends might wrongly believe she was thinking about another man like that. It was too horrible to countenance.

So she told them again about Raphael's invitation to drive down the coast together, and how they had bumped into Jennifer outside the Witches' Museum, keeping her tone light and neutral. Like she was discussing a routine trip to the bank or the hairdresser's. Not an intimate outing with Another Man. In an offhand manner, she even passed off their restaurant lunch as a simple business meeting.

To her dismay, Penny looked knowing, and Bailey tutted

anxiously under her breath. Exactly as she had feared they might.

Lizzie, on the other hand, chased a last, solitary pea around her plate, head bowed as though not paying any attention. But when Hannah reached the part where she had spotted Jennifer glaring at them through the restaurant window, she said abruptly, 'Don't like that lady. She was rude to me. I don't hold with that kind of thing.'

They all looked at her in astonishment.

Bailey put down her knife and fork. 'Rude to you, Lizzie? Who was? Jennifer? I didn't know you knew her too.'

'Seen her out at Mr Tregar's place, haven't I? With Mr Tregar, once or twice.' Lizzie shrugged, seemingly reluctant to elaborate.

'And what did she say to you?' Penny prompted her.

'Didn't say nothing.'

'Then how was she rude?'

Lizzie hesitated, looking a little hunted. Then suddenly stuck two fingers up at Penny. 'Like that.' She turned her hand clockwise, displaying the same crude gesture to Bailey, and then to Hannah, before realising there was a blob of mashed potato stuck to one of her fingers. Disregarding her napkin, she wiped her hand carefully on her sleeve instead. 'That's what she done to me when I was walking home from town. Just coz the lane gets a bit narrow there, and I was in the way of her car. Not very nice, is it?'

'No,' Bailey said, and sat back in her chair. She seemed surprised as well as annoyed. 'Not very nice at all. Was she with Raphael at the time?'

Lizzie shook her head. 'He were out with the sheep, were

Mr Tregar. She drives up, bold as brass. Bangs on his door, then drives away again.' Her smile held a quiet satisfaction. 'I don't think she were very pleased.'

'I bet she wasn't,' Penny said drily.

'Is Raphael still after this place, Hannah?' Bailey asked, helping herself to more gravy. Everyone watched with fascination as the coagulated mass refused to budge, even when held at a near-vertical incline, then abruptly splurged out of the boat onto her remaining toad-in-the-hole. 'I know he came to see Mr Knutson about it a few times before you moved in. But he hasn't been back.'

'I'm not sure. He hasn't mentioned it recently.'

Bailey shot her a concerned look. 'But you've discussed it with him?'

'Once or twice.'

'You shouldn't really have done that, you know. Not without a lawyer present.' She sounded serious. 'I'm sure Raphael doesn't have a genuine claim. But if you even hint that he might have, that could be enough for him to take it to court.'

They finished their meal in semi-silence, Lizzie humming a jolly Christmas carol under her breath as though delighted that she had put two fingers up to everyone and not got into trouble for it. Perhaps it had been a lifelong ambition, finally realised. Hannah could certainly relate.

'Talking of Raphael, he found some letters at the farmhouse,' Hannah said at last, unable to keep it a secret any longer. 'Letters from my grandmother to Gabriel Tregar. Or so he says.'

'Oh my God!' Penny put down the wine glass she had been

fondling, and stared at Hannah in amazement. 'You're kidding? You mean, some kind of secret correspondence between them? That's awesome.'

'I don't actually know what's in the letters. Raphael hasn't shown me.' Hannah felt awkward now, with everyone looking at her, even Lizzie. 'He could be making it up as a way of gaining my trust or something.' She raised her eyebrows. 'Though that sounds like nonsense now I've said it out loud, especially since he didn't actually share the contents with me. Maybe I'm being suspicious for no reason.'

'In my experience, it pays to be suspicious,' Bailey told her frankly.

'Yes, but . . .' Hannah tailed off, not sure where that sentence was going or if she even wanted to know.

'But you like him?' Penny's clever smile threw her off balance.

Hannah did not know what to say. But once again, she realised with a shock, she was blushing like a schoolgirl. She put down her knife and fork, and clapped her hands to her cheeks, half laughing. 'You lot, what are you like? I ask you into my home, and all you do is make fun of me. I don't have a thing for Raphael Tregar.' She blinked, amazed to find tears in her eyes for no apparent reason. Bloody hormones *again*? Then she blurted out exactly the opposite of what she had intended. 'Not a *serious* thing, at any rate.'

'I knew it!' Penny jumped up and ran around the table to hug her, which was difficult with Lizzie in the way. Yet somehow she persevered. 'I think it's wonderful,' she boomed rather close to her ear, nearly deafening her. 'You've been looking so forlorn recently. You deserve a bit of romance in your life.'

'It's not romance,' Hannah said, hurriedly backtracking. 'I don't know why I said that. Please forget it.'

Bailey was shaking her head as though she hadn't heard that denial. 'Well, I don't think it's wonderful. I think it's dangerous.'

'That's only because,' Penny said, straightening up to glare at her partner, 'you always insist on thinking the worst of people.'

'Oh yes, says the most sarcastic woman in Cornwall, famous throughout the Duchy for her razor-sharp quips.' Bailey looked at Hannah with sympathy. 'Look, I'm not trying to make you feel bad about this. If you genuinely like Raphael, you should go for it. But just be careful, okay? You have to admit, you're in a vulnerable position right now.' She waved a hand vaguely towards Hannah's prominent bump. 'And you know his reputation.'

'Honestly, I didn't mean—'

'I'm only thinking of you, Hannah. I don't want to see you hurt.' Bailey got up and started collecting their dirty plates, her movements brusque and a little impatient. 'Jennifer got hurt, didn't she? Okay, I agree I may have been wrong there; she sounds like a nightmare girlfriend. Bunny boiler material. But maybe that's what he deserves.' She sighed, scraping uneaten food off the plates into the pedal bin. 'It's not what you deserve, though. You deserve better than to be messed about by Raphael Tregar.'

Lizzie, who had pulled in her chair so close to the table as Penny squeezed past that she seemed to be having trouble breathing, suddenly sucked air into her lungs and said in a determined gasp, 'That's all well and good, but what I want

to know is, what was in them letters? What did Trudy write to old Gabriel?'

Penny sat down again, giving her a wry look. 'Well, quite, Lizzie. That's the big question, isn't it?' She poured some more wine into her glass, her shrug eloquent. 'We won't know the answer until Raphael Tregar can be persuaded to give the letters up.'

'And what are the chances of *that* ever happening?' Bailey added, stacking the scraped plates in the sink for washing.

'Maybe we should sneak over to his farm one day while he's out with the sheep.' Lizzie pushed back her chair, looking a little flushed and dishevelled. She had been sharing Bailey and Penny's wine, and it seemed to have gone to her head. Her voice was slurring slightly. 'Find them letters and steal 'em.'

Bailey looked around at her, appalled. 'No stealing, Lizzie. That's a really bad idea. Breaking and entering is a serious offence. You don't want to get in trouble with the police, do you?'

'S'pose not,' Lizzie muttered.

Hannah bowed her head and pretended to inspect her fingernails, still processing what had just happened.

Not a serious thing, at any rate.

What on earth had possessed her to say such a stupid thing? It wasn't even true, she told herself. Not the way they had taken it, anyway. She liked Raphael, it had to be admitted. But that was as far as it went. And she was sure he felt the same.

Though at least her friends weren't all staring at her anymore like she had two heads. They were simply arguing amongst themselves.

As though she didn't exist.

Which right now she wished were true.

Not a serious thing.

Relieved that the focus of their attention was no longer her own pink face, Hannah got up, saying, 'Hang on, I'll be back in a minute.'

She stood in the cool, dark hallway for a moment, breathing slowly in and out to steady her racing pulse, then went to the living room and retrieved the wooden Chinese box. This she brought back and placed on the kitchen table in front of them all. She had polished it that morning, and the carved wood now gleamed richly.

It would make a fine distraction from her blundering *faux pas*, she thought, smiling around at them.

'I could be wrong,' she said. 'But I have a feeling the other side of that correspondence might be inside this box.'

'What?' Bailey almost shrieked, her eyes wide. She sat down at the table and drew the Chinese box towards her with careful reverence. 'Oh, look at that inlay. Where did you find this? It's beautiful, the carvings are so intricate . . . You never mentioned this before, you secretive thing.'

'I only found it this morning, when I was up in the attic with Penny.'

Bailey shot Penny an old-fashioned look. 'What's this? Been sneaking about in the dark with another woman, have you?'

Grinning, Penny nudged her in the ribs. 'Shut up. We were looking for the Colonel up there. And we found him.'

'I'm sure it must have belonged to my grandmother,' Hannah told them, studying the box. 'It certainly seems to have

been well-cared for. And I can hear what sounds like paper inside it, and maybe a ring too. But it's locked, and I don't have the key.'

'Ribbon,' Lizzie said lovingly, staring at the box as Bailey turned it carefully over to examine the base. 'Red ribbon.'

'Ribbon? Sorry, what does that mean, Lizzie?' Hannah asked, frowning. 'Have you seen this box before?'

'Course I have.' There was a touch of affectionate scorn in Lizzie's voice. She gave a sniff, gazing up at Hannah, then rummaged in her pocket for a mangled shred of tissue and blew her nose on it. 'Your gran, she loved that box. It was her special secret, she'd say. Always had it open, Trudy did, right here on this very table,' she confirmed, nodding to the patch of pine immediately in front of her, a few small flecks of potato and gravy indicating where her plate had been. 'And whenever I'd come in with my rabbits, she'd throw all the papers back inside, all higgledy-piggledy like, shut the lid fast . . . and *lock it*.' She lowered her voice, leaning across to Bailey and Penny with wide eyes, her air conspiratorial. 'Before I could see what she'd got.'

'And do you know where Trudy kept the key?'

'On a ribbon,' Lizzie announced proudly, and tapped herself on the chest, 'a proper red ribbon, always strung round her neck.'

CHAPTER TWENTY-SIX

'This time, don't forget to bring home a Christmas tree!' Penny yelled out of the back door just as Hannah finished scraping ice off her windscreen.

'I'll try, honestly,' she called back, climbing into the chilly interior of the car, glad of her generous pashmina. 'If I get time after the auditions, okay?'

'You need to make time.' Penny glared after her with mock-disapproval. 'We're into December now. This is like the house that Christmas forgot.'

Grinning at her through the fogged-up car window, Hannah pretended to tug her forelock, and then headed towards Pethporro down the winding lanes, her smile fading as she considered the tricky day ahead.

Since last week, auditions for roles in the Boxing Day pageant had been posted online and in the local newspaper. There had been quite a buzz about it, apparently, with hundreds of comments in the Facebook group, and Pethporro residents were leaving notes in the suggestions box at the library on an almost daily basis. Several local characters rang her up personally to insist they should be the ones to play the infamous Obby Oss or the Lord of Misrule.

Although she was trying to keep an open mind until the auditions were over, Hannah already had a good idea of the physical types she was looking for. Certainly it would be a gruelling day for any participants – nearly all of it outdoors in possibly sub-zero temperatures – and even with thermals on under the costumes, she did not feel comfortable about casting anyone who didn't look up to the task.

It was a shame Raphael had refused to play the Lord of Misrule. He would have been perfect. Not just physically, but in terms of his local importance. Chairman of the pageant committee, and well-known in the community – largely as a difficult man, it was true, but people respected him, all the same. And he was also an oddly liminal presence in Pethporro – he lived outside the town, somewhat aloof, yet he was still involved in running the place.

But Raphael had said no.

So she needed to look elsewhere for her Lord of Misrule. Someone with natural authority and charisma, someone to hold the whole thing together. After all, the Lord of Misrule had to lead an unruly pageant all the way from the starting line to the beach, and give the final toast at the end, once dusk had fallen.

The town hall car park was almost full when she pulled up. Luckily, someone had thought of this eventuality, and a hastily drawn sign was stuck on the wall near the entrance, declaring the parking space RESERVED H CLITHEROE. She got out of the car, stamping her booted feet and wishing she had worn thermal underwear herself. It was so cold she kept her gloves and scarf on as she hurried into the town hall.

'Goodness, it's freezing out there,' she said to

Mrs Cobbledick, Nancy's mum, who was standing in the foyer, handing out fliers to promote the pageant. 'Like the bloody Arctic.'

'Cold enough to snow, do you think?'

She turned, smiling as she recognised her grandmother's solicitor. 'Hello there, Mr Knutson. I didn't think it snowed all that often in Cornwall. Especially along the coast.'

'Oh, it happens here. We're not exempt.' Mr Knutson shook her hand. 'But it does tend to be a somewhat lighter sprinkling than they get upcountry.' His voice had a wonderful, deep booming quality, and his bushy eyebrows waggled when he talked. He always made Hannah think of a character from a Charles Dickens novel, but she wasn't sure which one. He smiled warmly. 'And how are you getting on at Kernow House? Bailey tells me you've taken her and Penny under your roof. Like the Good Samaritan you are.'

'I'm glad of the company. It is nearly Christmas, after all.'

'Quite so.' He had not let go of her hand, she noticed, still squeezing her gloved fingers with a thoughtful expression. 'I hear you tried to get Tregar Junior to play your Lord of Misrule, only he declined.'

Tregar Junior?

Presumably he meant Raphael.

It was hard not to smile.

'That's right.'

'So the main role is still vacant.'

Belatedly, Hannah understood the significance behind the prolonged hand-squeezing. 'Erm, yes. Absolutely. Are you planning to audition?'

'Oh, I hadn't actually . . . Still, that's a very flattering offer.'

Before she could say anything, his chin lifted, and Mr Knutson turned his head slightly, as though showing off his profile for a film close-up. 'Perhaps Bailey told you about me?'

'Told me what?'

'That I'd indulged in some amateur dramatics in my younger days. Noel Coward, Oscar Wilde, a few pantos. I even played Hamlet once.'

Not sure what to say to that, Hannah managed a faint, 'Really?'

'So you think I'd be good in the part? That I have the right bearing?' He winked at her, which was disconcerting. 'The Lord of Misrule . . .'

'I'm not sure, to be honest.' Carefully, she disengaged her hand from his, and then stripped off her gloves in what she hoped was a business-like manner. 'But come through to the hall, and I can put your name down for an audition slot.'

'Will do,' he beamed.

She nodded to Mrs Cobbledick. 'Nancy here yet?'

'Been here half an hour, my love. And loving every minute of it.' Her mother nodded inside the hall. 'At the reception desk.'

'Excellent.'

As Hannah and Mr Knutson walked into the hall together, she spotted Lizzie in the corner, looking bizarre and unkempt in a pair of Trudy's old denim dungarees, with a Christmas sweater on top. She had come into town earlier, catching a lift with Bailey on her way to work, and was now sitting on a table, swinging her legs back and forth as she waited for the auditions to begin.

'Sorry, Mr Knutson,' Hannah said with barely concealed relief, 'I've just seen a friend. Excuse me a moment, would you?'

He murmured something about being 'perfect for the part' as she slipped away from him with a smile.

'Lizzie, are you hoping to audition today?' she asked, taking off her coat and scarf. 'Or are you here to watch?'

Lizzie seemed astonished. 'Me? Audition?'

'Why not?'

Hannah glanced at her phone for a time check. She would be there at least five hours, by her reckoning. Would there be time to go shopping for a Christmas tree before driving home again? And could she even get one in Pethporro? There weren't any large stores, but she seemed to recall there was a garden centre somewhere on the coast road north of the town. Which seemed wildly out of her way.

'I don't know nothing about acting,' Lizzie said, looking worried.

'This won't really be acting. Nothing like on the stage. You get a costume, and have to walk through the town wearing it, that's all. All you need do is pretend to be the character you're playing.'

Lizzie was fascinated. 'Like the Obby Oss?'

'That's right.'

'I seen the Obby Oss before. He done run up and down the town,' Lizzie said excitedly, 'all in black and with a horse's head. Big teeth too.'

'Do you think you'd make a good Obby Oss, Lizzie?'

Lizzie stared, and said nothing.

'Well, I think you might. Worth having a go, don't you think?'

Now Lizzie's eyes grew round.

'Just put your name down over there,' Hannah told her calmly, and pointed to the reception desk, a trestle table near the door, where Nancy was bent over a sheet of paper, taking the names of people who wanted to audition, and handing out lists of possible parts. 'Go on, you might be good. You certainly know what's needed. Which I bet is more than most people here do.'

A small crowd had gathered in the narrow hall, the room growing noisier as people chatted amongst themselves. The walls were hung with tinsel and other festive decorations, and a small Christmas tree dominated one corner, strung with lights that were already on and flashing cheerfully. It reminded Hannah guiltily of the promise she'd made Penny.

She was starting to look forward to Christmas, after fearing its approach for several months, worried how she would survive her first holiday without Santos. So it was ridiculous not to have the decorations up yet.

Having three other women in the house felt like a buffer zone, a barrier against the coldness of the world. A coldness she had only noticed when she was stripped so abruptly of love and companionship, and had to learn to cope with everything on her own, not merely single, but a single mother-to-be. But every day she was lifting herself further out of what she suspected might have been depression, and Kernow House was starting to feel like home, not just the place where she slept. Plus, any day now they would surely find the elusive key to unlock Trudy's box of letters, and she could then learn more about her grandmother's secret, other life. Whatever that had entailed.

'When's it due?' someone asked, and as Hannah turned to answer the middle-aged woman, she saw Raphael sauntering through the entrance.

'Erm, March,' she said vaguely, her gaze locked on his tall figure, her heart beating hard.

He saw her staring, and smiled slowly across the room.

Her skin tingled.

Bloody hell.

'Pregnant at Christmas,' the woman said, smiling broadly, 'how lovely for you.'

Hannah managed to stammer something in reply, she had no idea what, and then excused herself, heading for the loos.

Once safely inside a cubicle, she had a wee – her bladder was increasingly under pressure, so she had learned never to pass a toilet without nipping in – and then closed the lid and sat on it for a few minutes, trying to regain her composure. Raphael had not said he would be here today.

How dare he walk in looking like that? Flat cap, scruffy farmer's waterproof coat, mud-flecked wellies ... and totally mouth-watering with it.

It simply wasn't fair, she thought, leaning her head against the cubicle wall. Especially when he was such a difficult man to read, prickly and sarcastic one minute, then charming the next. How much easier it would be if his looks matched his grim behaviour. Not that looks were everything. But when he was in a room, Hannah could not seem to take her eyes off him. Which was both ridiculous and annoying, and was also going to make it incredibly hard to concentrate on running today's auditions.

Just as she was beginning to feel calm again, and ready to emerge, someone came banging into the ladies. 'Hannah? Hello, you in here?'

It was Nancy.

God, how long had she been in the loo? How bloody embarrassing.

'Just . . . erm . . . a minute.'

Rolling her eyes, Hannah made a show of noisily rattling the toilet roll dispenser and then flushing the toilet. She counted silently to three before leaving the cubicle with a bright, cheerful expression.

'Hey, Nancy.' She headed for the sinks to wash her hands and check her reflection. A surreptitious glance in the mirror told her things were not so bad as she'd feared. In fact, she looked like she was *glowing*. Pregnancy, or the Raphael effect? 'Are we about ready to start out there?'

'I guess so, yes. Twenty-four people have turned up to audition, though more may come along later. Some have an acting background, but most haven't. Still, I've been telling them they don't need much experience. Just enthusiasm, in fact. And reliability. No point giving out a part only for them not to turn up to our rehearsals, or the actual event.'

'Quite right.'

'And the Morris dancers have arrived.'

'Excellent, I can't wait to see them perform. Tourists always love a good Morris dance, don't they?'

Nancy tucked her hair behind her ears, watching curiously while Hannah washed and dried her hands. 'I was surprised to see Raphael Tregar here.'

'You and me both. I didn't invite him.'

'I just spoke to him. He says he wants to "oversee things".' Nancy made a face at her reflection. 'Whatever that means.'

'Christ.'

She stalked out of the toilets and found Raphael hanging around as though waiting to speak to her. He'd taken off his tweed cap and thrust it into his coat pocket, where it was poking out. His dark hair was dishevelled and he had a tinge of hard red along his cheekbones, as though he'd been out in the frosty fields since early that morning. Which he probably had.

He turned restlessly on his heel, seeing her. He looked her briefly up and down, and then said, 'Hannah, good. I was just looking at your schedule for the pageant, and I want to put forward a change.'

'Oh yes?'

'I'd like to be the one who makes the toast at the end of the procession to the sea, not the Lord of Misrule.'

She took a deep breath. 'Well, if you'd like to take on the role of the Lord of Misrule as I suggested before, that would work out perfectly.'

'No, I told you. Taking part in a pageant, dressing up ... It's not my kind of thing.' He sounded dismissive. 'But it's important to close out the event on the right note, so I'll make the speech at the end. Okay?'

'You're the boss.'

His smile was dry. 'Yes, I suppose I am.'

For God's sake.

He was saved from a cutting reply – though she had not yet managed to think one up – by her phone buzzing.

Hannah grabbed it out of her pocket, rudely turned her back on him, and opened the message.

It was from Penny. A GIF of a dancing Christmas tree.

'Bloody hell.'

Raphael looked at the message over her shoulder, his hands in the pockets of his scruffy coat. 'Very festive. What does it mean?'

'Do you mind?' Crossly, she stuffed the phone back in the pocket of her trousers, checked her blouse was still tucked in, and then turned back to face him. Why did he have to stand so close to her? She felt almost hot again, and wondered fleetingly if she was getting a cold. 'It's just a reminder from Penny to pick up a Christmas tree on my way home. We've been so busy recently, we haven't got on top of the decorations yet. Now, if you'll excuse me, I have to work.'

He watched as she walked away, the intensity of his gaze practically burning a hole between her shoulder blades, then called after her, 'Look, forget about the tree. I've got one you can have.'

She stopped, baffled, and frowned back at him. 'We don't need your cast-offs, Mr Tregar.'

'It's not a cast-off. I know a man who does Christmas trees. He owes me a favour.' He looked her up and down again, this time his gaze distinctly mocking. 'What size do you prefer, Miss Clitheroe?'

'Big,' she threw at him defiantly. 'The bigger, the better.'

He laughed softly as she walked on.

CHAPTER TWENTY-SEVEN

Lizzie bounced up and down excitedly on the passenger seat, nearly hitting her head on the roof of the car, grey hair straggling down from under her woollen hat. 'I got it, I got it. I'm going to be Obby Oss!'

'Yes, you did, and very well done too. You were brilliant, Lizzie.' Hannah glanced at the dashboard clock. It was only three o'clock, but she felt like it ought to be much later, her voice hoarse from shouting and her feet aching. Not to mention her lower back, which was starting to suffer from the increased weight on her front. 'You were easily the best Obby Oss we saw all morning. And thanks so much for organising those sandwiches for our lunch. I was starving and they tasted delicious.'

'Nancy walked with me to the sandwich shop.' Lizzie glanced at Hannah's tummy, then added, 'She's having a baby too, I think. Or she's very fat.'

'No, she's definitely having a baby. Sooner than me too.'

As though aware that it was being discussed, a tiny kick landed against her right side, low down, and she grinned.

'Obby Oss,' Lizzie muttered, staring out of the window as they headed up the high street, passing shop windows lit up

WINTER WITHOUT YOU | 248

with Christmas lights, all looking very festive. 'Obby Oss, Obby Oss.'

Nestled in the dashboard well, Hannah's mobile buzzed.

'Can you see what that is, Lizzie? I'm not allowed to touch the phone while driving.'

Lizzie stared at her in consternation, then picked it up gingerly. 'How do I . . . ?' She stopped, and then tapped the screen with a hesitant finger. 'There's a . . . a message.'

'Who's it from? Can you see?'

Hannah suspected it might be Penny again, nagging about the Christmas tree. Though if Raphael was to be believed, they would not need to worry about that.

He had reminded her about it before he left the town hall. After watching the first hour of auditions in silence, he had finally unfolded his arms and strolled out, though not before murmuring as he passed her, 'One Christmas tree coming up, Miss Clitheroe. *Extra-large*.'

She had ignored him, intent on Mr Knutson's audition for the Lord of Misrule. To her surprise, the solicitor had not been bad at all. In the end, she cast him in the role, though still half-wishing it could have gone to Raphael, if only because she thought of him as that kind of figure: a Loki, a disrupter, a bringer of chaos, if only to her peace of mind.

'Bailey. It's from Bailey. It says . . .' Lizzie was holding the phone very close to her face. '*At the cottage. Can you come?*' She sounded unsure, reading the message very slowly. 'Then some letters and numbers.'

'The postcode.' Hannah waited until it was safe, then pulled to the side of the road. She took the phone from Lizzie, keyed the satnav coordinates into her TomTom, and

then headed off again. 'It's okay, don't worry. Bailey told me last night she might be visiting her house this afternoon. It's been flooded, remember? Like your van?'

Lizzie nodded, looking anxious. Her shoulders had slumped at the memory of her own disaster.

'Well, she said there were still a few things she wanted to salvage. You know, take them back to Kernow House, so they don't get ruined while the cottage is damp. I told her to text me if she needed a hand.'

'No work today?'

'For Bailey?' Hannah smiled. 'I think she's nipped out of the office, actually. There's no electricity at her place, you see, so she can only go there during daylight hours. And it gets dark so early these days.'

'Nearly midwinter,' Lizzie said knowledgeably, sitting up straight. 'The shortest day.'

Hannah glanced at her, surprised. 'That's right. I'd forgotten that. But after that, it's Christmas. A much cheerier thought.'

'Christmas cake,' Lizzie murmured.

'Exactly.'

'In three hundred yards, turn left on road.'

Hannah checked her mirror, then prepared to follow the repeated instructions, much to Lizzie's astonishment, who had apparently never come across a satnav before.

Lizzie leaned forward, peering warily at the graphics on the dashboard screen. 'Who's that speaking?'

'Nobody knows,' Hannah told her. 'But she's a real bossy-boots.'

*

They turned down the narrow road that led eventually to Peth-porro harbour, slowing to avoid some walkers with sticks and bobble hats. The ocean in the distance was a cold, metallic grey, flecked with white tufts; exactly like an oil painting of a seascape, Hannah always thought; she never tired of looking at it. She continued driving slowly for another few hundred yards until they reached the first bend and their destination.

She parked in the semi-circular space opposite the river bank, marked Loading Only, hoping nobody would mind if they were longer than five minutes, and pointed to the row of low, whitewashed cottages along the riverside.

'That must be where they live,' she said, pulling on her scarf. 'Come on, let's go and find Bailey.'

The two of them battled against the wind towards the row of cottages. The gusts blasting off the sea were sharp and icy, cutting through the various layers of her clothing to leave her shivering. Those dark, heavy clouds Hannah had seen in the morning were still lurking on the horizon too, threatening rain, or what might become snow if the temperature dropped any lower.

The door to the third cottage along was open. Bailey emerged, looking a bit flushed and weary, a smear of mud on her forehead. She was wearing a protective apron over her work clothes, and wellies instead of shoes; it was obviously very dirty work.

Bailey waved a hand as they approached, clearly relieved to see them. 'Glad you could make it. I wasn't sure if you'd still be in town.'

'Happy to help. Just point me in the right direction. What do you need first?'

'Come in and I'll show you. Oh, and I found two boxes of Christmas decorations in the loft space. Tinsel, garlands, baubles, lights, angels and tree ornaments, the works. You can take them back to the house if you like.'

'Sounds like a plan.' Hannah picked her way carefully down the garden path, which was strewn with debris from the flood, and peered through the door into the cottage. She recoiled, a hand to her nose. 'Oh my God, the smell!'

'Sorry, I should have warned you to bring nose plugs. The place stinks to high heaven.' Bailey looked back into the house, her expression grim. 'It's all the mud and shingle and assorted detritus from the river. Plus the walls and floor-boards are full of damp; apparently they could take months to dry out properly.' She sighed. 'But you soon get used to it.'

'May I?'

Bailey stood aside for her and Lizzie, who was looking at everything curiously. 'Please.' As they both stepped care-fully into the hall, onto recently-laid newspaper that was already soaked through in some areas, she added, 'Best not go too far. Or you'll ruin your shoes.'

The narrow hall was mud-coloured to about waist-high on the walls, fading into what must have been a beautiful mauve, with occasional damp spots now marring the paint.

Lizzie was very pale, sniffing the air. 'I know that smell. Like my van after the roof leaked.' She shuddered. 'All nasty and . . . rotten.'

'You okay, Lizzie?' Hannah asked, studying her face. 'You don't have to come in if you'd rather wait in the car. I know this must be hard for you.'

'I'll be a'right.'

But she noticeably hung back, letting Bailey go ahead down the hallway.

The hall led first to a cosy front room that faced the river. It had been emptied of most of its furniture, Hannah realised, peering inside. And for good reason.

The stripped antique pine floorboards must have been Bailey and Penny's pride and joy. Now they looked ruined, awash with shingle and unrecognisable bits of rubbish from the riverbed. Here again, the walls had waist-high water damage; strips of dainty flower-patterned wallpaper hung off in places, some bowing almost to the floor.

Hannah carried on towards the kitchen, and found cold daylight pouring in over a scene of wreckage. A series of damp planks served as a walkway over a sea of mud and silt. Some of the doors on the damaged kitchen cupboards hung askew, heaps of broken crockery and glass on the floor in front of them. There was a red Aga squeezed between a Welsh dresser and a glass-fronted cupboard. The Aga looked like it needed a damn good clean and the cupboard was in a dreadful state, all the glass silted up from the inside.

The whole place looked forlorn. And smelled like something that had been dredged up from the sea bed, possibly with a handful of dead fish inside.

'We're working on getting all the odds and ends out first,' Bailey said from behind her, 'then we're told we'll be able to hire a generator and a dehumidifier. Remove the worst of the damp before we start renovations.'

Bailey's voice was light and easy, clearly trying to sound as though all this disruption was no big deal. But Hannah was not fooled for a minute. She had accidentally overheard

a late-night discussion between her and Penny, and knew that they were both struggling to come to terms with what had happened. Struggling and mostly failing.

'It's a lot of hard work,' she said gently.

'Penny's going to do most of it, because I'm needed in the office more or less full-time for the next few months.' Bailey peered past her into the muddy kitchen, strain in her face. 'Once she can bring herself to come down here, that is.'

'She's taking it very hard, isn't she?'

'This is her dream home. She's spent the last few years getting everything perfect, exactly as she wanted it. And now this . . .' Bailey shook her head, looking away to hide the tears in her eyes. But it was too late; Hannah had already seen them. 'She's got a tough exterior, Penny. Doesn't show the knocks much. But don't let that fool you. She's broken-hearted.'

'Well, whatever we can do to help . . .'

'Yes, of course, sorry.' Bailey ran a hand over her face, leaving another smear of mud behind, this time along one cheek. 'Could you help me shift that dresser?' She saw Hannah's shocked expression, and added hurriedly, 'It comes apart, don't worry. Top and bottom. It's an antique, and it's been standing in mud all this time. We were going to move it before, but there was so much to do, and we just ran out of steam.'

'Where's it going?'

'Upstairs, if we can get the top half past the turn. It's a bit narrow, but worth trying. I've put down plastic sheeting along the landing. If we can just lift the unit up there, when Penny comes along, she'll scrape the mud off it and . . . do the rest.'

'I've got some wellies in the car,' Hannah said. 'Let me put them on first. Then we'll get that dresser up the stairs.'

'Thanks.'

On impulse, she hugged Bailey, who promptly burst into noisy tears. 'Hey, there, there. Hush.' She rocked her back and forth for a minute, rubbing her back, then gave her another quick squeeze before releasing her. 'It's going to be okay. It's just mud and water.'

'And sh – sh – shingle.'

'Yes, and shingle. But it's all salvageable.' Hannah gave her a wobbly smile, trying not to cry too. What is it about other people crying, she thought, that instantly makes you start to tear up as well? Like yawning. One person yawns, and everyone's at it. 'Nobody died.'

She blinked, suddenly thinking about Santos, and how that situation had not been even remotely salvageable. 'Look, let me grab my boots from the car.' She glanced along the empty hall. 'And find out where Lizzie went.'

She found Lizzie sitting on the muddy river bank, knees hugged to her chest, staring down at the icy, rushing water.

'You okay?' Hannah asked, a little hesitant in case she was prying.

'A'right.' Lizzie sighed, then made a face. 'I don't like coming into town, is all. Pethporro.' She paused. 'Can't help thinking back to . . .'

Hannah caught her breath. Of course.

Lizzie had been attacked here years ago, and her van set on fire. That was why she had moved out to Long Field, and the relative safety of her cliff-side isolation near Kernow House.

Feeling guilty, Hannah bit her lip, then dropped onto the grassy bank next to Lizzie. It was freezing under her bottom, but she ignored the discomfort. The water gurgled along beneath them on its way to the sea, reflecting an iron-grey sky. She wondered again if they would have snow in the next few days.

The river seemed surprisingly calm today, she thought, considering the devastation it had wreaked so recently in the cottages opposite. Strange how nature could change so suddenly, shifting from benign to malevolent in a few hours, and then back again as though it had never happened.

'I'd forgotten about those thugs. I should have thought. I'm sorry.'

'Ain't your fault.'

'Do you want to talk about it?'

Lizzie shook her head slowly. Then she said, with a sudden ache in her voice, 'I don't know why, but people don't seem to like folk like me.'

'You mean, because you're . . . different?'

Nodding, Lizzie twisted a long grey strand of hair between her fingers, sucking it into her mouth. 'That's one word.' Her voice was muffled. 'They might use another.'

'They?'

Lizzie jerked her head back towards the town. 'Them, up in the town.' She frowned at Hannah. 'Not you. And not Bailey or Penny. Or Mr Tregar, neither. You all look out for me.'

'That's because we're your friends.'

'Friends.' She seemed to savour the word. 'Yeah, my friends, you are. But *they* aren't.'

'Those stupid boys who—' Hannah saw Lizzie stiffen instinctively, as though expecting a blow, and changed what she was going to say. 'They've all grown up or gone away, Lizzie. That was a long time ago. Nobody's going to hurt you now.' She lay her arm lightly along Lizzie's shoulders, unsure how she might take a full-on hug. 'I promise. You hear me?'

Lizzie nodded, though she still seemed sad. 'I shouldn't be Obby Oss though,' she muttered, staring gloomily at the river below. 'Let Bailey do it. Or Penny. Or anyone. Not me.'

'But you're perfect for the part, I told you.'

'I'll make a bloody mess of it,' Lizzie said forcefully, pulling away from her arm. 'Make a bloody mess of everything, I do. You'll see.'

'How will you make a mess of it?'

'Forget what I'm supposed to do. Go wrong. Fall over on my face.' Her lip was trembling now. 'And everyone'll laugh. Like they always do.'

'Oh, Lizzie.' Hannah stood up and offered her a hand. But Lizzie shook her head and scrambled to her feet without any help. 'You won't make a mess of it, okay? I understand, though. I get scared too. Scared by new things.'

Lizzie looked at her, baffled.

Pointing to her bump, Hannah said quietly, 'I'm scared about this. What it's going to feel like, having a baby on my own. If it's going to hurt. Or what if my baby gets sick, or something goes wrong at the birth? I'm not just scared, I'm ... I'm bloody terrified.' She gave a shaky laugh, then took Lizzie's hand and squeezed it before she could pull away again. 'But you can't go through life being scared. Or

you might as well be dead. And neither of us are dead, are we? Because we're survivors, Lizzie. We made it, and we're going to carry on making it.' She paused, breathless, smiling as her voice rose. 'Not just that, but enjoying ourselves too. Yeah?'

Lizzie laughed and squeezed her hand in return. 'That's it. Survivors.' She started to walk away, nearly slipped on a particularly muddy patch of grass, and laughed again when Hannah grabbed her arm. 'See now? Survivors.'

Hannah let her head back towards the cottage, then hurried to the car for her wellies. As she pulled them on, hopping awkwardly on one leg in the freezing lay-by, she thought about what she'd told Lizzie. Was it true? Was she genuinely *terrified* by the thought of having her baby? Or had that just been a way of cheering Lizzie up?

It was disconcerting to realise that she didn't know.

CHAPTER TWENTY-EIGHT

They had nearly finished a chicken casserole dinner that evening when the back door opened, letting in a great gust of cold wind that stirred all the newly hung decorations, and brought a hint of white flakes with it.

Bailey jumped up to catch her flyaway napkin, exclaiming, 'What the hell ...?' and then stopped, frowning at the newcomer. 'Hello?'

Turning in surprise, Hannah saw Raphael framed in the doorway, capped and scarved, and with half a pine forest on his back, by the look of it. A Christmas tree, just as he had promised. Its branches were dusted with tiny, already melting white flakes. Like he'd lugged it all the way here from the North Pole.

Was it snowing at last?

A childlike excitement rose in her at the thought, only to be pushed aside as she focused on their visitor instead. And his gift.

'Oh my God,' she said blankly, and put down the spoon she had been using to capture the last of the casserole.

'I told you I'd bring you a tree,' Raphael said, his deep voice somehow alien and startling in this house of women.

He began to drag it inside, panting slightly. 'It's still got a root ball if you've got a pot you can fill with soil. Just remember to keep it damp or you'll be finding pine needles under the rug until next Christmas. So where do you want it?'

Penny stared at Hannah, who said nothing, and then at Bailey. She said faintly, 'The living room, I guess? Since nobody else seems to know.'

'No, the dining room,' Hannah said quickly. 'I – I've set up office in the living room. I don't think there'll be room in there for a Christmas tree.' She paused, still stunned. 'Not one that size, anyway.'

'You did say *the bigger the better*,' he said, shooting her an ironic glance.

'I didn't think you were serious.'

'I never make empty promises.' Raphael eyed the trunk. 'I think it's eight foot. Too high to fit?'

Penny shook her head. 'Perfect, I'd say.'

He put one arm around the tree, getting a better purchase on the generous branches, then raised his brows at Hannah. 'Dining room's the one on the right, yes?'

She nodded.

They watched in baffled silence as Raphael heaved the vast pine through the kitchen, leaving bits of dirt and sprigs of fragrant needles behind. He wedged the door to the hall open with his back, struggling to get the wide boughs through the narrow space.

Lizzie seemed excited, though. 'Hang on, Mr Tregar, I'll help. There's some of Trudy's old tree decorations in the attic. They'll do nice, if Hannah don't mind.'

'I don't mind,' Hannah said, blinking. 'I didn't even know they were there.'

Scooping up spoonfuls of her chicken casserole as quickly as possible, not seeming to care if she missed her mouth, Lizzie finished her meal and then followed Raphael into the hall. 'Here,' she said, and lifted the root ball end, which was wrapped in some kind of white webbing, 'I got it, Mr Tregar. And there's a pot we can use in th' cupboard under the stairs. I'll fetch soil from out front, shall I?'

'Thanks, Lizzie,' he said unevenly.

As soon as the door had closed behind the two of them, Hannah looked at Bailey. She felt awkward about the intrusion, especially halfway through the delicious meal she and Penny had cooked. 'Sorry – in all the chaos today, I forgot to mention Raphael had offered us a Christmas tree. Actually, I wasn't kidding just then. I really didn't think he meant it.'

'Is it free?'

'I believe so, yes.'

Bailey still seemed dumbfounded, staring at the door. 'I don't understand. I feel like I'm going mad. Raphael brought you a Christmas tree. That's . . . kind of him.'

Penny nodded. 'It's certainly very generous.'

'But he's Raphael Tregar. He's never kind or generous.' Bailey paused. 'Well, maybe to his sheep and his dogs. But not to . . . you know, *human beings*.'

'I can't explain it either,' Hannah said, and took her plate to the sink, battling against the horrible suspicion that he was still after Kernow House, and this was some new ploy to influence her.

'Can't you?' It sounded as though Penny was teasing her, which was just mean, given Hannah had done nothing to invite his attention.

'No,' she said, and left the kitchen after rinsing her dinner plate, only too aware that the other two were exchanging knowing glances behind her back.

As soon as the door closed behind her, she felt bad about snapping at Penny. It was Raphael she was angry with, not her friends. He had come here uninvited tonight and just walked in without even knocking, bearing a gift she had every reason to think was bogus.

Right, I'm going to give that bloody interfering man a piece of my mind, she thought crossly, and about time too.

She stormed into the dining room, rolling her sleeves to her elbows as though poised for a fist fight, and stopped dead, the angry words dying on her lips.

Facing her was the most gorgeous natural Christmas tree she'd ever seen. Its top almost brushed the high ceiling, lush pine needles bristling with vitality, its lower branches spread out like a wide green skirt. Its trunk was planted in a gold-painted pot that had belonged to her grandmother, set in the corner beside the window. The fresh pine fragrance was intense, like walking into a forest, or back into memories of childhood. She almost expected to find a jolly Santa in a beard and red suit, handing out presents.

But the only person there was Raphael.

He straightened from behind the trunk and came around, an odd smile on his face. 'Lizzie's gone upstairs to root out the decorations for it. Apparently, your grandmother had a

bag of baubles and tinsel, but she's not sure where it was stored.' His gaze met hers, and for the first time she felt something akin to intimacy between them. Strange idea, she thought, and shivered. 'Cold?' he asked at once, coming closer. His dark eyes never left her face. 'So, what do you think?'

'Of what?'

His lips quirked in a rough smile. 'The tree, of course.'

'Oh.'

'I hope you're not disappointed,' he said, glancing around at its luscious perfection. He seemed pleased with himself for having found it. And with good reason – it was truly breath-taking. But she did not dare say so, in case it gave him ideas. Ideas she did not want to be having herself. Yet could not manage to suppress, it seemed.

'I'm . . . surprised.'

Slowly, his smile faded. 'Because?'

'You know why.'

'Because I'm Raphael Tregar,' he said flatly.

She hesitated, suddenly unwilling to be openly rude to him, despite her previous desire to blast him back to his own farmhouse. It would have felt like an overreaction, and ungrateful too, given how beautiful the tree was and how much work it must've taken to get it. It was beyond generous.

Instead, she raised her shoulders gently, then let them drop. It felt like a delicate enough response to an indelicate question.

He was hurt. Possibly deeply. Which was absurd, of course. And yet there it was: his lips tightening, his brows drawing together, his chin lifting slightly.

'I see,' he drawled, and turned away.

'Raphael,' she said abruptly, and caught at his coat sleeve. It was damp. Snow, she thought, and shivered again. He was looking down at her, his eyes intense. 'I'm sorry. Thank you. For the—'

But the word 'tree' was lost as his head descended.

She ought to have pushed him away. Said no.

But of course she didn't.

Instead, she closed her eyes and lifted her mouth to his, almost greedily. As though she had been waiting for this moment ever since the first time she had seen him, sitting in his tractor, staring up at Kernow House like he already owned it, bloody arrogant bastard that he was.

CHAPTER TWENTY-NINE

His kiss was softer than she had imagined it would be.

In her daydreams – and yes, there had been daydreams involving their mouths meeting, and other body parts too, much to her embarrassment – he had been rough and demanding. Almost a beast, throwing her to the floor in his urgency. Not an unrequited urgency either. That was his reputation locally, wasn't it? A man who took what he wanted and didn't care what happened to the unfortunate woman afterwards.

But to her surprise, Raphael was careful, almost wary, his lips parting hers experimentally; when his tongue found hers, it was a cautious exploration, not a brutal invasion.

She sighed, and grabbed hold of his short dark hair, drawing him closer. Take a hint, damn you, she was thinking, her mouth glued to his.

His arms came around her, gathering her up as their kiss deepened. Then his lips broke free, muttering, 'Hannah,' as he buried his face in her hair. 'God, Hannah.'

That was more like it.

But before things could get much hotter, she pressed against him seductively, and was suddenly aware of her prominent

bump between them. A physical and very tangible reminder of Santos. Her dead lover, who was no doubt looking over her at this very moment with a dark, forbidding frown. Calling down the wrath of all the Greek gods on her faithless head. Though Santos had been easy-going in life, not particularly prone to jealous fits, so perhaps that was her own guilty conscience talking.

He drew back, as though also aware of her bump. 'Well . . . That was . . .'

'Yes.'

His hands had moved to her shoulders, stroking her through the bobbly white jumper she was wearing. 'You have . . . erm . . . a spot of . . .'

She looked down, following his gaze. There was a splodge of chicken casserole on her sweater, caught up in the white wool.

Fan-bloody-tastic.

'It happens more and more these days,' she said faintly. 'The . . . bump. I can't lean forward far enough.'

His smile was devastating. 'How very unfortunate.'

Hannah looked at his mouth, curved upward in momentary amusement, and could not quite believe what had just happened. What she had wanted from him.

And God, the way she had wanted it too! Nothing polite or well-mannered, not the energetic pleasures she and Santos had enjoyed in the bedroom, but something rough and exciting and probably quite shocking.

She felt heat in her cheeks, and could not say another word.

He leaned forward to kiss her again, and this time his kiss felt more serious. But it was too late. They both heard feet

thundering down the stairs, then Lizzie burst into the room, vast and wild-haired.

'I found 'em!' she announced, holding up a plastic bag crammed with Christmas decorations. 'Up the attic, they were, behind a rocking horse.' She barely looked at them embracing, but strode straight to the tree and poured the contents of the bag onto the floor beside it. 'You want to do tinsel, Hannah, or baubles? I like tinsel best, because baubles is fiddly. But you can choose.'

'I'm fine with baubles,' Hannah managed to say, not daring to look at Raphael, who finally released her. Dazed and breathless, she sleepwalked over to the tree, crouched down beside Lizzie, and grabbed the first bauble that came to hand. 'This one looks ... nice.' She attached it to a pine branch with fingers that trembled, and hoped nobody would notice. 'There, perfect.'

'Is there an angel?' His deep voice was right behind her.

'Somewhere in here, I'm sure.' Lizzie rummaged amongst the tangled heap of tinsel. 'I seen one in the bag. Ah, proper job!' She produced a slightly crumpled-looking clothes-peg angel, with white cloth robes, a tinselly halo and a faded, hand-drawn face. 'Can you reach the top of the tree, Mr Tregar?'

'I've told you a thousand times, Lizzie, you should call me Raphael.' He took the angel and reached up to fit it to the top, but the tree was too high even for him. 'Hang on,' he said, and fetched a chair from the dining set.

'Look at this,' Lizzie said, and handed her a short strip of faded red ribbon, with a knot tied in it. 'That's like what she had round her neck, old Trudy.'

Intrigued, Hannah took the ribbon and examined it. It looked like it had been cut off a longer piece, and perhaps used to attach a bauble or other ornament to the tree. She wanted to question Lizzie further, but did not dare with Raphael present. It might be ridiculous, but some inner caution urged her not to tell him about the Chinese box, or the key Trudy had worn around her neck on a ribbon just like this one. Instead, Hannah tucked it into her trouser pocket and turned back to the baubles, some of which were broken and would have to be discarded.

'This angel's a bit the worse for wear. And dusty as hell. Must be twenty or thirty years old, at least.' Raphael sneezed, his head turned away. 'You could do with a new one.'

'Perhaps we should put you on top of the tree instead, Mr Tre—Raphael,' Lizzie said, with a loud snort of laughter. 'Keep you out of mischief, that would. No mistletoe up there.'

Raphael, who was busy lodging the scruffy angel on top of the tree, shot Hannah a startled glance, then looked at Lizzie's bent head as she sorted the tinsel into piles of red, gold and silver garlands.

'Mistletoe?' he repeated warily.

'For kissing, of course.' Lizzie did not look up, but her voice was suddenly sly. 'Best not try that with me. I don't hold with kissing. Not even at Christmas.'

Raphael finally secured the tree-topper, and got down from the chair. His face was slightly flushed, as though from exertion, but Hannah knew better. 'I'll bear that in mind,' he said seriously, then glanced back at the angel, forlorn and lopsided on the top branch. 'It looks home-made.'

'I expect my grandmother made it,' Hannah said, pinning on baubles for all she was worth. 'It may look a bit wonky, but I don't want a new one. It's like having Trudy here with us. Don't you think?'

'What, looking down on us all, you mean?' He bent to help her with the baubles, uncomfortably close. 'And judging us, perhaps?'

She met his gaze with a start, recalling her guilt over their kiss. How could he read her thoughts so easily?

She looked around for Lizzie, embarrassed by the abrupt shift in their conversation, but she didn't appear to be listening. Too busy trying to weave some silver tinsel between the back branches, her expression preoccupied.

'I'm sure my grandmother wasn't that kind of woman.'

'But you never met Trudy, did you?'

'Only because I didn't know she was alive.' He raised his brows at that, but she hurried on, unwilling to talk about her difficult childhood. 'What did you mean, anyway?'

He shrugged. 'I have some letters from your grandmother, remember? Letters that are quite revealing, in places.'

'So let me read them.' She held his gaze, her job forgotten. 'Please?'

He studied her in silence for a moment, then took the bauble from her hand and attached it to a branch higher up. '*Quid pro quo*,' he murmured.

'Sorry?'

His gaze dropped to her mouth, a promise in his dark eyes. 'It's a famous Latin saying. It means, what will you give me in exchange?'

'For what?'

'For letting you read your grandmother's letters to Gabriel Tregar.'

Her face flared with heat. 'Oh, get lost,' she said, and pushed him rather too vehemently away. Looking startled, he lost his balance, falling on his back amongst the tinsel.

'Oops,' Hannah said.

Lizzie, still painstakingly threading a silver garland through the branches on the other side, emerged with pine needles in her hair to stare at him. 'Mr Tregar? What are you doing down there?'

'Getting my just desserts,' he said, and struggled back to his feet.

Hannah did not apologise. Why should she?

And to think she had let him kiss her.

'Goodnight, Raphael,' she said coolly, deliberately not looking at him as she chose another bauble. 'Thanks for the tree. You can see yourself out, can't you?'

CHAPTER THIRTY

Hannah couldn't sleep that night, lying in bed and staring up at the dark ceiling in a kind of weary trance. The wind had increased after Raphael had left, and was now howling about the house like a furious ghost, which was hardly a thought conducive to sleep. It had been a long and exhausting day, and she desperately wanted to turn off her brain and get a few hours of shut-eye. But *That Kiss* kept going round and round in her head like a goldfish in a bowl, the start bumping into the end every few minutes. What the hell had she been thinking, grabbing him like that? And what about all that tongue-play just before Lizzie burst in?

Raphael must consider her a dead certainty now, which was so far from the truth as to be laughable.

He was a shepherd. He wore a flat cap, for God's sake!

Finally, she groaned and sat up in bed, abandoning the futile attempt to sleep. The wind was so noisy now, she couldn't even concentrate on berating herself. Perhaps she could read instead. There was an American thriller on her bedside table, which she was dipping into occasionally. Maybe some death and mayhem in New York would take her mind off the Tregar Incident.

But when she groped for the bedside lamp, it didn't turn on. She flicked the button back and forth a few times, then wondered if perhaps the bulb had gone. Though it was quite a new one.

Swinging her legs out of bed, Hannah tiptoed to the door. To her dismay, the main light switch didn't work either.

'Bloody hell, not the fuse box again,' she muttered, then hunted for her slippers in the dark. She eventually got them on, realised they were on the wrong feet, swapped them over, and then stood a moment, thinking.

There was a moon, but it was a cloudy night and the room was gloomy. Even armed with the light from her phone, the stairs would be a deathtrap, not to mention damned spooky. Especially if Colonel Mustard was out there somewhere, lying in wait so he could jump out on sleepy humans, as he often did at night. Perhaps she should simply crawl back into bed and leave the fuse box until morning.

She checked the time on her phone.

Ten past two in the bloody morning.

It was too early for her to ignore a power outage. The freezer might defrost while they were sleeping, she thought grimly. And what about the timer on the new heating system that had cost her a small fortune, almost the last of her capital? If the boiler didn't kick in at six-thirty sharp, they would be getting up in an icebox tomorrow.

She then remembered the mini-torch she'd put on top of her grandmother's chest of drawers when she spent her first night upstairs at Kernow House. The squat old piece of furniture had not been moved because it was so heavy, so there was a good chance the light would still be there.

She waved her phone along the top of the dresser, using its faint screen light to search. Her hand met something hard, which rolled away and fell to the floor with a clatter.

'For God's sake . . .'

Hannah knelt down and hunted reluctantly under the cabinet, steeling herself against the possibility of encountering spiders. The bedrooms had all been cleaned, but only in a desultory way and not under the older furniture. And some of the arachnids in Kernow House were unspeakably vast and hairy, like prehistoric monsters from some horror movie. So when something brushed her hand, she gave a shriek and jerked her hand back at once.

Then her brain kicked in.

Spiders didn't feel like that. Like *fabric*.

Gingerly, Hannah slid her hand back into the narrow gap and groped about. No cloth this time, but the cold aluminium of a small, cylindrical object.

Her torch.

She drew it out with relief, then turned it on and shone the thin beam under the chest. Kneeling lower, she took a quick peek. Then caught her breath, her heart beating faster at the sight of something unexpected. Something that was clearly red, but dusty and cobwebbed too. It looked like it had been under there a long time. Several years before she had even moved into the house, by her guess. Maybe longer.

Reaching under the furniture, she began to withdraw the ribbon. As she pulled, it snagged on something.

She tugged, and heard a faint clunk.

Metal?

Eventually, by wiggling her hand about, she managed to

get the object free, and brought it out from its long captivity. Shaking off the worst of the dust, she stared down at it in the dazzling light of her torch. It was indeed a loop of red ribbon, exactly like one that might be worn about the neck, with a small ornate key threaded onto it like a pendant.

A key small enough to fit a keepsake box.

It wasn't the fuses, Hannah realised, on having made the scary trek downstairs in the dark, Trudy's key strung about her neck on its faded ribbon, the Chinese box lodged safely under her arm.

She shone her torch up, but the fuses were all perfectly in place; none had been tripped. Yet the downstairs lights were also not working, and neither were any of the plug sockets. The internet hub lights in the hallway were off – which meant no phone and no Wi-Fi – and so was the standby light on the television.

Going to the front door, she peered out cautiously through the frosty glass. She couldn't see any lights in the direction of town either, though it was true that bad weather often obscured the view. Kernow House was pretty remote.

The most logical explanation was that the high winds had brought down a tree between here and town, which had brought down a power line in its turn, and so the electricity had snapped off. In which case, the only thing to do was wait. Though first, she used her mobile – which had one bar, to her relief – to report a power cut at her location via an online form.

Something shifted in the dark hallway as she clicked 'send', making her stiffen in sudden alarm, her heart

thudding unpleasantly. Then the shadow gave a plaintive miaow.

'Is that you, Cat With No Name? I nearly jumped out of my skin.' Hannah bent to stroke the tabby behind her ears, then followed her through to the kitchen. 'You still need a proper name, don't you? Poor thing. Even the geese have names.' She checked the box of kittens, but they all seemed to be asleep, one opening a sleepy eye to gaze up accusingly at her too-bright torch. They would all need names too, she thought. 'Sorry.'

She went into the pantry to fetch candles, and found herself shivering in an icy draught as she stood on tiptoe to reach the top shelf.

'Ridiculously cold in here,' she muttered, hurrying back into the kitchen. At least there it was warm, kept so by residual heat from the Aga. Small wonder the kittens were still curled up in their box, drowsy and contented, despite the howling wind outside.

Lighting the candles, she placed them strategically about the kitchen, then sat down at the table with the Chinese box in front of her. The eerie flickering glow of candlelight suited the moment, she thought.

She was so pleased that she would not have to break it in order to discover what lay inside. Increasingly, she had feared that would be the only way to get in. She had been considering calling the locksmith, to avoid damaging the box itself; it was so beautiful and worth preserving. But now she had found the key. At least, she hoped it was the key. Trudy had kept it on a ribbon around her neck, Lizzie had said, and seemed sure enough of her information. This had to be it, threaded onto a red ribbon for safekeeping.

The wind gusted violently against the kitchen window, shaking the glass in its frame and making the candle flames dip. She really ought to wait until daylight. But she felt driven to open the Chinese cabinet, to solve the puzzle that had been nagging at her ever since she found it in the attic.

Colonel Mustard appeared from nowhere, startling her. He hopped up onto the pine chair opposite, gazing at her bolt-eyed across the table. He must have heard her talking to the other cat, she decided, and become jealous. He was that kind of tom, always needing to be Cat Number One.

'Right,' she told Colonel Mustard, removing the ribbon from around her neck. 'All three paws crossed, please. If this doesn't fit, I'm going to be extremely annoyed.'

The cat watched her solemnly.

Her hands fumbled as she fitted the key experimentally to the small, gilt lock, half expecting it not to be a match. But to her amazement, the key slid into place perfectly. With one gentle turn, she heard the internal mechanism shift, and gave a little gasp.

The box was unlocked.

Holding her breath, she lifted the ornate lid.

CHAPTER THIRTY-ONE

Inside the velvet-lined interior was a creased and faded colour photograph on top of a stack of neatly folded white envelopes. Every one was addressed to her grandmother in the same flowing hand. No postal address, only a boldly written *Trudy*. Hand-delivered, then? Some of them were crumpled as though by repeated handling, the name faded to an inky smudge; others were almost pristine. At a rough guess, there looked to be about twenty-five in total. Hannah rustled them between her fingers; some were considerably thicker than others. These had to be letters, she decided, all written by the same person. But not ordinary letters to be thrown away after reading, or left lying out where anyone could find them, nor pushed to the back of a drawer and forgotten. These had been hoarded like treasure. Treasure kept locked up in this beautiful Chinese box for years, by the look of it, to be taken out and re-read only when nobody else was about.

One side of a secret correspondence?

Pulling a candle a little closer, but not so close it might spill wax on the box, Hannah put the envelopes carefully aside, and studied the photograph up close.

It looked as though it had been taken in the early seventies or late sixties: a group of young people in flares and wide-collared shirts and crocheted cardigans standing outside a building she recognised as the local Pethporro theatre, now an arts cinema, apparently only open during the summer months.

'Who's this, then?' She glanced at the cat, who started licking his fur with fierce concentration as though to indicate complete disinterest in her findings. 'Bit before your time, I expect.'

Peering at each face in turn, she decided the woman left of centre was probably her grandmother. She had the family face, which had been described more than once as being long and narrow; 'like a horse', as some had unflatteringly put it. And her blonde hair looked just like Hannah's own mop. Though Trudy's was rather better groomed, falling to just below her shoulders, a stylish red bandana tied across her forehead.

How old was she here? Late teens, perhaps?

She looked radiantly happy.

Early seventies.

Hannah did a few rough calculations in her head, and decided it could only have been the early to mid-seventies when her grandmother married Jack Clitheroe and started living here at Kernow House. Her mum had been born shortly after that, as she recalled. Though Mum had always been vague about her childhood, putting Hannah off with promises to 'tell you all about it later'. But then she died before she got around to telling her anything.

Everyone in the photograph was smiling at the camera,

she realised, except one young man, to the far left, whose head was turned; he was staring straight at Trudy.

Hannah examined that face closely. Unless she was imagining things, he looked like a younger version of the man in the photograph in Raphael's bedroom, posing in front of a tractor with his arm around his adopted son's shoulders.

'Gabriel Tregar,' she whispered.

The candle flames fluttered again in another violent gust of wind, and she heard a long moan in the walls.

She forced herself to put the photo aside, then unfolded the top letter and studied it by the light of the candle. It was written in a simple but consistent hand in neat lines, with wide margins and tiny drawings inserted at intervals. No date, no address, and when she turned over the sheet for the last few words, she saw the signature was simply G.

Surprisingly, there were no kisses after that stark initial, and certainly no great declaration of love. Frowning, she began to read through the letter, pulling her dressing gown tight about herself to fight the draught coming from under the pantry door.

My darling T.

I saw a hare in Long Field this morning, just after dawn, and thought of you. She was sleek and supple, and kicked out with her hind legs when I tried to come near her, startling and racing away through the long grass. So strong, so powerful, no man could hope to catch her. That is how I know Jack could never love you as you need to be loved, with his coarse mouth and even coarser mind. You deserve better, my love. And you will get better, even if I have to wait for ever.

Halfway down the page was a rough sketch of a hare, dashing along with its long ears flying backwards, alongside a few scribbled lines of poetry that she did not recognise.

After the drawing, his letter continued in a similar way, with some discussion of a previous meeting in 'town' – presumably Pethporro – where it seemed Trudy had studiously ignored him, and Gabriel had picked a quarrel with Jack. His reference to her grandfather as 'your husband' made Hannah a little uncomfortable. So her grandparents had been married by the time this letter was sent. She did not think of herself as a prude, but still . . .

Trudy had married Jack Clitheroe, not Gabriel Tregar, which suggested strong attachment on both their parts, whatever this letter stated. She was not keen on the idea of her grandmother having committed adultery; her mum had never mentioned anything like that, though, which made it less likely as a possible interpretation of this correspondence.

Had Gabriel pursued Trudy against her will after her marriage?

If so, why hoard his letters and not simply consign them to the fire as soon as they arrived? Why keep them so secretly, and for so many years, squirreled away in this box under lock and key? To prevent Jack finding them? But destroying the letters would have solved that problem. Hiding his letters suggested she had taken pleasure in receiving them. Yet if Trudy had been in love with her neighbour, perhaps even having an adulterous affair with him, why did she not get a divorce and marry Gabriel instead?

Hannah unfolded the next letter in the pile.

'*My darling T.*,' it began, exactly like the first. But it soon

became more empassioned. It seemed 'G' was intent on per-suading Trudy to leave her husband, despite her refusal to encourage him.

'I received your last letter, and its coldness burnt me. You are like the moon reflected on the tide, pure silver, beautiful and aloof. But I have not given up hope. I know you love me too, and must change your mind in the end. One stupid mistake cannot be allowed to ruin both our lives. So I will be patient, waiting for that day.'

One stupid mistake?

Gabriel made no overt demands of Trudy, she noted. He merely set up comparisons between himself and Jack Clith-eroe, and illustrated each letter with gorgeous hand-drawn pictures suggesting the beauty and complexity of the natu-ral world. Hannah opened the third letter, catching her breath at his stunning artwork. From the note of increasing desperation, it was clear that Trudy was still showing no signs of wanting to leave Jack Clitheroe.

'You tell me it's over. That I should give up the struggle. Stop writing out my thoughts to you,' read one hastily scribbled post-script. 'Yet how can I? You are my everything. You might as well tell me to stop breathing and have done with it.'

Gabriel had not stopped writing.

And Trudy had kept his letters. Not thrown them away in anger.

Hannah rubbed her forehead, perplexed. Whatever way she looked at it, the thing was a puzzle. What she needed was to get a look at the letters her grandmother had written Gabriel Tregar in return. That would give her a better idea of their relationship.

But that would mean striking some kind of bargain with

the devil, she thought. Or Raphael Tregar, as he was more commonly known in these parts.

The fourth letter she read, not surprisingly, was in much the same vein as the previous three. As was the fifth. She was aware of needing to go to bed, her body aching with fatigue. But Gabriel's writing style was so bold, and the tiny sketches of animals and plants that adorned his margins so vibrant and eye-catching, she was drawn in again and again, unable to stop reading . . .

The wind rustled the letters on the table some time later, and she looked up, startled by the creak of the kitchen door opening.

A pale face peeked around at her. It was Bailey, wrapped in a pink-and-white striped dressing gown, her hair dishevelled. 'Hannah, what on earth . . .?' She glanced at the clock, then back at her. 'It's nearly five o'clock in the morning. I came down because the electric's gone off.' She stopped, clearly registering the candles dotted about the kitchen. 'Not the fuse box, I'm guessing?'

'Power cut.'

Bailey stumbled in, yawning, then halted at the sight of the open Chinese box. 'Oh my God. You found the key?'

'I found the key.'

'That's amazing.' She came around to stare at the contents, rubbing sleep out of her eyes.

'Letters from Gabriel Tregar to my grandmother.' Hannah held out the first letter she'd read. 'Love letters.'

'Requited or unrequited?'

'Unrequited, so far. Very, very unrequited.'

Bailey took the pages, and then went to sit down oppo-site, only to jump up again with a start. 'Colonel!' She looked down with wide eyes at the ginger tom, who glared back at her accusingly. 'I nearly bloody sat on you.' Pulling out another chair, she sat there instead, scanning the letter, her lips moving silently as she read. 'Oh my God,' she whispered, reaching the end, 'this is so romantic.'

'My grandmother was married, remember?'

'Oh yes, right.' Bailey hurriedly made a disapproving face. 'That's bad. Sounds like he was a sex pest, then.' She read the letter again. 'But quite an eloquent sex pest.'

'What I don't understand is, why did she keep them? Why not throw them away as soon as they arrived? Burn them?'

'Evidence?'

'Of what, though? It's not illegal to write love letters. And if she'd wanted my granddad to thump him, surely one would have been enough.' Hannah ran a fingertip over the velvet lining of the box. 'And this is such a precious object. You'd keep something cherished inside it. Not evi-dence of sexual pestering.' She handed Bailey the photo. 'And there's this.'

Bailey studied it and tapped the blonde. 'That has to be Trudy. Wow, she was a stunner when she was young.'

'And that one, on the end, has to be Gabriel.'

'I don't know that I ever met him. Are you sure that's him?'

Reluctantly, Hannah told her about the photograph in Raphael's bedroom, and endured Bailey's knowing smile at the location. 'Yes, I was in his bedroom. For about three min-utes, that's all,' she said severely. 'Nothing happened.'

'Of course not.' Bailey looked at the photograph again.

'Gabriel's not bad-looking either. Is your granddad in this shot?'

'I don't think so. Though they both look quite young there. It may have been taken before she married Jack.'

Bailey nodded, going back to the letters. She frowned. '*One stupid mistake* . . . What does that mean, I wonder?'

'I spotted that too. It's not explained.'

'Intriguing.' Bailey fell silent again. 'And what's this?' she asked a moment later, holding out another letter, one Hannah had not read with much attention, as it had seemed to be largely about sheep. Including a sketch of a wild-looking ram in the margin. Not the most romantic topic, she'd thought, skipping on to the next one with a grimace. 'Some reference to a "cave." It sounds like they met there secretly.'

'What?'

Hannah took the letter and read it more carefully. '*Come down to the cave once Jack's asleep. I'll wait, even if it takes all night*,' she read out loud, and looked up at Bailey, her heart beating fast, as though the letter had been written to her, not her grandmother. 'Good God, I missed that. A clandestine meeting.'

'I wonder where this cave is.'

'I wonder if she went.' Hannah made a face. 'I wouldn't have gone. I mean, look at that, he's practically ordering her to be there. And talk about emotional blackmail . . . *I'll wait, even if it takes all night*. Like a three-line whip.'

'I didn't even know you could get down to the beach from here. Surely the nearest path to the sea is back near town? It must be a good fifteen or twenty minute walk along the cliff edge. Not very safe in the dark.'

'It certainly doesn't seem very chivalrous, expecting her to climb down the cliffs in the middle of the bloody night.' Hannah dropped the letter in disgust. 'What a bastard.'

Bailey was reading another letter from lower down the pile. 'Listen, here it is again. *When we met at the cave last night* . . . So she did go!'

'And did what, though?'

Bailey scanned the rest of the letter, then shook her head, her expression disappointed. 'He doesn't say. The letter just goes all mushy and poetic after that.'

'Typical.'

The door creaked again about half an hour later, and they both looked around in the flickering candlelight, suddenly conspiratorial.

It was Penny this time, a thick pashmina wrapped over her PJs, her broad shoulders hunched. 'Bailey?' She flicked the light switch, but nothing happened. 'None of the lights are working. Wh – what's going on? Christ, it's bloody freezing in here. Like a cold spot in a haunted house.' Her voice drowsy with sleep, she shuffled into the kitchen, then spotted the open Chinese box and started, suddenly properly awake. 'You found the key.'

Bailey explained hurriedly, and soon all three of them were seated around the kitchen table, letters in hand, exclaiming and reading extracts to each other. Colonel Mustard sat up to squint at them, clearly puzzled and unsure why everyone was up in the middle of the night, but glad of the company.

'His writing is so passionate, isn't it? And these gorgeous

little sketches in the margins . . . Look at this robin perched on a branch, it's almost real. I wish I'd known him.' Penny came to the end of the letter she'd been reading, and peered into the box. 'What else is in here?'

Hannah glanced at her, still lost in the romantic spell of Gabriel's prose, then put down the letter she'd been about to start and leaned in with her. 'Looks like even more of them. He seems to have written her dozens over the years. If only he'd dated them, it's frustrating not being sure . . . Oh!'

She stopped, having lifted the last few letters to find something rectangular beneath them, wrapped in what looked like red silk.

'What is it?' Bailey whispered.

Slowly, Hannah unwrapped the silk, and a deck of cards spilled out over the table. Not playing cards, she realised, turning a few over, but picture cards. She frowned, holding one up to the candle flame. It depicted a handsome man on a throne, crowned and holding aloft a huge sword.

'Good God, is that . . .?' Penny drew her chair closer, staring.

'The King of Swords,' Hannah read aloud, then handed the card to Penny, who was obviously fascinated. 'He looks like he means business.' She picked up another one, turning it over to reveal an apocalyptic scene of destruction. 'The Tower,' she read, and made a face. 'Not a very good omen, judging by that picture.'

'Tarot cards.' Bailey picked up another one, and gave a little shriek. 'Oh my God, look at these hairy legs! "The Devil". Except he looks more like a goat than a demon. With two stark naked minions too. Rather rude.'

'What were Trudy and Gabriel up to, messing about with these fortune-telling cards?' Penny handed the King of Swords gingerly back to Hannah, who returned it to the pack. 'Perhaps that's what they did in this mysterious "cave" all night,' she said, with a wink and a crooked smile. 'Not love-making, after all, but magic spells and tarot readings.'

'Nonsense,' Hannah said crisply, though she had to admit to feeling a bit weirded out, poring over all these old letters and tarot cards by flickering candlelight in a remote farm-house, an icy wind whistling around the walls.

'Here, let me.' Penny took up the pack and shuffled them gently, then laid a few cards out face down in a semi-circle. 'I had an aunt who used to read the cards at Christmas and birthday gatherings. Like a party trick. She could tell your fortune from tea leaves too. Mad as a box of frogs.'

'My grandmother was not mad.'

'Course not, sorry.' Penny started to turn over the cards very deliberately, then said, 'I see a tall, dark stranger coming for you through the snow ...'

Hannah laughed. 'Shut up.'

Bailey had pulled the box towards her, and now frowned, reaching into the tiny, velvet-lined well under the space taken up by the tarot cards. 'There's something else in here,' she said, and excitedly produced another key. 'Now what the hell does this one open?'

'Curiouser and curiouser,' Penny murmured.

Taking the key, Hannah turned it over in her palm, frowning. 'It's far too big to open another box like this one. So it's got to be a door key, don't you think? But an old door

key.' It felt heavy, made of rusty iron, and the lock shape was simple and thickly cut. 'Possibly Victorian?'

'Or maybe older, if it opens one of the doors here,' Bailey said eagerly. 'Kernow House was renovated in the early 1800s, and the original home dates back centuries. There was a settlement here in the Middle Ages, remember?'

'This key's not medieval, though. And neither are any of the doors that I've seen in this house.' But Hannah frowned. 'But you're right, I think it's older than Victorian. I'm no expert historian, but maybe ... late eighteenth century?'

'May I?' Penny took the key and weighed it thoughtfully. 'I agree. And I bet it fits a cellar door. Something unlikely to have been replaced when the house was rebuilt.'

'There aren't any cellars at Kernow House,' Bailey and Hannah said almost in unison, then grinned at each other.

Lizzie came into the kitchen, swathed in a blanket and shining a large torch over each of their faces in turn, dazzling them. Clearly she had been prepared for an apocalyptic event. 'Power's off,' she said unnecessarily, then swung the wavering torch beam over the letters and cards strewn across the kitchen table. 'What you all doing down here, then? Playing a game?'

'You want me to tell your fortune?' Penny asked gleefully, and made a spooky noise under her breath, turning over another tarot card.

The electricity came back on at that exact second, as though the act of turning the card had somehow precipitated it.

Lizzie screamed, and ran out of the kitchen and back up

the stairs, yelling, 'Don't show me! Don't show me them bad cards!'

Bailey glared at Penny. 'Now look what you've done.'

'I didn't do a thing!'

'You scared her.'

'She doesn't like tarot cards, that's all. I don't know why, it's just a bit of fun.' Penny sounded upset though, and a bit shaken too. She blew out the candle nearest to her, and then stood up, looking tired and washed-out in the suddenly over-bright kitchen. 'I'd better go upstairs after her, find out what on earth—'

'Wait,' Hannah said sharply, and pointed. 'Look, that's what she saw. That's what frightened her.'

They all stared at the tarot card that Penny had turned over for Lizzie.

It was Death.

CHAPTER THIRTY-TWO

At pageant rehearsals all the following week, Hannah kept herself busy with preparations for the Boxing Day festivities, and tried not to think too hard about her discoveries in the Chinese box. The sentiments in Gabriel's letters had been disturbing enough, but the tarot cards had astonished and worried her, despite Penny's assurances that they meant nothing. Tarot cards suggested a side to Trudy that Hannah had never before considered, and was not sure how to handle. She didn't mind other people using tarot cards or even casting the odd spell, but it was startling and a little unnerving to think that her own grandmother might have done the same. It was not knowing for sure that was troubling her most, she decided. Not having the *facts*. Only guesswork and supposition. And a one-sided correspondence that suggested a secret love affair, without any actual evidence to back it up.

For years, her dead, unknown grandmother had been a benign and passive figure in her imagination. A grey-haired, bespectacled granny, maybe a bit on the plump side, sitting in a rocking chair with a lapful of knitting . . .

Now Hannah not only had to contend with the uncomfortable vision of her grandmother as a passionate seductress,

meeting her lover in some dark cave at midnight, but one bestride a broomstick, with a black hat and perhaps a toad as her familiar.

Small wonder she was studying pageant logistics with such enthusiasm!

After a brief period of withdrawal, Lizzie threw herself back into rehearsals with renewed enthusiasm. She even became a go-to person for Hannah. Her suggestions were wise and unerringly accurate, often highlighting places where Hannah had missed something important. Indeed, she could probably not have prepared for the pageant so thoroughly without her help.

All the same, she was increasingly aware that Lizzie was not as joyful as she had been in the beginning, when she got the coveted part of the Obby Oss. Sometimes she caught Lizzie sitting on her own, staring across the icy fields with a faraway look in her eyes. Once, she asked what she was looking at, and Lizzie replied cryptically, 'Ghosts.' Hannah had not known how to reply to that. But it was clear the past was on Lizzie's mind a great deal the colder the weather became. Not that the cold snap kept her indoors; whenever the pageant work was finished for the day, Lizzie would go trudging about the countryside in wellies and anorak, checking her traps. When at home, she'd sit alone in her bedroom, having taken against the kitchen as a place where tarot readings might spontaneously occur. Though at least she had started to emerge for meal times again since Penny had moved supper to the dining room to alleviate her fears.

Lizzie had always distrusted the cold pantry, of course, which she would only enter shivering and under protest.

Perhaps she saw 'ghosts' there too. But now that she disliked the kitchen as well, even breakfast had become a challenge. Hannah had started placing a bowl of cereal or two hard-boiled eggs with toast at the bottom of the stairs, and then scuttling out of sight, like someone leaving offerings for an invisible god.

But dinner was a more sparkly affair these days. They sat around the vast eight-seater dark wood table for dinner most evenings, admiring the Christmas tree of epic proportions that stood in the corner. Bailey had brought home a string of excess Christmas lights from her office decorations, and the tinsel-laden tree flashed on and off at various speeds, a mesmerising sight during dinner. The lights seemed to please Lizzie, though she was still oddly subdued.

It was hard not to think of it as 'Raphael's tree'.

Raphael himself drifted in and out of rehearsals. He caught her eye from time to time, but never once tried to speak to her, not even during those rare intervals when Lizzie and the others actually left her alone for a few minutes. They saw each other at the pageant committee meetings, of course, and once he even spoke to her briefly after she had given an account of her work to date, but it had all been very business-like. Friendly, but no more than that. Almost as though they were strangers now.

Had Raphael lost interest in her after that kiss?

The thought piqued Hannah, a sting that kept her awake several nights in a row. Which was ludicrous; it reminded her of a time when a boy she'd danced with at a school disco had gone out with someone else, and for a long time she had been too hurt to even look at him.

Well, she wasn't a girl anymore, and would soon be a mother. Wasn't it time she put aside childish things and concentrated on being a parent instead?

Towards the end of that week, she spent a busy morning with Fenella discussing the catering for the post-pageant event, a meet-and-greet coupled with a storytelling session for younger visitors. Several marquees had been ordered for the big day, with matching tables and display units. The food itself was to be presented alongside a display of traditional Cornish flags, the distinctive white cross on a black background, known as the flag of St Piran. Fenella had already been working on a menu, so they went through her selection of traditional fare. Top of the list were Cornish pasties, then mini-tubs of shrimp and Newlyn crab, saffron buns and hevva cake for the sweet-toothed, and Cornish fairings. After agreeing to the prices and amounts required, Hannah stayed on for a coffee with Fenella. It was not long before they were discussing Bailey and Penny's flooded cottage, and how the renovations were going.

'Bailey's not been herself lately,' Fenella said, clearly concerned for her daughter. 'She loves living in that cottage. It's such a shame. For her and Penny.' She hesitated, then added sharply, 'We need better flood defences down by the river. Or this kind of disaster will keep happening. I hope you'll take that issue up with Mr Tregar.'

Hannah was astonished. 'Me? What do you think I can do about it?'

'Now, don't come the innocent with me. Everyone knows about you two.'

'Sorry? Everyone knows what, exactly?'

Fenella shrugged, looking uncomfortable. 'That you're . . . close.'

'Not that close! Besides, this sounds like a county matter, not local council.' Hannah felt her cheeks go warm under the older woman's silent scrutiny. She drained her coffee cup, then stood up, gathering her things. 'Thank you for the coffee, but I really should be going. If you want to complain about the flood defences, I think a letter to Cornwall Council is the way to go.'

Fenella looked at her with a sceptical expression, but said nothing more, much to Hannah's relief.

That difficult conversation haunted Hannah on the short drive home. Snowflakes that had been drifting lightly at the start of the journey thickened and began to whisk about on the icy wind, forcing her to put on her windscreen wipers. Normally, she would have been studying the dark clouds and calculating the possible snowfall ahead. But for once she was not fascinated by the prospect of a white Christmas, nor worried how bad weather might affect the Boxing Day pageant. Instead, she stared past the busily scraping blades at the road ahead, her mind elsewhere.

Was she really the subject of local gossip? Did people believe she had some hold over Raphael Tregar? That she could influence him over town council matters?

It was too horrible.

Yet the true horror was yet to come.

There was a striking bright yellow Citroen parked outside her house. A woman in a bobble hat was leaning against

the bonnet with a fulminating expression, arms folded, long legs encased in stylish leather trousers that matched her black jacket. Her boots were high-heeled and her make-up was immaculate under the woollen beanie.

It was Jennifer Bolitho.

As soon as Hannah got out of the old Land Rover, Jennifer headed towards her. Close up, she looked as though she had been crying, her tone almost hysterical as she demanded, 'Are you sleeping with Raphael?'

Collecting her bag from the back seat, Hannah glanced around at her in disbelief. Jennifer was the second person that day to suggest that she and Raphael were having an affair.

'What?' Where the hell was this story coming from, she wondered? They had kissed once. In the privacy of her own home. Yet apparently the locals already had the two of them in bed together, doing it non-stop like the last two bunnies in Cornwall. 'I don't have a clue what you're talking about.'

Jennifer's eyes bulged. 'There's no point lying to me. I know what Raphael's like. He's a total bastard. A liar. He led me on, made me think he cared about me. But he only cares about himself.'

'Jennifer, it's snowing and very cold.' Hannah stayed as calm as she could, given the provocation. 'I'd like to go inside my house, thank you.'

'You think you're being clever. But he ruined my life. And he'll ruin yours too.' She stopped, then swallowed hard and pointed at Hannah's bump. 'Is that his? Oh God, what a fool I am. How long has this been going on? Was he sleeping with you even before I took the job?'

Hannah's hand itched to slap Jennifer around the face. But she had never been the kind of person who met abuse with physical violence. And she was damned if she was going to start now.

'Please go away.' She headed for the house through whirling snow, clutching her bag tightly to her side.

But Jennifer was not to be dismissed so easily. She ran after Hannah, sobbing and dragging on her sleeve. 'Tell me the truth! I need to hear it from your own lips. Do you love him?' She made a grab for Hannah's hair. 'He's always had a thing for blondes. Is he in love with you?'

'Get your hands off me!' Hannah was suddenly furious. 'How dare you? The father of my child is dead. Don't you care whose feelings you hurt, throwing wild accusations about like that? Get off my property and don't ever come back.'

Jennifer stared at her. 'I'll put a spell on you.' Her eyes were fixed and malevolent. 'Don't think I can't.'

'Ridiculous nonsense!'

'Your grandmother didn't think so,' Jennifer said, leaving Hannah speechless. 'She knew the old ways. And so do I. You've been warned.'

Then she stalked back to her Citroen, revved the engine noisily as she reversed, turning the car, then accelerated away down the drive.

Hannah stared after the yellow car until it was out of sight. Fat snowflakes landed on her cheeks and eyelashes, and she brushed them away, blinking. *She knew the old ways.* What the hell did that mean? *I'll put a spell on you.* The woman was mad. Then she recalled that Jennifer was into

that kind of thing. Some kind of expert, in fact. Folklore and old country spells were the subject of the books and articles she wrote, Raphael had said. And they had met her coming out of the Museum of Witchcraft at Boscastle.

Bloody hell.

They might be living in the wilds of Cornwall, but this wasn't the Middle Ages. There were no such things as witches. Not really.

Or were there?

She turned and walked into the house, and found a pale and clearly distressed Penny turning away from the kitchen sink. She was nursing a nasty cut on her hand, and there was blood on her pink hoodie.

'Thank God you're home,' Penny said as soon as she saw her. Her voice wobbled. 'I called Bailey but she had to attend the magistrate's court in Bodmin this morning, and traffic on the way back is impossible.' She pointed to the Chinese box on the table, the lid open, its contents spilling out. There were tears in her eyes. 'I'm really sorry, Hannah. I tried, but I couldn't stop her.'

CHAPTER THIRTY-THREE

'Slow down and start at the beginning,' Hannah said as calmly as she could, though her heart was beating so rapidly she felt almost sick. It was that strange encounter with Jennifer, she told herself. What a horrid woman. And now it seemed something else had gone wrong. 'You couldn't stop who from doing what?'

Penny was normally unflappable, though it was true that the flood at her cottage had left her more fragile than usual. Whatever had happened, Hannah thought, it was obviously serious. Not least because of the cut on her hand, which was still bleeding. But Penny was lost in tears and could not manage a coherent reply.

'I . . . Oh, this is awful.'

'Please don't cry, Penny. Whatever's happened, it's not worth getting upset over.' Dropping her bag on the table, Hannah ignored the Chinese box for now. This situation had to take precedence. 'Let me look at that cut. You need some antiseptic on it, and maybe a bandage.'

'There's no time. You need to go after her. I can't face it.' Penny sounded distraught. 'She attacked me.'

Hannah stopped. 'Are you talking about Jennifer Bolitho?'

'What?' Penny stared. 'No.'

'Then who?'

'Lizzie, of course.' Penny nodded to the open Chinese box. 'I found her with that. She'd got hold of the key somehow.'

Instinctively, Hannah touched her chest. But of course she had taken the ribbon necklace off days ago, leaving it in her bedroom. It had not seemed so important now that they knew the contents of the box.

She still did not understand though. Lizzie had taken the key from her room and unlocked the box. But for what purpose?

'She took Gabriel's letters?'

Penny shook her head, impatient. 'Not the letters. The cards.'

'Sorry?'

'The tarot cards. She said they were evil. That she had to get them out of the house before it was too late. Or destroy them. I don't know exactly, she was hysterical.' She ran her cut hand under the cold tap, wincing. 'I tried to take them away from her, but she scratched me and ran out.'

'Going where?'

'No idea. Hannah, she wasn't wearing a coat. She had wellies on, thank God, but only a jumper and jeans. And it's snowing heavily now. She'll freeze to death out there.'

Hannah did not know what to make of this fantastical story. Launching a physical attack on Penny seemed out of character for the normally cheerful Lizzie. Though she had been distressed when she first saw those tarot cards. But there was no time to figure it out. Penny was bleeding and clearly distressed. Hannah brought down her first aid box

from the shelf beside the Aga, and pulled out the antiseptic cream.

'Here,' she said, and tended to Penny's cut as quickly and efficiently as she could, then wound a bandage around her hand, securing it with a safety pin. 'Thank God it wasn't a deep cut.'

'I'll be fine. It's Lizzie I'm worried about.'

'Poor thing, what on earth can have set her off like that?'

She checked her grandmother's Chinese box. The tarot pack was gone, its length of red silk discarded on the floor under the kitchen table. The cards hardly seemed important; not when compared to the treasure trove of love letters from Gabriel to Trudy. But clearly they were important to Lizzie. *Evil*, though? There was something deeper to this business, but her mind could not settle to working it out. And Lizzie was probably the only one who could shed light on her own bizarre behaviour.

The rusty key was still there, lying on the table among the letters. She picked it up and popped it into her coat pocket for safe-keeping.

'I'm going after her,' she said firmly. She kicked off her outdoor shoes and dragged on her wellies, which were better in the snow. 'You don't know which way she went?'

'Sorry, no. The whole thing kicked off less than ten minutes before you walked in. I tried Bailey first, then left a message on Raphael's machine.' She paused, glancing covertly at Hannah's tummy. 'Perhaps you should wait for him to arrive. It's not safe out there in this weather. And Raphael knows better than anyone else all the secret paths along the cliffs here, all the hiding places.'

'Where is he, then?'

Penny shrugged helplessly. 'In town? Out with his sheep?'

'So he could take an hour to arrive. Maybe more. I can't wait that long. Lizzie must be beside herself, or she would never have hurt you like that.'

'I know.' Penny sat down, looking defeated. 'God, this has been the worst year I can remember. First the cottage, now this.'

Hannah hesitated, then gave her a quick hug. 'Look, it's all going to be fine. Bailey will be back soon. And I'll find Lizzie and bring her home.'

'But—'

'If Raphael rings, tell him I've gone out to look for Lizzie, okay?' Hurriedly, Hannah took a spare waterproof coat for Lizzie and draped it over her arm. 'I'm taking my phone, though you know what the signal's like out there. Intermittent at best. But I'll keep it on, just in case.'

'Please be careful.'

'I will, absolutely.' She smiled. 'Try not to worry.'

With a confidence she was far from feeling, Hannah took a deep breath and dashed out into the snow.

It had seemed like an easy enough task at the time, Hannah thought drily. A quick trudge out to the camper van in Long Field, retrieve Lizzie, and hurry back to Kernow House with her before they both turned into snow maidens. But Hannah didn't have much experience of heavy snow, having lived too long in Greece, and the low visibility on the cliff edge took her by surprise. Not to mention the freezing

conditions, which made her movements and brain slow, leaving her unable to think clearly.

The Atlantic Ocean was gloomy and barely visible today, the muffled boom of the tidal surge against the cliffs sounding far-off, though it was only fifty feet to her right. A pale haze was descending on the land, smothering everything in white.

In a moment of cowardice, she thought of heading back.

But then she pictured a hapless Lizzie stumbling along in only a jumper and jeans, probably bawling her eyes out, and became more determined to find her. They had grown close recently. Lizzie had become a good friend, in fact. She couldn't imagine life at Kernow House without her. Penny, Bailey, and Lizzie. They were a foursome now, they fitted together perfectly. And if Lizzie had run away because she didn't think she could trust her new friends anymore . . .

Hannah had to find her.

Head down against the storm, Hannah left the crumbling perils of the cliff path, and slogged her way through brambles and rough grass towards Long Field. But as she crossed the undulating land, she began to feel doubtful of her direction. Should she have headed further inland than this? She peered about, using the spare coat as a shelter over her head, but did not recognise any of the landmarks, by which she meant mere lumps and bumps in the snow, or low-growing shrubs, twisted out of shape by the prevailing winds.

Bloody hell.

What an idiot she was not to have waited for Raphael. She

had only passed Lizzie's rackety old camper a couple of times while out walking, which did not help. Long Field itself was vast, as the name suggested, and she had never explored it thoroughly, only cut across the upper half nearest the sea. So her blithe assumption that she would easily be able to spot Lizzie's van, which was itself predominantly whitish-grey, in a whitish-grey snowstorm, in a vast field and in gathering dusk, had been foolish in the extreme.

Alone out here in the dark, she could perfectly understand why Lizzie clung to the old Cornish belief in ghosts. As the wind howled eerily about her head, she began to feel a little spooked herself.

Just as she was considering retracing her footsteps to Kernow House – if that was even possible now, with the snow laying thickly all around – she spotted a looming grey-white shape in the haze, a few hundred yards to her left. Solid and rectangular, with the hint of a tattered blue awning, flapping in the wind.

Lizzie's van!

She half-ran, half-stumbled, calling out, 'Lizzie! Lizzie!' in a tearful way reminiscent of a scene from *Wuthering Heights*, and grabbed at its door. It opened easily, much to her relief, and Hannah bundled herself inside, flushed and out of breath, dragging it shut behind her.

It was dark inside the van.

Dark, grim, and empty.

She shivered, staring about at the gloomy interior, which smelt strongly of damp and something smouldering.

Had there been a fire in here?

'Lizzie?' She took a deep breath, and then said more

calmly, 'It's okay, Lizzie. It's Hannah. Nobody's angry with you. But you need to come home.'

There was no answer.

She felt awful, her stomach twisted with anxiety.

Where was Lizzie?

Hannah took a few more steps into the darkness, and cried out, tripping over something on the floor. A saucepan, she realised. Picking it up, she sniffed at it. That was where the unpleasant burning smell was coming from. And the metal was still slightly warm.

She dropped the pan in the sink and slumped against the cooker, unable to believe her bad luck. Lizzie had been here, and recently. But where had she gone now? And in such appalling weather, no less?

Checking her phone, she saw there was no signal. And the battery was quite low, only about thirty per cent left. It must be the cold, draining it more rapidly than usual. Plus all the searching for a signal.

'God, I'm freezing.'

Thinking to warm herself by its flame, she fumbled with the stove. But it seemed to be out of fuel, though she could smell gas when she bent close. Perhaps Lizzie had got the same idea, or had tried to make a hot drink.

But what about the burning smell?

Using the light from her phone screen, Hannah investigated the contents of the abandoned saucepan. Bits of card, some burnt almost to ashes, others merely singed. She frowned, holding one of the less-damaged fragments to the screen light. It depicted an old bearded man in a cloak, carrying a lantern, though the bottom of the card had been burnt away.

Trudy's tarot cards!

Lizzie must have tried to burn them. Penny had said she stole them because she intended to destroy them. But then the canister ran out of gas, and ...

Raising the light, Hannah looked down. She was not standing on rubbish, but pieces of her grandmother's tarot pack, cut into dozens of haphazard pieces. A pair of scissors lay beside their scattered remains. Lizzie had cut up what she could not burn, then for some reason had fled her old home, and gone back into the freezing storm.

Shivering violently now, Hannah sat down on the damp bunk. It was so cold, she thought, it was like being inside a meat locker. She rubbed her arms but could not seem to get warm. Her teeth began to chatter, and it was increasingly hard to think. One thing was sure, though: if she could not get warm, she would soon start to develop hypothermia.

And what would happen to her baby, then?

She rubbed her bump, trying to sing to her unborn child as though it needed comforting. But her lips felt thick and rubbery, and all she could manage were moaning little breaths. She needed to warm herself up, and quickly. And the best way to get her blood pumping again was to move. Which, given the cramped interior of the van, meant following Lizzie's example, even if it seemed crazy on the face of it, perhaps even suicidal.

'I've g – got to g – get out of here,' she muttered, and drew Lizzie's spare coat over her head before wrenching open the door and falling out into the snow.

It whirled about insanely, striking her already cold face like frozen shards of glass. She bent her head under the

cover of the spare coat, and trudged painfully away from the camper, in the opposite direction to the one she'd come. Perhaps if she made for Raphael's farm, she'd get a signal on her phone and be able to call for help. Though whenever she peered through the violent flurry of snowflakes, she could see absolute zero in every direction. Just white, white, white, with a grey nothingness between.

Suddenly, she butted up against something knee-high. It moved at once, crying out in alarm.

Hannah yelped too, panicked and recoiling. 'What the hell . . .?' Then saw what it was, and laughed weakly under her breath.

It was a sheep.

Starting to walk again, she hit another sheep a few feet away. Then another. The animals bleated wildly at her, as though accusing her of not looking where she was going.

'Sorry,' she kept saying, increasingly tired of trying to sidestep these blasted beasts, snow sneaking under the coat and clustering uncomfortably down the back of her neck, her limbs suddenly heavy. 'Sorry.'

The flock was all around her, she realised belatedly. She had stumbled into their midst, and could not seem to shake them off. Then something butted her from behind, as though nudging her on, and she turned, realising with a shock that the little blighters were following her.

'G – go away, go and . . . find sh – shelter!' she told them crossly, waving her arms in a threatening manner, but they ignored her.

Strange slanted eyes peered out at her through the whirling snow. Bodies banged against her. It was as though they

WINTER WITHOUT YOU | 308

were herding her, she thought, herding her in one particular direction ... But where? A few of them bleated, but mostly they were silent, staring at her, pushing and following on behind as she stumbled through the formless snow towards a blanked-out horizon.

I'll put a spell on you.

Jennifer Bolitho's words went round and round in her head, sibilant and frankly terrifying. Had she been serious about being a witch? In this white-out, it was easy to imagine some malevolent force was behind her predicament. Soon she began to hear a dim roaring in her ears too, almost like the sea, though she was fairly certain she couldn't be anywhere near the cliff edge.

What was it Jennifer had said about Trudy Clitheroe?

She knew the old ways.

In these wild surroundings, she could almost believe her grandmother had been a witch too. And as capable of working mischief as Jennifer Bolitho seemed now.

Suddenly, she thought she heard someone shouting, but couldn't make out the words.

'Hello?' she shouted in response.

No reply.

Still sheltering under her coat, she stopped to listen. The sheep stopped too, turning and bleating in panic, milling helplessly about. For a moment all she could hear apart from their cries was that soft roaring that she couldn't place. Then, carried on the whining lilt of the wind, the call came again.

'Trudy!'

Bewildered to hear her grandmother's name instead of

her own, Hannah lifted the coat from over her head and stared through the tiny cold pinpricks of flakes hitting her cheeks and eyelids.

There was a dark figure a long way behind her, barely visible, shrouded in snow, its outline blurred. But she could tell it was a man, moving slowly towards her, head down against the storm's blast, holding a shepherd's crook.

'Hello?' she shouted again, her voice a mere croak, probably inaudible. 'Over here! I'm over here!'

It was useless. The snow battered at her face, the sea winds gusting more violently, and she had to squint at the man from behind a raised hand. With relief, Hannah thought for a moment that it must be Raphael, come to check on his sheep in the snow. Only this man with the shepherd's crook seemed older, more thick-set than Raphael.

Good grief, she thought, staring in disbelief.

Was that Gabriel Tregar?

CHAPTER THIRTY-FOUR

A sheep nudged the back of her knees, and she nearly fell over again, steadying herself with difficulty. Turning, she glared down at the foolish animal. When she looked back into the whirling snowstorm, she couldn't see the man with the shepherd's crook anymore. A sense of panic and isolation set in, making it hard to breathe.

Where had he gone?

All she could see ahead of her was an ancient gnarled tree growing at an absurd angle, its trunk and long-fingered branches bent almost horizontal, thanks to the power of the prevailing sea winds.

She was going mad.

It was the cold, she decided. Numbing her brain. The snow whisking insanely about was making gnarled old trees look like people who couldn't possibly be there.

The sound of roaring had grown louder and more distinctive. Not the tide, she realised with a sudden flood of relief, but the approach of a diesel engine, chugging noisily towards her across the undulating field. Another blurry outline this time morphed into a lumbering green tractor, plastered with snow, its headlights on full.

She waved both arms hysterically, so little strength left that it was all she could do not to collapse in the snow.

'Over here!' she cried out with a last effort, scattering the panicked sheep. 'Help!'

The tractor stopped a few feet away. The door opened and out jumped Raphael Tregar, flat cap and all. No snow mirage but a real, live person. And a very welcome sight he was indeed. He whistled and his two dogs flew out of the cab, rapidly driving the flock into a wedge-shape and then pushing them away into the snow.

Raphael reached her side, his expression furious.

'What on earth did you think you were doing, setting out in this God-awful weather? You could have been killed!'

She stiffened, immediately reconsidering how welcome a sight he was. Horrid cross man. 'Oh, yes, that's right. I can hardly stand up. But you go ahead, keep telling me off.'

He took one look at her face, and caught her as she wobbled.

'You idiot,' he muttered, and then scooped her off her feet as though she weighed no more than a pregnant ewe, which was frankly impossible. She clutched his shoulders, too weak and cold to protest, and a moment later was deposited in the exquisitely warm and bright cab of his tractor. 'Stay there,' he ordered her, a ridiculous thing to say under the circumstances, and slammed the door shut.

The space was claustrophobic, and she had a large steering wheel crammed against her belly. But there was no snow, which was a miracle, and hot air was pumping out of a vent somewhere. She shivered and groaned quietly, and wondered if she would ever be able to feel her toes

again. Just as she was beginning to seriously worry about frostbite, the door opened and Raphael climbed into the cab with her.

'There's no room,' she said, but was ignored.

He climbed over her in the most brutal fashion, then pushed her against the side window and put the machine in gear. The tractor, which had been shuddering gently the whole time, sprang into noisy life; the suddenness of it broke something in Hannah and she buried her face in Raphael's coat, bursting into tears. She had no real idea why she was crying. Except that it felt like the right thing to do.

He looked down at her. 'Are you crying?'

Mutely, she sat up and shook her head.

'Don't lie,' he said drily. 'Your face is wet.'

'From the snow.'

'Whatever.' He turned the wheel, bouncing them across the snow-white field, his wipers racing frantically to brush away flakes. 'I'm taking you to mine.'

'No, no ... Lizzie's still out here,' she said urgently, and tugged on the heavy wheel as though planning to turn the tractor around herself. 'We can't leave. We have to find her.'

Raphael wrenched the wheel back under his control. 'No, we don't.'

'But—'

'Lizzie's fine, you mad woman.' He peered ahead through the whirling snow. 'I dropped her back at Kernow House not ten minutes ago,' he said, adding tersely, 'and don't touch the steering wheel again. Long Field isn't the bloody cricket green. It's dangerous terrain, especially when I can't see where I'm going. You could turn us over.'

Now it was her turn to stare, drying her tears on his jacket sleeve. 'Wait, what did you say? You found Lizzie?'

'She found me, actually. And told me where you'd be.'

'You'd better explain.' Hannah straightened, starting to feel better, though a little foolish for having blubbed. She wasn't the weepy sort. It must have been the bitter cold, she told herself. It had left her incapacitated. But she still felt bloody silly. 'Lizzie was at her camper van only a short while ago. I know she must have been, because I tracked her there.'

He raised his eyebrows. '*Tracked*?'

'Followed her, then. Oh my God, you're so literal.'

'Only because I had a sudden vision of you doing your best Sherlock Holmes impersonation, checking for bent blades of grass or wellie-shaped footprints in the snow.'

'I still don't understand. How did Lizzie find you?'

'She came to the farmhouse. I was actually out looking for the sheep, who had strayed in the snow, but saw her torch.'

Her eyes widened. 'She had a torch?' Now why didn't I think of that? she asked herself crossly. 'That was clever of her.'

'No, she let herself into the house and took my spare torch from the hall stand. Then signalled me, hoping I was close enough to see the light. Which I was, luckily.'

'Lizzie signalled you with a torch?' Hannah gaped. 'Now who's Sherlock Holmes?'

'If she'd been Sherlock Holmes,' he pointed out, 'she might simply have picked up the phone and called me.' He patted his jacket pocket. 'I've got my mobile on me. How do you think I knew you two were gallivanting about the cliff edge in a snowstorm?'

'I can't speak for Lizzie,' she said hotly, 'but I never galli-vant anywhere. Besides, I was nowhere near the cliff edge.'

'Is that so?'

'I must have been smack bang in the middle of Long Field when you found me.' Hannah paused, alarmed by his silence. 'W – wasn't I?'

'You may have been at one point. But by the time I arrived, the sheep looked to be heading for the cliffs, and driving you along with them. There's an old pen near there. I imag-ine they were making for that, hoping to find shelter from the storm.'

'Oh God.'

'You were probably safe enough. There's an electric wire to prevent the flock straying too near the edge.' He made a face, tilting back his flat cap. 'Though it may have been down because of the storm.'

'In which case, if I'd carried on . . .'

'You could have gone straight over the cliff, yes,' he said, his tone matter-of-fact. 'You and the sheep. But you didn't. And the dogs will have brought them back to safety. So no point dwelling on it.'

She did dwell on it though. And felt chastened.

'But how did Lizzie know I was out looking for her?'

'I drove her home to Kernow House, hoping you'd have turned back by then.' His voice sounded rough. 'But Penny said you were still out. She wasn't sure where you'd gone,' his voice was rough, 'but Lizzie knew straightaway. That woman has some kind of sixth sense. She more or less told me exactly where I'd find you.'

Hannah sat in silence for a moment, glad to see the

familiar hulk of his farmhouse ahead, its solid walls and lit windows emerging out of the snowstorm. And not just because she was sick of being bounced about on the tractor. If she hadn't stopped to respond to what she'd thought was the ghost of Gabriel Tregar . . .

She asked abruptly, 'Before you found me, did you get out of the tractor at any point and search for me on foot? With a shepherd's crook?'

He shook his head. 'My crook's at home. I only tend to take it out with me when I'm going to be handling sheep.' His voice dropped, a note of humour in it. 'Not women.'

'Oh.'

Raphael frowned, slowing the tractor as they passed through the open gate opposite the farmhouse. 'Why do you ask?'

'I thought I saw someone, that's all.'

'Someone with a crook?'

'That's right.' She smiled at him brightly, sitting up straight. 'But I couldn't have done, could I? So that's that.'

'You sure you didn't bang your head out there?'

'Yes, very funny.' She hesitated. 'Though the sheep were behaving scarily at one point, pushing me all over the place. Like they were herding me in a particular direction. I began to think they were under a spell. And not a very nice one.'

He halted the tractor in the farmyard, and turned off the ignition. Snow fell against the windows, its near-silence oppressive after the noise of the engine.

'Listen,' he said quietly. 'There's nothing supernatural about what just happened. Frightened sheep are unpredictable in their behaviour, and the snow at night can do funny

things to your mind. You'd be amazed what I think I've seen out there in the dark, especially in blizzard conditions. Cornwall is an ancient country, and when you add bad weather to an overactive imagination, anything can happen.'

She glared at him for the 'overactive imagination' remark. She was not given to being fanciful. But she couldn't deny the good sense of what he said.

Yet, at the same time, it did feel possible that someone or something had been watching over her out there. Perhaps Gabriel Tregar really had flickered back into existence between the whirling snowflakes, like a glitch on a film track, just long enough to warn her away from the edge of the cliff before he vanished again.

'Seriously, are you okay?' Raphael opened his door, jumped to the snow-packed ground, then held out a hand to help her down. 'Because I could call out the doctor.' He studied her face intently. 'I can even drive you to the hospital myself if necessary. I expect the roads aren't so bad where they've been gritted.'

'I don't need a doctor.' She let him swing her down from the cab, their bodies briefly brushing together before he let her go, his expression reluctant. 'A hot drink would be very welcome, though.'

He led her towards the farmhouse, but she hesitated in the doorway, looking back into the icy black evening, snow spitting in her face as though desperate to be rid of her.

'What's the matter now?' Raphael was frowning.

'Your dogs.'

'They're doing their job, getting those stray sheep back into the right field.'

'But in this snow . . .'

'Merry and Pippin know their way home.' When she continued to stare at him, Raphael sighed and went back to the gate. He put two fingers to his lips, gave a shrill whistle, and then waited.

The fields remained silent, nothing moving out there. Snowflakes began to settle on his flat cap and the shoulders of his jacket. Then suddenly, making almost no sound, two wiry black forms came barrelling out of the snow and under the gate, milling about him, tails wagging.

He laughed, patting the sheepdogs on the head, then nodded towards the house, and in they ran, barging past her with little curiosity, and disappeared.

'If only I could get you to come to heel that easily,' he drawled, sauntering back down the snowy path towards her, jacket drawn back, thumbs hooked in his belt.

She went inside the house, and shut the door in his face.

'Hey!'

CHAPTER THIRTY-FIVE

Hannah made her way into the hall with a wry smile, hearing him swear under his breath as he wrestled with the stiff door catch.

'Thanks for nothing,' he said drily when he finally caught up with her. Removing his snow-covered jacket, he hung it up. 'Do make yourself at home.'

There was a sturdy-looking rug at the entrance to the hall, and she stopped to drag off her wellies there, not wanting to tread snow and mud through the house. It was tough work, and she had to lean against the wall to manage it. She said nothing though, unwilling to admit how weary she felt. He would only fuss. Her socks were sodden and freezing, but she felt awkward removing them in someone else's home. Even the Big Bad Wolf's. She padded across to hang Lizzie's spare coat on a wall hook, but kept her own coat on, hunched into it for warmth. The old farmhouse was less chilly than being outside in the snow, but not exactly Bermuda.

There was a light flashing on his phone cradle in the hall.

She glanced at it, then at Raphael as he pulled his own wellies off, throwing them down without ceremony beside her own neatly arranged pair. 'Is that a new message?'

Impatiently, he leaned over and stabbed the Play button.

'Raphael, it's Penny at Kernow House. You're not answering your mobile. Can you give us a ring, please? Lizzie's fretting about Hannah.' Some noise in the background of the call. Penny added wearily, 'She says if you find her, to tell Hannah she's sorry. That she made a mistake. Call us, would you?'

He made a face and handed Hannah the handset. 'Something for you to deal with. I'll put the kettle on.'

She called the house back, and was rewarded with shrieks of relief from all three women on the other end. 'That's fantastic news. Are you coming back tonight?' Bailey put the call on speakerphone so they could all hear Hannah. 'Lizzie was sure you'd gone over the cliff. She's been so worried. We all have. And there's food warming on the Aga for you.'

Hannah hesitated, listening with her other ear to Raphael moving about in the kitchen, giving his dogs snacks by the sound of it, the kettle boiling in the background. 'That's really sweet of you. And Lizzie, thank you so much for suggesting where I'd be. If Raphael hadn't found me when he did . . . Oh, and I'm not sure exactly when I'll be home.' There were more shrieks on the other end, and what sounded to her like Lizzie clapping. Which seemed odd. 'I'm fine, honestly. I just need to sit down and have a hot drink first.'

A hand grabbed the phone off her.

Raphael said sharply into the receiver, 'She's staying the night here. It's shocking weather out there, not fit for driving. I'll bring her over in the morning.' He listened to some response, then grunted. 'Leave it to me. Goodnight.'

Then he dumped the handset back on the cradle, and

jerked his head towards the sitting room. 'Go and sit down. And take those wet socks off. And the coat. I'll find you something dry.'

'I was talking to my friends!'

'And I'm talking to you.'

'What was all that nonsense about shocking weather, anyway? I thought you said the roads were probably fine.'

'It's called a lie, and it's useful for getting you out of things you have no desire to do.' Raphael pushed her towards the gloomy open doorway to his sitting room. 'I'll be in to make up a fire in a couple of minutes, and check you over properly, make sure that baby's come to no harm. Now, sit.'

'I'm not a dog, thank you.' She put her hands on her hips, glaring at him. 'Or a sheep, come to that, which I expect is the only pregnant thing you've ever checked over.'

'Go and sit down, woman!' he said loudly, and the dogs came running out to see what was happening, surprised at his tone. He toed them aside, and steered her into the living room. 'There's the sofa. Get yourself on it.' He groped for the light before returning to the kitchen, calling back, 'Sugar in your tea?'

'I stopped taking sugar in my tea when I was fifteen,' she retorted, and wandered back out of the living room, unable to settle. 'Can I use your, erm, bathroom?'

'Downstairs loo, you mean? Blue door, opposite the stairs.'

Raphael put sugar in her tea anyway. 'For the shock,' he said, grinning at her horrified expression on tasting it. Then he made up a log fire with ease; soon the room was warm and cosy, and she was relaxing on the sofa in thick dry

socks – his, of course – and a baggy jumper, also his. He tried to make her take her damp trousers off too, but she refused stoutly, not sure where that would lead.

Her phone had come to life now there was a signal. Eleven notifications popped up noisily one after the other, the mobile buzzing in a deranged fashion and making Raphael look around at her drily.

Guilt welled inside her as she scanned through the various messages. There were several panicked-sounding voicemails from Penny, asking where on earth she was. Two on the same subject from Raphael, though typically terse. The texts all seemed to be pageant-related, mainly last minute flurries of queries and worries, but also a message from Patricia Cobbledick that said simply, 'Good luck!'

Raphael plucked the mobile from her hands as she attempted to answer one of the more urgent pageant queries. 'No more work.' He threw the mobile onto the adjacent armchair. 'Not tonight.'

'But Fenella's table displays haven't arrived.'

'Is there anything you can do about that right now?'

'No,' she said reluctantly. 'But I could reassure her.'

'Fenella's a grown woman. Trust me, she can reassure herself.' He shook his head, swiftly blocking her from reaching for her phone again. 'Not a chance. Look, we didn't hire you so you could work yourself into the ground. You've been out in a snowstorm. You could have died. So take the rest of the night off, okay?'

'But . . .'

'Here.' He sat down beside her with what looked like a glass of brandy. 'This will warm you up. Drink it.'

'I can't,' she said, pointing to her bump.

'Not even a sip?'

Hannah shook her head firmly, and was amused when he shrugged and knocked back the brandy himself.

Her amusement did not last long, however.

Raphael put down the glass and turned to her with an odd look in his eyes.

She held up a pre-emptive hand. 'No more kissing!'

'I was only going to check that the baby was okay.'

'Really?' Her eyebrows shot up. 'And what are your credentials for that?'

He shrugged. 'You said it yourself. I've handled plenty of pregnant ewes.'

'And like I said, I'm not a sheep.'

'But you are *pregnant*.' His smile was ironic. 'Two minutes, that's all. Or don't you care if the baby's okay?'

'Of course I care,' she said sharply, feeling ruffled.

'Well, then.'

He removed his flat cap. At last, she thought with secret relief, watching him chuck the offending item onto the coffee table before smoothing down his short dark hair, but said nothing. Then he placed a hand on top of her bump through the jumper, but cautiously, as though ready for her to bat him away.

'No aches and pains?' he asked, studying her face.

She shook her head.

'No nausea?'

Again, she shook her head.

'So far, so good.' He moved his hand slowly over her swollen belly. 'Nothing out of the ordinary, then?'

Catching her breath, Hannah shook her head for the third time. She tried hard not to give in to the sensations his gentle exploratory hand was causing. But she was only human. And very, very lonely.

She was still grieving for Santos, of course she was. But Santos was not here, and part of her was empty and yearning for . . . She did not know what, and didn't really want to pursue that disturbing thought. But it was difficult not to let her mind wander in that direction. He was sitting so close to her now, and she could smell his tangy outdoor scent, all fresh wintry air and aftershave.

She had always thought of Raphael as the opposite of Santos: dark versus light, rough versus smooth, cold versus warmth. But in fact they had far more in common than she had realised. Raphael Tregar was a strong, active, outdoors man, just as Santos had been. Except that he spent his days herding sheep and traipsing across cold, muddy fields, not climbing mountains or water-skiing on the Aegean. And suddenly his hand felt warm and smooth across her belly, not cold at all.

'How about movement?' he asked, breaking into her thoughts. 'Have you felt the baby kick recently? Since you went out in the snow, I mean.'

Hannah hesitated. 'I'm not sure.' She frowned, thinking back over the ordeal she had suffered. 'I . . . I don't think so, actually.'

Perhaps sensing her sudden trepidation, his gaze locked with hers, their faces mere inches apart. 'Look, it's okay, it's probably nothing. You were very cold out there, and the baby may have responded to that by staying quiet, that's all.'

'Oh God.'

'Don't panic. Breathe.' He stroked her bump comfortingly. 'That's it. Keep breathing. Nice and slow.'

'Perhaps I should get checked over by a doctor, after all,' she said, her voice high and shaking. She struggled to get up and he pushed her back onto the sofa, shaking his head. 'No, I have to get up. When they don't move for ages, that's a really bad sign. I need a scan. You have to drive me to—'

Then she stopped.

He stared at her arrested expression. 'What? What is it?'

'Oh!'

'Hannah, I swear to God if you don't tell me—'

She put a hand to her bump. 'It moved. The baby moved.'

'What?'

She grabbed his hand and dragged it to the spot where the baby had kicked. But the jumper was too thick for him to feel the tiny movement. She pushed it up impatiently, and pressed his hand to her bare tummy.

'Feel that? She's kicking me.'

'*She?*'

'It's a girl. The sonographer told me.'

'A girl.' His smile warmed her. 'And she's fine. There you are, I told you she'd be absolutely—'

The baby kicked under his hand, and he stiffened into silence, staring down at Hannah's prominent bump. He frowned, as though not sure what had just happened.

Then the kick came again.

His eyes widened. 'I . . . I felt something.' He spread out his fingers, and waited, jerking in surprise at the next, well-aimed kick. He laughed incredulously. 'My God, she's really putting the boot in. I think we woke her up.'

'I take it back. Maybe you are a baby-whisperer, after all.'

'You see?' He stroked down her tummy, grinning stupidly as the baby seemed to follow his hand, kicking again. 'I wasn't exaggerating before. I *do* have experience with babies.'

'*Baa!*' she bleated at him.

Raphael threw his head back and laughed, a deep, rich sound that left Hannah breathless and staring. 'Bloody woman!'

Hannah laughed too, but the sound broke in the middle, turning into a kind of mad, breathless sob. To her relief, he did not seem to notice. His hand was still lying on her skin, so warm and intimate, and for a few terrifying seconds she was horribly tempted to sleep with him. Or to suggest it, anyway.

He might turn her down, after all.

Yes, he'd kissed her before, when they were putting the Christmas tree up. But kissing and sleeping together were two very different activities. She was pregnant with another man's child, and it had been months since she'd had an even passable figure. And her cheeks must look red-raw after being out in the snow, and as for her hair . . . It was damp and uncombed, and probably frizzed up like hell.

Their eyes met, and all that nonsense was forgotten.

He bent his head just as she raised her mouth towards his, and they met with a dizzying collision. Oh my goodness, she thought, linking her arms about his neck, he's such a good kisser. Even if he does taste of brandy.

She probably shouldn't trust him, she thought.

Mr Knutson had reminded her at rehearsals only the other day that Raphael might yet present them with Jack

Clitheroe's gambling IOU and demand some share of the estate, if not the whole of Kernow House. It had been clear from the solicitor's tone of gentle reproof that Bailey must have mentioned Raphael's increasing visits to the house, and maybe his recent gift of a Christmas tree. Or perhaps Lizzie had spotted their secret kiss, after all, and been shocked enough to share that piece of salacious gossip with Bailey and Penny, who had then generously shared their concerns with Mr Knutson.

There were dozens of excellent reasons not to give in to her desire right now. Not least that she was round with child. There was also the small matter of his other women, of which local gossip suggested there were many, including the vindictive Jennifer. Those two had been lovers once, by his own admission. But her brain was not fully engaged at the moment. It was her body doing the negotiations, not her mind. And he certainly knew how to get her attention, his mouth moving persuasively on hers, his hands warmly cupping her face.

To her surprise, he suddenly stopped and knelt before her. There was something gratifying about seeing the aloof Raphael Tregar down on his knees, as though reduced to begging. But for what?

'Raphael . . .' She began the sentence, but then stopped, unsure where it was going.

He stroked her cheek with his fingertips. She felt the calluses on his skin. It was the hand of a working man, a man of the land, a shepherd.

'Hannah.' His voice was hoarse. 'Say no if you must, but I want to . . .' He drew an unsteady breath. 'That is, I need . . .'

'Me too.'

His eyes narrowed on her face, then he smiled wolfishly. He drew back only to drag his shirt off, revealing a hard, muscular chest and abdomen. Hannah stared, unprepared for the sheer wave of lust that engulfed her at the sight of this half-naked man on his knees in the firelight, his eyes glittering with desire.

'Take me to bed,' she said, then laughed when he sprang to his feet and bent to lift her from the sofa. 'I didn't mean that literally. One heroic feat per night is enough, even for you.' When he ignored her, hoisting her into the air, she said hurriedly, 'Careful, you'll put your back out. I can make my own way up – Oh!'

Raphael had put her down again. But not on the sofa. He had placed her on the thick rug in front of the fire, and now slid a large, springy cushion under her head. He smiled into her eyes. 'Comfortable?'

She licked her lips. 'It'll do.'

Raphael wasted no time in lying down beside her. He hooked one leg demandingly over hers, and then surprised her by turning his face into her blonde hair. 'Your hair always smells so amazing.'

'Makes a change from the smell of sheep's wool, I guess.'

He looked up, showing her his teeth. 'If you're not careful, Hannah Clitheroe, I'll throw you back out in the snow.'

'What, and ruin your tale of a daring rescue?'

Holding her breath, she ran a hand down his chest and flat abs while he watched her. They felt like iron, she thought, her mouth dry with longing. She was aware that she could still change her mind at any point, yet did not

resist when he began unfastening her trousers. She was feeling rather overheated, and only too ready not to have any clothes on.

'My God, that fire's hot,' she muttered, helping him with her remaining clothes. 'How many logs did you throw on it? I feel like I'm going to spontaneously combust.'

'Have you considered it might not be the fire causing that?'

'You egotist.' But she kissed him back when he bent over her, his hands exploring her wonderfully ripe, naked body. Then he stroked between her legs, and she closed her eyes, gasping with shocked pleasure. All thoughts of changing her mind vanished in a torrent of desire. 'I can't believe I'm about to have sex with a man who wears a flat cap.'

'Be quiet,' he muttered, kissing her throat, 'or I'll put it back on again.'

CHAPTER THIRTY-SIX

Next morning, Raphael came upstairs to tell her there was no milk in the fridge for tea or cereal. He had already been out to check on the sheep at first light, leaving her to sleep in his bed – they had left the fireside rug eventually, sometime in the early hours, for a rather more comfortable round two of lovemaking – but now suggested they drive into town, since the cupboard was bare.

'There's a café on the seafront that does a good fry-up,' he said, grinning at the sight of her sitting up boldly in his bed for a stretch and a yawn, not even bothering to conceal her nakedness. 'My treat.'

Hannah readily agreed, her tummy rumbling after having missed dinner the night before. When he left to see about the dogs' breakfasts, she had a quick wash and got dressed. To her relief, her clothes from the night before had dried in front of the fire, so she didn't have to wear his outsized jumper into town and risk making it obvious they had spent the night together.

Silly, perhaps, but she was eager to avoid gossip. There was always the chance that the unhappy Jennifer might be

back for another row. Or would start leaving voodoo dolls stuck full of pins on the back step.

It was a chilly day, the sun glinting off a steel-grey Atlantic that looked perfectly flat and still and not a bit as though there had been an appalling storm mere hours ago. The roads in Pethporro were slushy but passable, just as Raphael had predicted. The council gritters had been out on the main roads overnight, and snow was already melting on any smaller lanes and side roads that had missed out on being gritted. But he still drove more carefully than usual, as the verges were dangerously soft and there was a risk of skidding on tight corners. Plus, Hannah was in the passenger seat, glaring in a meaningful way whenever he tried to accelerate.

After ordering two fried breakfasts – described defiantly on the menu as 'a full Cornish breakfast' – with a pot of tea for two, Raphael leaned back in his chair and studied her face. The place was almost empty and he had led her to a table right by the window overlooking the sea.

'How are you feeling?'

'Fine.' She met his gaze shyly. It had been an amazing night. 'Better than fine, actually. Though I take it you don't mean physically?'

He nodded slowly.

'I have a few niggling doubts.' She bent her head, playing with her cutlery. 'But that's only natural, and I'm dealing with them.'

'Because of Santos?' His tone was very matter-of-fact, perhaps even distracted. But she was not deceived.

'I am carrying his child, remember.'

'True.'

'And I'm not over him yet. I still love him. Or am in love with him. I'm never quite sure of the difference.'

'I wouldn't have expected anything less,' he said gruffly, looking out to sea.

'Besides, you're not much of a keeper.'

He turned his head to stare at her, a flash of something dangerous in his face. 'What the hell's that supposed to mean?'

She hesitated, then told him about Jennifer and her visit to Kernow House. His face darkened with anger as he listened, then he swore, falling silent when the waitress appeared with their cooked breakfasts. The woman glanced at him, her eyebrows raised at the bad language, but made no remark, putting the plates down with a snap.

He waited until she was out of earshot, then leaned forward, his voice urgent. 'It's not true. I told you before, that thing with Jennifer, it was a one-off. A mistake.'

'She clearly doesn't see it like that.'

'That's hardly my fault.'

'And there have been others, according to local gossip.'

'Utter rubbish.'

'No smoke without fire,' she murmured.

He shook his head, glaring down at his breakfast plate as though he blamed bacon and eggs for all his misfortunes. 'That has to be the least logical saying on the planet. Of course you can have smoke without fire, everyone knows that.' He buttered his toast. 'Apart from that one night with Jennifer, I haven't . . . That is, you were . . . I haven't exactly been playing the field.'

Hannah stopped, a forkful of mushroom dripping with egg yolk paused on the way to her mouth. 'What?'

His head was still bent, a hard tinge of red along his cheekbones. 'You heard me.'

'Heard but didn't quite understand.' Her eyes narrowed on his face as she went through what he'd said. It couldn't be true. 'Are you saying Jennifer was your *first*?'

'Not quite my first. I had a couple of girlfriends after I left school, but . . . I was always so busy on the farm, and Gabriel needed me. Then he got sick, and I didn't like to leave him alone for any length of time. Afterwards, nobody really appealed. Except Jennifer, and I knew immediately that was a mistake.' Raphael shrugged, not looking at her, a defensive note in his voice. 'I got out of the habit of dating, that's all. No crime in it.'

'Of course not.' She bit back a smile. 'Well, your lack of practice didn't show last night. Trust me.'

He grinned at her, and then focussed on his plate again, eating with great appetite. 'This is very tasty.'

She agreed, chewing thoughtfully on her mushroom. It was the most mouth-watering mushroom she had ever eaten. In fact, the whole breakfast looked and smelt unspeakably delicious. And the sun on the sea was so inviting, the rugged cliffs beautiful in the morning light. She was suddenly seized by a desire to walk along the cliffs and breathe in the fresh Cornish air. Walk for miles and miles, with Raphael by her side, the two of them holding hands and talking.

'But your reputation . . .'

He flashed her a dry smile. 'I said I hadn't dated anyone. Not that I hadn't flirted.'

Hannah caught her breath, her gaze locked with his. Oh God, she thought in sudden anguish, and looked away hurriedly, her heart thumping.

'What's the matter?' he asked at once, putting down his knife and fork. He took her hand across the table. 'Hannah?'

'Nothing, I . . .'

'Is it the baby?'

She shook her head, half laughing, and turned to stare at the sea. The light was so bright and blinding it brought tears to her eyes. Her voice shook a little as she said, 'It's so gorgeous here, that's all. I'm really glad I came to Cornwall. That I didn't sell Kernow House.'

He said nothing, withdrawing his hand.

She returned to her meal, burningly conscious of him sitting opposite her, every mouthful he took, the way he looked at her, and then away.

I'm really glad I came to Cornwall. That I didn't sell Kernow House.

Well, that had shut him up.

Was it possible Raphael was still after her grandmother's legacy? She turned the thought over in her mind, heat creeping into her face. The heat of humiliation and despair. The food that had been so delicious moments ago now tasted like ashes. Had Raphael slept with her to gain some kind of seductive influence, so he could wheedle the house out of her? Was he lying about his previously monk-like existence? It did seem strange, given his looks, for a man of his age to claim he was a loner by choice.

For all she knew, he'd bedded every unattached woman of a certain age in the town, and was simply a gilt-edged liar.

Her chest suddenly hurt like it was being crushed by a heavy weight. Crushed and squeezed at the same time. God, was she having a heart attack? Indigestion, more like, she told herself angrily. She was pregnant; she had to remember that and behave more sensibly. She had wolfed down her breakfast like a teenager and was suffering for it now. It was nothing to do with her stupid bloody heart.

Raphael finished his meal, pushed away his plate, and then checked the time.

Like nothing had changed.

I've fallen in love with you, she wanted to shout.

Except that was unthinkable. She was still in love with Santos. The father of her child, the man of her dreams, about as different from Raphael Tregar as it was possible to get.

Or was she?

When had she last spent quality time thinking about her poor darling Santos? When had she last curled up on the sofa to cry over his photograph and tell him in a whisper about her life now, and how their child was growing inside her? When had she last felt the sharp pang of loneliness as she lay in bed without him by her side, and wished he was there, making love to her?

She could not remember.

The truth of that inner realisation shook her into silence, and she sat, stunned and breathless, looking anywhere but at Raphael.

I've fallen in love with you ...

How the hell had she allowed that to happen?

*

'You never explained what made Lizzie run off like that,' Raphael said when she'd finished eating, pouring her a cup of tea and pushing it towards her.

The tea was lukewarm but she drank it again, aware of his gaze on her face. 'Didn't I?' She shrugged. 'She was freaked out by Trudy's tarot cards. Poor woman. I'm not sure why, but she seems to hate anything like that. So she stole them and took them back to her van to burn.'

He stared at her.

'Oh,' she said faintly, and put her cup down in its saucer. 'I didn't tell you about the tarot cards, did I?'

'No.'

'I found them in her Chinese box, you see.'

His brows rose. 'Sorry?'

'It's probably not Chinese. I only call it that because it's got oriental-looking patterns carved in the lid.'

'And it belonged to your grandmother?'

'Yes.' She drew a deep breath, deciding she might as well tell him the whole truth now, having blurted that out about the tarot cards. 'It was locked. I didn't want to break in, so I didn't actually open it for ages. But then . . .'

'You found the key.' He folded his arms, leaning back with an unreadable look on his face. 'It seems quite a lot has been going on that I know nothing about.'

'Because it was none of your business.'

'Do I need to remind you that the coastguard could have been out searching for your remains right now if I hadn't found you last night?'

It was a fair point.

Briefly, she told him about the key on the ribbon, and

what she had found in the box. Raphael listened intently, and stiffened when she mentioned the letters.

'Counterparts, presumably,' he said, 'to the letters I already have from Trudy to Gabriel.'

'I would imagine so.'

His gaze tangled with hers, causing all sorts of wobbly sensations in her tummy. 'We should put the two sets of letters together,' he said, 'work out some kind of timeline. Maybe find answers to some difficult questions.'

'You mean, work out if they were actually having an affair?'

His mouth quirked. 'Oh, I'd be amazed if they weren't.'

'But maybe Gabriel was like you. A thinker, not a lover,' she said, before thinking how that would sound. Too late she tried to snatch the words back, but her apology tailed off in silence at his expression.

'Thanks,' he said.

'I didn't mean . . . That came out wrong.'

'It doesn't matter.'

'Yes, it does. And I'm probably wrong anyway. In his letters, Gabriel mentioned meeting her somewhere secret. A cave, or something like that. Though I suppose it could have been code. Or even a euphemism.'

He shook his head, and said coolly, 'No, it's a real cave.'

'What?'

'Gabriel often went down there. When I first came to live with him, he had a small boat, and he used to keep some of his fishing stuff in it. Winter storage, you know. Ropes and lobster pots.' Raphael made a face. 'He fancied himself a fisherman, though he hardly ever took that boat out. Then

he sold it. But he still went down to the cave a few times a year.' His smile was wistful. 'I always thought it was strange. Now I know why . . . That was where he used to meet her.'

Hannah felt inexplicably sad, imagining the two star-crossed lovers meeting in some dark little cave, unable to be together.

But if Trudy was in love with Gabriel, why not simply leave Jack?

'I wish I understood all this,' she said.

'Me too.' He nodded, reaching for his wallet. 'So let's go and find out,' he said. 'The tide's nearly at its lowest ebb. No time to waste.'

She stared at him, not understanding.

'You can only get to the cave at low tide. It's a short walk around the headland.' He eyed her bump. 'Think you can manage it?'

Hannah laughed, jumping up. 'Try and stop me.'

The cave looked like a mere indentation of the rocks, protected by a craggy outcrop sunk in the pale shingle and sand of the beach, until they came closer and Hannah was able to see the opening. It was incredibly low to the ground, which she had not expected. But there was no way she was turning back now.

Raphael went first, crouching almost to the ground in order to clear the low hanging rock at the entrance. 'Come on,' he called back to her. 'It's perfectly safe.'

Her heart beating fast, which she told herself was due to the unusual exercise of clambering across rocks, Hannah followed him inside. To achieve this, she had to drop to her

hands and knees, crawling several feet through a claustrophobic passage, into a dark cavern.

Raphael was waiting for her on the other side. He helped her to her feet, and fumbled in his coat pocket for a torch. It was small, barely larger than his palm, but the beam was bright enough, and he waved it across the damp walls, highlighting water running down to pool in tiny puddles in the rocky floor below.

'Do you go anywhere without a torch?' she asked.

He grinned. 'Not usually, no. That's the life of the sheep farmer, I'm afraid. I'm always having to plunge into the night with only this coat over my pyjamas, for one emergency or another, especially in lambing season. If I didn't carry a torch everywhere, I'd end up falling down a hole or off a cliff. Or losing a birthing ewe in the dark.'

He held out his hand again, and she took it uncertainly.

With a gentle squeeze, he reassured her. 'Look, if your grandmother was willing to come out here in the middle of the night, then surely you can manage to explore it in broad daylight, with me and a torch for company.'

'There's not much broad daylight from where I'm standing.'

'Come on, it's easy. Walk where I walk. The ground is uneven here, but it gets better around the corner.'

'There's a *corner*?'

He laughed, leading her through the narrow entrance, and around an even narrower bend in the rocks, to where the cave opened out into a larger chamber, much to her relief.

It felt dry in the bigger space, or rather, less dank than

the opening, which presumably took in the sea at high tide. This part looked relatively untouched by the water.

Towards the back of the cavern, Raphael's torch picked out broken lobster pots and coils of rope, and a few old planks leaning against the wall in a kind of alcove. The ground was part solid rock, part shingle, with a few large pebbles scattered here and there. It made for difficult walking. But they were both wearing wellies, which helped.

'Well, this is the cave from their letters. Hardly the stuff of romantic fantasy, is it?'

'It's certainly bloody cold.'

He glanced at her. 'You need my coat?'

'I'll survive.'

Raphael turned on his heel, shining the torch over the high, rocky, dark-veined walls. The salty air was moist and chilly, and their voices echoed as they spoke, bouncing off the stone. She tried to imagine Trudy and Gabriel meeting here in secret, perhaps even making love. Perhaps they brought a blanket to lie on, she thought. Intimate it was, to be sure. But like he'd said, hardly an ideal place for a romantic encounter.

'In one of the letters Trudy sent Gabriel,' he said thoughtfully, 'there was mention of a passageway. I always assumed she was talking about the entrance we just came through. You know, where you had to crawl in because of the low overhang?'

'Sure.'

'Well, now that I'm standing here again, I can't believe that's what she meant. It was so specific. I think she even mentioned steps. But there aren't any here, are there?

Unless . . .' He clambered over the higher levels of the rocky floor, until he reached the alcove-like space where the old planks had been left to rot against the wall. 'I wonder . . .'

Shining the light behind them, he gave a muffled exclamation, and then put the torch down and began to drag the stacked planks away from the wall.

'Over here, Hannah. Quick, come and see.'

Going anywhere quickly was not within her power. But she did her best. By the time she reached him, treading gingerly over tangled heaps of rope and slippery, pock-marked rocks, Raphael had cleared most of the stained planks and grabbed the light up again. Looking past him, she could see there was a gap in the rock-face, a gap that the old planks had been concealing.

It was a narrow space, about five foot in height, and barely wide enough for two people.

Breathing fast, Raphael beckoned her closer, his face illuminated by the wavering torch beam. His body felt warm beside hers, his breath steaming out on the cold air. She looked him up and down, suddenly excited. Perhaps this place had its own rugged brand of romance, after all.

'Look at this,' he said urgently, pointing the light inside the gap, 'there's a hidden passage back here. And I can guess where it goes.'

CHAPTER THIRTY-SEVEN

'Bailey said there was a rumour about a secret passageway in Kernow House,' she whispered, 'but nobody had ever been able to find the entrance.'

'Well,' he said, 'maybe this is it.'

Beyond the gap in the rocks was a flight of rough-hewn steps, carved out of the cliff itself, black and damp and hellishly slippery-looking. They stood at the base of the steps and stared into darkness. Raphael shone his torch beam up the steps, but it was a long way, and the beam only reached so far.

There was only one choice.

Without a word, he took her hand, and they began the long and arduous ascent. Several times, Hannah wanted to stop and go back. But then she reminded herself that her grandmother had climbed the steps, and descended them too, maybe in the middle of the night, with a torch just like theirs. As Raphael had pointed out, if Trudy Clitheroe could do it, so could her granddaughter.

The stairs zigzagged at odd intervals, so they paused at each widening of the stairway to catch their breath. It was a steep ascent.

Just as Hannah was beginning to question who had laboriously carved out these steps, and why, Raphael said in her ear, 'Smugglers. That's why this secret passage is here. They would have moored a small boat just off the beach, or run it aground, and then rolled the merchandise into the cave.'

'Merchandise?'

'French brandy in barrels, I should imagine. Maybe silk too, brought in from the Far East, and sold secretly without paying local taxes. The smugglers must have brought the contraband in here, and then up these steps into Kernow House. Right under the noses of the revenue men, who would have shot them on sight.' He gave a hoarse laugh. 'I should have realised. Gabriel always said smuggling was rife in Cornwall. And all the time, he must have known about this secret passageway. Probably used it himself.'

'To visit Trudy?'

'I imagine so. He certainly wasn't carrying kegs of brandy up these steps. It must be nearly two hundred years since there were smugglers in Cornwall.'

'I wonder if Jack knew about this place?'

'I doubt it.'

'Then how would Trudy have known?'

Raphael hesitated. 'Gabriel must have told her. Who else? His family had been farming here for generations. So had the Clitheroes, of course, but not all secrets get passed down parent to child. And as a family, they have always been noto- riously close-mouthed. Perfect smuggler material.' He gave her an odd, teasing look. 'Clitheroes like secrets. Secrets and games.'

She raised her eyebrows. 'Sounds more like a Tregar trait to me.'

His laughter echoed strangely in the confined space.

They had reached the top.

Ahead stood a door set into the rock, with crumbling brick about it. The door was low and wide, made of some ancient dark wood. Oak, possibly. There was an iron ring handle, rusty with age. Raphael shone his torch beam at the ring, tugged on it several times, and then swore.

'What is it?' she asked.

'Bloody thing's locked, of course. Too much to ask for this to be easy.' He stood back a few inches to let her see the iron ring handle. 'There's a keyhole.'

'What's behind this door, do you think?'

'Kernow House.'

'I can't believe this door opens somewhere inside my house. What, into a cellar, do you think? I didn't know we had any. There aren't any shown on the plans.'

'I guess we'll have to bang on this door until someone hears us and opens it. It's either that, or go back to the cave.' He shone a torch down the winding, narrow steps reaching into darkness, and she shuddered. 'Exactly.'

'I vote we bang on the door.'

'Yes, and hope somebody's in. Unless . . .' His sideways look was wry. 'I don't suppose you have the key?'

He was being sarcastic, of course.

But Hannah stared at him silently. Then put a hand in her pocket, and drew out the key from her grandmother's Chinese box.

His eyes widened a fraction, glittering in the semi-darkness.

'You're kidding, right? Is that the key? Where on earth did you get it?'

'One guess.'

Raphael gave a bark of incredulous laughter, then shone the torch beam onto the lock. 'Be my guest.' Holding her breath, she bent forward and inserted the key in the lock. It fitted, but would not turn. She struggled a moment, biting her lip in frustration. Then he handed her the torch. 'Let me.'

He jiggled the door about in its frame, which was difficult as the door looked very heavy. He swore under his breath a few times, then finally the key gave. As soon as it had turned in the lock, he gave a triumphant cry, and dragged on the ring handle.

Nothing happened.

He tried again, but the door did not budge.

'Perhaps it's a push, not a pull,' she suggested in a whisper.

He glanced at her, then back at the door. This time, he pushed. And this time, something happened.

The door moved. But again, it stopped.

He pushed again, this time harder. The door thumped up against something on the other side. Something heavy and solid. But there was daylight filtering through the gap, and now Hannah could feel fresh air on her face, not the stale, salty air of the passageway. She could also smell something.

She grabbed his shoulder. 'Cake,' she said, almost gabbling in her hurry to get the words out. 'Christmas cake.'

'Trust you to think of food at a time like this.'

'No, you idiot. Use your nose.'

He opened his mouth to say something dismissive, no doubt, then shut it again. He took a deep breath, sniffing the air. Then smiled. 'Christmas cake,' he repeated, almost dreamily.

Hannah banged on the door with her fist, as loudly as she could. She shouted into the gap, 'Hey! Anyone in there? Hello? Can you hear us?'

Silence.

'We're stuck behind a door somewhere in the house,' Raphael shouted, his voice much louder than hers, echoing deeply in the narrow space. She imagined he could be heard all the way down in the cave. 'Follow the sound of our voices and let us out!'

They kept this up for another minute, shouting and hammering on the door, until suddenly the gap widened, with a terrible scraping of wood on slate. Oh God, Hannah thought at that ominous sound, not more scratches on the slate floor! But there was no time to worry about the damage, because suddenly Penny was there in the doorway, staring into the dark hole in utter disbelief.

Behind Penny's head were the familiar shelves of the cold pantry, loaded with tins and cans and other odds and ends. Of course! The secret passageway had been concealed here, a space so chilly that Penny had suggested it was the cold heart of the house, where somebody must have died in the distant past and still haunted the spot.

Now though, the reason for the cold atmosphere was obvious. A draught blowing up from the cave below and under this door, especially in bad weather, had created the

cold spot. Not a ghost. And the door itself had been hidden away behind a hideous, gigantic Welsh dresser that had always looked too heavy to move.

Good job Penny was so strong, Hannah thought, as her friend wrenched the dresser back another few inches to let them escape.

'Where on earth did you two come from?' Penny asked, her mouth agape, but got no answer, the two of them clutching each other in helpless laughter, unable to say a word.

Once they had all taken some time to examine the door hidden behind the pantry dresser, Hannah suggested a slice of Christmas cake. Penny had been making some last-minute, mini-versions for the pageant feast – that was what Hannah had been able to smell through the gap in the door – but her large, family-sized one was ready to eat, and in a tin on the table. Sitting down with Raphael with a sweet and coffee seemed like a perfect opportunity to talk to him about his claim on the house, which had been worrying her ever since making the decision to go to bed with him. It was possible, after all, that his seduction – if it could be called that, given how she had grabbed him back – had some ulterior motive. A thought which left her feeling a bit hollow and unhappy. It was a possibility she had to face though, and could not dismiss until they had discussed it properly.

Raphael hesitated, glancing first at his watch and then outside at the bright sunshine. 'I should probably . . .'

'Penny's Christmas cake is famous.' She opened the tin, then set out some festive red-and-gold side plates, smiling as Penny disappeared upstairs, no doubt sensing that a

relationship chat was imminent and making herself scarce. 'Come on, ten minutes downtime won't hurt you. Besides, I want to ask you about Gabriel's IOU.'

His gaze came back to her face, his expression unreadable. 'I see.' He drew out a chair and sat down slowly. Then jumped up again, startled. 'Good God!' Peering under the table at what he'd nearly stood on, he hesitated, then picked up the tortoise, who instantly tucked in his legs and head. 'What the hell . . .?'

'Sorry, that's Slowtop. Penny's tortoise. Just put him on the floor over there, he likes to wander.'

His brows still raised, Raphael set the tortoise gently back on the slate floor and then sat down again. 'That cake does smell good.'

She made coffee, humming as she watched him nibble on a rich, fruity slice. At least now they could have that long-delayed conversation about his claim on Kernow House. Her intention was thwarted, however, when Lizzie burst in through the back door, two scrawny-looking rabbits dangling from her hand.

'Haven't lost me touch, look! I got these out at Long Field,' Lizzie began cheerfully, then stopped, silenced by the unexpected sight of Raphael Tregar in their kitchen, sitting down with Hannah, a tin of Christmas cake between them and fresh-made coffee in the cafetière. 'What are you . . .? Miss Clitheroe? Mr Tregar?'

Hannah jumped up to give her a hug.

'Lizzie, I'm so glad you're okay,' she said quickly. Penny had told her how upset Lizzie had been on hearing Hannah had gone looking for her in the snow. 'I was really worried

about you. We all were. Please don't ever run off like that again. You gave us all kittens.'

Then Hannah half laughed, glancing at the box by the Aga, where the tabby kittens were wide awake and playing noisily with each other. They looked even bigger than they had yesterday, she realised. They would soon need new sleeping quarters. Or better still, new owners.

'And we've already got enough kittens!' she added.

'I'm so sorry,' Lizzie said, and her eyes were shiny with tears. 'Miss Clitheroe, I'm really sorry.'

'Hannah,' she corrected her, smiling. 'Please can't I persuade you to call me Hannah?'

'Oh, Miss—' Lizzie hugged her back, awkward and ungainly. 'Hannah.' She wiped her face on her sleeve. 'Mr Tregar brung me home in his tractor. But they said you'd gone after me. I . . . thought you was lost.'

'It's okay. And thank you so much. If it wasn't for you, Raphael might never have found me. How did you know to tell him where to look?'

'Dunno.' Lizzie smiled at last. 'Just had a feeling to look by the cliff, is all. Is that where you was?'

'Yes, and thanks to your directions, Raphael found me. I stayed the night at his place because . . .' she hesitated, then finished calmly, 'because it was too late for him to drive me home. Not in all that heavy snow. So no harm done.'

Lizzie drew back to peer uncertainly at her bump. 'Baby . . . okay?'

'Baby is kicking like she wants to come out early,' Hannah said, putting a hand to her tummy, then saw all their horrified expressions and laughed. 'I'm sure she won't, though.

Just a turn of phrase. I've still got about three months to go before she pops out.'

She crossed her fingers though, superstitious enough to worry that her little incident last night – not just getting lost in the snow, but what came after – might have had some kind of effect on the baby's well-being.

'Why don't you join us, Lizzie? We're just about to have some of Penny's Christmas cake. And we found a secret door.'

Lizzie's eyes lit up at the mention of cake. Then her face darkened again. 'A secret door?'

'Don't worry, it's nothing spooky. It goes down to a cave at the base of the cliffs, that's all.' Hannah smiled. 'A smugglers' cave. Isn't that exciting?'

Penny bustled into the kitchen at that moment, her arms full of washing, and, seeing that Lizzie was there now, said that she would join them for coffee too. 'And I could do with a bite of that cake,' she said, winking at Lizzie as she fetched some extra plates, 'considering that I made it.'

She went to call Bailey from the bedroom, who came downstairs whistling cheerfully, obviously having been told about their unorthodox arrival. Bailey examined the secret door, and then sat down with them, demanding to know all about the cave too.

'Oh, before I forget,' Penny said to Hannah, 'you had a few phone calls while you were gone.'

'A few?'

'Eight or nine, actually. We lost count,' Bailey chipped in. 'The phone's been ringing nonstop all morning. I stopped answering it in the end.'

'I'm so sorry.' Hannah looked guiltily from Penny to

Bailey. 'Pageant business, is it? I suppose people are panicking last minute.'

'I think panicking is an understatement. Fenella was nearly in tears. She says the marquees for her refreshment stalls are the wrong size, and none of the St Piran flags she'd ordered for the table displays have arrived and she doesn't know what to do. Patricia Cobbledick rang to say the street jugglers have cried off, and should she ask the Morris men to do two spots back-to-back instead? Bethany from the fishmongers wants to know if it's okay to substitute mussels for prawns because one of their storage freezers broke down yesterday and they've lost all their shellfish. And Mr Knutson's wife says he's feeling peaky.'

'Peaky?'

'Gas attack. Apparently, Mr Knutson often gets bilious when he's nervous. But he should still be fine to play the Lord of Misrule come Boxing Day. Fingers crossed.' She smiled grimly at Hannah's despairing groan. 'There's more. Much more. I made a list. And said you'd get back to everyone once you were home.'

'Thanks,' she said drily.

Sinking back into her seat, Hannah met Raphael's wry gaze across the table. So much for having a private chat with him, she thought, a little annoyed. Damn it.

But at least Lizzie seemed unharmed by her own little adventure in the snow last night. It would be good to wheedle the truth out of her, if possible, about why on earth she had destroyed Trudy's tarot pack.

It seemed Raphael had read her thoughts again.

'So, Lizzie,' he said, solicitously pouring her a cup of

coffee and passing it across, 'you don't like tarot cards. Perfectly understandable. I don't believe in them myself. But why go to such a length to get rid of them?' When she stared at him, apprehensive, he added quietly, 'Hannah went to your camper van last night. She saw them – or rather, what remained of them.'

'I'm sorry, Mr Tregar,' Lizzie said again, twisting a clump of straggly hair around one finger as she looked around at their faces. 'I didn't mean nothing by it.'

'Nobody's angry with you, Lizzie, so there's no need to be upset.' Hannah kept her voice soft. 'But I think we're all curious. Why did you feel the need to *burn* the cards?'

'Coz of old Jack, that's why.'

Hannah frowned at her. 'You mean my grandfather? Jack Clitheroe?'

Lizzie nodded, her look conspiratorial now. 'She done the cards for him, didn't she? And that's when it happened. That's why I had to get rid of them. I couldn't leave 'em in the house. Not with Miss Clitheroe and the baby here. Them cards be too dangerous.'

Raphael held up a hand. 'Hang on,' he said, looking confused, 'let's backtrack a minute. Trudy did a tarot reading for her own husband?'

'That's right.' Lizzie looked petrified. Her voice dropped to a whisper. 'And that card was there, right on the end. The *evil* one.'

Bailey put down her slice of cake, untouched. Her face was serious. 'Do you mean to say the Death card came up in that reading?'

Lizzie nodded, her lower lip trembling.

'Well, that doesn't mean actual death,' Penny said, in a matter-of-fact way. 'It could simply indicate the end of something. Or even a new beginning.'

'No, no.' Lizzie shook her head, her eyes wide with remembered horror. 'Old Jack died that night. And he hadn't even been ill, or nothing. He just ... died. Stroke, the doctor said. But Trudy knew better. The cards done it, she used to say, and kept 'em locked away where they couldn't harm nobody else.'

CHAPTER THIRTY-EIGHT

They all looked at Lizzie in silence.

'Oh God, how awful for poor Trudy,' Bailey said at last, her face stricken. 'She must have thought . . .'

'That she caused his death?' Hannah suggested.

'Come on, that's impossible.' Raphael finished his coffee, and put the cup down firmly. 'Like Lizzie said, the man died of a massive stroke. I remember Gabriel telling me. Probably had arteries as clogged as the town drains. Nothing supernatural about that.'

'Of course it wasn't Trudy's fault,' Hannah told him, reaching across to squeeze Lizzie's hand, who was looking distressed. She hated to see her like that. 'But I can see why she might have felt guilty. Perhaps she thought it precipitated some kind of crisis in my grandfather.'

'You mean, the tarot reading may have brought on the stroke?' Penny looked at her thoughtfully. 'Yes, I can imagine how that might happen with someone suggestible. But was Jack Clitheroe suggestible? I rather thought he sounded quite the opposite sort of man.'

'It was them cards,' Lizzie insisted darkly. 'They done for him.' Then her look became defiant. 'So I done for them in

return. Now they're gone, all burnt up or cut to pieces, and you can sleep easy, Miss C—Hannah. You and the baby.'

Hannah was genuinely touched by Lizzie's loving concern. Not only for her, but her unborn child as well.

'Thank you, Lizzie. I know why you did it, because you wanted to help. That means a lot, it really does.'

Lizzie met her eyes, then gave a nod. 'You're welcome, Hannah.'

Clearing his throat, Raphael pushed back his chair and rose. 'Well, that cake was delicious, Penny. Thank you for that. But I really must be going. Sheep farms don't run themselves, and I have to pick up my car from Pethporro.'

'Let me give you a lift back to town,' Hannah said. 'No point you trudging all the way down there on foot when I've got a car outside.'

He agreed, and she found her car keys, then followed him outside.

Raphael was standing in the yard, head tilted back, looking up at a flock of birds circling in the cold, bright sky. She studied him from the back, his dark head, the casual way he was lounging, one hand in his coat pocket, the other shielding his eyes against the sun. There was something almost boy-like about him, she thought with a smile, and then suddenly wondered if he would ever be intimate with her again.

It was an odd question to be asking, given the passionate night they'd spent together, and the way he had laughed with her when Penny eventually let them out of that dank passageway. But there had been more than a touch of hesitancy about him this morning, as though he was already having regrets. She did not know why. But it had made her question her own

desire for him, suddenly afraid that feeling too much emotion for Raphael Tregar might devour her, and at a time when she needed to stay in control. To be sensible and grown-up, for the sake of the child inside her. Santos' child.

Was that why Trudy had rejected Gabriel, despite feeling enough for the man to meet him behind her husband's back?

Maybe his love had made her feel young and carefree, and that had clashed with her maternal instinct to protect her daughter and provide a stable home for her. She was guessing, of course. Her mum had never discussed her childhood much, and had been even less forthcoming about Hannah's grandmother. Once she became a teenager, the two of them had not got on. 'A personality clash,' her mum had said once, and shrugged, leaving it at that. Nor had Hannah thought to push for more information later, wrongly believing her grandmother to have died years before.

Yet the same war was going on inside her at the moment, these scary feelings of conflict and desire.

'I haven't forgotten your suggestion in the café, you know,' she said lightly, coming up behind him. 'And I agree, I'd love to see Trudy's replies to Gabriel, put the two sets of letters together.'

Raphael turned at once, and his gaze searched her face almost hungrily. There was a glow about him this morning that had nothing to do with the exercise they'd just done. She knew she had the same: when she'd nipped to the loo earlier, she'd seen her own eyes shining, and her skin dewy and lit up, as though she were seventeen again.

'I'll show you mine if you show me yours.'

Hannah held her breath, her smile uncertain. She loved to

be teased, but it felt like he was always making a joke out of what was most difficult and serious for her. Could she trust him to show her Trudy's letters if she brought Gabriel's over to the farm? She also badly wanted to ask about her grandfather's gambling debt, the IOU that might mean her house lawfully belonged to him, not her. They had come so close to discussing it but now she was wondering if she dared.

It would be more than she could bear if Raphael admitted to having slept with her because of that bond. Because he thought she might surrender the house more easily if she was sexually involved with him.

'Come on,' she said, deliberately not answering him, and unlocked her car. 'Jump in, I'll take you down to the harbour.'

He said nothing during the short, slushy drive into Pethporro, and she kept silent too, but her palms felt damp on the wheel despite the wintry chill. Would he expect her to kiss him goodbye? Hannah was seized with a sudden, terrible shyness and did not think she could handle him touching her again. What on earth was that about?

To her relief though, he got out in Pethporro without even offering her a kiss, murmuring a polite 'Thanks for the lift' instead.

But it seemed her brain was not strong enough to counter the urging of her body, because she leaned forward and heard herself say, 'Look, why not come to Christmas Day lunch, if you're not otherwise engaged? Penny's cooking, and I'm sure there'll be plenty to go round.' She hesitated. 'Maybe you could bring Trudy's letters over with you.'

His smile was dangerous. 'Maybe I could.'

Waking early on Christmas morning, Hannah stretched and yawned, then remembered what day it was and closed her eyes.

'Oh, Santos,' she whispered to the empty room.

Her first Christmas without him.

She had been too harried by the stress of work to think about it much over the past few weeks, though it had haunted her thoughts from time to time, bringing her down. But now, with a buffer zone of twenty-four hours before the frantic activity that Boxing Day would bring, Hannah had plenty of time to experience the reality of her bereavement. No Santos to kiss first thing on Christmas morning, no Santos to shower with gifts, no Santos to cuddle with after lunch, enjoying the peace and quiet of a day without work. All those little traditions they had built up as a couple, a blend of British and Greek, were all gone. Perhaps if she had stayed with his parents in Athens ...

But no, she did not regret leaving Greece, even if it did mean facing her daughter's birth without their support.

Here she had found independence, and some kind of solace in solitude, albeit one that was short-lived. Even now she could hear people moving about, floorboards creaking, the toilet flushing, and then the sound of carols playing down in the kitchen. Then she heard Lizzie shriek and footsteps thud along the upstairs landing.

Did she regret asking those noisy three to join her at Kernow House?

Not a bit.

In fact, despite her grief, she had probably never felt happier. Never so fulfilled and optimistic, at any rate. She was

busy, she had friends, and she had a gorgeous baby to look forward to. Whatever lay ahead, she was confident that she could deal with it.

Except possibly Raphael Tregar.

She had bought him a present, but it was a tongue-in-cheek one. Would he have bought her a present in return, though? If not, that could be awkward. Actually, the whole thing felt awkward. She did not even know if they were having a relationship or not, despite having spent the night with him. Which was an unfamiliar problem for her.

The door burst open and Lizzie tumbled into the room in old PJs borrowed from Penny, the top half buttoned up askew. 'Look, look!' She was holding aloft a gigantic old sock, gripped around the neck like one of her unfortunate rabbits. 'Santa came!' Then she pointed to the foot of Hannah's bed. 'He came for you too, Miss Clitheroe! You must have been a good girl.'

'I haven't been a good girl in years.' Hannah sat up in amused disbelief, then belatedly realised there was indeed a gigantic sock on the end of her bed too, presumably the fellow of the one in Lizzie's hand. The foot end bulged oddly, as though stuffed with a number of items. 'Oh my God, I got a stocking.'

She knelt up to retrieve it, and peered inside. There were several somethings wrapped in silver foil; one turned out to be a tangerine and the other a small lump of coal. Reaching into the toe of the sock, she found a candy walking stick, a multi-coloured party horn, a couple of uninflated balloons, and a packet of genuine Cornish fudge.

A little note stuck onto the fudge read, *Merry Christmas, love, Mrs Santa x*

She half laughed, feeling tears spring into her eyes at the same moment, and to her horror, burst into tears.

Lizzie stared, then dropped her sock on the bed and came to administer an awkward hug. 'What's the matter, Miss C— Hannah? Was it the coal? I got coal too, please don't cry. It's lucky to get coal in your stocking.'

'No, it's not the coal . . . I'm really pleased, honestly.' She tried to control her sobs, returning the hug as best she could, hampered with the goodies on her lap. 'I don't know why I'm crying. But this is so lovely, I can't seem to help it.'

Lizzie nodded, good soul that she was, seeming to find this perfectly acceptable logic. She perched on the bed next to Hannah, studying the contents of her own stocking before pulling out a party horn and blowing on it experimentally. 'I think Penny's Mrs Santa,' she whispered, and dropped the party horn back into the sock.

'I think she might be, yes.'

There was a pause, then Lizzie brightened. 'I'll go show Bailey. I bet she done got a stocking, too.'

Out she raced, and then stopped abruptly, hurrying back to the door to shout, 'Merry Christmas, Hannah!' before heading off again to Bailey's room, laughing and cheerful.

There were different levels of happiness, Hannah thought with a grin, listening to the excited chatter a few doors along. Today Lizzie was right up there on the top. If only she could reach those heights too. But there were so many steps, and she was not sure her heart was open enough yet.

CHAPTER THIRTY-NINE

Christmas morning seemed to fly by, and suddenly it was one o'clock, the time when Raphael had agreed to arrive for lunch. Penny appeared to be cooking the biggest turkey in the world, courtesy of a local farmer whose mother attended her Cornish language classes.

Preparations for lunch smelt delicious, the aroma of roast turkey and potatoes filling Kernow House, even filtering as high as the bedrooms, where Hannah sat cross-legged on her bed, wrapping the last of her presents for her friends. Later, she would have to make some final tweaks to Lizzie's costume for the Obby Oss, which was swathes of black chiffon with twisted black and red crepe ribbons, plus of course the horse's head, a massive papier-mâché creation she and Lizzie had made together in the kitchen, much to Lizzie's amusement, who had loved playing about with the strips of newspaper doused in glue.

Hannah only hoped everything else was in place by now for tomorrow's pageant. Boxing Day was almost at hand.

'He's here!' Bailey put her head around the door without knocking, and hurriedly recoiled at Hannah's high-pitched shriek of warning. 'Sorry!'

'You can't come in, you might see your present.'

'I can't believe you haven't wrapped it yet. We're going to be opening them right after lunch.'

'Erm, been rather busy, okay? Making Lizzie's costume,' she said, quickly folding gold paper around the perfume she'd bought for Bailey, 'not to mention finding last minute replacements for people who've dropped out of the pageant tomorrow.'

'If you say so. Anyway, come down, would you? You're a good friend but I can't be expected to entertain the local ogre on my own. After all, he's your ...' Bailey hesitated, then said delicately, '*guest*.'

The unspoken word, *boyfriend*, hovered in the air as she retreated down the stairs, still laughing.

When she'd gone, Hannah stuck a final piece of sticky tape on the parcel she'd been wrapping, then jumped up and examined herself in the mirror. She needed a haircut, she thought critically, and possibly a manicure too. But she'd do for a relaxed Christmas lunch with friends.

She hesitated before the mirror, inserting a pair of sparkly earrings she'd picked up in one of the lovely Cornish boutiques in Pethporro, and decided against any make-up. Friends, she reminded herself firmly. It could not be denied that Raphael was more than a friend, of course. But what was he?

Not my *boyfriend*, she thought firmly.

She wasn't ready for that.

But her heart seemed to know better, beating fast as she skipped downstairs, arms full of presents, hearing his deep voice in the kitchen, and the reassuring sound of laughter from her friends.

'Hello,' she said shyly, pushing through the kitchen door to find everyone there waiting for her. Bailey grinned, Lizzie waved cheerfully, and Penny held a spoon aloft in greeting, busy stirring something on top of the Aga. Bread sauce, by the look of the white gooey blob that dropped off her spoon. 'Looks like I'm last up – Oops!' One of the presents she was carrying fell to the floor – luckily nothing breakable, only some fluffy socks for Penny, who often trod the house barefoot – and she grabbed for it, missing. 'Damn.'

Raphael bent and retrieved the parcel, handing it back to her with an equally uncertain smile. 'Hello.'

'Thanks,' she said huskily, then headbutted the door-frame as she turned abruptly to retrace her steps. 'Ow, that hurt.' She straightened. 'I – I should probably put these under the tree.'

'Here, let me help you.'

Raphael followed her into the hall, accompanied by a tangy, Christmassy scent of citrus and spice. His aftershave, she guessed. He was wearing all black again, her absolute favourite. Black round-neck sweater over a black shirt, with his casual black jeans. Even his boots were black.

She felt the hairs rise on the back of her neck, deeply aware of him behind her as they entered the dining room. Someone had lit the fire in there, and the room was cosily warm, the lights flashing on the tinsel-clad tree, baubles glittering in the firelight. The eight-seater table was laid with a white damask tablecloth and shining cutlery and a glorious holly and ivy centrepiece with bright red berries dominated the table between two festive red candles, giving off a spicy fragrance as they burnt. Each setting boasted a

thick, red cloth napkin in a golden napkin holder, with a traditional Christmas cracker along the top.

'How beautiful!' she gasped, and he hurried forward to take some presents away from her, as though afraid she was about to drop the rest too. 'Thank you.' Hannah avoided his gaze. 'Under the tree, please.'

Together, they knelt to arrange the parcels under the tree. The space there was narrow and restricted, already heaped with parcels in shiny wrapping paper, decked with gold and silver bows, some tied up in red ribbons. The tree itself still looked and smelt marvellous, the fresh pine scent almost overwhelming.

With a somewhat bemused expression, Raphael peered up through the glittering, flashing branches. 'This tree certainly looks impressive now it's fully dressed,' he said with a wink, and got back to his feet. He turned to help her up. 'It was only ever me and Gabriel at Christmas. I'm not used to all this relentless festivity.'

'Me neither. My mum was never a big Christmas person.' Hannah made a face. 'Some years we didn't even put up decorations. And of course I didn't know my grandmother was still alive. Otherwise I would have come here.' She paused. 'And with Santos . . . Well, our Decembers tended to be spent organising skiing holidays for other people. So we rarely got a chance just to enjoy the season.'

'Poor Hannah.' He was smiling, almost mocking her, but there was a serious note to his voice too. 'Well, you're making up for all that "Bah, humbug" regime now.'

She nodded without speaking, her mouth suddenly dry.

They were standing very close, hands still touching. She

swore she could hear his heart beating, which was surely impossible. Yet there it was, a soft hammering just audible above her own. She stared into his dark eyes, and saw his pupils dilate, reflecting her own desire.

'Merry Christmas, Hannah,' he whispered, leaning forward, and touched his mouth to hers.

A mere brush of his lips at first, then the kiss deepened compulsively, and before she knew it, her arms were around his neck and she was pulling him against her.

Oh God, what was she doing?

He must have felt her stiffen, because he drew back and looked into her face. 'What's the matter?'

'Too fast,' she managed to say, pulling away. 'And too soon.'

'Too soon after Santos?'

She put a hand to her bump, her laugh a helpless croak. 'That,' she whispered, agreeing, 'and come on, this is hardly your responsibility.'

He studied her for a moment in silence, his face more sombre than she had ever seen it, no hint of laughter there now. 'Hannah,' he began carefully, but had no chance to continue as the door flew open.

Lizzie came in, bearing a stack of gold-edged dinner plates that Hannah had bought specially for Christmas. 'Food's nearly done,' she said breathlessly, and barged past them to slap the plates down on each setting. 'Penny says to wash your hands and help carry in the food. And you,' she said, nodding at Raphael, 'can carve, if you like. Though Penny says it's not because you're a man, it's because she's busy serving and you're the only one she trusts to do it right.'

Raphael looked at Hannah, who bit her lip in chagrin and

moved away, straightening one of the plates Lizzie had put down accidentally on top of a fork.

'Right,' he said, and disappeared into the hall.

Lizzie stared after him, suddenly downcast. 'Mr Tregar don't look too happy. Don't he want to carve?'

'No, it's not that.' Hannah rubbed Lizzie's arm. She felt things so strongly, Hannah thought, watching her friend with an aching heart. The slightest upset could send her to the dark side. 'Raphael's got something on his mind, that's all.' She managed a faint smile. 'Hey, nearly finished that costume for you. Just a few tweaks. You up for a last fitting tonight?'

Lizzie's eyes shone as she nodded. 'Pageant tomorrow, isn't it? Presents today, pageant tomorrow.' She grinned, and waved a cracker at Hannah. 'I like Christmas this year.'

Lunch tasted incredible, the best and definitely the largest Christmas meal Hannah had ever had. The turkey was moist, melting in the mouth under a coating of gravy, and the roasties were crisp on the outside and soft in the middle, exactly as they should be. They had sprouts with cracked almonds, a new experience for Hannah, oodles of buttered carrots, and the most gorgeous roast parsnips, done to perfection. Bailey served everyone a glass of champagne, though Hannah declined, not sure it would be wise in case she didn't stop at one glass. They all toasted Penny as head chef, who blushed but looked deeply pleased, especially when Bailey poked her with the business end of the carving fork; apparently this was a mark of affection. After the vast meal, since none of them felt inclined to move to the sofas

in the living room, they stayed at the table for party games and gift unwrapping.

Lizzie insisted on pulling several crackers with everyone, shrieking at each loud bang, so ended up wearing three paper crowns at once, her place setting piled high with cracker gifts. It was lovely to see her so happy.

They divided into two teams to play charades for half an hour, Hannah and Raphael paired against the other three, which left them all helpless with laughter. In the end, they called it a draw, and Bailey began to check gift tags and hand out presents to everyone, claiming she had always wanted to be one of Santa's elves.

Bailey seemed delighted with her perfume, kissing Hannah on the cheek, which started Penny growling, until she opened her pink slipper-socks and matching wash bag, shouting, 'Perfect! How did you know?'

Unwrapping a stylish new dressing gown from Hannah, Lizzie was left speechless for a short while, then recovered enough to jump up and hug Hannah so enthusiastically she found it hard to breathe.

As for Raphael, she had bought him a carved wooden shepherd's crook, picked up from a farming warehouse just outside Pethporro.

He opened his present with a grin, the shape of the parcel instantly giving away its contents. 'What's this, then?' he said, joking as he ripped away the festive wrapping. 'An umbrella?' Then he fell silent, stroking the neck of the wooden crook, admiring its lines. 'Thank you, Hannah,' he said in the end, his voice husky. 'I'll treasure this.'

She was surprised as well as pleased when he handed her

a small, plainly wrapped present at the end. 'You didn't need to . . .'

'Yes, I did,' he said firmly, and waited with obvious impatience until she had unwrapped it.

Hannah stared down at the small cache of letters inside the parcel, the folded paper a little worn, ink faded. 'Trudy's letters to Gabriel?'

He nodded.

'Oh, thank you.' She got up and kissed him on the cheek, but chastely, aware of everyone else in the room watching them with interest. Sitting down again, she hungrily pulled out the top letter, then checked everyone else had finished opening their gifts. 'May I? Does anyone mind?'

'Are you kidding?' Penny said, laughing. 'We all know what Gabriel said to Trudy – thanks to you finding the key to that box – now we're desperate to hear what she said in reply.' Having said that, though, she collected up the plates and left the table, saying casually, 'You start on the letters. I'll be back in five minutes with Christmas cake and coffee. Bailey, Lizzie, you want to help?'

The other two trailed out and shut the door, leaving her alone with Raphael.

He laughed. 'That was discreet of them, if a bit obvious.' Getting up with a groan, he threw another few logs on the fire. 'God, that meal was filling. I may not need to eat again for a week.'

But Hannah was already reading the first letter, head bent, finding it rather more difficult to decipher her grandmother's closely-written, flowing script than Gabriel's loose, spidery scrawl. She was vaguely aware of Raphael's voice

continuing, but his words were soon lost in the world of her grandmother's forbidden love triangle.

When she did not reply, Raphael sat down beside her at the table, and put a hand over hers. 'Hannah?'

Dazed, she looked up. 'What?'

'You didn't hear a word I said, did you?'

'No, I'm sorry.' Hannah put down the letter, glad to hear amusement in his voice and not reproach. 'I was reading. My God, thank you so much for bringing me these. This is fascinating, incredible stuff . . . I can hardly believe it.'

'I'm sure.'

She smiled. 'You were asking me something.'

'That's right.' Raphael stroked a long finger over the back of her hand, making her shiver. 'I wondered if you'd like to spend tonight over at my place. Then we could drive down to the pageant together tomorrow, get everything set up before the main event begins.'

Another night with Raphael. It sounded like the perfect end to a lovely day. The words 'yes, please' were on her tongue, but for some reason she couldn't say them.

Instead, she held out the letter she'd been studying.

'Read it,' she said quietly.

He hesitated, and then shook his head. 'If only I could. I've muddled through most of those letters several times already, and only managed to catch a few things. I'm afraid Trudy's handwriting has defeated me.'

'It was difficult to follow at first, but oddly enough, it's not dissimilar to my mum's handwriting, so I've got the hang of it. Here, listen to this.' Hannah put the letter back on her lap, ignoring the slight trembling of her hands, and

began to read aloud from it. '*It broke my heart when Cynthia wrote to me in London and told me you were engaged. I rang the farm, and your dad answered. He said it was true, and I had no reason not to believe him. I thought it was all over between us. That me going to London had been the final straw for you. So when Jack turned up, looking for me at the nurses' home, I let him take me out. You have to understand, you'd left me so cold and alone, any comfort was welcome. Even Jack Clitheroe.*'

She stopped and looked up at him eagerly, but his face was distant and expressionless.

'Well? Don't you see what happened between them?' She tapped the letter, her eyes stinging with unshed tears for the woman she had never known. 'Gabriel and Trudy were in love when they were younger. But then she must have gone off to train as a nurse in London – I do recall Mum saying something about Trudy having worked in a hospital before she married my grandfather – and while she was gone, Gabriel started seeing someone else. So Trudy did too.'

'It sounds more like she got the wrong end of the stick. Or was misinformed.' He raised his eyebrows when she began shaking her head. 'Think about it. That Cynthia girl wanted him for herself, I expect. Or maybe Gabriel's father disapproved of their relationship. I don't think Trudy's family had much money. Perhaps he reckoned if he could put her off Gabriel, she'd look elsewhere for a boyfriend.' His ironic smile did not reach his eyes. 'And she found one easily in Jack Clitheroe, didn't she?'

'Sorry, how on earth do you work that out?'

'*I had no reason not to believe him,*' he quoted.

'You think Gabriel's dad was lying to her? And this friend

of hers, Cynthia . . .' She studied the letter again, frowning. 'You're suggesting Cynthia put Trudy off him deliberately, so she could go out with Gabriel instead?'

He shrugged, almost laconic. 'Why not?' He took one of the other letters and glanced down at it. 'All these letters have a similar theme. She says she loves him. That she was heartbroken when he went off with someone else, and that's why she fell into bed with Jack.' His voice sounded brooding. 'But it seems to me that she was the one who left. She abandoned Gabriel, not the other way around. Then came home and married Jack Clitheroe.'

'Yes,' she said angrily, 'because she was pregnant by him.' She shook the letter at him. 'She says so right here at the end.'

Raphael looked at her face, no doubt taking her flush as a consequence of sitting too close to the fire, and then dropped the letter he'd been holding onto the table.

'I rest my case,' he said softly.

'Oh my God.' She stared at him in disbelief. 'It sounds almost like you blame Trudy for what happened.'

'Maybe I do.'

'Let me read you the rest of the letter.'

'I'd rather you didn't.' He drained his glass, and then added, 'Look, the others will be back in a minute, and you haven't given me an answer about tonight.'

'That's because I haven't made up my mind yet,' she said, her voice shaking, and picked up the letter again. 'Going by what she writes here, by the time Trudy discovered Gabriel wasn't in fact engaged or involved with someone else, it was too late and she was carrying Jack's child.'

'She didn't love Jack Clitheroe,' he said flatly. 'That's the simple fact of the matter. She loved Gabriel, and he loved her. Yet despite knowing that, she went ahead and married the wrong man. And ruined both their lives.'

'Good grief, what earthly choice did she have?'

'We always have a choice.'

'Not every time. And not everyone. Especially when a child is involved.'

'We always have a choice,' he said again.

Hannah studied his impassive face, barely able to believe this was the same man who had made love to her so passionately. The man she had fallen in love with, if her heart was to be believed.

She paused, then asked, 'Do you seriously believe Gabriel Tregar would have married Trudy after what she'd done, knowing he'd be raising another man's child as his own, and in full view of the Clitheroes, too?'

'Yes, I do.' Raphael stood up. 'Because I'd do the same myself, without a second thought.' Then he bent to kiss her cheek, his lips cool and impersonal. Collecting the carved shepherd's crook, her Christmas gift to him, he left the room, saying over his shoulder, 'Thanks for lunch, Hannah. No, don't get up. I'll see myself out.'

CHAPTER FORTY

The morning of the Boxing Day pageant dawned bright and clear, much to Hannah's relief. She had feared a downpour, or even a repeat of the freezing snowfest they'd suffered the week before Christmas, but the weather couldn't have been better. The sun shone benignly on the ocean and a light wind ruffled the rough cliff grasses as Hannah carried Lizzie's elaborate Obby Oss costume to the car, where she called back to Lizzie to hurry up. 'I've got to meet a few members of the pageant committee before it all kicks off, so I hope you're ready to leave. The others are driving down on their own later.'

Hannah put her own costume in the back of the Land Rover, a green and yellow satin affair with a ribbon-festooned headdress, having decided to dress up as a Cornish 'piskie' for the pageant. By the time she was seated behind the steering wheel, Lizzie had arrived, flushed with excitement, her long grey hair having been plaited into pigtails by Bailey after breakfast, and then pinned together on the back of her head, ready for the horse mask to slip over it.

She tucked herself in beside Hannah, and struggled with the seat belt. 'Ready now.'

'Right, here goes.' Hannah had her fingers crossed as she turned the car around in the muddy yard, which was difficult enough, hoping to goodness that nothing went wrong today, nobody else called in sick, none of the tourists had any accidents, and the elderly tea urn they'd hired for the refreshments tent didn't explode, which Fenella had suggested might be a possibility. 'Pethporro pageant, here we come.'

She roared along the narrow Cornish lanes like she'd been born to them, too stressed to care if anyone was coming the other way, her mind racing as fast as the tyres.

She'd purposefully put Raphael out of her mind overnight. The pageant was her job and had to come first. Also, she was aware of a strange feverishness whenever she remembered their conversation yesterday, an uncertainty that came of not knowing exactly what he had meant, nor why he had left so abruptly. Presumably he was equating Trudy's situation with her own, simply because of her pregnancy, though in fact it was in no way similar.

Santos was dead, and she had loved him first. No similarity there. But if Raphael was saying that he would happily raise her child as his own . . .

Well, she did not know what to say to that, and was a little afraid of such a fierce commitment, not least because she herself was still unsure of Raphael.

Or rather, unsure how she felt about him.

It was probably love, because everything wobbled inside whenever she thought of him, a sure sign from her youthful days of dangerous infatuation. But was it a love that would last? Would their feelings survive the howling stress of the first months of life with a new baby? And then there was all

the rest of it, including raising Hannah's daughter until she was old enough to leave home, a stern responsibility without having fathered her himself.

Reading her grandmother's letters to Gabriel last night had been an eye-opener. 'One stupid mistake', that's what Gabriel had blamed for the irrevocable split in their relationship.

Was she making a similar mistake now, pushing Raphael away out of guilt, worried about betraying Santos' memory?

'Slow down!' Lizzie pointed to a fox in the lane ahead, and Hannah hit the brakes and swerved, though of course it was already through a gap in the hedge by then. 'Foxie,' Lizzie said with obvious relish, twisting around to see if she could spot it in the field beside them. 'Vixen, she were. Hope she don't come too near town. It's not safe for the likes of her.'

Hannah frowned, shaking away her tangled thoughts with difficulty. 'You're not still nervous about going into town, are you?'

'Not so bad these days. Not when I'm with you.' Lizzie beamed at her. 'Even if you do drive proper Cornish now. You was giving th' hedges a close shave back there. Just watch out for foxies and badgers, and hoot your horn on corners, case of deer. Them wild ones don't look for cars.'

'You know so much about country life,' Hannah said, impressed.

'Oh, you will too, soon enough,' Lizzie said, nodding in a reassuring manner, 'if you marries Mr Tregar. Then you'll have two farms between you.'

'If I marry . . .' Hannah slowed, staring at her. 'What on

earth are you talking about? What have Bailey and Penny been saying to put that idea in your head?'

She squirmed in her seat, uncomfortable. 'Nothing.'

'Lizzie!'

'Only that you and Mr Tregar spent the night together when the snow came. So now you'll be married.' Lizzie paused, looking worried. 'Won't you?'

'Of course not. We're not living in the Victorian age.'

'Right.' Lizzie nodded, staring resolutely out of the window as they entered Pethporro. 'Just as well, any how. Mrs Clitheroe, old Trudy, she wouldn't have held with that. A Tregar in Kernow House. Definitely not.'

Hannah frowned. 'What makes you say that?'

'Only that she said it often enough herself.' Lizzie shrugged. '*I won't have no bloody Tregar in my house*, she used to say when Gabriel came past in his tractor. Called him rude names too, and didn't care who heard her. Old Gab tried to come round after Jack died, oh, many times. But Trudy, she'd fetch her shotgun and fire out the window at him, even when it was dark and she might hit him. *Get away from my house, Tregar,* she'd shout. I used to hear her in the night, shouting the odds at him.' She grinned. 'So poor Gabriel, he had to go home again, without even a kiss.'

'Good God.' Hannah was shaken. 'I had no idea.'

'It was just like in them letters of hers you read last night,' Lizzie said simply, playing with one of her plaits. 'She didn't hold with adul – adul—'

'Adultery,' Hannah said, then glanced at her sharply. 'Don't pull on your plaits, Lizzie. Please, don't. The horse's

head won't fit if you mess up your hair.' But she bit her lip. 'But if Jack was dead . . .'

'She didn't want no man after Jack Clitheroe,' Lizzie said darkly. 'That's what she'd say to me.'

'Was Jack that bad a husband?'

It was horrible to think of her grandfather as a possible wife-beater, even if she had never known him.

Lizzie shrugged. 'Don't rightly know the ins and outs of it.' Then she pointed ahead, suddenly excited, forgetting all about Trudy's tangled affairs. 'Look, Morris men! Morris men in the road!'

Hannah slowed to a crawl, conscious of Lizzie's mild air of apprehension as they reached the built-up area of the town, and drove carefully past the group of Morris men. The traditional dancers appeared to be practising on their way to the refreshments tent which marked the start of the pageant route. Enchanted by their strange green-and-white costumes, and their sticks and bells, Lizzie stared after them even longer than she'd stared after the fox. Then she settled back in her seat afterwards with a sigh, saying dreamily, 'I love them Morris men.'

'Perhaps you could dance with them during the pageant.'

'*Dance* with the Morris men?' Lizzie turned huge eyes on her, apparently shocked by that suggestion. 'Oh no, no . . . I couldn't do that. They keep away bad spirits.' She pursed her lips. 'Bad men, too.'

Hannah grinned.

They had all sat around the dining table yesterday, long after Raphael had gone and well into the dark evening,

reading Trudy's letters to Gabriel, and setting them alongside Gabriel's letters to her, trying to find a timeline and a likely order, given the lack of dates on both sets. It had become increasingly obvious that Gabriel, although deeply in love with Trudy, had failed to get her into bed. And that Trudy, while rejecting his amorous advances, received his secret letters with obvious pleasure, and replied to them with a contradictory mixture of anger and affection. She had spoken of duty towards her husband and daughter, and a desire to do things 'right' even if it meant her unhappiness.

The letters appeared to have been left down in the cave, either collected from there or exchanged in person, to avoid Jack knowing about their continuing relationship, if it could be called that. But there was no hint that they had slept together after her marriage to Jack, or indeed after Jack had died, though the letters must have stopped long before that event, since there was never any mention of his death in any of them.

She had always assumed that once her grandfather had died, Trudy might well have permitted some intimacy between herself and Gabriel.

But the bitterness that leaked through in the early letters must have made Trudy regard him as an enemy once they were older. Because Lizzie's account of the old lady's behaviour when Gabriel did finally come courting – firing a shotgun at the poor man in the dark – would seem to suggest there was no physical desire left by then. Or none that Trudy planned to act upon.

It was awful, she thought sadly, turning into the public car park at Pethporro, to think there had been such love

between them once. Yet one stupid misunderstanding, fuelled by jealousy and insecurity, had driven two lovers apart who were probably otherwise perfect for each other.

The most interesting thing was that Gabriel had never married, even after it must have been obvious that Trudy would not leave Jack Clitheroe for him.

Had he hung on after her marriage, hoping Jack might die young, or even divorce her, and he could then claim Trudy for his own? If so, he must have been so hurt and disappointed when his chance finally came, but instead of a welcoming kiss, he nearly got his head shot off.

She could not imagine Raphael hanging on that long for another man's wife.

Nor did she think she would ever shoot at an old friend out of a window, just because he would not take no for an answer.

Though maybe if he kept on at her long enough . . .

Once she had parked, they walked swiftly back into the town centre from the car park, carrying their costumes under their arms.

'We'll change later,' she kept reassuring Lizzie, who was fussing, concerned that she ought to be wearing her horse's head. They passed Nancy going the opposite way, who had left her scarf in the car. She looked absolutely massive and about to pop at any moment, but grinned cheerily at Hannah and Lizzie. 'I don't know where everyone is going to park,' Nancy called out. 'There are so many people already here, this is going to be mega!'

Several dozen people were assembled near the refreshment

tent, which was flapping in a stiff breeze from the sea. Patricia Cobbledick was inside, chatting with a group of local dignitaries, including the mayor. Turning swiftly away before she could be roped into some long-winded conversation, Hannah spotted Fenella and her helpers, carrying in the dodgy tea urn.

'How's it going?'

After listening to Fenella's list of complaints about what wasn't working, and who had called in sick, Hannah reluctantly headed over to meet the mayor and the few members of the committee who had bothered to turn up for the pre-pageant consultation.

Raphael was not among them, she noted, dismissing the little stab of hurt at his absence and pinning on a bright smile instead.

Everything went smoothly until about half an hour before the pageant was due to start, when it transpired that Mr Knutson had come down with what sounded suspiciously like man flu, and so would not be able to take on the role of the Lord of Misrule. Instead, he had sent the costume down with his wife and a note of apology.

'You're joking?' Hannah read his note, and felt like weeping openly in the street. 'We can't do this without a Lord of Misrule.'

Luckily, Penny and Bailey had turned up by then, bearing home-made cakes and sandwiches for Fenella's various refreshment stalls. They persuaded Hannah that someone could be found to replace Mr Knutson, even last minute.

'Honestly, we'll be able to find someone to do it,' Penny said, examining the costume with a thoughtful expression.

'I can even be Lady of Misrule myself if necessary. I'm about the right height.' She smiled at Hannah. 'Relax, we're on this. Go do your job.'

Hannah turned her attention to health-and-safety matters instead, checking the pageant route was clear of traffic and any dangerous obstacles. She left Lizzie struggling into her costume with Bailey's help, and briskly walked the route with a clipboard in her Cornish piskie costume, ticking off all the risk assessment points she'd agreed with the council.

By the time she got back, the street was packed with tourists in thick coats and woolly hats and scarves. A camera crew from BBC Spotlight South West had arrived to film the event, and the pageant was almost due to start. She spotted Caroline in the crowd, the nurse looking tall and elegant as ever in a knee-length blue coat, and lifted a hand in greeting. Her next antenatal check-up was due in just over a week.

Freezing in her satin piskie costume, the thin material straining a little over her baby bump, Hannah stopped and ran her gaze down the pageant line.

Still no sign of Raphael, she thought, frowning.

He had not stated categorically that he would attend, of course. But as Bailey said, waiting impatiently alongside her, hair blowing in her eyes, 'It seems odd that Raphael hasn't turned up yet, considering this is his baby.'

Hannah almost choked.

The marching band was right at the front, all the dancers and costumed actors in their pre-arranged starting positions behind them. In the middle of the pageant came the Morris men, followed by a series of Cornish-themed floats, mostly sponsored by local businesses. After that came a

primary school group of tiny, red-hatted children acting out the Hunt of the Wren, with a troupe of traditional musicians, including drummers, guitarists, fiddlers, and a wild-haired accordion player bringing up the rear.

It was annoying to note the continuing absence of a Lord of Misrule. But she had no time to worry about that; she would give the final toast herself if Penny and Bailey were unable to find a replacement. It was more important to start exactly on time, not least to beat the grim clouds gathering on the horizon.

The mayor of Pethporro appeared in his robes and heavy-looking gold chains to give his opening address, bowing comically to everyone for some minutes before Hannah finally nudged him to speak.

The crowd listened politely and then clapped at the end, except for a baby in a buggy who screamed all the way through his speech. 'With due solemnity, therefore, I pronounce our first-ever Pethporro Boxing Day pageant . . .' The mayor paused for effect, then finished with a roaring shout, 'Ready to be off!'

Relieved, Hannah gave the signal for the music to start, and the marching band set off with a dramatic roll of drums, the crowd applauding on all sides. The costumed dancers followed on, waving long ribbon streamers, with the actors coming after in their masks and festive outfits.

At that instant, she saw a tall, dark figure with a beaked mask emerge from a side street and insinuate himself into the pageant.

The Lord of Misrule!

Hannah wondered who Penny had got to play the part.

Somebody taller than Mr Knutson, she thought, because the black robes were a little short, brushing the ground rather than trailing behind as they were supposed to.

Jumping into the pageant as it wove past the refreshment tent, she tried to ignore the nagging ache in her ankles. She squeezed past Gog and Magog, the two 'giants' wobbling along impressively on stilts, and fell in behind Harold from the bakery, who had come dressed as a Christmas pudding, and was handing out discount fliers for cake as he waddled along. She decided not to say anything, but frowned at him in her best Cornish piskie way.

Thank God, she kept thinking, smiling madly and waving at the crowds of tourists on either side of the route. The pageant was finally happening, and so far nothing had gone wrong. Fingers crossed, she thought, looking ahead to the ruffled waves of the sea out in Pethporro Bay.

The pageant took longer than anticipated to reach the sea, largely because the marching band got into difficulties at a crossroads where someone had ignored the makeshift barriers and driven a farm trailer across, blocking half the road while they stopped and tried to remove the barrier on the other side. After some delay, Hannah hurried forward to see what was happening, and finally managed to clear the obstruction so the pageant could move on.

As she tried to find her place again among the Cornish characters, a hand grabbed her arm, whisking her around in a mad dance, then releasing her back into the group. Startled, she peered up at the beaked mask of the Lord of Misrule. Before she could say anything he had already gone, a long

ribboned stick of some kind in his hand, his black cloak whirling about his figure.

As she stumbled after him, staring, Lizzie appeared between the people in her Obby Oss costume, neighing frantically, her huge papier-mâché horse's head bouncing on her shoulders. It looked uncomfortable, but Lizzie seemed to be enjoying herself immensely. It was like Christmas morning all over again.

'Watch thou for the Obby Oss!' Lizzie kept shouting, her voice echoing strangely inside the head. 'Or get thee with child.'

Bit late for me, Hannah thought ironically.

All the same, she protected her bump as the large black 'horse' barged past her. This was Cornwall, after all, and stranger things had been known to happen here. She didn't want her baby to turn out to be twins.

Lizzie's large black cape spun out, just catching young women in the crowd, who shrieked with laughter and ducked away. Behind her came two Teasers, men with sticks and what looked suspiciously like sheep skulls, which they shoved towards the shrieking women. Then they chased Lizzie too, who galloped off singing a song she'd apparently recalled from some long-ago midnight procession, the lyrics of which sounded very rude. But she was having tremendous fun, so Hannah let it go.

It was a long and circuitous route through Pethporro, and by the time they finally reached the sea, dusk was beginning to fall. The pageant followed the slipway onto the shingle beach, heading for the sea, the tide already on its way out. There were paper lanterns along the way, and

flaming torches stuck into the sand at intervals. The second of their refreshment tents was on the beach itself, serving alcohol and snacks, and was lit up by hundreds of flashing Christmas lights, powered by a generator.

They passed the tent, the musicians playing traditional Cornish songs now instead of carols, and headed for the water's edge. There, amid cheers and applause, the pageant came to a halt. Hannah pressed through the crowd to the front, dazzled by the flaming torches and blinking at the dark. She saw Jennifer among the people watching, standing beside Caroline, and held her breath. Were the two women friends? That might explain why Caroline had spoken so harshly about Raphael during her first antenatal check-up.

The Lord of Misrule began to speak, his voice deep and booming in his beaked mask, and everyone along the shore fell silent.

He was praising the people of Pethporro and wishing them a peaceful year ahead, a good harvest from the sea, and the wisdom of the ages. And as he spoke, he scattered white flower petals into the water, which was lapping in frothy waves about his feet and the wet hem of his robes.

Hannah, staring at the Lord of Misrule, become aware of someone beside her. It was Penny. 'How did you manage it?' she whispered.

Penny smiled. 'Manage what?'

'To persuade Raphael to be the Lord of Misrule.'

But there was no answer, and when she turned, surprised, she saw Penny drifting away from her in the crowd, a smile on her face . . .

*

Locals and visitors alike danced on the beach until it was pitch-black out to sea, and the threatening clouds began to spit rain, finally silencing the musicians. Slowly, in twos and threes, the crowd began to disperse, some still hugging plastic beakers of Cornish ale, until the only ones left were members of the pageant committee and the clean-up crew. And Lizzie, still dashing about the sands in her Obby Oss costume, neighing like a horse at anyone who would listen, not even remotely drunk, but loving the moment.

There was no sign of Jennifer again. With any luck, she had only turned up in the hope that Hannah would make a mess of running the pageant, and she could gloat over her failure.

Except she hadn't made a mess of it. More by luck than judgement, perhaps.

But still.

Shuffling with fatigue, Hannah collected a binbag and began to hunt for rubbish on the sands before the tide turned to sweep it all away. But as she bent for her third discarded beer can, a hand clamped about her wrist.

'What do you think you're doing?'

It was Raphael, still in his beaked mask, his hair a mass of black ribbons. He looked down at her as though from a great distance, his head slightly turned because of where the eye-holes were situated in the mask.

She frowned, straightening. 'Tidying up, of course.'

'Leave that to the cleaners. That's what they're paid for.' His grip tightened when she tried to continue. 'For God's sake, Hannah, you must be exhausted. You've barely stopped for weeks.'

'I can sleep all day tomorrow. And the next day too. Tonight, I intend to help with the clean-up.'

He took away her binbag. 'You're about to fall over.'

'No, I'm not.' She swayed, her eyes nearly closing, and wished he wasn't such a bloody know-it-all. He certainly looked the part in that sinister mask, she thought. 'Please go away, Raphael, there's a good ogre.'

'Come on.' He removed his beaked mask and gave her a direct look. 'You've done a fantastic job here. But now it's over. I'll drive you home.'

'I don't need a lift. My car's in the car park.' Hannah tried to snatch her binbag back. With an infuriating lack of effort, he held it out of her reach. 'And what about Lizzie?'

Lizzie came galloping past at that moment, neighing and spattering them with sand. 'Oops, sorry. You two going home? Can I come too? It's a long walk back to Kernow House.' She sounded plaintive, and was shivering. 'I won't get in the way if you want to kiss.'

'Lizzie!'

Raphael merely grinned, however. 'You can come with us, and welcome. But there'll be no kissing, I promise.'

Hannah felt a bit cold suddenly, and pulled away from him. He glanced at her through narrowed eyes, but said nothing.

'I'll drive you home,' she said, linking arms with Lizzie and hugging her close. 'Unless you'd rather go with Raphael.'

Lizzie looked from her to him, and then whispered in her ear, 'Best give him a chance to have his say, Miss Clitheroe. He don't mean no harm. He's not the type.'

Hannah was astonished.

But she gave in at that point, and either he heard Lizzie's hoarse whisper, or sensed Hannah's acquiescence, because he gave her a little smile and took her other arm.

'Come on,' he said.

If that smile had held even a hint of triumph, she would probably have grabbed that binbag and strangled him with it. But it was carefully neutral, giving no clue to his feelings.

Raphael steered them away from the clean-up operation, past the men taking down the beer tent, and up the torchlit path towards the roadway. At some point he must have brought his car down to the strand, she realised, because almost as soon as they were off the beach, he produced his key, and helped her inside his flashy BMW. Lizzie scrambled into the back seat, and within minutes they were in the warm darkness of his car, purring up the hill back out of Pethporro.

What were they doing together? She kept asking herself that question, and only came up with the most depressing answers. He was a loner, and she was ... bereft. Hardly a promising combination.

At Kernow House, Lizzie dashed straight inside with a cheery goodbye to Raphael. No doubt she was exhausted after her matchmaking efforts, Hannah thought, watching her disappear. The lights were on downstairs, so presumably Bailey and Penny had also returned and were still up, perhaps having some late night cocoa.

'Why did you change your mind?' she asked, still on her

mettle. 'I thought you had something better to do today than play the Lord of Misrule.'

'I only refused because I knew I'd have to turn up to rehearsals in town week after week, and—'

'You didn't want to see my face that often.' Suddenly weary and forlorn, Hannah groped for the door handle. 'I get it.'

'No, wait,' he said, and touched her cheek. She turned at once, seeking out his face in the gloom. 'It was the other way round. I didn't think you'd want to see *my* face that often. In fact, I thought it would be better if we kept apart. At least until you knew what you wanted.' He met her eyes. 'Do you know yet? Or do I have to wait a little longer?'

She stared, speechless, not knowing how to answer that, and he leaned forward to kiss her. Tiredness fell away at his touch, and desire flickered inside her instead, suddenly fierce and hungry. She did know what she wanted, she thought hotly. She wanted to ask this man up to her bedroom. To spend the night with him again, whatever people in Pethporro might be saying behind their backs.

Then she remembered Jennifer on the beach tonight, the cold, intent expression on her face as she listened to Raphael's speech. Caution warned her to stay away from any man who could make a woman look at him so furiously.

Besides, Raphael had slept with her the night of the snows, then barely come near her since then. Oh yes, she thought bitterly, he had invited her home with him last night. But he was only after one thing, and it wasn't her body. Nor was he nobly waiting for her to make up her mind about him, as he claimed. Because Raphael Tregar still held

Jack Clitheroe's gambling debt, and increasingly that knowledge felt like a sword between them.

'No,' she said unevenly, and pushed him away before opening the car door.

He was surprised, staring. 'But you want me.'

'And you want Kernow House.'

He did not deny it. But she could see anger in his face.

Hannah got out and slammed the door shut. Seconds later he had turned the BMW and was gone, only the red rear lights showing in the murky distance as the car vanished down the lane. From inside the outbuilding, she heard one of the geese give a belated honk of alarm, then fall silent again.

Raphael Tregar had got the message. In fact, she doubted he would ever come to see her again. It was a thought that ought to have made her ecstatic.

Odd, then, that she felt so empty inside.

CHAPTER FORTY-ONE

Hannah woke early to the sound of music. It was barely dawn and Kernow House was cold and quiet, as though caught into sleep under some spell of winter. Frowning, she lay listening to the music for a moment, until she had identified it as jazz of some kind, then swung her legs out of bed. Her feet and legs still ached from walking the entire pageant route – three times, if she counted checking it beforehand – and then dancing until late on the beach. But she took a deep breath and found her slippers, shuffling to the bathroom before heading downstairs.

Her trips to the loo were becoming increasingly frequent, she thought, aware of that fluttery sensation again. The baby was moving inside her. Turning around, perhaps? Then a kick made her eyes widen.

'Gently now,' she said in a reassuring murmur, and put a hand to her stomach. She had found herself talking to the baby recently, as though her child could hear and understand her, which was probably nonsense. But it made her feel better to have these little conversations with her unborn daughter. 'I know it's early, but I need to find out who on earth is downstairs, playing jazz of all things.'

When she got downstairs, she checked in all the main rooms, but they were empty and she could not isolate the source of the music. Yet it was clearly coming from somewhere. She was not imagining it.

She stood at the back door, shivering and staring at a few desultory flakes of snow drifting past in the grey dawn light. The rain had blown away overnight, and the temperature had dropped sharply, leaving frosted window panes and icy puddles in the yard.

And now these beautiful snowflakes were falling . . .

Abruptly, the music stopped.

Some high-pitched squeals caught her attention instead, and she turned with a frown, closing the back door quietly. The squeals came again from the pantry, where a chill draught was still blowing through into the kitchen. Penny and Raphael had shoved the Welsh dresser further along the wall until it was no longer obstructing the once-hidden entrance. But easier access had only exacerbated the air blowing up from the cave.

Hannah guessed it must be a kitten she could hear squeaking. The mother cat was sitting upright near the Aga, licking her fur without much interest, but several of her kittens were missing from the high-sided box.

'Hello, kitty, are you in here?'

She pushed the pantry door open, and laughed at the sight of two of them rolling on top of each other in a play-fight.

'Naughty kitties! Come here, you two.' But the litter-mates scattered as soon as she headed for them, dodging back between her legs into the kitchen. She didn't follow

them though. There was another kitten in the pantry, a delicate tabby with one white-tipped ear. It was scratching at
something lodged under the door to the secret passage.
Something that looked like a discarded piece of paper. 'Hang
on a minute, puss-cat, I don't think you should be playing
with that. What is it?'

She bent and scooped the kitten up in one hand, and the
torn piece of paper in the other. To her surprise, it wasn't a
lost bill or receipt, but a tatty old napkin, with something
written on it in faded ink.

She read aloud, '*I, Jack Earnest Clitheroe, owe you, Gabriel
Tregar, the deeds to my property, Kernow House, Pethporro,
Cornwall . . .*'

Her voice died away.

Hannah jumped violently at a knock on the other side of
the door to the secret passage. Her heart sped up, and her
grip on the kitten tightened so much the poor thing
squeaked in protest.

'Sorry,' she muttered, stroking its head.

The tiny kitten seemed to forgive her at once. It began to
purr, a warm ball of fluff in her arms, kneading her with
surprisingly sharp claws.

Hannah stared at the old door. It was still shut and locked,
the key sitting in its ancient lock. So who on earth could be
standing in the smugglers' passageway, knocking to be let
through into the house, especially at this godforsaken time
of the morning?

The answer was so obvious, it made her catch her breath,
half in fury, half in delight.

'Bloody man, scaring the life out of me and the cats!'

Still holding the kitten, she folded the napkin IOU into her fist, then wrestled with the key. As soon as the door was unlocked, it began to open, and she hopped backwards, staring crossly.

Raphael Tregar.

He was shivering too, she realised, despite wearing his thick coat and a black scarf wound twice around his throat. He wasn't wearing a cap though, and his dark hair was damp and slicked back.

'Good morning, Miss Clitheroe.' He stopped on the threshold when she did not move aside, raising his eyebrows at her terse expression. 'Come on, who did you expect it to be? Barnacle Bill? Or perhaps some Cornish smuggler with an eye-patch, come to sell you brandy?'

'What are you doing here, Raphael?'

He looked down at the floor, as though hunting for something, then spotted the paper napkin trapped in her fist. 'You found it, then?'

She said nothing, waiting.

'I've been here for hours,' he said huskily. 'I tried knocking at first but nobody heard me. Too early, I suppose. So I started playing music through the door on my iPhone, to get your attention. Finally, I heard someone come downstairs, so I pushed that note partway under the door. Special delivery.' His smile faded when she did not say anything. 'Someone pulled it through from the other side, so I thought . . . But then the door stayed shut.'

Hannah showed him the kitten. 'Here's who you delivered it to.'

'Oh.' He stroked under the kitten's chin, his look rueful. 'I

wanted you to be the first to read it. Then I was going to go home, job done.'

'So why didn't you, then? Why knock on the door too?'

She was being rude and adversarial, she knew, but couldn't seem to stop. Yes, he had brought her the IOU she had wanted to see. But why? It was so hard to understand his motives. And her own head was such a tangle of messy emotions, she couldn't cut through them to find the right response. Except that she knew it was over between them. They had established that without question last night. Hadn't they?

Raphael paused, then said reluctantly, 'The tide's still blocking the entrance to the cave. So I can't safely leave that way. Or not yet. I reckon another hour or so.' He met her gaze. 'I can go back down those steps and wait in the cave if you prefer. But it's very damp and cold.'

She stood back and let him into the house, then struggled to push the door shut. He helped her, then locked it again.

'In case of smugglers,' he said, when she raised her eyebrows.

Automatically, she handed him the kitten, and then went through into the kitchen to put the kettle on. She was desperate for a tea, if only to distract herself from his presence. Besides, Raphael looked half-frozen. She could hardly leave him there without a hot drink, waiting for pneumonia to strike.

He sat at the table and watched her, stroking the kitten until it squealed again, struggling to be free. Then he put it gently down on the floor, where it scampered away to be with its brothers and sisters. Out of the corner of her eye,

Hannah noticed the tortoise, Slowtop, helping himself to some lettuce in his dish near the kitchen door.

'You must have gone into the cave almost immediately after dropping me off last night,' she said, frowning. 'The tide was on the turn when we left Pethporro, and you said the cave is inaccessible at high tide.'

'I went home first,' he said, nodding. 'Fed the dogs, walked out with them to check on the sheep, then drove back down to the beach. The tide was coming in strongly by then, but I anticipated that and wore these specially.' He slapped his thigh, and she glanced at him, startled, before realising that he was wearing thigh-high boots, like the ones trout fishermen wear in streams. 'Useful things, waders. I imagine that's how Gabriel got back and forth across the beach for his meetings.'

'And Trudy would have nipped down the steps with a torch once Jack was in bed,' she said, 'or waited until he was out on the farm.'

'Yes.' His smile was wry. 'Only once it was high tide, I was stuck there. For hours.'

'Serves you right, creeping about underneath other people's houses in the dead of night.' She made a pot of tea and handed him a cup, bringing milk to the table in a jug. It was hard to sit opposite him in this domestic setting, a disquieting intimacy in pouring the milk for him as though they were husband and wife. 'Why not simply drive around this morning if you wanted me to see that IOU? Then we could both have enjoyed a lie-in.'

He stared at her intently. 'I had to do something. I couldn't sleep last night. I was on fire for you.'

'Dear me.' She pushed the teapot towards him. 'That sounds uncomfortable.'

His laugh was grudging. 'Yes, all right, maybe I do sound like a teenager in the grip of an infatuation. But to be totally frank with you, I feel like one. Like my head is going to explode.' Their eyes met, and she felt an answering ripple of desire inside herself. 'Except this isn't infatuation, Hannah. This is—'

'Don't!'

He fell silent at her protest, but his jaw worked with frustration. Then he looked pointedly at the IOU slip, now lying beside the teapot. 'That means nothing, then? After what you said last night, I finally realised how important it is to you, that damn napkin. So I brought it to you.' He hesitated. 'Only now you've got it, apparently it makes no difference whatsoever.'

Hannah put down her cup, her tea untouched. 'You mean, you're not just showing it to me? I can have it for good?'

'Of course.' He flicked it towards her with one contemptuous fingertip, his voice rough. 'Take it. I don't want your bloody house. I never have. Besides, I doubt it would ever stand up in court. Any lawyer worth their salt would be able to tell you that. Jack was reputedly as drunk as a lord when he wrote that IOU, and if Gabriel never pressed his case at the time, it's highly doubtful any judge would find in my favour now, decades later.'

'Then why not give it to me before now?'

'I thought it would be fun to see your face when I mentioned it. The new owner of Kernow House, all high-and-mighty, just flown in from Greece.' He made an explosive

sound under his breath. 'Fun!' She had never seen him look so angry. 'I was a fool to do it. All I achieved was ruining my chances with you. And for what? For a practical joke!'

'Raphael . . .'

'I swear, I had no idea you were pregnant. Or recently bereaved. I knew next to nothing about your life. But when I saw you from a distance, I thought—' Raphael swallowed convulsively. 'I thought you looked like an angel.'

'An angel you might want to manipulate into bed?'

'It was never like that, I swear it. By the time we were that close, I'd forgotten all about that stupid gambling slip. I'd forgotten everything except how much I missed you when we weren't together.' He looked at her urgently. 'Because by then, I had no other thought in my mind except how to persuade you to say yes.'

'*Yes*?' She repeated the word, puzzled. 'To what?'

'To marrying me, of course.'

Hannah stared at him, her heart thudding so loudly she wondered if the baby could hear it.

'Tell me it's not too late,' Raphael said, leaning forward. 'Say something, for God's sake. Even if it's to tell me to get out. At least then I'd know where I stand.' He ran a hand raggedly through his hair. 'I love you. Did I say that yet?'

Mutely, she shook her head.

He loved her?

'There are a couple of things I need to tell you,' he continued. 'Things I'm . . . embarrassed about.'

She opened her mouth, then shut it again, suddenly unsure if she wanted to hear more or not.

'My real name's not Raphael,' he said hurriedly. 'It's Ralph.'

Oh, that.

'I know.'

He stared. 'Really? How?'

'Bailey told me when we first discussed your claim on the house. You changed it to Raphael because of Gabriel, she said.'

'He could be very Old Testament. I thought he'd prefer it to Ralph.'

'I think I prefer it too,' she said drily.

'And you hated that whole business with Jennifer, didn't you?' He sounded ready to walk out, to give up on her ever loving him back. 'But you have to believe me, I wasn't lying when I said I didn't lead her on.'

'I believe you.'

'I'm not a womaniser. Not even remotely.'

'I said, I believe you.'

'I'm so far from being a womaniser, in fact, I could barely control my nerves when you finally agreed to go to bed with me. Didn't you notice? I was shaking like—' He stopped, frowning. 'What did you say?'

'I believe you.' She reached across and took his hand, pleased when his fingers curled instinctively around hers. 'I saw Jennifer on the beach last night. With Caroline, my antenatal nurse. When I got back, I was telling Bailey and Penny about it, and they told me Caroline is Jennifer's stepsister.' She gave him a crooked smile. 'Don't you see? That's why Caroline was so quick to blame you for what happened, why she tried to suggest you were the one who'd behaved badly, not Jennifer. I was too quick to believe her, though it didn't help that Bailey and Penny had given you bad press

too. But they only did that because of the rumours Caroline and Jennifer had been spreading around, telling everyone who'd listen that you were some kind of sex-mad Lothario.'

'God, I wish!'

She arched her brows at him. 'Well, I don't,' she said tartly, but then could not sustain her sharp tone and found herself smiling at him instead. 'You didn't help your cause much though, the arrogant way you behaved when we first met. All that cloak-and-dagger stuff over the IOU.'

'I'm sorry about that,' he said quickly, and moved closer, raising her hand to his lips. His eyes gleamed when she pulled her hand away, as though undeterred. 'I didn't want you to know how attractive I found you. Not at first. And then later, I was just plain scared.'

'Scared?'

'Of having my insides pulled out by you.' He grimaced. 'Anyway, you can't blame a man for trying not to become a total slave. Not when the woman in question is as beautiful and brave and bloody crazy as you. Coming here after Santos died, starting out again on your own with a baby to raise. That can't have been an easy decision. And it wasn't just about independence, though I can see that in you. It took courage too.'

'I thought you said I was crazy?'

His lips quirked into a smile. '*Slightly* crazy,' he corrected himself. But she could see strain in his face now, and a certain intensity that made her shiver. He was still waiting for an answer to his question, she realised. An answer she was not ready to give. Not definitively, at any rate. 'And very, very beautiful,' he finished softly.

She tried not to be swayed by the hungry look in his eyes. The household was stirring above them, probably due to the sound of their voices drifting upstairs. She could hear water heating in the pipes, and someone heading for the bathroom, and then the creak of floorboards overhead as Lizzie got out of bed.

Soon their privacy would be invaded by noisy, chattering women, all curious to know what was going on and why Raphael had paid them a visit so early in the morning. And what would she tell them?

Coming here after Santos died, starting out again on your own with a baby to raise. That can't have been an easy decision.

Hannah felt a shiver run through her as she considered the truth of that statement. And the underlying questions it raised in her mind.

Was she ready to move on?

Or was she still too much in love with Santos to give herself wholeheartedly to Raphael? Because she didn't want to go into this while still pining for another man. Raphael deserved better. And so did she.

Back when she'd first moved into Kernow House, living here alone in the chill winds of a darkening winter, she would have said yes, absolutely, she was still in love with Santos. And she would have angrily rejected the notion that anyone could sway her from that position. Her love for him had been so powerful, her grief at his loss still so raw. Now though she would alter that slightly. It hurt to let go of the beautiful soul-love she had once shared with him, there was no denying that. It was the hardest decision she would ever make, in fact. But letting Raphael into her heart and her life

need not mean she was letting go of Santos' *memory*. That could never happen.

And she would make sure their unborn daughter knew all about her father. That she was shown photographs and holiday films, and told the stories about how they first met and the things they did together. And Hannah would take her to Greece to see her grandparents and where her parents had once lived and worked together.

She would make sure Santos was never forgotten.

But it was time to look to the future now, to what might lie ahead for both of them as a family, not back at what she'd lost.

First though, she needed to be absolutely sure of this man's intentions.

Hannah picked up the IOU and read it again in a cool voice. '*I, Jack Earnest Clitheroe, owe you, Gabriel Tregar, the deeds to my property, Kernow House, Pethporro, Cornwall.*' She looked at Raphael, her tone sharpening deliberately as she added, 'So this means nothing to you anymore? It's mine now?'

'All yours, love.'

She took a deep breath and tore the paper napkin in half, then in quarters. She mashed up all the fragments in her fist, walked over to the recycling bin, and dropped them inside. Along with all the soggy vegetable peelings from Christmas dinner.

'Well, that's the end of that nonsense.' When she looked back at him, Raphael was smiling, but sadly. As though at a dear memory, now lost. That look gave her hope. She had made her decision, and she was sure it was the right one. But she needed him to be sure too. Even if it meant testing

him a little further. 'What's the matter now? Wasn't that what you expected me to do with it?'

'Of course. But that was my only real bargaining chip. What am I supposed to use now to get you to say yes?'

'You genuinely want to marry me?'

'It's all I've been able to think about for some weeks now. That,' he added, with a lopsided grin, 'and how to get you into bed.'

'Even with this on the way?' She rubbed her bump through her dressing gown. 'Because it's not going to be easy, parenthood.'

'Nothing good ever is.'

'Plus, I snore.'

'I'll wear earplugs.'

'Not when you're on baby duty, you won't.'

Raphael opened his mouth, then shut it again. Then said, 'Did you say, *baby duty*?' His smile was slow, but incredulous. 'Hold on, is that your way of telling me you'll consider my proposal?'

'I've already considered it.'

And she had considered it, a ghostly image in her head of Gabriel Tregar trudging through the snow in Long Field, endlessly searching for her grandmother, who had decided they could never be together, perhaps afraid that she was to blame for her husband's death, or that it was too late to change her mind . . .

He stood up jerkily and came towards her, his eyes fixed on her face. 'Then don't keep torturing me like this, woman, for God's sake. I swear to you—'

'Yes.'

He stopped, dumbfounded. 'What?'

'The answer's yes,' she said firmly, and would have said more, only he caught her in his arms and swung her around several times.

An impressive feat given her girth, she thought, squeaking in surprised pleasure. Then he pressed his mouth to hers, making the whole world go away for a few wonderful moments, and did not stop kissing her until the kitchen door creaked open. They both turned to see Bailey and Penny standing there, Colonel Mustard in Bailey's arms, and Lizzie staring over their shoulders, a hand at her mouth, her grey hair still in pigtails. She must have slept in them, Hannah realised.

'That Mr Tregar, has he been kissing Miss Clitheroe again?' Lizzie whispered, wide-eyed, barely suppressing a giggle.

'It certainly looks like it,' Penny said in mock-accusation, making a tutting noise.

'Oh, that's my fault, that is.'

'How do you figure that, Lizzie?' Bailey asked, concern in her eyes as she sought out Hannah's face. No doubt she was still a little worried that her friend was being strung along. 'From where I'm standing, I'd say Raphael is the one to blame here. Not you.'

'On account of my mistletoe,' Lizzie said simply, pointing to the kitchen ceiling. They all looked up to see sprigs of fresh mistletoe strung along the exposed beams, one particularly bushy example dangling mere inches from Hannah's head. 'That's good for kissing, that is. Why else d'you think I strung so much of it up? To stop this silly old pair messing everything up with their argy-bargy.'

'Argy-bargy?' Hannah opened her mouth to remonstrate

with Lizzie, then shut it again. Perhaps they had been a bit silly, she accepted. A very little bit.

'So basically, I have you to thank for this, Lizzie,' Raphael said, looking at her solemnly.

Undisguised glee in her face, Lizzie nodded. 'That's right.'

'In that case,' he said, 'I'd better come clean with you at once. Now I know how you feel about . . . argy-bargy.'

Raphael took Hannah's hand and kissed it in an exaggeratedly gallant fashion, much to everyone's amusement. He drew himself up straight to face his accusers, his dark eyes glinting with humour.

'Please don't throw me out on my ear, ladies. She's probably stark staring mad, of course, but I'm proud to say Miss Clitheroe has just agreed to be my wife.'

Bailey gave a little shriek of delight, and Colonel Mustard leapt out of her arms in alarm, nearly colliding with the tabby cat, who hissed at him and then retreated under the kitchen table to sulk. Under cover of the chaos, one small kitten made a spirited attempt to climb onto the tortoise's back, a horrified Slowtop hunching back into his shell just as Penny stooped to rescue him, grinning around at them broadly.

'Now look what you've done.' Hannah bent to reassure the cross tabby under the table, who merely glared up at her balefully. 'You've upset The Cat with No Name. You know how crabby she gets when it's noisy.'

'Crabby?' Penny raised her brows, musing. 'I think you've just named her at last. Crabby the Tabby. Not bad.'

'Marry *Raphael*?' Bailey mouthed to Hannah during all this confusion, clearly incredulous. 'You sure?'

Hannah straightened and nodded, embarrassed now at being the centre of everyone's attention. 'Ouch.' She put a hand to her bump as the baby kicked violently. 'Seems someone else is excited about the news too.'

'Can I be your bridesmaid?' Lizzie asked, sidling up to her, very earnest.

Hannah looked across at Raphael, and he smiled.

'You can all be my bridesmaids if you like,' she told them shyly. 'We could hold the wedding reception here, maybe in a marquee out on the field.' Then an unexpected thought struck, almost knocking her sideways with its force. Hannah turned on him, suddenly breathless with indignation. 'Oh my God, Raphael, I've just realised. You ... you gave me my grandfather's IOU to tear up. But if you marry me, that means you get to live in Kernow House anyway.'

Raphael dragged his flat cap out of his coat pocket and fitted it carefully to his head. 'Erm, I suppose it does, yes.' He pointed out of the kitchen window. 'Hey, look, it's started snowing again.'

'Why, you dreadful, conniving—'

'Not in front of the tortoise,' Penny said calmly, and handed Slowtop to Bailey, who carried him safely out of earshot so that Hannah could curse her new fiancé as roundly and comprehensively as he deserved.

Acknowledgements

I began writing romcoms as Beth Good in 2014, and self-published them as a hobby. It was an adventure and I loved that so many readers were willing to give my ebooks a try. But four years on, with the publication of *Winter Without You*, that journey enters a new phase, as my first Beth Good paperback romance reaches out to a whole new readership.

Firstly, my heartfelt thanks to my literary agent, Danielle Zigner, and to Luigi and Alison, and the whole team at LBA, who have remained with me throughout the often-thorny process of being a writer and getting this very special book to bed.

I also thank my brilliant and inspirational editor at Quercus Books, Emily Yau, for loving this book as much as I did, and seeing its potential. Novels tend to be written by one person, but it can take an entire army of eager book-lovers to get that story into the hands of the reading public. So a big thank you also to Milly Reid, Hannah Winter, Molly Powell, and everyone at Quercus for their continuing help and encouragement.

Also, a huge debt of gratitude is due to my readers, whom I love and greatly admire for their loyalty and friendship over the years, and their seemingly unflagging enthusiasm for these stories I spin out of straw in my head. Without you, my

readers, there would be no point getting up in the mornings. I include here the wondrous cohort of book bloggers – often among a writer's staunchest supporters – who read and then spread the word about my novels, bless them. In particular, I'm thinking of Rachel Gilbey at *Rachel's Random Reads*, whose expertise and sheer kindness have made her a saint in my eyes. Thank you, all!

Lastly, as always, my loving thanks to my husband Steve, and our five long-suffering offspring – strictly in order of appearance: Kate, Becki, Dylan, Morris and Indigo. Well done for putting up with a temperamental writer in the house, especially once my noisy experiments with *Write Radio* had begun. It's not over yet though; there's a new novel in progress even as I write this. Keep those cups of tea coming . . .

First published in Great Britain in 2018 by

Quercus Editions Ltd
Carmelite House
50 Victoria Embankment
London EC4Y 0DZ

An Hachette UK company

A CIP catalogue record for this book is available
from the British Library

PAPERBACK ISBN 978 1 78747 639 4
EBOOK ISBN 978 1 78747 640 0

www.quercusbooks.co.uk

Typeset by Jouve (UK), Milton Keynes

Printed and bound in Great Britain by Clays Ltd, Elcograf S.p.A.

Winter Without You

BETH GOOD

Quercus